ALL NIGHT LONG

ALL NIGHT LONG

MELISSA MacNEAL

APHRODISIA

KENSINGTON PUBLISHING CORP.

http://www.kensingtonbooks.com

APHRODISIA BOOKS are published by

Kensington Publishing Corp.
850 Third Avenue
New York, NY 10022

All Kensington Titles, Imprints, and Distributed Lines are available at special quantity discounts for bulk purchases for sales promotions, premiums, fund-raising, and educational or institutional use.

Special book excerpts or customized printings can also be created to fit specific needs. For details, write or phone the office of the Kensington special sales manager: Kensington Publishing Corp., 850 Third Avenue, New York, NY 10022, attn: Special Sales Department, Phone: 1-800-221-2647.

Aphrodisia and the A logo are trademarks of Kensington Publishing Corp.

ISBN: 0-7582-1411-1

First Kensington Trade Paperback Printing: November 2006

10 9 8 7 6 5 4 3 2 1

Printed in Mexico

For Geoff
Many thanks, over many years, for the ideas and information
that inspired parts of this story. (The good parts, of course!)

Acknowledgments

Thank you to Ms. Rinat Glinert, Mr. Chris Dionaldo, Mr. Ador Agbisit, and Ms. Svetlana Kovaceviz for answering my questions and giving me a personal tour of crew areas and security facilities. Special thanks, as well, to Captain George Paraskevopoulous for his gracious attention while I was aboard his *Vision of the Seas*. It was a special honor to share tea and conversation with you in the bridge, sir!

1

"Welcome aboard the S.S. *Aphrodite* for Fantasy Cruise Line's adults–only adventure in the Caribbean! I am your captain, Skorpio Skandalis, and—"

"Yeah, *you* say 'skahn-DAH-lees' and *I* say scandalous," Lola teased the TV in her stateroom. "Captain Scandalous. That would be you, Big Boy."

"—I am committed to satisfying your wildest desires and making your fondest fantasies come true!" the Greek seaman crooned.

His accent flowed like olive oil, slick and smooth and musky. And when he flashed his white smile at her, Lola could only stare, her brushful of Very Cherry nail polish poised above her hand.

God, but he was a fox! Bronze complexion. Raven hair gone silver at the temples. A five-o'clock shadow that suggested rough–cut masculinity—and sometimes she *liked* to play rough! And with those smile lines radiating from his snapping black eyes, he became Mr. Greek God of Sensuality. Mr. Caribbean Heat. Mr. Peel-Down-My-Panties-and—

Lola snickered. She wasn't wearing any.

How many times had she watched this closed-circuit cruise orientation these past two days, letting Captain Scandalous seduce her with his accent and come-on smile? His was the first voice she'd heard as she entered this room Sunday afternoon, and she'd watched him a few times yesterday while they were sailing to Aruba, too.

When she was alone, of course. Fletch wouldn't get it.

Could a girl ever get too much of a man in uniform? Bravado and balls, all decked out in those crisply pressed whites. The reruns of *The Love Boat*—and *Fantasy Island*!—had become her reality on this little getaway, and she was, by God, going to soak up every bit of ambiance and sizzling sexuality the captain was promising her in his welcome address! At least until Dennis came back to dress for dinner.

Or not, if he caught her here, naked this way.

Fresh from her afternoon shower, sitting cross-legged on the queen-size bed, Lola Wright was in a fine, feisty mood: tonight was the Captain's Gala Reception, where dressed-up guests would meet the crew, standing so virile and fit in their white uniforms. She'd get to shake this Greek tycoon's hand—

"Or whatever else I might grab," she whispered with a grin.

The idea of sneaking a feel—right there in the reception line, while others watched—dared her to *do* it! Hadn't he just promised to make her fondest fantasies come true? She'd slip down the zipper of those trim white trousers . . . let her fingers find the band of his bikinis, and the warm, coarse hair bristling just above his—

Lola gasped. A cold blob of nail polish had plopped on her nipple, and if she breathed—or if that nipple jutted out any farther—there'd be a crimson stain on the ivory comforter. She'd have to explain to Enriqué, the room steward, and tip him big-time to make up for such a mess!

So, with a quick swish of the brush, Lola coated her nipple

with the nail polish. The contrast of that brazen red shine against her baby-pink skin kicked something wayward into gear, and she painted the whole puckery circle around it. Didn't want to look off-balance, so she colored the other nipple, too.

"Whadaya think, Skorpio?" she murmured, shimmying at the Greek on her TV screen. "About the time you feel my fingers in your skivvies and get a load of *these* babies, we may have to leave the reception!"

But Fletch would be here any minute now, and he'd be gawking at these hooters. He liked it hot and raunchy—Mr. Lewd and Crude, that was Dennis Fletcher! So, knowing these brazen red tips awaited him beneath her low-cut cocktail dress, he'd be looking for a place to lift her skirt while everyone else swilled their champagne at the gala. Tonight, Ms. Wright would be the girl most likely to! In a public place, no less!

She looked toward the picture window, where walkers and joggers made their rounds just inches from the end of her couch. Captain Scandalous was now saying the windows on the Promenade Deck were one-way mirrors, so passengers could look out but walkers couldn't see in. One of the many fine features of the *S. S. Aphrodite* he was so proud of.

With a wicked grin, she got up to test this theory: standing in front of the window naked, she cupped herself from the sides, offering up her luscious handfuls to passersby.

Two little old ladies ambled past, chatting, but the one looking right at her didn't blink.

"Must be true," she murmured.

Lola glanced at the clock. Time for some serious primping before her fiancé got back from his winning streak in the casino. If he smiled just right and ground against her on the dance floor, Dennis Fletcher might get lucky yet again after dinner—and she'd keep him coming back for it all night long. That fantasy alone made the price of this trip worth it.

She'd gone through a long, sometimes rocky romance with

her financial advisor, a man who played hardball with the markets while she'd played hard to get. But only enough to keep him panting like a puppy, since she was every bit as hot for it as Fletch was.

Lola had finally convinced him they should elope to the Caribbean for one of those romantic cruise ship weddings. She and Mr. No-Strings-Attached were finally tying the knot! So he deserved nothing but the finest—in other words, *her*, totally tricked out—as a reward for making such a sound decision. Not only would she be the wife of a savvy, handsome man, but her business would benefit, too: she could spend her time expanding Well Suited instead of working so hard for Fletch's attention.

Lola flicked her auburn hair back to keep it from smearing her wet nipples. God, but they looked tacky, like they belonged on trailer trash—or some chick in a cheap porn flick. Which meant Dennis would go nuts. They might not even make it to the Captain's reception, or get dressed enough to go downstairs for dinner.

Yet she *did* want to wiggle into that little black cocktail dress and then announce her arrival with a click-click-click of her stilettos. A girl didn't get many opportunities to fox herself up and split zippers. And even though she was crazy for Fletch— because he *was* a fine catch; the money man who'd sent her business soaring—Lola hoped she'd never outgrow her power to make other guys *look*. And then put their hands in their pockets.

Rap-rap-rap.

Fletch! Lola quickly capped her nail polish, so she could sprawl suggestively on the bed for his entrance.

"Yehhhhhhs?" she crooned toward the door. "Who *is* it?"

"Message for Meese Wright. I leave eet here, een your box."

With an impatient sigh, she opened the door and stuck her head out. Must not've been much of a message, if Enriqué didn't wait for a tip! She glanced up the long, narrow corridor to see if Fletch was on his way, hoping he wasn't so engrossed in his poker game that he'd lost track of the time. It was her night to *shine*, dammit! To romance the night away with a man in a tux who couldn't take his eyes off her.

But then, if he was really raking it in at the tables, maybe she could forgive him for being a little late. Dennis Fletcher was the luckiest man she knew, when it came to playing Caribbean Stud. And that diamond on her left hand hadn't come cheap.

She snatched the message from the clip on her door, which she shut with a swing of her bare butt. No envelope, just a folded slip of paper. Fletch must really be cleaning out the house—but then, cell phones didn't work here on the ship, so maybe he'd scribbled a note instead of coming upstairs.

Lola, said his familiar scrawl. *I've found my true soul mate! A woman who knows how I need my freedom—who won't boss me around, or insist on having the last word. And she doesn't call me Fletch—much less bark it like she's giving her dog a command. I've left the ship to get better acquainted at her sea- side villa, so don't come looking for me.*

I didn't want to break it off this way, but it's for the best. Have a nice life, babe, You can bet I will! Dennis.

2

"That goddamn double-crossing sonuva *bitch!*"

Lola crumpled the note and threw it at the bed, but that didn't nearly relieve her anger. Who did he think he was, saying he'd met somebody else—his true *soul mate*, for chrissakes! Dennis Fletcher wouldn't know a soul mate if she slapped him in the face!

She threw open the closet door, slamming it hard against the jamb. What if he'd been planning this all along? Just said he'd get married to shut her up, so he could abandon her on this swanky ship and not have to pay his bar tab and casino—

But his clothes were still hanging there. The blazers she'd chosen to make him look wider across the shoulders. The slacks that hugged his sexy ass and played up the bulge in front.

Lola yanked out the top drawer, still muttering.

"Must not've thought he'd need underwear, either, to go sashaying off to some rich bitch's seaside villa. Some bitch from *Aruba*, no less!" she jeered, hurling his undershirts across the room. "Probably met her in that onshore casino we walked through this morning. In the time it took me to *pee*, no less!"

Still pissed, Lola flung his socks at the picture window, wondering why any moron would roll them up into such bulky balls. "Well, I hope she's loaded, cause Fletch'll let on like he's *so* the Caribbean stud—and then go through her cash faster than Tarzan's chimp can swing through the jungle!"

Dennis *did* bring to mind a monkey, come to think of it. An albino monkey, with his close-cropped blonde hair curving around his temples into a widow's peak. She should call and tell him *exactly* what she thought of him right now! Make monkey noises in his ear—

But no. He'd see her name and number on his cell screen and ignore her. And she certainly didn't want to interrupt whatever he and his *soul mate* were doing!

"You can't call him," she muttered, throwing his skimpy swimsuits to the floor. "No cell signal, remember?"

But she *could* play detective.

Lola grabbed the *Aphrodite Ahoy!* newsletter that listed today's schedule and events. Since they didn't sail until six, she had forty-five minutes to run ashore and—if he thought for one minute she'd let him dump her for some—

Lola sucked in a shuddery breath. That's exactly what Fletch had done. He'd *dumped* her, for some sleazy broad with a villa on Aruba . . . a woman who wouldn't put him in his place, or suggest that his tightie-whities were shot—or too tacky for a guy marrying a—a woman who advised high-level execs about dressing for . . . success.

Dammit, I did NOT say his name like he was a dog fetching something!

Lola fondled the silk bikinis she'd bought him, but the rainbow they made in his drawer taunted her like his note had.

She would *not* cry over this jerk! Instead, she grabbed the closest thing—her swishy silk robe from Victoria's Secret—and stepped into her kitten-heel sandals with the rhinestone vamps. She snatched her SeaKey from on top of the TV, where Captain

Scandalous was once again assuring her he was about to make her wildest dreams come true.

And Lola headed out. A bitch on a mission!

Down the narrow hallway she rushed—around the corner, to race down the stairs—no time to wait for elevators!—until she reached the gangplank on Deck One. Sweaty, overbaked passengers were swarming aboard, their Sea Key cards making a steady *ding! ding!* as they passed through the security checkpoints. Uniformed crewmen watched their x-ray monitors, while other men in whites handed out antiseptic wipes as guests reclaimed their bags from the conveyor belt. A sense of urgency filled the bustling room, where everyone was thinking about squeezing into their formal wear in time to guzzle free champagne at the Captain's reception.

But not Lola. She surveyed the scene, and then trotted up behind a Filipino watching a monitor off to the side of the incoming lines.

"Please, can you tell me if a Dennis Fletcher has come back on board?" she asked breathlessly. "I was expecting him hours ago, and I'm afraid something *awful* must've happened if—"

The agent flicked his gaze her way. "Sorry, ma'am. Can't give out that information."

"But he's my husband!" she pleaded, widening her eyes as she gripped the front of her filmy robe. "He went back ashore to get me a—"

The man in whites refocused on his screen. "Stateroom number?" he murmured.

"7010, Promenade Deck," Lola wheezed. Then she realized he'd ask for her SeaKey next. "I—when I saw it was getting so late, I rushed down here with just my key—"

He plucked it from her hand. *Ding!* went the scanner. Up came her registration info, and that lousy photo they took when she first boarded the ship. Then he keyed in a few other numbers.

"Sorry, Miss Wright. He's not back y—"

"What time did he leave the ship?" she demanded, but then she exhaled plaintively. Better to sound like a worried wife than a diva who's been dumped.

"I'm so sorry," Lola wheezed, swiping at her eyes, "but Dennis gets shaky in this heat and—the ship won't *really* leave before we find him, will it? I'm worried sick about him!"

Mr. Efficiency raised an eyebrow, as though he saw through her little story. He handed back her SeaKey. "Mr. Fletcher disembarked at 3:09 PM. And yes, ma'am, the *Aphrodite* pulls away at six o'clock sharp. The gangplank closes in five minutes, however, so don't even think about going after him. We'd have to leave without both of you, ma'am. It's cruise line policy."

Lola's mouth snapped shut. Fletch left *hours* ago! All this time she'd assumed he was parked at a poker table in the ship's casino! She'd spent the afternoon anointing herself for the biggest night of his life, while *he'd* been galavanting around with some floozy from Aruba! Was probably naked in her jacuzzi by now, laughing his ass off about the clueless, *bossy* broad who thought she'd have him roped and branded by tomorrow.

Flummoxed, she strode to the open doors to scan the pier area, where the last stragglers were hurrying up the gangplank.

Like he'd really be there, she chided herself. *You should've known he'd never change! You should've taken a clue from all those times he walked out before. But no, you had to wheedle and coax and spread your legs to keep him coming back for—*

"Pardon me, Mrs. Fletcher?"

"I don't *think* so!" she spat, wheeling around to face the crewman who'd dared to interrupt her inner rant.

Lola's jaw dropped. Golden-brown eyes drank her in. Sun-kissed, sandy hair framed a slender Mediterranean face. A wicked little mustache curled around lush—very kissable—lips that curved in a polite smile.

Then she realized her arms were crossed so hard she was hanging out the front of her robe. "I—sorry—"

He bowed slightly, graciously maintaining eye contact while she tucked herself in. "Rio Benito DeSilva, Chief of Security, at your service, Miss—"

You can service me any time, honey.

"—Wright," he crooned. "I understand we're about to leave a passenger behind, and that you're concerned about your husband's—

Not any more, he's not.

"—weakness in this heat."

"So it's not just me?" Lola breathed. "It really is *hot* in here?"

Rio clenched his teeth to keep from chuckling. In an ivory silk wrap that left little to his imagination, with her wavy red hair drifting in disarray around her heart-shaped face, Lola Wright looked like she'd jumped out of one man's bed in search of another. Never mind those crimson nipples.

He hoped his instincts were right, about Miss Wright being brassy on the outside but far too . . . naive to be involved in Mr. Fletcher's situation. He couldn't discuss it right now; didn't want to upset her more than she already was, or speak before he had the facts. Rio felt the overwhelming urge to tuck this lovely woman into a hug and protect her from the cruel truth, but he mentally stepped away.

"While we must maintain our schedule," he continued quietly, gazing into eyes as deep and green as a primeval forest, "we will do everything possible to contact Mr. Fletcher and instruct him on how to meet us at the next port of call. This probably seems terribly inconvenient—"

The ship lurched, pulling away from the pier. Lola gasped, shifting to keep her balance—or was it because DeSilva had grasped her shoulders to steady her? She couldn't decide if his mustache belonged on Don Quixote or Zorro, but she wanted to keep him talking so that low, Spanish accent would caress her ear again. So she could watch his lips move.

"—but I assure you that the staff of the *Aphrodite* will do all in our power to put your vacation back on track," he continued. He glanced at the crewmen securing the exits, and at the passengers in the hallway impatiently awaiting the glass elevators.

"This way, please," he said, gesturing around the corner, toward double doors painted the same beige as the walls. "If you can describe Mr. Fletcher for me—if his cruise documents are in your stateroom—this will expedite finding him onshore. And it will prevent the local authorities from detaining him, if he's fallen ill and doesn't have his passport with him."

Cruise documents? Passport? It would serve Dennis right if the cops hauled him in! But then, his *soul mate* wouldn't have required a photo I.D., *would* she?

The doors slid open, and Lola stepped into a staff elevator, which was very plain, compared to those glitzy glass ones for the passengers. She hugged the back wall, feeling the cool stainless steel through her silk robe. When she shivered, her nipples seemed determined to show off, just when she needed to behave herself. She'd been in such a hurry to get back at Dennis, and now this robe she'd thrown on in the heat of the moment had probably made her the talk of the boys in white.

Her escort pushed the 7 button. He smiled like he was trying not to notice what she wasn't wearing, even though the fit of his zipper hinted otherwise.

This ride might become extremely . . . intimate, if Mr. DeSilva took two steps toward her. His eyes were soft and sympathetic, like a golden retriever's, and with his hair feathered back from his suntanned face, rakishly brushing the top of his collar, he looked like anything but a security agent.

But if he was escorting her to her room, to see Dennis's cruise docs . . . Lord, were they even there? DeSilva had probably heard her sob story from the Filipino at the monitor, so the little lie she'd set into motion to get Fletch's departure time would unravel pretty fast if she didn't—

"Are you all right, Miss Wright?"

"Please—call me Lola," she blurted, suddenly undone by this man's debonair *kindness*. Cop or not, he seemed sincerely concerned about her predicament. "I—I'm just upset. Thank you for asking."

"Understandably so. You're quite welcome."

You're quite welcome. How long since she'd heard that phrase? These days people said "no problem!"—as though her thanking them *was* one.

When the elevator stopped on the Promenade level, she walked ahead of him nervously, SeaKey in hand. Lola felt like a little girl being herded to the office for lying to the teacher. Or for not wearing panties to school. The nuns would've fainted—or gotten out the paddle—at *that* sin!

"I'll wait right here. Take your time," DeSilva said as she slid the key card into the lock.

"Ah. So it was only my fantasy that you'd come into my room," she quipped, and then her cheeks flared with embarrassment. "I'm so—that was inexcusably rude, to—"

Rio sucked in his breath. Here in the dimmed lights of the corridor, with her ivory face flushed and her robe clinging to curves that called out to his hands, it was a fantasy he certainly shared. He looked through her open door to rein in his runaway thoughts, and then grabbed her by the shoulders.

"Wait! Someone's been in here, rifling through your room! You'd better stay right here while I check for an intruder."

Pulse pounding—from the thought of intruders, and from the heat of his skin through her robe—Lola grabbed the door jamb as Rio stepped into her stateroom.

"Anybody here?" he demanded, throwing open the bathroom door. He was bristling with business now—not a burly man, but not one she'd want to get crossways with, either. Rio DeSilva's angles looked sharp enough to slice like a saber.

As she peeked in after him, Lola let out a long sigh. With Fletch's undershirts and socks strewn everywhere, the place *did* look ransacked. And when DeSilva leaned down to pick up a crumpled piece of paper, she knew she had to come clean.

Lola stepped inside. Leaned against the door to close it. "I have a confession," she breathed.

Rio's heart skipped a couple of beats. He felt like anything but a priest. Lola's robe had fallen open again, enough to tease him with her pale pink cleavage . . . round and firm and sweet. His tongue flicked the roof of his mouth, wondering how those painted points would feel—and taste.

He cleared his throat. This was an adult cruise, yes—the fantasy Captain Skandalis alluded to in his welcome spiel—but he was strictly forbidden to be in a passenger's room while she was in it, too.

"Yes? I'm listening," he replied. He was uncrumpling the paper he'd picked up out of sheer habit—*searching for clues, about a possible intruder or Dennis Fletcher's situation*, he would say if the captain quizzed him about this breach of behavior.

"That story about Dennis going ashore to—and maybe being too sick to come back?"

Lola hated it that her eyes were tearing up over the way Fletch had jerked her strings, but dammit she'd loved the guy! Or thought she did.

"Well, I made it up. He—he left me that note you're holding, saying he—he's found a woman with a seaside villa—and—well, I got pissed off and threw his clothes out of the drawers!"

Rio stopped fidgeting with the note. "So you went down to the gangplank area, to see if you could chase after him?" *Dressed like that?* he almost added.

Lola sighed, yanking the lapels of her robe together. "I was so—so *irked* that he'd taken off with somebody, when we were supposed to get . . . married tomorrow. . . ."

"I'm so sorry."

It was the merest whisper, yet it carried the weight of his concern: the key that opened the innermost room of her heart. A room Dennis had never known, or cared, how to reach. Lola slumped, letting her hair fall like a curtain so DeSilva wouldn't see how ugly her face got when she bawled.

"Please excuse me, I—"

"There is no excuse for the shabby way he's treated you," Rio stated, more fervently than he had a right to. Lola couldn't know yet just how true that was. Every nerve ending in his body warned him to step away, to get himself out of her room and out from under her spell while there was still time.

Her shoulders shuddered pathetically when she tried not to cry. To keep from pulling her into his arms, Rio skimmed the note.

—found my true soul mate—someone who won't—boss me around—have the last word—get better acquainted at her seaside villa—

The lying bastard deserved to rot in jail for this! DeSilva looked up from the note before Lola could catch him reading it, and took inspiration from the small safe in the open closet.

"Is his passport—any sort of identification—still here?" he asked in his most official-sounding voice. "It will help the authorities process him. Or help you, if you need to—what's wrong, Lola?"

She opened the safe, surprised it hadn't been locked, and then frantically yanked the drawers open below it.

"My cell phone's gone! I put it in this top drawer when I came back to take my—and my purse!"

My Camels! The bastard took my only pack of—

She scanned the room, her gaze raking the top of the TV, the corner desk and its open shelves, the glass-top coffee table, and the upholstered love seat. "I brought it back from shopping on-shore, after lunch, and I put it—if that bastard took—he's got my credit cards! My checkbook's in there—and so is *my* pass-port!"

Fletch knew damn well I'd get crazy if he took my security smokes!

Rio's jaw clenched as he watched her desperately search every inch of the stateroom, her expression growing more alarmed by the second. As well it should! Here on board her SeaKey was all she needed, but stepping ashore in any Caribbean port without identification was risky. Not to mention the pre-dicament it would put her in when she went through Customs on her way home.

"Why on earth did he have to take my—it's not like he's hurting for money, but God! My cell had all my clients' num-bers, and my appointments, and—"

Lola stopped rummaging around the bed's comforter and pillows, engulfed in a deep chill. Ah, jeez, now she was shaking like a junkie, just at the thought that he stole her—

"What is it? What else has he taken?" Rio stepped toward her, determined not to touch her because just recalling her soft skin and the fresh scent of that bare body had him reeling.

"Cigarettes," she finally mewed. Then she screwed up her face, which was already blotchy from crying. "I—I *quit*, dammit! For good this time! But I carried around one single pack of Camels, still wrapped. With strapping tape around it to remind me *not* to open them, no matter how jittery and desperate and bitchy I got!"

Lola cast another miserable, futile glance around the ran-sacked room. "I had them in my purse this morning, when we were shopping onshore!" she rasped. "He must've—"

Her insides twisted into a tight knot. She held herself, know-ing it made her look like a nympho going into withdrawal, but things were suddenly a whole lot worse than Dennis's note had led her to believe. What he'd said about his new soul mate was humiliating enough, but what he *hadn't* said was that he'd ripped her off, big time, when he jilted her!

"After we got back on board, he went to the casino while I took a shower," she breathed, shaking her head forlornly. "He had to've come to the room . . . figuring I wouldn't hear him with the water running. And it matches up with the time that security guy at the gangplank gave me."

Rio sighed heavily. Gave in to the urge to touch her, just letting his hands rest on her shoulders to reassure her.

She was shaking like a scared rabbit. Frightened out of her mind, on top of being upset because the man she was to marry had backed out on her so crassly. Betrayed her in ways they had yet to discover, if he had access to her clients and her plastic.

"We'd better report this immediately," he suggested.

Lola nodded, wanting to cry and vomit and curl up in a ball. Hoping someone would tell her this mess had been straightened out—that Fletch had played one of his colossal jokes on her, and was on his way upstairs now to smooth things over.

But that wasn't going to happen, was it? Fletch had never truly been hers, and she was paying now for refusing to see that.

"You're right," she sighed. "Let's go."

3

"This is Clive Kingsley, our concierge," Rio said as he escorted Lola behind a counter and into a small, colorful office.

The man at the glossy walnut desk, stood up with a debonair grin. "So pleased to be of service! And how may I assist you, Miss—"

"Miss Wright has just discovered that her purse, cell phone, and cruise documents are gone," the security agent filled him in. "Not to mention her passport. And we suspect her fiancé—"

"*Ex*-fiancé," Lola muttered.

"—Dennis Fletcher, has taken them ashore and not returned to the ship," DeSilva finished pointedly.

"Well, isn't *that* nasty?" Kingsley exclaimed with a horrified expression.

His face softened when he looked at her, and the way he'd said *nah*-sty, with a British accent that flowed like hot fudge, would've sounded utterly delicious if she weren't in such a pinch.

"But rest assured, Ms. Wright, we will get to the *bottom* of this! Mr. DeSilva here is the *best* security man sailing today, and the *Aphrodite* is equipped with cutting-edge technology."

"Perhaps you could file the report and notify the credit card offices of this theft," the agent went on, "while I check out a few other details."

"Most certainly," Kingsley said with a crisp nod. "Put out my sign as you leave, please, so we'll have no interruptions. This is far more important than passengers wanting to book shore excursions or sign up for ballroom dance lessons. Shall we?"

The concierge, so dapper in his navy blue suit, gestured toward a doorway behind her. Feeling indecently underdressed, Lola preceded him into a cozy little sanctum decorated in brilliant jewel tones, where a flat-screen computer hummed quietly.

"Now, sit yourself down, my dear, and we'll get you squared away so quickly you'll still catch the captain's champagne reception before dinner. Just let me bring up your account . . . and you're in which stateroom again, please?"

"7010. Promenade deck." She tried not to slump dejectedly, but the sleek wooden chair was so slick her silk robe gave her no traction. Gripping the edges of the seat, she thought about how *ready* she'd been to attend that gala reception—before this thing with Dennis came up, that is.

"And you would be Miss Lola Wright of Portland, Oregon, sharing the stateroom with Mr. Dennis Fletcher—"

Kingsley clicked through some screens and then glanced at her. "And you don't have a single shred of identification, darling?"

Lola swallowed hard. Here again, under different circumstances she'd find Clive Kingsley's baritone voice and dark, curly hair most alluring. His blue eyes glimmered with sympathy and perhaps even . . . interest.

"Not a shred," she echoed. "The best I can figure, Dennis

came up from—*supposedly*—the ship's casino while I was in the shower. Stole my purse, my phone, my passport—"

"We'll *get* him for that!"

"—and left me a note about finding his true soul mate, if you can believe that! Some woman with a seaside villa on Aruba!" she continued, fueled by her anger. "And this on the evening before we were to get married tomorrow, at sea!"

"Oh, and the ceremony is lovely!" Clive cut in, his fingers flying across the keyboard. "Our chef, Alphonse, outdoes himself on the ten-tiered cake—and the champagne punch cascades as a waterfall into an ice sculpture of a couple frolicking nude in a jacuzzi. This *is* an adult cruise, and we make every opportunity to keep our guests in the *mood*—"

Kingsley squinted slightly, and then slipped on a trendy little pair of reading glasses that hung around his neck. "Oh, my. My, my, my."

Lola stiffened, straining to see the computer screen. But the concierge, whether to reduce the glare or protect her from what he saw, tilted the screen with a flick of his finger.

"*What?*"

Kingsley sighed and sat back. "I've brought up the various charges to the credit card with which you booked your cruise, dear. The account *is* in your name, correct?"

She nodded, getting that sick feeling again. "And?"

"It seems numerous charges have already been made to the ship's bars and boutiques on Mr. Fletcher's SeaKey—"

Lola cringed. They'd only been aboard for a day and a half! And *she* certainly hadn't received any gifts from the fabulous shops here! What the hell had he bought? And what had he done with all that stuff?

"—so I'm wondering, since you mentioned he was in the casino—"

"How hard did he hit the ATM before he ditched me?"

Clive Kingsley's face was a study in utter dejection. "I don't show that information here, but I'd better find out. Excuse me while I make a call."

Nodding, Lola pretended to study the array of appliquéd fabric montages depicting Caribbean street scenes. The vivid colors and textures played with her eyes, and she wished she were in the mood to appreciate such unique artwork. But who could possibly enjoy a vacation that had turned into the cruise from hell when her fiancé filched her plastic?

God, but I need a smoke!

Lola scootched back upright in the slick chair, while trying to keep her legs together and her boobs from falling out of her robe. A nicotine fit would be the *pièce de résistance*, far as impressing this courtly concierge. He was probably working so urgently just so he could get her out of his office.

Indeed, Mr. Kingsley's low grunts into the phone, and the way he scribbled figures on a miniature legal pad, appeared anything but encouraging. Lola blinked rapidly and looked away, trying not to embarrass herself further.

Kingsley hung up. Did the math with quick, efficient strokes of his gold-plated fountain pen before focusing doleful blue eyes on her. "If it's any consolation, dear girl, you're better off without this—"

"*What*? Just *tell* me, already!"

"Mr. Fletcher's casino ATM withdrawals total more than ten thousand—"

"Holy shit! My credit limit's only—"

"Yes, I'm afraid we've got a problem there, too." He handed her the little legal pad and a sleek black pen promoting the *Aphrodite*. "You'd best list all the credit cards you were carrying, while I call their hotlines, so you can report them as stolen."

Dazed, Lola jotted down all the Visas and Discovers and American Expresses she could recall, ready to kick herself because some of them were accounts for Well Suited. Ordinarily she left those cards at home as a security precaution, but she'd hoped to do some buying on this trip—find novel Caribbean accessories and clothing designs her upper-crust clients would pay top dollar for.

If Dennis had accessed those accounts—

But dammit, as her financial advisor, he didn't even need her plastic to do that! He had her account numbers. Knew her business inside out, as far as her finances went. Including her credit limits.

"Thank you," she wheezed when Kingsley handed her the phone.

He was genteel enough to leave the office and shut the door, but his gesture didn't save much of her dignity. There was damn little of it left.

The lady rep was courteous and efficient, but it was still the conversation from hell. When she hung up, Lola felt so numb she couldn't move from the chair. Might as well die right here, because now she couldn't afford to be buried anywhere else. A simple wrapping of her body . . . it would slide down the board for a burial at sea, just like in the old movies. . . .

Her thoughts were spiraling downward from there, and she sat gripping the lapels of her robe when Kingsley poked his head in. Knuckles white with her fury, she began to shake all over. More than revenge against Dennis Fletcher, what she really needed right now was that pack of Camels.

"As bad as we expected?" came his genteel British inquiry.

She nodded, staring blankly at the top of his desk. "Not only my personal accounts, but my business ones, too. Fletch cleaned them out, systematically—like the thorough financial manager he is. The day before we left home."

Mr. Kingsley's brows puckered as he let out a sympathetic gasp. "I'm rather surprised you weren't notified about such large withdrawals—"

"Oh, the rep said she'd been trying to call me about all this unusual account activity, but I wasn't at home or at the office—

and Fletch *conveniently* stole my cell phone today, before I could check for messages." Lola rolled her eyes in disgust and desperation. "I made a point of turning that damn phone *off* for this romantic vacation! Obviously a huge mistake!

"Which means," she wheezed, wishing her humiliation would just swallow her whole and get it over with, "that he planned this whole thing before we ever left. Had that floozy from Aruba all lined up—one of his brokerage contacts, no doubt. Had that seaside villa reserved because—because—he never *intended* to marry me! I booked the cruise, but it seems Dennis Fletcher took *me* for the ride."

Kingsley's sigh filled the little sanctum. "I'll do my very best to rectify this, Miss Wright. You have my word on it. Please feel free to remain here until you've composed yourself, my dear. I'll be right outside, and your wish is my command. Tea, sympathy—a good stiff drink. You name it."

A pack of Camel Turkish Jades and a Bic to flick, she almost blurted.

And why didn't she? It was a simple request, even if she'd have to stay on the starboard side of the decks, which were designated for smoking, or in the bars where they still allowed pariahs like her to puff.

Picked a helluva time to quit, didn't you? And you did it for Fletch, no less. Because he challenged you to, and you loved him!

Lola smacked her palm with her fist, disgusted with the way this whole thing was coming down. Here she sat in the concierge's office, having a meltdown nicotine fit, when her entire world was coming unstuffed like a feather pillow Fletch had stabbed again and again . . . much like he'd played slasher with her heart and mind and soul. Why had she ignored the signs? And the remarks her friends had made about how fast and loose Fletch liked to play?

Which was one of the things you adored about him. A risk-taker, just like you, babe!

But she couldn't sit here all night, beating herself up.

And, as Lola thought about it, the credit card rep had said she'd get right on it: stop payment on those charges, to keep her credit rating from going down the toilet with the *whoosh* of a cruise ship flush button. It would take some time, considering the amount of damage Dennis had done, but everyone was on her side. They weren't blaming her for all those bills, or holding her accountable for her poor choice of financial managers.

She was a free woman.

Well, she'd been left in a very expensive predicament, but her *problem* was gone now, wasn't he? And his funds had been cut off. Dennis Fletcher could sponge off that floozy from Aruba now: sweet talk *her* with the same pretty lines he'd used while they planned this cruise.

I'm free—unattached! And I kept my trophy diamond!

The sparkle of the rock on her left hand made Lola smile. She wouldn't be the only patsy. She wasn't the only fool who'd fallen for the illusion of love or for a shyster's lies. Someday that vixen with the villa would be in a world of hurt, too.

She let out the breath she'd been holding. Automatically reached down to where she would've set her purse, and then rolled her eyes at this habitual gesture.

Habits! Who needed them? Maybe it was time to break a few—and pick up some new ones while she was on this trip. After all, it was paid for before they left home. It was *her* trip, and by God she might as well enjoy what was left of it!

After all, I'm free now! A single woman on an adults-only cruise!

Lola's pulse picked up and she stood—tummy tucked, shoulders back, head held high! If she couldn't enjoy a fantasy situation like this, well, she *did* have a problem. And it had nothing to do with money.

4

When she stepped out into Kingsley's desk area, the concierge was talking in hushed tones with Rio DeSilva and another dashing man in dress whites. The three turned with encouraging smiles—which meant they'd been talking about *her*.

See there? You ARE important enough that the most gallant, handsome men aboard this ship—

Lola's jaw dropped. The man in the uniform of blinding white, with the Mediterranean tan and laugh lines, and that raven hair laced with silver, was none other than Captain Scandalous! He was even more of a Greek god in person than on TV. And he was smiling at *her*. Drinking her in with obsidian eyes that sparkled with *plans*!

"Miss Wright, let me express my regrets for the unfortunate situation Mr. Fletcher has left you in," he crooned, oozing with ambiance as he offered his hand. "Captain Skorpio Skandalis. Pleased to meet you, despite such unfortunate circumstances."

Lola felt his warm hands enfolding—no, *enslaving*—hers. "Captain Scandalous! I mean—Skahn-DAH—it's such a pleasure to—*so* not me to be this—"

His midnight eyes lit up with mirth. And why wouldn't they? Could she turn any more shades of red or trip over her tongue any faster?

"You are understandably upset," he assured her, still holding her hand captive between his. "But you surely realize that we must have a *plan* to pay for the items Mr. Fletcher charged in the ship's shops and—"

What was wrong with *this* picture? With a firm tug, Lola freed her hand from the captain's.

"Wait a minute! You think I *planned* to get ripped off?" she retorted. "After I *finally* convinced Fletcher to come on this trip—and to set a wedding date!—and I arranged to be away from my business for eight days—"

The men's smiles were tightening, probably because guests were parading by in their finery, on the way to the Captain's Gala Reception. Lola paused, to pull her foot from her mouth again.

"I'm sorry. I detest women who make a scene, or who whine and play helpless," she said in a lower tone. "But dammit, I didn't come on this cruise to get broadsided by a jerk who's allergic to commitment—and who's run off with a woman he just met! Not to mention a helluva lot of my money!"

"Please, Miss Wright," the concierge said, his eyes shining like a summertime sky. "Fantasy Cruise Line understands such emergencies, and I'm sure we can work these matters out. Now that we've reported the theft of your credit cards—"

"If you could create the man of your fantasies, who would he be, Lola?"

She sucked air at the intensity of Rio DeSilva's topaz gaze. His voice soothed her like warm, sweet brandy. Such a question came like a bolt from the blue—an *outrageous* question, from a man she'd met just today!

But he was serious. He was still focused on her, standing tall yet relaxed; just his *presence* suddenly settled all the conflicts about Fletch and her credit cards. Or at least she forgot all about them as her lips parted and she returned his soulful gaze.

This wasn't idle chitchat he was making. He expected an answer! And with *three* handsome men in uniform watching her, Lola sensed she'd better come up with something coherent.

If you could create the man of your fantasies, who would he be, Lola?

It didn't help that the captain and the concierge were smiling expectantly, as though they could see through their cohort's ploy—and her silky robe, as well. As though they might decide their course of action after hearing her reply to Rio DeSilva's loaded question.

She blinked, tugging her lapels together. She was a free woman now, so she could answer this security agent's question any way she liked, right? So why not lay it all out? These three heroes of the high seas might as well know *exactly* what she expected of any male she might create!

"I want a man who'll make a home and a family with me," she replied in a thoughtful murmur. "A man who'll be king of his castle and treat me like a queen. *His* queen."

Rio's sensual mouth softened with a wistful smile.

"A refreshing revelation, in this day and age," he replied with a nod. "And what man wouldn't want to build his world around you, Lola? To lavish his love upon you in a hundred ways each day? But surely there's more."

Lola's eyes widened. Why had they gone from discussing repayment plans to writing a script for *Fantasy Island*? Would the floor open up and send her swooping down a chute into the open sea, if she said the wrong thing? Captain Scandalous and Mr. Kingsley looked like guys who played by Old World rules. She'd better beware of stepping on their chivalrous yet chauvinistic toes with that *attitude* Fletch had always ragged her about.

And why don't you just play along? the voice in her head piped up.

It's your vacation, remember? A girl doesn't get many chances to make men LOOK—and here's yours, honey!

"Well—since this *is* a fantasy, after all," she went on in a bolder tone, "I want a man who respects my intelligence and business savvy! A life partner who understands that I must work very hard to maintain my accounts and my professional reputation!"

Her heart was pounding now, her need for nicotine over-ridden by Rio's invitation to dream *big*!

"A man who enjoys my success as well as his own," she added emphatically. "Yet he'll cuddle me when the chips are down, and—and help me believe in myself again!"

The area behind the crescent information desk rang with a silence so profound, it blocked out the sounds of the well-dressed crowd going to the gala.

Clive Kingsley smiled, his face alight with interest. "And what is it you do, Ms. Wright?"

While he was the most reserved of the trio, in his conserva-tive navy blue uniform and a tie that matched his eyes, Lola sensed a sincere interest in her professional accomplishments. And perhaps her personal attributes, as well.

"I've created a chain of menswear stores called Well Suited," she replied, standing taller. "I operate on the premise that men on any level rise higher faster if they're better dressed—not just designer suits and high-end Italian shoes," she added fervently, "but *advice*, from my specially trained staff, about which styles play up their bodies to their best advantage. How to present themselves well for any occasion, whether it be corporate inter-views or class reunions."

"The classic 'clothes make the man' concept, eh?" Clive's grin held a delicious secret: he was choosing his words as carefully as he'd select truffles from the high-end chocolatier on the ship. "Not an easy sell, in this era where khakis and polo shirts are considered acceptable business attire."

Lola beamed her appreciation at the insightful Brit. Then she let her gaze linger on his imperial physique.

"You wear slacks with a thirty-four inch waist and take the same measure at the inseam, don't you, Mr. Kingsley?"

He stood taller, his interest—and his zipper—more piqued than before.

Lola's voice lowered into that seductive tone she reserved for closing deals with tightwad tycoons, selling them three suits rather than two. "And you've wisely chosen pleated pants, because that jock sock you call underwear holsters an eight-inch pistol, I'm guessing. And it's half-cocked right now."

DeSilva and the captain snickered, but the way Kingsley shifted, his eyes widening with admiration, made Lola feel bolder. After all, this was an adult cruise and these three men were here to ensure her *pleasure*, despite the havoc Fletch had wreaked upon her finances. It was their place to *serve*, which implied she was their mistress.

Lola liked that idea!

"While I'm on a roll, I'm going to press for the *ultimate* fantasy," she continued with a shimmy that made her nipples whisper against her robe. "I want a man who'll drive me over the edge with passion, until I come—and come again, dammit! A lover who'll spend the time I need to—who'll *take* control until I *lose* it! A man who'll keep me coming all night long!"

Skorpio Skandalis stuffed his hands in his pockets, his nostrils flaring like a stallion's as his eyes lit up with a wicked awareness of her. The temperature of the little alcove rose with his body heat.

"Well, gentlemen, there we have it!" he proclaimed, his Greek accent edgy now. "Miss Wright has stated her needs, and it's our duty to meet them—while finding a way for her to repay the charges accrued in her name. How shall we go about this?"

Kingsley flashed them all a pointed smile. "I'm sure we'll find myriad ways for a woman of Ms. Wright's abilities to—*right* herself, if you will. And should you need assistance with formal wear—and you *will*, my dear—"

"Need assistance? Or formal wear?" she challenged.

The sexual energy these three generated sent her pulse into overdrive with a heady mix of testosterone and adrenaline. She was outnumbered here—in over her head. But she dealt with high-powered men every day, and she was getting too damn tingly to care!

Clive's grin waxed cryptically British. "I hope you'll allow me to be of service," he replied with a slight bow. "While we have three boutiques that specialize in bling, only one carries clothing befitting a woman of your classic tastes and expertise—"

"No, no, no," Rio DeSilva interjected.

On any other man, his stiletto mustache would look ridiculous, yet the security agent resonated with an eloquence harkening back to Spanish nobility. A Don Quixote of the open seas, he was . . . or perhaps a pirate of the Caribbean, considering the playfulness that bubbled like champagne in his tawny eyes right now.

"This is not about adhering to *our* agendas," he reminded his colleagues, "nor is it about that loser who left her in debt, or about following cruise line rules and regulations. It's about Lola. Whatever Lola wants."

As Rio stepped forward to clasp her hands, Captain Skandalis looked on with a glimmer in his onyx eyes. "I couldn't agree more," he murmured. "From here on out, our policy shall be 'whatever Lola wants, Lola gets.'"

"*So*, Ms. Wright," he continued, stepping up beside DeSilva to nail her with his bottomless black eyes, "what shall it be?

Would you rather be removed from the *Aphrodite* in cuffs—handed over to the authorities at our next port? Or will you work off your debts at my discretion?"

Lola's jaw dropped—and then she bristled. "That's a helluva way to—"

"Whatever Lola wants," the captain quipped in a clipped voice. "Make your decision. I'm late for my reception."

Where did this guy get off, threatening to remove her from the cruise in *cuffs*? As though *she* had charged those things in the boutiques, with no intention of paying for them?

Lola slipped her hands from between DeSilva's and planted her fists in her hips. It was a clichéd move, but it improved the view she was giving them. Perhaps her Very Cherry tips would change the Captain's mind—or convince his cohorts to rescue her.

"Are you telling me what I can or cannot do?" she challenged. "Dennis Fletcher made that mistake, and I won't miss that about him! You know damn well I'll honor my obligations—my own *legitimate* expenses—no matter who—"

"A wise choice!" Skandalis crowed, his eyes flashing. "You've just become my love slave for the remainder of the cruise, Ms. Wright. I've already had your belongings transferred to more suitable quarters, and I've assigned you a personal companion to—"

Why did this suddenly sound like house arrest with a warden? And premeditated, no less!

Lola widened her eyes at Captain Scandalous. "You can't just—"

"I am the captain, Miss Wright," he stated with rich simplicity. "You've given yourself into my service, as a consenting adult. So for the duration of this trip, you belong to me, and me alone."

The Greek leaned forward, until his chiseled nose and those

deep, dark eyes were mere inches above her own. Persuasive, to say the least.

"You will relinquish all *control* to me, little lady," he said in a voice that forced her to read his lips. "Control over your schedule, your personal problems and finances, your . . . sexual desires. You will be mine, and mine alone, Lola. Do we understand each other?"

Something told her not to sass him about that "little lady" thing. She blinked her *yes*, not dropping her gaze; not wanting to, even though every fiber of her body throbbed with resentment toward this chauvinistic goat who thought he was God's gift to her fantasy life.

That *was* resentment she was feeling, right?

Skandalis snickered, flicking a nipple that had slipped from the front of her robe.

"Fine! We've reached our agreement!" he said in a wicked whisper. "So now you will go upstairs to your new room, to prepare yourself for my pleasure. And then you'll report to the spa. Half an hour. Naked."

5

When the door to the staff elevator slid shut, enclosing them in a cocoon that felt intimately risky, Rio knew better than to make any moves or telltale remarks. Lola Wright was trying to disappear into the corner across from him, filling the little cubicle with waves of her barely repressed wrath.

Lord, but she was all the more tempting when the roses bloomed in her cheeks and those eyes narrowed with catlike contempt! She'd given up all pretense at modesty: her robe gaped open beneath its sash, and her crossed arms bared most of those delectable breasts. He longed to ask why a nice girl like her—because he believed she *was* one—had painted her nipples red. But discretion got the better of him.

"You seem . . . upset."

"*Upset*?" she retorted, hugging herself like he wanted to. "You haven't *seen* upset until—"

"But your problem's solved. Skandalis is letting you work off your debt—"

"Skandalis can screw himself! '*You will report to the spa— half an hour—naked!*'" she mimicked. "But you know the worst part? For a brief and shining moment, I believed you and Mr. British Gentility would step up to the plate and rescue me! All that talk about Lola getting what she wants! And that's not how it came down at all!"

Rio fought back his laughter. "Pardon me if I'm overstepping, but when a woman visits the concierge wearing only a revealing robe and sexy little sandals, she's sending a clear message about what she *wants*. And when three men see her in this—*suggestive* state of—"

"How was *I* to know all three of you would gang up on me? I thought you and Kingsley were on *my* side!"

He closed his eyes against the image of lying with her, Lola on her side and he on his, leaning into each other, kissing with mad passion. When she swung her leg over his hip so he could slide inside her, that sparkly screw-me shoe dangled from her toes.

"And we are, my sweet. At the captain's command, I could have—"

"I'm not your sweet! Go to the chocolate shop if you want candy!"

"—escorted you to the brig instead of to your new suite. My sweet."

"And you see a difference?" Lola threw him an exasperated frown as she stepped out of the elevator ahead of him. "My cuffs might be invisible, but they're *here*! If this ship had a jail cell, you could just—"

"It does. Remind me sometime, and I'll show you what a romantic little hideaway it can be, down there in the bowels of the ship."

She stopped in the corridor. Glared up at him with those feline green eyes and that auburn hair flying in crazy, alluring disarray around her face. "Get real. And just get it over with, will you?"

He slipped his master key card into the door, reminding

himself that once they stepped inside, he was *not* to touch her. She'd declared herself a free woman, with thought, word and deed—but that was before Skandalis pronounced Lola *his* conquest.

"Are you ready?" he asked patiently. He opened the door just enough to stick his foot inside, which left him standing so close to her he could follow the rise and fall of those breasts . . . could still smell the herbal scent from her shower . . . could count the delicate freckles on skin that shimmered with health and . . . a very blatant sexuality.

Why hadn't he gone to Kingsley himself with Lola's dilemma? Let the concierge and his computer solve her problem? Then this volatile, voluptuous redhead would be so damned grateful—would be *his* instead of—

"Ready for what?" she asked tartly.

With an inward groan, Rio opened the door and waved her inside. "Your prison, Miss Wright. The captain wants you to do nothing but *suffer* for the sins of your fiancé."

"*Ex*-fian—"

Lola halted in the foyer, on a floor of mosaic tiles that glistened like stained glass. Her mouth fell open.

"Holy shit. This must be the Presidential suite, or the—"

"Castle's keep?" Rio quipped. He glanced around, to be sure they were still alone. "Solitary confinement at its finest, wouldn't you say? The Aphrodisia Suite's a bit of an upgrade from your stateroom where the joggers could gawk in at you."

Lola's eyes widened. "It's one-way glass, that picture window."

"So they say."

Before she could spin off into another conversation that would only make him silence her with a ravenous kiss, DeSilva walked to the center of the spacious front parlor to point out its amenities.

"Living room here, complete with home theater entertainment and a sound system with speakers throughout the suite. Fresh flowers to welcome you, compliments of your despicable Captain Scandalous—"

She stopped gaping at arrangements of tropical lilies and red-orange hibiscus. "How'd you know I called him that?"

He grinned. Thought about hedging, just to get her more riled up. "You said it to his face, remember? Not that you're the first. He secretly loves that nickname, so you made some points—along with winning favor by painting those *other* points."

She pulled her lapels together, miffed again. "He's an arrogant bastard and you know it! Please don't tell me you obey his every rule and whim."

DeSilva kept his gaze steady, considering how much to reveal.

"He's the captain of the ship, Lola. When he says you're his alone, I must honor that command. And besides," he went on, gesturing toward the large bedroom to their right, "didn't you get what you wanted? Nearly a week with a man so hot he makes you melt—who has put you in this room and provided you a companion—and you're complaining! Or so it would seem."

Lola glanced at the lush king-sized bed swaddled in plush and pillows, and the balcony that beckoned her through French doors. The entire suite was done in cranberry and royal blue with ivory accents; lots of gold and glass details to make it a sumptuous hideaway any woman would love to wile away endless weeks in.

So why was Rio's point hitting home? Why *was* she acting so pissy, when she had indeed won the attention of that Greek god she'd gawked at on TV?

"OK, so I got what I wanted," she replied. "But it was on *his* terms!"

"Skorpio's a man who craves control. Again—that's what you said you wanted."

It was all he could do not to laugh at her—not to make love to her on that huge bed that just called out for a man and his woman to get lost in its cushioned depths. Lost in each other.

But thoughts like that would get him into more trouble than he could afford right now. While he didn't like it that Lola was disappointed in him, for not being her white knight, it was the best way to keep this relationship at a safe distance. Because that's where it had to stay.

Her sigh lingered in the room, like the languid scent of the scarlet roses on the dressing table. Lola's expression told him she wasn't accustomed to such luxury; her wistfulness suggested she didn't feel she belonged here—or deserved such a room.

Perhaps his new mission should be to change that attitude . . . to convince Ms. Wright with every bit of his body and soul that she was a woman who should be living out those fantasies of becoming a man's queen. He could see her now, wearing only a royal purple robe trimmed in ermine, which would slither off her to provide them a cozy pallet on the floor, where he could—

The door opened, and Rio's brief fantasy ended. "Ah—and here's your companion."

"My new best friend," she said with a roll of her eyes. But when she turned to get a look at him, Lola stopped in her tracks.

The warden Skandalis had sent looked to be about twenty-something years old. Had a lithe body and a mop of sun-streaked, tangled curls that partly hid his eyes. He walked with the easy grace of a guy who'd sauntered along hundreds of white sand beaches, and who had no higher ambition than to spend the rest of his life doing that.

And why wasn't she surprised that he had a cell phone at his ear? Or maybe it was some sort of walkie-talkie like DeSilva wore on his belt, for staff communications.

Then, when the kid grinned at her as he listened, it hit her full force: *Cabana boy. Omigod, I've got a cabana boy to die for!*

"Lola, this is Aric," Rio announced. "He's at your beck and call for the rest of the week, so don't hesitate to keep him busy. And Aric—"

Beach Boy held up one finger while he finished his conversation.

"Yes, sir, I understand. She's right here, and I'll have her in the spa waiting for you." He holstered his walkie-talkie on the loop of his low-rise boxer trunks, giving her a slow once-over. "The captain sends his regards, Ms. Wright. Fifteen minutes. Naked."

"Send the captain *this*!" she replied with a flick of her middle finger.

Aric's grin rose like the sultry Caribbean sun. "He'll like that. I'll let you deliver the message yourself, though."

Lola bit back what she'd been about to say. Back home in the real world, she'd never dream of flipping somebody the bird—not even clueless drivers who cut her off because they were yacking on their cells. So why was she acting so damn hostile? So *rude*, when so many good-looking men were just waiting around to be of *service*?

"I'm sorry," she murmured. "I'm behaving badly. I'm lowering myself to Fletcher's level, and neither one of you deserve that."

"Apology accepted," Rio replied. "And, since I'm responsible for the security of this ship for another hour, I'll leave you two to get acquainted. Keep the lady out of trouble, Aric."

"Will do, sir."

DeSilva nodded and went to the door, not liking the kid's

expression one bit. It was like Skandalis had assigned a sly young fox to watch a very vulnerable, very desirable bird, simply to rub *his* nose in it, too.

"Mr. DeSilva? Rio?"

Lola's voice curled around him as though she'd cupped him from behind. He turned in time to catch a look of wanting on her face; an expression that made his body ache to reply in kind. "Yes, *mi corazon?*"

She nipped her lip, and the sight of those white teeth against her lush mouth made him wish such an endearment hadn't slipped out. Where had that come from, anyway? Why was he letting on like he was on her menu, when the captain had declared her *his* dish?

"It *is* one-way glass in those picture windows, right?"

Whatever she'd done in that room on the Promenade Deck, he wished he'd seen it. He smiled at her, wishing he could do so much more . . . like getting rid of her watch dog.

"In broad daylight you're relatively safe, yes," he assured her.

But with me? Never!

—

6

Unlike Rio DeSilva, her cabana boy leaned against the same wall of the elevator as she did, standing close enough that their arms nearly touched. Not a bad thing, except, well—he was *young.* Which meant he either had the hots for her—

Oh, get real! You're old enough to be his . . . aunt.

—or he wanted to make damn sure she didn't escape when the doors opened downstairs. He was tall enough that he could gawk right down into her cleavage, and in the reflection of the stainless steel wall across from them, Lola could see he was doing just that. Probably ogling those Very Cherry nipples she was wishing she hadn't painted. Probably because Captain Scandalous had clued him in about them.

It was too damn warm in here. Too quiet, with just the thrum of the elevator going all the way down from the penthouse deck.

"*So,*" she said, desperate for conversation, "I guess after you've worked your summer on the cruise ship, you'll be going back to college?"

"And give up a cushy job like this?"

Smart aleck! If Aric weren't so hot, with that medallion hanging among the sparse hairs on his chest, she'd smack him for sounding so insolent.

Lola shifted to her left, trying for a little more space. But damned if he didn't shift, too.

"So this is your life's work?" she challenged. "I suppose you play escort—bodyguard—whatever—for a different woman each week? The captain impresses me as a man with a lot of *steam* to let off."

"You think I'm gonna answer that?"

She glared up at him, a teacher ready to put this wise-guy student in his place.

But his expression made her swallow her retort. Aric's eyes were taking their own sweet time checking her out. They were a silvery green, those eyes, and his lips were parted just enough to make her think he modeled for magazines; had maybe gotten some botox shots to make them look so professionally pouty.

But, hey—he was looking at *her*! None of Fletch's judgmental advice or left-handed compliments on his mind. And, actually, he was discreet and intelligent—at least about keeping the secrets of the man who signed his paychecks.

"Nice robe," he said matter-of-factly. And damned if he didn't run his finger up her arm, just enough to make her breath catch. "Silk?"

"Yeah. On clearance at Victoria's Secret," she breathed.

Now *that* sounded classy! Not only had her man—ex-man—run off with her plastic and her cell and her business accounts, but she was so high-class as to admit she wore stuff nobody else would pay full price for.

"I like it."

Lola blinked. But she saw no smirk on his face or heard no telltale edge in his voice. Just a man of few words, making conversation. About her.

"Thank you, Aric."

"No problem."

So much for her rising opinion of him—but then, she hadn't exactly been a shining example of the social graces, had she? "I—I want you to know that I'm not ordinarily so mouthy or—"

"Don't go there."

The elevator doors slid open with a seductive whisper, and he gestured for her to go first. They stepped out into a hallway she hadn't seen—but then, she'd had little time to explore the ship. Incense, or maybe candles, filled the air with the subtle scent of sandalwood and Aric opened a carved door with elegant gold lettering that said THE GODDESS SPA. He was leaning down just enough that his face was level with hers. Kissing level . . .

"We'll have lots of time to share secrets this week, Miss Lola," he continued with a crocodile smile. "Why waste them on elevator chitchat, when we've got the Aphrodisia Suite all to ourselves?"

Was that a promise or a threat? Lola wasn't sure how to answer him, now that he was stringing more than two or three words together.

"Miss Christy'll be here in a minute. So I might as well relieve you of that robe."

She blinked. Was this kid going to peel it off her? Right here in the spa lobby, where just anybody might walk in and—

He glanced at his watch—quite possibly a Rolex, but probably a knock-off. "Fifteen minutes—with two to spare. And naked. Right?"

A young man who took his work seriously. Lola turned her back to disrobe, but a huge gilt-framed mirror reflected Aric's face then, right above her own, as she untied the sash. His eyes held hers in the glass as the silk slithered down past her shoulders, baring her breasts.

At least he didn't tweak those lewd nipples, like the captain had. His smile was slow and sensuous like a lover's, rather than a warden's, and it occurred to Lola that maybe solitary confinement with Stud Boy here would be a welcome relief from working off her debt with the captain.

"Hey, sugar! Just in time!" a honeyed drawl accosted them. "Let's get you into that little room and *ready*, shall we, darlin'?"

Was the masseuse talking to Aric, or her? Miss Christy's enthusiasm was outdone only by her ample assets: she was a curvy blonde with hips that would've looked oversized had she not needed them to balance out the golden pillows pushing up out of her lacy pink pajama top. Lola hadn't worn baby dolls since she was a kid, but this woman had just brought them back into vogue in a very adult way.

"I—nice to meet you, Miss—"

"Miss Christy. So glad to be helpin' out!" she chirped, pumping Lola's hand. "Nice to see a gal from the good ole U. S. of A.— not that these Greeks aren't good-lookin' and reeeeeal good about tippin'!"

Somehow, she'd expected a more ... soft-spoken, New-Age, mystical type down here in the Goddess Spa. But then, what had gone like she'd expected it to?

Miss Christy gave Aric a cheerful salute—the changing of the guard—and then guided her toward a room behind the ornately carved check-in desk. The lobby, decorated in pale sage and maize and teakwood, was dominated by a larger-than-life statue of a goddess with raven waves cascading down her sun-kissed body.

"Let me guess. Aphrodite?" Lola said to make conversation.

"You got it, honey! Some guests like to rub her nubs for luck, but hey—you're Skorpio's *girl* tonight! Lady Luck is already playin' your song!"

That was one way to look at it. She didn't have much time to look at *anything*, however, the way Miss Christy was hustling her into a dimly lit room with two massage beds and candles that flickered seductively in wall sconces. A fountain bubbled in the corner, next to a table covered with vials and jars.

"You know, don't you, that the line's two other ships cater to a little different crowd," the masseuse said, patting the cushioned table. "The *S.S. Athena* specializes in, well—*girly* things—"

Lola sensed she wasn't talking about chick trips with your sister.

"—and the *Pandora*, now *that's* where you get into heavy metal and leather. *You* know—the little whips, and the manacles chained to the walls, and the room stewards wearin' spiked dog collars?" she went on nonchalantly. "You picked the right ship, sugar!"

"I—I certainly did!"

"And there's nobody I'd rather look at nekkid than Skorpio Skandalis. Now you just get comfy here—"

Lola settled herself on the soft, scented sheet, thinking maybe this wasn't such a bad way to repay Fletch's debts.

"—while I slick you down a little," the masseuse chattered. "More fun when you don't have any friction. Just warm, oiled skin. . . ."

Warm, thick liquid dribbled down her spine and Lola caught her breath with the intense sensation. Miss Christy had a fine set of hands: gentle fingers smoothed the oil into her neck and shoulders, to release the tension she'd been holding there. On down her ribcage they went, until Lola buried a giggle in the small pillow.

"Ticklish, are we?" Miss Christy whispered. "Ooooooh, this is gonna be so much fun! Just you wait!"

As her body went limp, rocking with the firm rhythm of the massage strokes, it occurred to Lola that she *was* waiting. Where was that damn captain who'd insisted on fifteen minutes?

At the Gala Reception, silly. You think he's going to leave all those admiring, sequined women for YOU?

She would've realized this earlier, had she been her rational self. And now, with these skillful hands lulling her into a heavenly state, Lola told herself not to think about Captain Scandalous— or that other jerk who'd gotten her into this mess in the first place. It was a fine, fine thing to lie here and be blissfully oblivious, rocked like a baby in the arms of the ocean . . .

"Good evening."

The words flowed near her ear with that seductive Greek accent, yet Lola heard undertones of Bela Lugosi doing Count Dracula. Like she could care, in this relaxed state. She lazily opened one eye, almost wishing the captain had stood her up.

He was nude. Smoothly muscled and sleek, like she knew he'd be. And that *thing* standing at attention, right at eye level, was *not* a cocktail weenie he'd brought her from the reception.

"It pleases me that you've followed my instructions, Miss Wright," he went on in a voice dusky with desire. "I plan to reward you accordingly. May I introduce my personal masseuse, Odette."

Things began to spin out of kilter when she raised her head from the pillow. Why would this man want a different masseuse, when Miss Christy with the magical hands obviously adored her boss? And hadn't he requested the pleasure of *her* company tonight?

Looking at Odette, however, kept Lola from voicing these demands. She was willowy and tanned and pampered, with the smile of a satisfied cat on her classically elegant face . . . a cat who saw a canary and intended to make it squawk. She could've been Skorpio's twin, except he wasn't exactly kissing her like a sister. As their bodies pressed together, Lola got the icky feeling they intended to put on a show—like the ice dancers in the Olympics, who'd honed their performance during months of practice. Except those folks wore clothes!

And as the Greeks eased onto the other massage table in the small room, Miss Christy peeled off her lacy pink baby-dolls.

Then the masseuse mounted *her* table—straddled *her*, while she was laid out on her stomach, naked and defenseless!

"What kind of a deal is—"

"Shhhhh, sugar, don't fuss now!" the blonde whispered in her ear.

Pale hair fell like a curtain around her face, and Lola felt the warm weight of that voluptuous body beginning to rub . . . to lightly writhe against her butt and spine. Those double-Ds were resting against her back, and Miss Christy's nips were prodding her. *Hard.*

"Everybody's gonna have a real good time tonight," she promised. "Play the game by Skorpio's rules, honey buns, and you'll get yours. Oh, you're gonna get it reeeeeal good, girlfriend."

Lola clenched her jaw, not to mention the rest of her body. It wasn't so much what Miss Christy said, as the way she'd said it. As though the masseuse felt inclined to be *girly* and get some for herself while she was at it.

Meanwhile, Captain Skandalis was lying on his back not five feet away, with Odette straddling *him*. His laugh lines arched above his cheek as he smiled fondly at his partner, fondling the taut line of her jaw . . . letting his fingers skim down her honey-colored skin until they found her pert, bobbing breasts.

Lola clenched again, somewhere lower this time. God, the way he handled that woman! The way he cupped her and murmured encouragements.

Not once did Fletch ever gaze at me that way. Or caress me with such genuine affection.

But her ex was the furthest thing from her mind when she caught a glimpse of the captain's cock. He'd slipped it between Odette's outer lips, and was encouraging her to slide up and down it, with his hands indenting her hips. Her head lolled back, and her tortoiseshell comb came loose, sending waves of midnight hair cascading down her back as she let out soft, desperate moans. Meanwhile, there was that tip of him, like a wine-colored mushroom, bobbing up and then disappearing beneath Odette's little Mohawk of black thatch.

Lola gripped her pillow. Modesty guilted her into looking away, yet her eyes wandered back to that sensuous scene with every gasp and lusty grunt Captain Scandalous let out.

"You want that cock up *your* cunt, don'tcha?" Miss Christy whispered. "I can feel your heat down there, Lola. And I can tellya Skorpio hits all the hot spots and lets his woman come first. Right, Captain?"

The handsome Greek flashed a grin that told Lola he *loved* this game. He intended to make her watch, until she couldn't stand it any more!

"Give it to her, stud!" the masseuse said in a hoarse whisper. "Shove it up her cunt and pump her full of it! Lola here can't wait much longer."

This encouragement was punctuated by those rock-hard nipples prodding her back. Lola was too appalled at her body's reactions to protest what Miss Christy said or did: their rhythmic rubbing against the sheets made a suggestive whisper all its own. And with the weight of her captor pushing her mound into the mattress, it wouldn't be long until she needed more direct relief.

And damn the captain! He chose that moment to lift Odette a few inches above his body, giving Lola full view of his rampant erection before lowering his lady onto his shaft, inch by inch.

Odette cried out, bucking wildly. The massage table creaked with their shifting weight, and the musky scent of their sex made Lola writhe in spite of herself. Skandalis was gorgeous, lying there fully in command of himself and his partner: his muscles tensed and bunched with each deliberate thrust as Odette rode him. She was rocking faster against him, her pert breasts shimmying as her hips wiggled feverishly against his.

Then Skorpio jammed her down and held her absolutely still.

The little room held its breath. And so did Lola.

As he raised his head, Odette lowered herself enough for him to suckle her breasts. He lapped gently at one peak, releasing it with a wet, sucking sound that made Lola clench where she hoped Miss Christy wouldn't notice.

Her own nipples ached as she watched, so she pressed them harder into the mattress. Would that man never tire of teasing every woman in this room? Did he think they'd all worship him while he took his sweet time with his partner?

Skandalis clamped his lips around Odette's other breast and she shrieked. Began to pump the man with an abandon that took Lola to the end of her tether. Her sigh rasped between her clenched teeth, and damned if Miss Christy didn't scoot off her and slip an arm beneath her hips.

"I'm gonna give you what you want Lola," the masseuse said, reaching beneath the table. "I can't stand your agony any longer. I know your pain, girlfriend, and Miss Christy's gonna fix it."

The masseuse, strong from the rubdowns she gave each day, effortlessly lifted Lola into a position that left her backside pointing up and her legs parted. This sent her weight onto her forearms while she clutched the mattress.

"If you think for one minute you're going to—"

"Don't even have to think about it, darlin'. Just followin' my rule about how the customer comes first." When Miss Christy chuckled, her breath feathered against Lola's slit. "Open wide, and then close hard. Try not to let the people upstairs hear you screamin', baby doll."

Lola squeezed herself shut, determined not to let this *woman* have her way, when it was that man on the next table she wanted. But then she felt a very warm, solid *something* coaxing her open down there.

"Whatever that is, you're not going to—"

"It's a glass dildo, sugar. All warmed and oiled and just ready to slide inside your—"

"I want it *that* way," Odette rasped, pointing at Lola. "I want to be the bitch in heat while you fuck me like a dirty dog, Skorpio."

Lola's breath left her in a rush as the lithe Greek woman scrambled into position, pointing her firm backside so her slick lips were visible between long, shapely legs. Skorpio's smile had a desperate edge to it, yet he was ever the captain in control. He knelt behind Odette, his rod as rigid as a piston, and then entered her with enough force to make them both gasp.

Lola's groan rose to a cry of sheer need as Miss Christy plied the glass toy with perfect timing, matching the captain's thrusts, stroke for stroke. Was that a thumb tickling her clit, or a knuckle?

Not that it mattered. Too far gone she was; didn't care what rubbed her there as long as it didn't stop.

"Doesn't that just make you wanna whimper and pant, Lola?" the masseuse demanded slyly. "I'm gettin' mine just watching that sweet little ass of yours spasm . . . oooh, and here comes the honey!"

Odette's low moan escalated, filling the little room with a keening need that made everything spiral upward like a turning screw. She arched up to balance on her knees, her ebony hair swinging above hips that ground backwards into Skorpio's. Her long fingers curled over her breasts. The gorgeous woman's breathing became ragged and rough, and at the moment she grimaced, Skandalis shot.

Unable to control her wiggling hips any more than she could stop that wicked masseuse with the slick toy and fingers, Lola gave in to it. Closed her eyes and lost herself in the extreme sensations of solid girth and warm length and the wetness dribbling down her leg. Gritting her teeth against a scream, she convulsed. Again and again Miss Christy slid the dildo inside her, high enough to inflame her g-spot, as well.

Lola collapsed forward, which canted her ass toward the

ceiling. Her thoughts were still swirling in a sated haze when she heard the captain's low laughter.

"What a lovely creature you are when you lose control, Lola," he murmured, stroking her hair away from her damp forehead. He was standing beside the massage table with his other arm around Odette, smiling indulgently. "It will be a great pleasure indeed to hold your body close to mine as we waltz tonight in the grand ballroom."

Lola blinked, which was all she could manage at the moment. Now the captain was hinting at other intimate activities, but she wasn't betting any money she'd make it to the ballroom—or anywhere else—as rubbery as she felt.

"Be dressed and ready to dance the night away when I come for you," he crooned, lowering his face so those obsidian eyes were level with hers. So she could see how handsome he was as she caught a whiff of the sex he'd shared with Odette; so he could lord it over her that even after making mind-numbing love, Skorpio Skandalis remained the supreme commander of everyone and everything aboard his ship.

"I want you to look nothing less than electrifying when I show you off, my dear," he finished, "because you are *mine*."

7

"Wipe that smirk off your face and get me outta here," Lola muttered.

Aric had appeared out of nowhere, and had the gall to hold her robe like a perfect gentleman would hold a lady's coat. Once again his silver-green eyes took a leisurely tour, this time lingering on the wisps of hair clinging to her sweaty neck, and on the trails of wetness that had dried on her thighs.

"Rode hard and put away wet?" he teased.

She whirled around to smack him, but he caught her by the wrist.

"You knew!" she rasped. "You *knew* Skandalis would just tease me while that nympho Miss Christy shamed me into—"

"So you find pleasure shameful?" Keeping hold of her hand, Cabana Boy opened the door for her. "Funny, but from the looks of you I'd swear you found shame pleasurable. You just won't admit it."

"Bye, now! Y'all come back!" a cheerful chirp followed them out of the spa.

Lola strode down the hallway with what little dignity she

could muster. Were the other guests still at the gala, or had they gone to dinner by now? She could *not* be seen by normal, decent people looking like she'd been ravaged!

Especially since she hadn't. Not the way she wanted, anyway. And not so much as a towel or a cigarette or a kiss-my-ass when Miss Christy sashayed out of the massage room, sniffing after the captain. Just *left* her there, feeling sticky and—*used*.

"Why do *you* find it so amusing that—why do you call it *pleasure*, what Miss Lusty Busty did to me?" she demanded. "You think it's *funny* that the captain got me all hot and bothered, and then made me watch him put it to that—that other woman?"

Aric's lips curved in a secretive grin. "Why do you think I'd know about this stuff?"

"Oh, get real!" she cried. "Skandalis would've bragged to you on his way out. Don't pretend he doesn't keep you informed—so you can be sure I don't have a single moment to consider *escape*."

They stepped into the staff elevator. Once again, Wonder Warden leaned against the wall right beside her, lithe as a tiger. Looking sexy as hell just pushing the UP button.

"OK. So he told me I was to get you showered and fed before I hustle your buns downstairs to find a formal dress," Aric replied with a hint of impatience. "You think I have it easy? You think I *like* playing cop to a prickly little bitch who *whined* because she got moved to the penthouse level? And is *whining* because she *came* in the spa?"

Lola straightened her shoulders, yanking her lapels together. Those silvery eyes were looking for her Very Cherries again, and he didn't deserve that view right now!

"I didn't whine," she simpered. "I merely. . . ."

She sighed. Why was his point so very damning? So damned accurate?

Suddenly very tired, Lola went limp against the cool steel

wall. "What would it take for you to let me just crash tonight? It's been a helluva day, you know?"

"Sorry, babe. I'm not for sale."

The elevator door slid open with a low swoosh, and then Aric unlocked the suite's door. In their absence, the room attendant had turned down that big, beautiful bed and left mood lamps burning on the tables. It seemed a shame to have such a gorgeous suite and no chance to spend time in it.

She spotted two wrapped truffles from that high-end chocolate shop downstairs, and snatched one off her pillow. "So tell the captain I'm sick. You know damn well he only wants to—"

"Take your shower. You'll feel better."

"—get me all hyped up to dance with him, and then he won't—"

Aric's single raised eyebrow said *don't make me take you to that bathroom myself, lady.*

With a loud sigh, Lola unwrapped her candy, smoothing its foil when she saw a message printed inside.

You're about to meet a wild, wonderful lover!

"Yeah, right," she muttered. "In my dreams."

She popped the truffle into her mouth and then paused, letting the sweet mocha filling ooze over her tongue while her teeth tested the dark chocolate that surrounded it. Her toes curled into the plush carpet.

My God, this is fabulous. Good thing I breezed into that candy shop and breezed right back out when I saw the price tags on these things. I can already feel my ass getting fatter.

Cabana Boy, who was staring right at it, didn't seem to notice. So she wadded up her robe and threw it at him, for spite. She padded toward the bathroom, aware he was watching her every move.

"Do you know how many women on this ship would give their right legs to dance with Captain Skandalis?" he shot at her bare back.

Lola stopped, tonguing the chocolate off her teeth as she thought about that. "Not if they really intended to *dance* with him, they wouldn't," she teased.

"OK, I've got it now! You don't know how to dance!"

She slammed the shower door on that remark, twisting the faucet handle with a vengeance. What did a girl have to do to get a little peace and quiet? So much *lip* that kid was giving her! Another Yes Man for the captain, just like Rio DeSilva.

Closing her eyes as the warm water pulsed against her chest, Lola let herself relax against the glass wall. Let her head fall forward to catch the water. This was the best thing to happen to her all damn day!

But why? What's so tough about playing along with Captain Skandalis and your cabana boy? In the end, you go home a free woman! Your credit gets fixed, and it'll be business as usual.

But that was the problem, wasn't it? She'd planned to go home *married*.

While she prided herself on being independent and savvy, Lola Wright still believed, deep down, that once you had that MRS in front of your name, life had direction. You had a road map to maturity, and a more secure future—and your family and friends would stop speculating about whether you were too impossible for any man to put up with. Or . . . girly, that way.

And once you got past the Big Three-O, the biological time bomb ticked like a grandfather's clock marking time in a funeral parlor. Even though she'd been running a successful business for years, she felt lacking as a woman because she didn't have a family of her own.

What ever happened to that woman who'd believed she could have it all, and do it all? And why couldn't you just order the perfect guy online and get a set of smart, adorable kids to go with him?

Sighing, Lola lathered her hair and then scrubbed herself all over with her net scrubbie and the gel on the shower shelf. Scents of eucalyptus and green tea wafted around her in the steam, refreshing her more than she anticipated. The chocolate and sugar and caffeine from the truffle kicked in, revving her pulse.

Maybe there was hope for this evening, after all. Maybe she could give the captain an eyeful of woman he couldn't possibly refuse—or at least get a kick out of showing herself off.

When Lola opened the door, the cloud of herbal mist filled the bathroom with a heady sense of wealth and well-being, as though a woman of mystery—a goddess!—was emerging to rule this night like the moon!

"And here I am!" she whispered, raising the back-scrubber like a scepter. "The High Priestess, stepping from her Gilded Tarot deck to dance divinely above the waters of insight and illumination!"

A low laugh came from the doorway. "Bet the captain's never heard *that* one!"

Aric appeared in the mist then, holding out the thickest, fluffiest towel she'd ever seen.

"Thank you, dear," she murmured. Despite his smart-ass remark, she maintained her regal tone and posture. "Never forget who you're dealing with here. A Priestess has powers and secrets no mortal man can fully comprehend. Captain Scandalous doesn't stand a chance!"

It was a head game, a pretense to get her through the night. But what could it hurt? It beat whining and feeling sorry for herself—and being told she was.

So Lola lotioned—no, she anointed—herself. Then she ate the fabulous lobster stir-fry Aric had ordered up from the galley, while he dried and arranged her hair in a sleek topknot with a riot of ringlets springing out of it. Not a style she'd ever consider in the real world, and yet . . . there was something very goddesslike about appearing younger and more spontaneous and—

"Very sophisticated. Yet playful." Aric circled her, studying the overall effect of his efforts in the vanity mirror.

"That's what you tell *all* the captain's girls, right?" Lola eyed the lanky young man with a thoughtful eye, trying to figure out if his talents in cosmetology *meant* anything. Like, about his sexual preferences.

"So how'd you get into doing hair?" she fished as she tested the spring in those ringlets. "Or did you just write 'miracle worker' on your job app, so Skandalis hired you?"

There was that secretive grin again, as he peered at her from beneath his own tousled curls.

"I'm not done yet, Priestess," he whispered, his breath tickling her ear. "Sit still, or Cinderella's gonna be late for the ball."

He worked the same sort of magic with her makeup, using the cosmetics she'd brought from home. He made her eyes grow greener and more feline with a flick of the eyeliner. Gave her a polished, classy glow she'd never achieved on her own.

Lola could only stare into the mirror, wondering who that woman was; believing the Priestess had emerged for real, and could make men kneel at her feet. A goddess like that could make the captain *beg* for it!

"Whatever's on your mind right now, hold that thought!" her warden murmured. "Now let's get you downstairs for an evening gown—"

"And what's wrong with mine? I've got a black strapless number that—"

His raised eyebrow shut her up again. The kid was way too good at that move—and Lola was feeling way too good to jinx this new mood he'd created with face paints and hair spray.

By God, she'd show Captain Scandalous who he was dealing with! She'd play by his rules, all right—but this time she'd *win*!

* * *

Why wasn't she surprised that Clive Kingsley, the courtly concierge, awaited them in the boutique Aric escorted her to? These guys on the *Aphrodite* must take as much time conferring on their walkie-talkies as teenage girls spent on their cell phones.

She didn't complain, however. The dapper Brit had set aside three of the most exquisite dresses she'd ever seen, in colors that called out to her. And all of them were her size.

Lola tried not to gape like a clueless schoolgirl as she admired each of the gowns. "But how did you know—"

"You're not the only one who has a practiced eye at . . . sizing things up," he replied with a smug smile. "And sometimes, others have a different impression of us because they have a fresh focus. I've chosen colors and designs you might not try on your own, assuming they just wouldn't be *you*."

Oh, but each of these gowns spoke to something deep within her: the woman who would be Queen, but feared someone would lift the hem of her royal robe and discover her scuzzy sneakers. While she could make an ordinary businessman look like a million bucks, Lola Wright spent little time choosing her own wardrobe. Tailored suits with blouses and pumps got her through nearly every occasion.

So what a treat it was, to revel in the first gown's diaphanous layers of pale ivory, and then to giggle at the glitzy way its iridescent beads flashed like shooting stars. When she tried it on, she felt like a fairy princess—until she stepped in front of the mirror in the main room.

Two red bull's eyes and a patch of thatch jumped out at her.

"My God, you can see right through the—well, you can see *everything*," she said with a gulp.

Clive smiled, his gaze wandering below her waist as he smoothed the shoulder seams.

"Perhaps a wax job and some nail polish remover would be

the thing before you wore this one. Or not," he added with a coy shrug. "Bait your hook for whomever you're trying to catch, my dear."

Right. That wild, wonderful lover I'm about to meet.

"I'm sure you'll agree that wearing a slip would ruin the effect."

Rolling her eyes at the concierge—a man who obviously enjoyed this part of his job—Lola took the second dress into the fitting room. Sleek and smooth, made of deep green satin, it seemed a better choice because it at least covered her uh, assets.

"I chose this one to accent your lovely hair and eyes, of course," Kingsley crooned. "But don't let that limit you! A gorgeous girl like yourself can wear a *kaleidoscope* of colors well! And your figure is *so* suited to styles most women can't carry off. You should celebrate that."

Celebrating herself! Now *there* was a novel concept!

Yet it impressed Lola anew as she slipped into a gown of eggplant and claret stripes: it left one shoulder bare and set the other off with a pleated sleeve cap that rose boldly into the air like a butterfly wing. Wayyyy too out-there and Parisian for a girl who grew up in Oregon! She only kept it on to humor the kind concierge, yet she was amazed by what she saw when she stepped in front of the triple mirror outside the dressing room.

"I look like someone from a different galaxy or—"

The *hissssss* that escaped as Clive exhaled shut her up. And when he met her gaze in the mirror, over her bare shoulder, Lola swore she saw smoke from the fire in those blue eyes.

"Guess I'd better take this one, huh?"

"No one else can even try it on, now that I've seen *you* in it."

She felt a glow inside, yet habit made her reach for the price tag. Kingsley, however, grabbed it first and deftly tore the paper from its string.

"We're charging these to the captain's account," he murmured. "And since you're working off debts Mr. Fletcher left you, you might as well have something to show for it. Whatever Lola wants, Lola gets, remember."

"But I couldn't dream of—"

"Why not?"

Clive kissed her hand, challenging her with the glint in his eye. "If you can't dream here, on Fantasy Cruise Lines, then *where*? After all, you're appearing in the ballroom at Skorpio's command. If he's going to play, he's going to pay."

Finally! A man who's not kissing the captain's ass!

Lola grinned at the concierge, feeling grand and giddy. And very high-maintenance!

"Right you are! I'll take all three!" she crowed. "Now tell me which gown will wow Captain Scandalous tonight. And I'm betting you have just the right little *trinkets* to wear with it."

"Indeed, I do, my dear," he purred, grinning like the Cheshire Cat. "For this evening, I suggest the deep green sheath. I'll have the others sent to your suite."

Was this really happening? Lola quickly changed into the elegant dress that made her eyes look large and mysterious and . . . provocative. Lord, she'd never felt *provocative* in her life—not this way! The gown fit like a glove that was custom cut for her body. In the back of her mind, her mother was telling her to ask for the proper underthings—a slip, at least—to wear beneath this sleeveless creation that dipped low to show the tops of her unfettered breasts. It also had an open side seam that revealed most of her thigh.

But of course, underwear didn't *exist* that would do this dress justice! Why would she want a bra line? Or a slip that would flutter through that daring slit on the side?

And isn't YOUR slit feeling sleazy and free? Without even a thong to cover it!

Lola chuckled, hearing sex and cigarettes in her inner voice.

A killer combination, when the captain took her into his arms to dance tonight!

When she emerged from the changing room, Kingsley awaited her with the perfect accessories.

"Your magic slippers," he said, handing her a pair that were little more than clear straps with heels like icicles. "Fuck-me shoes at their finest, don't you agree?"

Lola's jaw dropped. Had this proper Brit really said that?

Yet the grin twitching at his lips made her giggle. And when Kingsley deftly fastened a strand of black pearls around her neck, she didn't have to ask if they were real. Not to mention terribly pricey.

"How can I ever repay—"

"Ah-ah!" He shushed her with a gentle finger, his face alight with sensual pleasure. "Wear it all and be wonderful, dear Lola. Wear it, and *believe*."

She returned his gaze, feeling like the princess in a fairy tale—thinking miracles just might happen, and she could indeed win some private time with Captain Scandalous. Maybe upstairs in that Aphrodisia Suite.

Was that why he'd put her there in the first place?

The phone rang and Kingsley went behind the counter to answer it. As Lola turned in front of the mirror, it struck her as odd that the concierge on a ship this size would be managing such a boutique. Surely he'd have full-time duties dealing with passengers, since a well-versed saleslady could've assisted her with these gowns.

Or perhaps Clive Kingsley had taken her on as his personal mission. An intriguing thought, as she sneaked a peek at his face in her mirror. Brits had always fascinated her with their wry humor and impeccable etiquette and—

He held her gaze in the glass with sexy blue eyes that then wandered along her profile.

Lola melted. He *did* have intentions, and they went beyond seeing that Skorpio Skandalis treated her like a queen rather than a captive! Perhaps Clive intended to challenge the captain for the pleasure of her company!

"I see, sir . . . yes, of course, captain. I'm sure she'll understand," he spoke stiffly into the phone.

But she bloody well won't like it, was what he didn't say.

Lola frosted over. "I suppose he's come up with some excuse—"

"Actually, our captain has been called away to an emergency. So he sends his regrets—and me," came a voice from the doorway.

In strolled Aric, looking young and wonderful in a close-cut tux of navy blue with a cravat and cummerbund of bright lime and silver stripes. On anyone else such a combination would look outrageous, yet Lola couldn't help gaping at him. His hair hung in loose, gleaming curls that made her fingers itch to get lost in them.

He offered her an elbow. "I guess you're stuck with me, Priestess. Shall we dance?"

8

All right, so it really wasn't such a sacrifice, walking into the grand ballroom with the stud muffin who'd given her this miracle make-over. Aric eased her out of the doorway to pause for a moment—either so he could read the room, or to give her a chance to make a grand entrance. Lola wasn't *pleased* that Skandalis had stood her up, but she wasn't surprised, either. Of *course* he'd get called away, just when she'd turned from a caterpillar into a butterfly! Wasn't that how her luck was running on this trip?

But here in this ballroom aglow with crystal chandeliers and champagne punch, where more than a hundred gloriously dressed guests swayed to the beat of a small orchestra, Lola decided to *shine on*. In the past hour she'd gone from feeling utterly exhausted and peeved to feeling like the High Exalted Ruler of the Universe. Way beyond a mere Priestess.

Not a sensation to be wasted. No matter *whom* she'd planned to be dancing with.

So as Aric led her to the parquet dance floor, she didn't balk at being shown off. Didn't protest when he extended his arm like a dancer in a competition, gripping only her fingertips as he held her in his dramatic gaze. And then they walked—no, they were gliding—to the center of the floor. On cue, the trumpets announced them with a fanfare, and the orchestra seguéd into the high style of a Viennese waltz.

It was no time to tell him she was a little rusty; that she'd forgotten all but the ONE-two-three of the beat she'd learned in a college ballroom dance class.

Not a problem, his silvery eyes said, and he cut the theatrics to lead her in a very basic waltz pattern. Soon they were surrounded by other couples, some who'd spent *many* hours on the dance floor, and Lola relaxed. Simply enjoyed feeling like she was in one of those scenes from a grand old movie, where the entire roomful of dancers turned and dipped gracefully.

"Thank you for this, Aric."

He blinked. Either thinking of something else, or totally immersed in Strauss.

"For this wonderful evening," she explained. "For the way you made my hair and face look like some swanky model's, and the way you've escorted me here at the last minute, and—"

"Not a problem."

Lola stifled her sigh. Any fantasy this Cabana Boy co-starred in would have its limitations, right?

But it's still a pretty wonderful feeling, isn't it? To be dancing like I know what I'm doing—like I deserve to be the belle of the ball just this once?

Her lithe partner stepped back to raise her arm, leading her into a showy spin. With a grin she obliged him—until the squeeze of his hand at the top of the turn made her grimace. Her diamond had turned, and was now being driven into the flesh between her fingers.

Aric's pouty lips parted in confusion. "Did I step on—"

"No, this thing's rubbing me the wrong way!"

Stepping out of the other dancers' path, Lola yanked the

ring from her finger and stuffed it into his tux pocket, behind his lime-striped kerchief.

"Fletch will *not* ruin the rest of this day!" Lola whispered with a triumphant grin. Her finger looked naked without the rock she'd sported these past several weeks, yet the sense of freedom she now felt made her grin giddily at Cabana Boy.

"Dance on, sir! I think I'm getting the hang of this Priestess thing!"

With a sly smile her warden complied, easing them gracefully into the flow of the waltz. He really was a treat, all tricked out and squiring her around this way—not that she'd swell his head any more by telling him so. It was enough to float from one downbeat to the next with his hand on her back, telling herself he'd left duty behind to join her in this grand fantasy. Wondering if Aric had any inclination to take it farther. . . .

It was then Lola spotted him: a figure in dazzling dress whites that set off his olive face and raven hair. He was whirling and gliding with an innate grace no mere Arthur Murray graduate could attain, because his supreme confidence carried him across the floor with a silver-haired lady who dripped in diamonds. Tall and slender, she, too, wore a sophisticated white—

Sophisticated, maybe, but she looks like a cigarette with tits.

Lola nearly choked when Captain Skandalis caught her eye. *Winked* at her, no less!

"By God, if he thinks he can—"

Aric twirled her expertly under his raised arm, so she had to shut up and concentrate. Good for him, sensing she was about to make an ugly scene.

But damned if, the next time she spotted him, Skorpio Skandalis wasn't dancing with a *different* partner! This gal's hair was bottle-black and her strapless, red sequined gown gaped open above wrinkly boobs that didn't do it justice.

He must've felt her temper flaring, because this time Aric guided her to the edge of the dance floor and then twirled her into the crook of his arm. So she couldn't run up and claw out the captain's laughing eyes, obviously.

"It's Skorpio's obligation," her escort spoke soothingly into her ear. Still holding her in that clinch, he lifted a flute of champagne from a passing waiter's tray. "Those ladies have paid extra for the privilege of the captain's company tonight. Most of them are longtime friends. Rich widows who cruise just for something to do."

"Which he knew about before he stood *me* up, right?"

Lola tossed back half her champagne, nearly choking on its intense fizz. She didn't ask if any of those bejeweled beauties were once the captain's love slaves. Didn't such a harem speak for itself—and for Skorpio's priorities?

And here he came now, sauntering up to the dessert buffet—but of course taking time to squeeze and kiss the ladies who fawned over him along the way. Served him right to have three different colors of lip prints on his cheek.

Taking champagne from the table, Skandalis bowed elegantly. "To the most beautiful woman in this room," he crooned as he clinked his glass to hers. "Miss Wright, you astound me, the way you've appeared here like a goddess in—"

"This is *quite* the emergency you're tending to!" she rasped.

Captain Scandalous chuckled seductively. "I got called to a fire, my dear. You see how it is with me? So many flames—so little time to fan them all!"

And before she could reply, the arrogant Greek quaffed his bubbly, grinned devilishly—and strode to the end of the table with his arms open wide, to where the next flame was wagging her finger at him.

"Fire, my ass!" she muttered at his retreating backside. "Those old broads could start a weenie roast with their hot flashes! And I hope yours gets *torched*!"

Aric let out a loud laugh, but squelched it when some of the people around him turned to stare. "I can see now why the captain requested a companion for you, Miss Wright. He really wanted a bodyguard for himself."

"Yeah, well, if he'd behave like a gentleman—follow through on his promise—I'd mind my manners, too."

Lola realized then that her fist was planted in her hip and she was tapping her foot: Skandalis had taken his new partner in a clinch and was cheek-to-cheek in a tango position so close they were making love through their clothes. He was obviously going to bait her all evening; had no intention of dancing the night—or even part of a song—away with her, by the looks of the glittering, silver-haired entourage that cheered him on from the punch fountain.

She snagged another glass of champagne and downed half of it in a gulp. It was getting easier to do that.

"I appreciate your being such an understanding escort, Aric," she said. Her voice was getting as slurred as her thoughts, but what did that matter? "I'm gonna sit the rest of them out. I don't exactly feel like dancing anymore."

"But Miss Wright, you're the—"

"And knock it off with the 'Miss Wright' thing, OK?" she muttered. "Bad enough that Captain Scandalous is making me feel like such a wall flower, without feeling old enough to be your mother, as well."

"You think I'd dress this way for my mother?" he countered, turning her chin with his finger. "We might as well enjoy—"

"You talk a good line, Aric, but you're being paid to be my keeper, right?" Lola sighed, gently smoothing his lime-striped tie back into place. "I'm guessing any number of young ladies on this ship would *love* to be with you. So why don't I just go back to my suite, and you can spend the rest of your evening—"

"Nice try, Priestess. Shall we sit over here for awhile?"

With an exasperated roll of her eyes, Lola traded her empty flute for another full one and allowed him to steer her toward a small table in the rear. Even after chugging bubbly, her spirits were deflating. Why was she feeling like a misfit at a middle school dance? So damn disappointed because the captain had snubbed her—when Cabana Boy here was trying his damnedest to show her a good time.

Sheesh, if she were with Dennis, he'd be schmoozing at the bar or working the room for new clients in this moneyed crowd, because dancing had never been his thing. Not even a simple slow dance like the one they were playing now—while Skandalis gazed haughtily into the enamored eyes of his third partner since he'd walked away from her.

Lola sighed forlornly. Instead of making her giddy, the booze was taking her down with the sheer exhaustion of this long, stressful day. Damn shame to be all tricked out but ready to bury herself in bed. Alone.

God, she wanted a cigarette. When she realized she was holding the stem of her empty champagne glass in the fork of her fingers, she shoved it away. Damn that Dennis! This was all his fault!

The orchestra struck up a sultry Latin introduction, and Lola could *not* watch Captain Skandalis faux-fornicate to another tango. "Look, I've got to use the little girls'—"

Damned if Aric didn't stand up, like he planned on going with her!

And then a hand landed on her shoulder and a soft voice murmured, "May I have the honor of this dance, Lola *mia*? I requested this song just for you."

Was she dreaming, or had every head swiveled at the raw longing in that voice? She turned to find Rio DeSilva smiling at her, within kissing distance, his Spanish eyes glowing golden-brown in the low light. He stuffed a folded bill into Aric's pocket. And when her warden didn't take the immediate hint, the security agent dismissed him with a pointed stare.

No dialog. No king-of-the-jungle guy games. Aric simply headed for the exit.

What was it about this man DeSilva? Oh, it didn't hurt that

his ivory tux and that black shirt with the tab collar rendered him fatally attractive . . . enough of a rebel bad-ass to make Lola suck in her breath as she returned his gaze. When those eyes wandered down to her lips, she licked them, wondering if her lipstick had held up through all that champagne.

His sigh sounded hungry.

Lola blinked, aware that Rio's warm hand still rested on her shoulder, and that the orchestra had slithered into a seductive rendition of "Whatever Lola Wants." Her mother used to ham up the lyrics of this song when she was a kid, acting like the spoiled princess she was . . . *whatever Lola wants, Lola gets.* . . .

She smiled. Swallowed. The willowy black singer in strapless red sequins crooned the opening line into her mike—surely a blatant message to Captain Scandalous, who would *not* be dancing this one with her. Rio's hand slipped down to the small of her back, and as he escorted her toward the dance floor, her pulse galloped.

This man was *not* her mother, nor was he hamming it up to humor her. Rio DeSilva knew exactly what Lola wanted, and he intended to give it to her. Maybe right here on the dance floor.

The brief flicker of that fantasy made her blink. Made her *think*, before she succumbed to the tang of booze on his breath— how would his tongue taste?—and the aroma of smoke that clung to his clothes.

"I—this is *so* romantic, that you requested this song for me," she bleated, "but it's been years since I learned to—"

"Give me thirty seconds in this dark corner, and the basic step pattern's yours," he said, effortlessly easing her out of the crowd and into tango position. "Give me another minute, and I'll be yours, as well, Lola *mia*."

Lola swallowed. It's all she had the strength to do, once his seductive words sank in.

Wasn't this the man who'd kept his distance earlier, saying he wouldn't cross the captain's line? Yet here he was, teaching her to tango in front of God and Skandalis and everyone.

"Gliiiide . . . gliiiiide . . . step, step, step. Gliiiide . . . gliiiiide . . ."

How had she come to be pressed this close to him, thighs rubbing and hips flexing in rhythm? Her arm was dramatically thrust forward with his, and he was whispering the dance pattern as though telling her how he wanted her to make love to him. All the moves and nuances that would take him over the top.

And she was so damn ready to take him there.

"Gliiiide—gliiiiide—step, step, step," he murmured again.

The singer's castanets did a sexy *click-click-click* to that same beat, and Lola realized then that she was *dancing*, right there on the dance floor, without having to think about what came next, or having to coax her partner along like she'd done in ballroom dance class. Somehow DeSilva had step-step-stepped her onto the parquet floor, and—like an illusionist making magical things happen—the man with the tiger eyes had her dancing the tango on intuition.

The debonair Spaniard held her gently against his hip, his lead so smooth as to be invisible: just the merest pressure and pull of the warm hand that held hers. She caught a glimpse of the captain, who'd paused on the sideline to watch them.

Lola straightened to flaunt herself, her head held high and proud—like she'd seen in the movies. Rio's grin flashed his approval: his eyes narrowed seductively, which cast the rest of his bronzed face into a mask of sheer seduction.

Gliiiide—gliiiiide—step, step, turn.

Without a hitch they negotiated the edge of the floor and insinuated themselves between other couples caught up in the passion of the dance.

Lola caught a whiff of brandy and fine tobacco, manly scents that increased his mystique and had her inhaling deeply: feeding her need for nicotine, yet firing her desire for something much more addictive. Rio Benito DeSilva was now a very seductive puzzle she longed to solve, slowly. Naked.

The music slowed to a dramatic halt, and as though he'd done it a hundred times, the Spaniard tipped her backwards into a dip that had her holding her breath. His face was mere inches above hers and the kiss on his lips had her name on it.

"Lola," he breathed.

As though on cue, the ballroom lights went down. How long would he hold her this way? How long could her leg bear her weight?

And yet, she felt no concern. Rio held her firmly against him as time stood still. There was only the silent shimmer of the mirror ball sending its sequins through the room, and those lips inching so, so close she could feel the warmth of his breath.

A vein fluttered above his collar.

Lola stretched to kiss the smooth skin between its rounded black tabs; to feel the beat of his pulse against her lips.

The soft strains of a rhumba brought her upright—through no effort of her own—and Rio led her into the secretive sway of impassioned prey and predator, circling . . . seducing. Step-step, pause . . . step-step, pause.

Somehow her feet followed the beat. Somehow her body followed his lead, for Lola's mind was too swept away to be of any assistance.

Were people really standing along the sideline, watching them? Did she *look* as perfect with Rio as this felt? It was a heady sensation, to merely let go and let this man take control of her with the power of those eyes. Eyes focused only on her.

And yet, Rio's gaze wasn't domineering or arrogant, like someone else's she knew—some Greek guy whose name escaped her now.

Around each other they went, circling and swaying. Her fingertips remained lightly against his palms so he could have his way—so Rio could lead her into another step pattern without saying a word. Why and how their bodies brushed and then parted, Lola didn't know. There was only the throb of the bass pulse and the whisper of the cymbals, and her hips found the rhythm as though she'd been born dancing this way.

The music ended, and Rio grabbed her hand. Quickly skirting the crowd, he led her through a door marked STAFF ONLY. As if that weren't enough to set her her heart racing, he whisked her down the short corridor and into a service elevator.

As its door closed, he smiled tightly. Punched the highest button.

"I saw Aric coming toward us, probably on orders from the captain." He stepped close enough that his knee parted her thighs, pressing her against the cool steel wall. "Why waste a woman like you on a kid like him?"

For a fleeting moment Lola thought he was calling Skorpio a kid, but she got so caught up in watching his lips—in catching that faint hint of liquor and smoke on his breath—that the words lost their meaning.

She did recall, however, that this was a change in course for the security agent. And not a safe one.

"But if Skandalis catches us—he was watching—"

"Yes, he was," Rio said with a happy snap of those eyes, "and if ever there was a man who wished *he* were holding you so close and so—but that's too damn bad! I say we give him a run for his money—if that's what *you* want, Lola *mia*."

Her sigh escaped with a little hiss as he moved in for the kiss she could already taste. Her eyes fluttered shut. She lifted her face to bask in the glow of him, parting her lips—

But Rio pulled away. Just enough that his question quivered between them in the dim, airless elevator. The shine of his eyes hypnotized her. She sucked air, struggling to think. What was it he'd asked her?

Whatever Lola wants. . . .

And what *did* she want? In the whirlwind of being ditched by Dennis Fletcher and then tormented by Skorpio's sensual power plays in the spa and the ballroom, she felt more alive than she had in *months*. Felt open to the *adventure* sparkling in Rio DeSilva's attentive eyes.

The elevator door slid open, punctuating his unspoken call to choose her fate.

9

She rose to meet him, feeling his thigh against her mound. His mouth felt hungry and hot, more predatory than she expected. Lola matched him breath for breath, lips writhing over his firm, moist mouth and reveling in the tickle of that feral mustache. In his eagerness he bumped her teeth a couple of times, but then slapped his hands to the elevator wall on either side of her head, pressing into her body, refusing to ease up.

Rio tried to fight it down, but it did no good. He'd known it would be this way once they danced and courted each other—once Skandalis saw how it was between them and wanted Lola, too, for more devious reasons.

But that was a moot point now: Lola was *his*. Hadn't she just taken that ring off her finger?

He felt it in her kiss, and in the sighs that escaped when she molded her mouth to his. God, he loved how she didn't back down—didn't come up for air—did *not* let go or shrink back! She was right there with him, sucking his tongue into her mouth and letting out those little groans that drove him nuts.

She was writhing against his thigh. Undulating like a snake

in that deep green dress that made her eyes look wide and childlike—especially with that outrageous hairdo, which shot curls from the topknot like a fountain spewing fireworks. It was a style so brash and unabashed, only Lola could wear it.

And her skin, God it was as soft as he'd dreamed, where her shoulders were exposed. He wanted to grab the dress by its low-slung bodice and rip it down the front, to get a good look at her.

But that would only prove what an animal lurked beneath the facade he'd cultivated since Katya left him. It was how he got through each day, telling himself he could tamp down those desires; could ignore the call of his body when he saw passengers who appealed to him, or made passes at him.

And they did that, women of every age. Every week their eyes sought him out and lingered, questioning as they flirtatiously lowered their gazes. Gratifying, but not the road he wanted to follow. Sometimes the staff rules were handy to hide behind.

So why break them now? Why with Lola? She was in more of a mess than she knew, and she'd probably shoot him when she found out just how deep the muck was. He had no choice but to drag her through it before the week was out.

But for now . . . for now there was only the soft give of her breasts, heaving beneath his chest, and the madness escalating between them. Her hands found his ass, as though she knew how he loved to be squeezed there. The elevator door gaped open, because he'd jammed the OPEN DOOR button mere heartbeats before he'd taken her this way. Anyone could come along—although, on this penthouse level, there was only one suite besides Lola's.

But he couldn't let Skorpio catch them this way. Couldn't let Aric see them, either—too soon for that. Too damned soon for *any* of this. When she slid her tongue in and out of his mouth, imitating what she really wanted from him, Rio reluctantly broke it off.

They panted, staring at each other.

Lola's makeup was wrecked, but he liked that. She looked more warm and willing, So sultry. So *eager*.

But not here. And not tonight—God, not this soon or the rest of the week would be a lost cause and they'd both be in serious trouble. If he could hold back—make her understand that he was using discretion as the better part of valor, as Clive the Proverbial was wont to say—maybe she'd agree to see him again after this week. After her cruise ended. After she found out the truth about Dennis Fletcher—if she was still speaking to him then.

Lola had to understand that his world was about to change, too, in a way that had nothing to do with Fantasy Cruise Lines. Real life had met him head-on, and she might not want to follow him there.

"Come on," he whispered, grabbing her hand.

He pulled out his master key card to let them into her suite. The lamps were lit and the bed turned down, but Rio ignored those wrapped chocolates and the rose on her pillow. He glanced around, his senses keen; listening for anyone who might be hiding in the bedroom or the closets.

It was useless against Aric or Skorpio, but he locked the door and hooked its chain anyway, to make her feel more secure. Resting against the solid coolness of the door, Rio let his body absorb its temperature to lower his own.

Like that would happen! Lola stood there with her hands on her canted hips, jutting her bust at him. Daring him to by God get himself over there and take up where they'd left off.

Any decent man would. He wasn't some clueless kid who'd led her this far and then didn't know where to go.

A square of pale moonlight on the carpet gave him his next cue.

"It's a perfect night for that balcony," he murmured. "Go out there and get ready, Lola *mia*. Let the wind play in your hair. Soak up the wildness of the sea breeze. Cast your inhibitions overboard, and we'll . . . see where this goes."

"You're not coming?" she replied with a sly smile. "Don't think for a minute you're going to strand me out there on the—"

"I have *never* stranded a woman—or even kept one waiting," he insisted with a flash of his eyes. "There's a bottle of champagne in your fridge. I want to catch up with you, now that I'm off duty—and now that *you* won't guzzle it to tolerate Skandalis and his games."

So Lola stepped out onto the balcony, leaving the French doors open to watch Rio move. He looked as lithe as a cream-colored tiger in that tux, and that black shirt made him so, so dangerous! She still had the scent of him on her skin and the taste of his tobacco on her tongue, and she wanted more of *everything*.

She wouldn't quiz him about this change of attitude. It was enough that he'd brought her here so they could be alone for the first time. And he wanted her *ready*.

Well, she'd been *ready* from the moment he'd whispered in her ear, back in the ballroom: *may I have the honor of this dance, Lola mia? I requested this song just for you.*

It was a heady combination, that elevated Spanish accent and the way he ran his words together in that low growl that made little shivers run down her dress with his breath. And then the tango lesson: as long as she lived, she'd *never* forget how he'd crowned her the Queen of that ballroom. Because he knew she needed to feel that way; feel like she was *worth* something, after all the shit she'd been through with Dennis.

The taste of that name made her mouth go sour. Enough of that!

Lola, still ogling the man in her kitchen, reached back to her zipper. It would be more romantic, perhaps, to ask for assistance with it—the age-old ploy for getting a man's hands on her.

Yet this moment in the moonlight called for something more direct. More provocative—the way he'd awakened *her* senses by dancing so close, so effortlessly, and by letting his words tickle her ears while his smile turned her insides to honey butter.

The zipper sang its randy song, and as the sea breeze teased her skin, Lola knew this was right. Knew this night, with that bright crescent moon beaming down like a secretive smile, was made for a couple who came looking for love.

And when they went back inside, is that what they'd have?

She wouldn't ask him. Better to go with the moment, to flow with the current Rio DeSilva had quickened within her. A loud *pop* announced the champagne he'd soon pour, and she wanted to be ready for whatever he did with it. When he took two flutes from her cabinet, she turned her back to him. Gazed out over the midnight blue canopy of night, where lights twinkled on the horizon and another cruise ship was outlined like a diamond broach on velvet.

She shivered, feeling his approach.

Rio stopped in his tracks. Lola was stepping out of that phenomenal dress, pointing her backside toward him. She was naked! What kind of woman wore *nothing* beneath a formal gown?

Dennis Fletcher's woman. You're crazy if you think you can—

He shook away that pesky thought. *Not anymore, she's not. Not if she entrusted that rock to Aric.*

Skandalis told her how to dress. She was following his orders.

The sway of that pretty pink ass, which flared delightfully from her narrow waist, made Rio realize precisely what he'd started here. He'd told her to shed her inhibitions, and he had to admit Lola'd taken his request to the limit. He shifted to relieve the pressure where the seam of his pants cut across his cock.

It was time. Katya was gone, and Lola would be, too, unless he took what she was offering. Skandalis could go screw himself.

God, the way she moved . . . letting the deep green dress slither down her skin to bare her body in a slow striptease. *Very hot.* His damn tux was cut with little room to spare even when he was sane, but all hell would break loose if he let it out of his pants. There'd be no stopping.

And that's what Lola wanted.

So he'd do his best to please her and sate her and drive her out of her mind. Rio wanted her—too long it'd been since he'd indulged in a woman—but he also believed in savoring the finer things, rather than gulping and guzzling them. Lola deserved nothing less.

The gown puddled around her ankles. She balanced herself with an elegant arm outstretched on the balcony railing, leaning forward as she stepped out of the dress. Graceful, like a dancer in slow motion. Knowing he watched her. Knowing he wanted her. Establishing her power over him in this simplest act of undressing while she looked the other way.

He gripped the two glasses. Jittery as he felt, he could ruin this mood in a hundred little ways—or just one. It only took one.

"Lola," he murmured from the open doorway.

"Yes?"

Little vixen was playing hard to get, standing with her back to him—as though she cared what the ocean looked like! Her reply drifted back to him on the breeze, low and sweet and oh-so-hungry.

And what did she do then, but reach up to unfasten her hair. She fumbled with the topknot—for a moment he thought about assisting her—but then that lush auburn hair fell like a rumpled curtain, wavy where the band had held it. Loose tendrils drifted with the breeze—tendrils he suddenly had to feel blowing across his face.

"Lola, I'd like to toast this moment," he offered, hoping she didn't hear that adolescent catch in his voice. "It's a special joy for me, when I please a woman for the first time, and I want to make it special for you, too. No rushing. No groping and fumbling in our haste to couple. I—I want you."

She turned, ever so slowly. First the tip of her breast became visible, siren red alongside her pale, shapely arm, Then the turn of her thigh revealed her sex to him, arrayed in a vee of tight auburn curls.

His zipper lurched. He'd figured her for the type who'd wax everything, so he was ecstatic at her natural beauty down there. The slightest bulge below her navel enthralled him; her ribcage led his eye higher, to those pert, lush breasts. She probably felt they were too small, but he found them delightful. Those jaded nipples glistened like cinnamon disk candies, suggesting an inner child who loved to play naughty big-girl games.

It was her expression that didn't fit.

"You're stalling, aren't you?" She could see the nobility fighting its way into his eyes. She'd hoped for something less . . . respectable.

"Why do you say that?"

She shook her head, which made those waves drift in the breeze—which was turning her nipples into rigid peaks of red.

"You have that look about you, like the white knight who sweeps the princess off her feet but not into his bed. Dammit, Rio," she finished with a sigh. "I've been naked today for two other men—and women—I just met, and all they wanted was a piece of me."

Rio flinched. He'd disappointed her, and he hadn't even dropped his pants yet. "I prefer to take my time with a woman, out of respect for—"

"Please don't tell me you're gay."

A laugh escaped him. Instead of taking that bait, Rio set down one of the champagne flutes and stepped toward a wide-eyed Lola, who now leaned back against the balcony with her arms resting along the railing.

He'd never seen such a sight, such an offering on the altar of the gods. For *him*.

He'd never knowingly provoked a woman's wrath, either,

but he wanted to see what Lola was made of. So he pitched the champagne, splattering her breasts with it.

Her cry rang out in the night. "You son of a—"

He was on her then. He held her beneath her arms while his mouth worked feverishly to keep any of that bubbly from going to waste.

She writhed but couldn't move. Was too astounded at this man's response—and too surprised by the champagne's chilly tingle against her skin. Rio's lips were roving over her breasts, his tongue lapping and licking. When that pencil-thin mustache brushed her painted nipple, Lola laughed out loud, not giving a damn that anyone standing outside would know where that laugh came from.

It came from that place between her legs, which was driving this whole show.

The railing cut into her back as she arched against it, but she could only hold on for dear life, letting her head fall back as he devoured her. DeSilva's mouth was covering every inch of her bare skin, and now that his initial affront had proven his point, he was gentler . . . downright worshipful as he wiggled his tongue in her navel.

Lola's laughter was like the cry of a wild bird above him. Her hips wriggled, and she tried to escape his mouth as he sucked and licked the wine from her skin.

But she didn't try very hard.

He was circling her navel now, relishing the swell of flesh beneath it before going lower. The top of her thigh quivered beneath his lips. He teased her by running his tongue above her mound, following the line of the coarse hair there.

"Wait—Rio, please—"

That made him laugh! This woman was begging for it now! Never again would she question his sexual preferences!

And damned if she didn't shift her weight to one foot, so she could drape the other leg over the back of the wicker chair next to her. Opening herself to him.

Rio knelt. Would there ever be a more alluring sight than those dusky lips rimmed in fur scented with her essence?

"I think the lady needs more champagne," he murmured. He was distracting himself so he wouldn't devour the delicacy before him.

"I think the lady needs a tongue job."

Lola gazed down at DeSilva, into eyes that reflected the moon's glow and the love within him.

At least that's what she told herself. Never had a man approached her from that angle with such a . . . prayerful expression. Yet his eyebrows had just enough slant in them to appear jaded with desire, and that mustache—that wicked thing that slashed downward from his nose, in such direct contrast to the soft lips beneath it—

"Whatever Lola wants," he whispered.

And damned if he didn't snatch the other glass of champagne from the table and wet his fingers, to coat her slit with a cool effervescence that sent shock waves through her. This time she nipped her lip to keep from wailing like a bitch in heat. She could only watch, mesmerized, as his fingertips dipped into the glass and then into her again, circling up inside her.

The fizz make her giggle. Lola couldn't hold still and she loved it!

The scent and heat of her arousal drove him wild. Rio poured more bubbly into his palm and then cupped her with it, pressing the wetness into her coarse curls . . . smearing it on the insides of her thighs.

"C-cold!" she yelped when the breeze kicked up. But she didn't move that suspended leg or the hands that gripped the railing.

He flashed her a grin. Then Rio parted her lower lips with his fingers and wiggled the tip of his tongue all over her damp, luscious flesh, lapping the champagne like a dog at a water bowl. Going for the overt and the outrageous, to show her he knew a few tricks, too.

Lola was quivering now, wiggling all over, which made it hard for him to hold his place. So he stuck his tongue up her. Closed his eyes and resonated with her low cries, urging her into a steady rhythm with his thrusts.

She glanced down and thought, *My God, if there was ever a more gorgeous sight, I hope I never see it.*

His face caught the moon's glow, and his closed eyes revealed long lashes that fluttered at the tops of those high cheekbones. His lips and tongue were in constant motion, tasting her and then creating suction against the tender, sensitive flesh there.

Rio felt the spasms beginning, deep inside her. He went after them, first with overt thrusts of his tongue flattened against her clit and then with a light flicking that avoided it.

"Please—Rio—just give it to me—"

Whatever Lola wants, he thought with a wicked grin. But how soon she got it was up to him, wasn't it?

DeSilva sat back on his heels. Looked up at her as he lapped her honey from his mustache.

He was a cat licking his whiskers. A wildcat with eyes that glowed in the night, as they would glow in her dreams for months to come. So damned proud of himself for catching her off-guard this way—taking advantage of her naked state while not baring his own body. Just teasing her—bringing her to the edge and then backing away!

Grasping the crown of his head, Lola pressed his face to her flesh again. "Finish what you started, DeSilva. I'll make you do this again and again, till you get it *right*."

He needed a lesson, and she was just the one to teach him.

Rio moaned. Grabbing the halves of her ass, he thrust his tongue up her again, running it around her rim until he felt her quiver.

Her hand was still on his head but she'd speared her fingers into his hair. She sprawled back against the railing to open herself farther ... to fully take what he was giving, like a cat stretched languidly to enjoy a belly rub. Lola's moans told him she was well on her way, but in no hurry.

So he pressed upward, *hard*, covering her sensitive flesh with the flat of his tongue.

When he sucked her in, Lola convulsed. She was suddenly surging forward, crying out with the most exquisite, excruciating climax. It throbbed inside her like a beast trying to break free, banging and aching until—

She fell forward, so limp Rio had to catch her. She was vaguely aware that he lifted her up on his shoulder—slung her over his back like a caveman's conquest—and she would've giggled if she'd had the strength. He lowered her onto the bed—that huge, beautiful, soft bed she sank into so blissfully—and then lowered himself for a kiss.

"DeSilva!" his walkie-talkie squawked from the living room. "Get yourself down here! Got footage you have to see!"

Rio grimaced. Being ordered away from this female by another one got on his nerves—especially since he was off duty. Lola wound her sweet arms around his neck, cooing contentedly, her eyes still unfocused.

"Goodnight, Lola *mia*," he whispered.

He slipped out of her grasp, putting his finger to her lips when he saw the protest in her eyes. God, how he wanted to stay here right now!

Backing, backing—he fetched his walkie-talkie from the coffee table to squelch it, before the message came through any louder or clearer.

Then Rio leaned in to blow her another kiss, but Lola was sprawled loosely on the sheets where he'd left her. She was already asleep.

10

Lola felt giddy when she awoke, like a girl who'd crashed after an all-night prom date and the biggest night of her life. Still muzzy from sleep, but fully awake in her head, she began reliving Rio.

When had a man ever lavished such thorough attention on her, knowing exactly how she wanted to be kissed and caressed? And sucked. Oh Lord, how that man could suck! Knew exactly where and how, and with how much pressure.

And what a picture he'd made, on his knees, gazing up into her eyes, with her muff where his mustache should be. Rio Benito DeSilva had *worshipped* her with his hands and mouth and those golden eyes!

Lola knew now that she *had* to have that Spaniard. Had to make love—completely next time—to the most strikingly sensual man she'd ever met. Captain Scandalous be damned! Who needed an arrogant Greek sailor bossing her around? Telling her she could look but not touch. Could get all dressed up but have no place to go with him.

Far better just to loll in this soft, pillowy bed and let her mind drift back to the man who'd pleasured her so masterfully last night . . . and let her body drift back, too.

She awakened in all those places Rio had aroused. Usually finicky about feeling *clean*, Lola ignored the stickiness between her legs, postponing her shower to go over and over her balcony encounter, replaying all the best parts. The intense fizzzzzz of chilled champagne on her sensitive flesh . . . the urgency of Rio's tongue as he guzzled and nuzzled her . . . the way he set aside his own pleasure to concentrate on hers.

When had *that* ever happened with a man?

She shifted, needy again. Too lazy and happy and rubber-muscled to get up for one of her toys—which, now that she thought about it, had been unpacked and put away somewhere by a total stranger, when she got moved to this room.

What an embarrassing—but kinky—thought! Which found her fingers riffling through the hair between her legs. That's why God made arms exactly the right length, wasn't it?

She let her thighs fall open, warming to fresh sensations. Rising to meet Rio's needs in her fantasy, because this time *he* was naked and she was sucking—

"Sorry to interrupt, Priestess, but official business calls. Seems we have information about your runaway roommate."

Yipping, Lola yanked her hand away. She whipped the sheet over herself, glaring at Aric. "You could've at least knocked, dammit!"

He shrugged, chuckling smugly.

She laid there with her pulse pumping, waiting for some sort of apology.

But it wasn't coming. Cabana Boy stood lounging against the door jamb with that insolent, low-lidded smirk that reminded her why she'd never chased after younger men.

"The sooner you get ready, the sooner you see DeSilva again."

Lola sat up, clutching the sheet to her chest.

"That's what I figured." Aric smiled slyly. "You might think about how much my silence is worth to you, Priestess. The captain won't be happy if he finds out Rio's getting a piece of you."

She grabbed for the nearest thing—hurled the two wrapped truffles at him—but he dodged them and slithered away, his laughter lingering to taunt her. Bare-chested and slim-hipped, her keeper was way too cute—and cutthroat—for his own good.

When she finished showering and dressing, Lola found him stretched like a cat on her couch, catching a *Playboy* movie. He was wearing a loose tee-shirt and shorts now, nursing a bottle of imported beer as he polished off her truffles. Considering the crisp uniforms the rest of the staff wore, she found it odd that Aric got away with beach bum attire.

"I have special privileges," was his only explanation as he escorted her into the elevator. "It's not what you know, but *who* you know. You know?"

Lola rolled her eyes. This conversation was going nowhere she wanted to be. "So where are we? I noticed the ship wasn't moving."

Aric checked his watch, his movements unhurried as the elevator began its descent. "It's Wednesday, November 9th, so this must be Caracas. Great place to catch some culture, they say."

Culture. She'd planned to do a tour of some nobleman's historic home here—until Fletch took his own little tour. She scowled at the thought of him, and how many fun things she'd forfeited for his foray in Aruba.

The steel door slid open and Lola stepped out first. The hallways down on this level were painted plain white—a stark contrast to the Caribbean colors and patterns up in the passenger areas.

When Aric gestured into a small office where security monitors lined one wall, she forgot about details of decor, however. Rio DeSilva sat at the desk, shrouded in the room's dimness, his face alight with the unnatural glow of the monitors.

His expression was anything but overjoyed when he looked up at her. It was like they'd never met.

"Please have a seat," he said, pulling up another chair. "We've put together some evidence that might help us with our case against Dennis Fletcher, and I thought you should see it. So you can make informed decisions, or press charges, or whatever."

Lola's spirits sank like the cushion when she sat down. Here she was with the man who'd had her screaming for it last night, alluding to pretty promises he might make—but reality was now about to smack her in the face. Rio DeSilva was the chief security agent, after all, and his cool demeanor and starched whites told her he was all about business now.

He dismissed Aric with a pointed look.

"Later, Priestess," her warden murmured. "Keep me hot in your thoughts, got it? Oh—and don't forget I still have your ring. Bet you're real glad you left the real stone at home, considering all the other stuff Fletcher snatched."

Her jaw dropped. "What do you mean—?"

Rio rose to close the door, scowling. What he didn't need was that smart-aleck stirring up more hornets than they already had swarming right now.

"What was *that* about?" he asked when they were alone. He all too aware of how intimate this setting was—and that other staff members would think so, too.

Lola swallowed. And swallowed again. That queasy, nervous need for a cigarette was roiling her stomach. "Seems Stud Muffin feels it's *worth* something, if he keeps quiet about what you and I did last night."

"Yeah, he says that to all of Skorpio's girls." DeSilva dropped his weak attempt at humor to choose his words more carefully. "What'd he mean about your ring? That was an impressive diamond, as I recall."

The tug-of-war on her face nipped at him. Lola was doing her damnedest to keep a stiff upper lip, her eyes distracted by the flickering images on the six security monitors.

"It slid around on my hand while we were dancing, so I

stuffed it in his tux pocket," she replied. "I don't have a clue about leaving a stone at home, but if Aric thinks for one minute—"

He laid a hand on her shoulder, really sorry this new issue had come up. "Some wealthy ladies have fakes made of their valuable gemstones, to wear when they travel. That way if somebody steals—"

"Well *I* didn't!" She wrapped her arms around her middle, unsure of what to believe. God, what she'd give for a smoke right now! "If he's saying my diamond was a—how would he *know*? Or why would he insinuate—"

"Let's not forget that younger men sometimes say things just for the effect."

Rio perched on the chair beside hers, struggling to keep his hands and remarks to himself. After all, Lola had painted her nipples a startling scarlet, presumably for the man who'd bought her that ring. While it was heartening that she'd removed the damn thing before they'd danced last night, it was still a very visible sign that Ms. Wright was spoken for—no matter *how* he'd had her howling on that balcony last night.

Poor woman looked ready to either throw up or pass out.

But with all the unfortunate information he had to pass along to her, he couldn't make any sympathetic moves right now; couldn't get the least bit personal, either, considering how Skandalis might walk in to be briefed on this Fletcher affair.

"I—I'm sorry to say, your ex-fiancé has an *effect* on the ladies, as well," he offered, aware of how inelegant he sounded. "We put together some footage from the security cameras in the casino, and from a lounge called Fedora's, that show him at his . . . most effective, I'm afraid. But first, fill me in on what went on before you read that message he sent to your room. It might help me fill in some blanks."

Lola blinked. So much had happened since she'd read that damn note, she had to stop and think.

"We—we boarded the ship in San Juan like everyone else," she faltered.

"And we were at sea all day Monday, en route to Aruba," Rio reminded her gently. "Did you notice anything strange about his behavior then?"

Her lips were parched and her voice was starting to crack.

"Strange?" she asked with a sarcastic little grimace. "Fletch was keen on casino gaming—especially lucky at Caribbean Stud poker. So I wasn't surprised that he wanted to play. Once I lose twenty bucks or so in the slots, I lose interest."

Rio nodded, encouraging her with his smile. So far, nothing surprised him. He'd figured Lola for a woman who worked too hard to drop a wad at the tables, and her face bore out her story. "So what'd you do while he played?"

She shrugged sadly. "Strolled in and out of the shops. Figured it was too early to spend a lot on souvenirs from the ship, before we got off at the ports. Looked at the display of art for sale at the auction, but I'm not into that, either. Played some Bingo."

"Win anything?" Damn but he wished they were talking about something else! Here was a woman on a Caribbean cruise, and words like *fun* weren't in her vocabulary.

"Nope. Sorta hung around till Dennis got back, just in time for dinner. Took in the show—"

Still she sounded like a shell of a woman: no excitement in her eyes or lilt in her voice, or details about what she'd eaten or seen in the theater. Damn shame she'd come on this trip to get married, because she sounded like anything but a bride.

Encouraging maybe, but sad. He dropped that thought so he could stay on track: his fingers itched to smooth her hair back from her pale, freckled face. When a tear slithered from the corner of her eye, it took all his strength not to wipe it away.

"And then you got off the ship yesterday morning, when we docked in Aruba?"

"For awhile, yeah. Went to the flea market shops near the

pier, and then walked into town," she mused aloud. "And of course when Fletch saw that snazzy casino, we had to go inside. Just as well, since I had to use the little girls' room."

She blinked, embarrassed that Rio had to be in on all this nitty-gritty—and that she had to reveal such a fiasco of a romance.

"I'm thinking that's when Dennis must've hooked up with the chick with the villa. Just like I now think he must've contacted her before we ever left home," she said with a sigh. "We came back to the ship and I wanted to shower . . . get all freshened up, since Dennis said he wanted to play the tables on board for awhile."

DeSilva watched her expression; didn't have the heart to point out that the casino on board remained closed whenever they were in port. Fletcher had fed her a big fish story, and she'd been too intent on getting caught—really trying for his attention, with that nail polish—to see the loopholes in his net.

But Lola's story did indeed confirm some suspicions, so he steered the conversation away from her feelings, toward the nasty business at hand. Might as well get it all out and get it over with.

"Well, here's what we've caught with our cameras—but I'll warn you, it's not complimentary," he said with a nod toward the bottom monitor. "Try to stay calm and fill in some blanks for me. It'll be a big help, all right?"

Lola glanced at the screen he pointed to, feeling sicker by the minute. The picture was fuzzy and the color wasn't clear, because the casino lights were dim, but that was Fletch, all right.

He was at the ATM near the teller windows. Slot machines and poker tables were teeming with business, and when the view flickered into a close-up, probably from the camera on the bank machine, she saw him snatch several big bills from it. Then he punched numbers for another transaction . . . which she recognized as the PIN for her Well Suited account.

She let out a sick groan, not wanting to watch yet riveted to this evidence all the same.

"Here's a printout of Fletcher's transactions from this ATM and others aboard the *Aphrodite*," Rio said, handing her a page that was nearly filled with entries. He turned on a small lamp.

Lola scanned the long list, which took awhile because her hands were shaking. "Not a surprise, considering what I learned from the credit card rep in Mr. Kingsley's office."

But then the scene on the monitor changed. Dennis was at one of the poker tables, where an attractive girl was dealing cards with dexterous flicks of her bangled wrists. By the looks of the bets, these players were devil-get-screwed wealthy—especially the classy blonde beside Fletch. Or at least she had an impressive stash near her hand—not to mention those two assets bulging out of her strappy little camisole.

Blondie batted her eyes when one of the other players collected his winnings, and then she and Dennis got up. Fletch ordered drinks from a passing waitress, flirting with his poker companion as she approached the ATM. She slipped in her card and punched the numbers with a long, dark nail that had to be fake.

Lola's jaw dropped. "Dennis has a memory for figures that won't quit—and not just chest measurements," she added shakily. "Do you suppose he's accessed *her* accounts, too?"

Rio remained silent, directing her back to the screen with his nod.

The tape flickered at a splice, and Dennis was again at a poker table with Blondie as a new game was being dealt. She bantered with the dealer—a sexy Jamaican guy this time—as she placed her bet, and meanwhile Fletch set his drink down near her fresh stash. He was teasing this gal to go for it, giving her the ole come-on eye contact, while, with a magician's quickness, his cocktail napkin landed on her credit card. Just that fast, he slipped it into his sport coat pocket!

"He—he never missed a beat chatting her up," Lola gasped. "Doesn't she know better than to leave her cash and card out where—"

Rio shushed her with a gentle finger, his gaze foretelling more unpleasant information.

"This next footage," he said, scrolling forward, "is from our cocktail lounge, Fedora's. After watching this a few times, I'm thinking Fletcher's new 'soul mate,' as he called her, is setting her hook. Her cash and card might've been her bait."

Lola watched in horrified fascination as Blondie, bulging out of her black cami top, wagged her finger playfully at Dennis. Never one to miss an invitation, Fletch devoured her with his kiss, right there on a leather love seat with other people looking on. His hand slipped up under one of those bazooms, as though one little tug would bare it.

"That goddamn bastard," she muttered. "Wasn't wiping out *my* accounts enough for him? He—he's a financial manager, you see. Invests his clients' accounts—*my* accounts—and has control over *huge*—"

She drew a shaky breath, looking away so Rio wouldn't see her tears. "I've made the mistake of my lifetime, falling for that man. *Trusting* him with my personal and business accounts. I—I never in a million years saw this coming. I feel so—so *stupid*."

"Don't." DeSilva stood up, clicking the monitor off.

"But—I need to see that part where—"

"It won't change anything, Lola," he murmured. "I'll walk you back upstairs now. I've given you plenty to think about."

The man in white was still all business, yet she sensed he was steering her out of that cozy little office to avoid temptation—and talk—as much as to remove her from the images he'd shown her. Lola kept seeing them, those incriminating pictures that rolled through her mind in fast-forward, as she and Rio got into the elevator.

"I suspect Fletcher is extremely charismatic," he went on in that low Spanish accent. He reached for her hand, to weave his fingers loosely between hers. "Attractive enough to charm the ladies, obviously—but an expert at presenting himself—presenting a facade to outfox even intelligent, rational women like yourself."

He tried to coax a smile from those trembling lips, but it didn't work. Lola still looked shell-shocked as they stepped into the upstairs corridor.

"If it makes you feel better, Fletcher has conned a lot of high-powered men, as well," he remarked. "Although I'm guessing he performs white-collar thievery, on paper, with them."

"What a relief," Lola jeered, still pissed at herself. "Such a comfort to know I'm not the only one!"

A tug on her hand made her look up at Rio DeSilva's kind smile.

"I never wanted to hurt you with this information. I just thought you should see first-hand how he's operating."

The slender hand inside his was quivering, and somehow Rio resisted kissing it. "The stats on the Fletcher Financial Group show nothing but a sterling reputation, which means some Fortune 500 executives gave him excellent ratings. Not a clue that he was ripping them off. So you're *not* stupid, Lola *mia*."

While she clung to that little endearment—finally, a sign that something had happened between them last night!—Lola grunted in disgust. "Yeah, well he had a way of making me *feel* stupid. As though I couldn't run my business without him. Or couldn't have *conceived* of it, and gotten the ball rolling enough that I needed his financial services."

When they stopped outside the suite door, Lola knew DeSilva wasn't coming in this time. He had that on-call look about him—and he did have a job protecting hundreds of other passengers, after all. She smiled up at him, wishing she didn't feel ready to bawl.

"Thanks for believing I could tango last night. And for making *me* believe," she murmured.

He put the key card in her door. She marveled again at the smooth, slender muscles of those hands . . . the way they'd taken her to unbelievable heights on the balcony last night.

Rio's hazel eyes said he was recalling that, too, while suggesting some sad secrets he'd never let Lola see. It was part of his white knight act, covering the chinks in his armor, she figured.

"Never assume you've cornered the market on feeling stupid," he whispered wistfully. "This world's full of liars and frauds who never come clean. Predators too slick to get caught before they've left a big hole where your heart used to be. Bank accounts can be reconciled, but hearts and spirits—well, that's another matter entirely."

His expression vacillated between that of a fallen angel and a lost, lonely puppy—a potent mix. A magnetism Lola couldn't resist. So she stood on tiptoe to kiss his cheek.

Rio smiled. Reminding himself to remain an enigma. "Tell Aric to escort you ashore, so you can enjoy Grenada today. I'll be in touch."

Lola blinked. Why did that sound like a kiss-off?

She watched him walk to the elevator, with that glide like a tiger's. Had she been stupid again, to fall for *this* man after one wildly ecstatic night?

Out of the frying pan, into the fire. Either way she got burned, right?

She had no time to feel sorry for herself, however. The red light on her phone was blinking, and it was Skorpio Skandalis giving another command:

"I want you to come to my quarters immediately," he crooned in that Greek accent that had first turned her on to him. *Now* she saw him for the shark he was, but what could she do? There'd be hell—and a lot of debts—to pay if she didn't follow through.

"You are to wear a tight black dress—the shorter, the better," the captain continued. "Nothing underneath it. Stiletto heels. Don't make me wait."

11

Was the captain finally going to give her what she wanted? Finally going to grant her fantasy and take control by making her lose it?

It was a head game, same as the ones he'd played on her before. Yet right now, a pretty pretense felt fantastic, compared to thinking about how Fletch had screwed her over.

And there was nothing like a tight black dress and stilettos to make a girl feel like *getting* some—even in the middle of the day. Even when exotic islands called and every *sane* passenger was going ashore to indulge in tourist-trap shopping and sightseeing in the Caribbean heat.

Sane. That left *her* out, didn't it? Why else would she have made this cockamamie deal with Captain Scandalous, when she could've called her lawyer—could've called the credit card companies again—to assure this cocky Greek he'd get his fucking money.

Without the fucking.

But no, here she was, swaying down the corridor with Aric keeping close watch. Close *appreciative* watch, at least, after she'd asked him to sweep her hair up into something provocative, and then touch up her face.

Hah! He'd painted her up like a slut, with extra eyeliner and lipstick that matched her Very Cherry nipples. Ah, those nipples—pebbling up as they rubbed her dress's built-in bra. Ready to party. It was kind of like Halloween for hookers, although she assumed she'd be the only one at the party.

Wrong.

She entered the captain's quarters—why hadn't she guessed his suite was the only other one on the penthouse level?—to find him lounging on his four-poster bed. He wore a shimmering robe of deep green Lola would've stolen for herself, except it showed off Skorpio's dark chest hair and an expanse of olive skin that veered downward, far enough to prove he had nothing on under it.

Far too masculine for her wardrobe . . . but damn, it did wonderful things for *him*. A hint of musky cologne suggested he was fresh from the shower.

Skandalis truly looked the part of Captain Scandalous as he sipped a drink and then chose from a tray of exquisite canapés. Lola hadn't had a chance for breakfast, so she eyed them longingly. But all he gave her was a crocodile smile.

"How lovely to see you, my dear," he crooned. "You look as hard and jaded as I hoped you would. High-maintenance. Well worth the debts I'm waiving for you."

Lola held his gaze, refusing to scowl at this reminder of reality. "Thank you, sir. How may I be of service?"

"Ah, a woman who knows her place."

His gaze raked over her as he gulped the rest of his drink. Not many men could control such a situation while appearing ready for a nap.

Then he snapped his fingers, three times.

"Yes, *mon capitaine*?"

In flounced Odette, wearing a very short French maid's uniform and seamed, patterned stockings attached to a garter belt. She fluttered to his bedside with a feather duster—

Yep, it's Halloween for hookers, all right.

—like a kiss-up debutante at a benefit ball. Except her eyes held a hurricane warning Lola didn't dare ignore. She'd almost laughed out loud at that clichéd, ridiculous uniform. Surely guys didn't *still* go for that fantasy?

Yet Skorpio's fingers found the inside of the housekeeper's thigh and began to stroke it. The rise in his robe said he was very much into this fantasy, and when he fondled higher up, Odette parted her legs to let him.

She wasn't wearing panties. Just that little Mohawk, framed by the black elastic bands that bisected her thighs.

"Do you like what you see, Lola?"

She blinked, frowning. But something told her not to get sassy with the captain today: those obsidian eyes narrowed with a predatory, proprietary air as her silence ticked by.

He was indeed going to screw her. One way or another.

"Odette, my love," he went on in that maddening accent, "I want you to strip Miss Wright. I want you to slowly peel off her cocktail dress so I may view her body in all its glory, wearing only those stiletto heels."

Skorpio paused to sip his drink and assess her reaction.

"And then, when I've looked to my heart's content," he continued in that lord-of-the-manor voice, "you'll take off your uniform and dress her in it. I'm guessing it'll be a nice, tight fit—don't you think?"

"*Oui, mon capitain,*" the masseuse-turned-maid replied gleefully. "Eet weel be far too short, ze uniform, and we weel have to punish her for letting her *poof-poof* show. *Non*?"

"No! Not a chance!" Lola replied, stepping back.

Except that damned Aric, behind her all this time, kept her from going any further. Meanwhile, Odette was moving in to do the captain's bidding.

And Skandalis, the jerk, was laughing at her! Making that robe shimmer over the tent pole beneath it.

"I like my women to know their place," he repeated, sitting up straighter to make his point—partly because that one point now jutted up out of his open robe.

"I like to watch them excite each other, too," he added, his nostrils flaring. "What a lovely contrast, when Odette lets down her raven hair to tease your pale breasts into hard, aching peaks. Like the one you see under my—"

"No way!" Lola made a cross with her two digit fingers, flashing it in front of the advancing maid. "I don't *do* women! You had your fun tricking me with Miss Christy, but—"

"You'll do as I say. Let's not forget our bargain, Miss Wright."

"This is no bargain!" Lola protested. "And whatever happened to 'whatever *Lola* wants'? Like we talked about with DeSilva and Mr. Kingsley?"

Skorpio Skandalis made a show of gazing around his bedroom. "They don't seem to be here right now. Do you recall that being part of the deal, Odette?"

"Oh, *non, ma cherie*!" the maid said a little too cheerfully. "Eet eez your ship! *You* are ze boss!"

"A woman after my own heart. Among other things." The captain gave his maid a mischievous swat on the backside. "Thank you, Aric. You're excused."

Cabana Boy's hands tightened on her bare shoulders. "I've seen how this woman defies you, sir, so perhaps I should stay to—"

"I believe I can handle her, Aric."

As much as Lola resented having a keeper—and considering how Stud Muffin could rat to the captain about Rio—she hated to see him go. Maybe it gave her a false sense of security, but she'd gotten to know Aric better than these other two, and maybe—if he saw something in it for himself—Cabana Boy would keep things from getting *way* out of hand.

But he let go of her. The door behind her closed.

It was just her and Frenchie and Captain Scandalous now. The energy in this room started whirling a little faster, taking on a sensual, pulse-quickening current, but Lola still didn't like the odds.

"How was I to know I made a deal with the devil?" she demanded.

Odette whirled her around with a quick grip on her shoulders. The captain's laughter taunted her, like the singing of the zipper in her little black dress.

"Time to give the devil his due, my dear."

Skorpio rose from the four-poster to stand a few feet in front of her, his eyes aglitter like onyx. A shrug sent his robe slithering down his taut body.

"You wanted a man to take control so you could lose it, Miss Wright, and I'm about to grant your wish," he said, taking himself in hand. "It's my game and I'll play it my way. Because I *can*."

The captain's voice wasn't all that had risen to the occasion. While she'd caught glimpses of his cock in the spa, Lola had to admit it made an impressive weapon when he pointed it at *her*.

"Any questions?"

After the way Rio had worshipped her last night, she found Skorpio's ego very annoying. But he was holding her to their deal—and for all she knew, the captain had already put the security agent in *his* place. Maybe threatened his job. Which might explain Rio's refusal to touch her this morning.

And Dennis *had* left her with quite a bar and boutique bill. Not to mention credit card debt that might not get canceled if Skandalis got pissed at her.

Lola closed her eyes as the maid tugged on her dress. "No, sir. No questions."

"Don't you dare patronize me!" came his coiled reply. "You're really rather ordinary when you give in, Miss Wright. So I expect you to fight me every step of the way."

Her eyes flew open, just as Odette bared her breasts. Oh,

this guy was a piece of work! Intended to have his cake and eat her, too. Well, if he wanted a bitch who could spit and hiss at him, he'd come to Miss Right!

"Get your *hands* off me!" she rasped, grabbing the female fingers that tweaked her nipples from behind. "If you think my peaks are so pretty, Odette, why don't we paint yours?!"

The maid's sly laughter began a volley of Greek between her two tormentors. While Odette's fakey French accent got on her nerves, it *really* bugged her that the captain and his maid were talking—probably about her—in a language she couldn't understand.

So she stepped backwards, nailing the maid's foot with her stiletto.

"Ayyyeeeee!" Odette shrieked—and then she squeezed Lola's breasts together, pointing them lewdly at the captain. Up came a knee to the base of Lola's spine, tilting her back so her legs flew apart and her hips thrust forward against her dress, which hung at half-mast.

Skorpio was loving it. He reached for his drink, his eyes never leaving her exposed body. He was fondling himself nonchalantly, as though he intended to play all day.

"Nicely done, Odette," he purred. "Show her who she's dealing with."

Lola gasped, amazed at the other woman's strength: as one slender arm snaked around her, beneath her breasts, Odette yanked her dress down with the other hand. Bad enough that this left her helplessly jutting out toward Captain Scandalous, but the dress she'd worn here so proudly was now a manacle of black fabric around her thighs.

"Step out of it!" Odette ordered.

"I can't move! That damn—"

Lola howled as the maid's fingers found her muff and ruffled it. She kicked and wiggled against her captor, jabbing backwards with her elbows.

At last! She was free of the cocktail dress, so she could really get her licks in!

But Frenchie had the upper hand—and it landed with a loud *smack* on Lola's backside.

"You sneaky bitch, that's not—"

Smack!

"—fair!" Lola yowled. "I might just have to—"

The room tipped way too quickly. Skandalis suddenly had her by both ankles. He could spread her legs as wide as he wanted.

The room rang with her exasperated gasp as she assessed this situation: when had he set down his drink? How the hell had she ended up with both feet off the floor?

And how was his maid supporting her weight with one arm? Odette's other hand skimmed her stomach with maddening slowness before landing between her legs again.

"*Poof-poof!*" Odette whispered victoriously, right beside her ear.

Livid, Lola struggled against both of them—which of course meant she was flashing the captain as he held her stiletto-clad feet, while grinding herself against Odette's chest. They were *loving* this! How twisted and kinky did they have to be, setting her up this way?

And how uh, twisted was *she*?

As the captain's lips lingered on the ankle strap of her shoe, Lola went limp. Held her breath. Watched the man with the raven hair run his tongue up her calf . . . felt the sandpapery scrape of that five-o'clock shadow that made him so dangerously alluring.

"You're very, very wet," he murmured. Just looking. Not touching her there. Yet.

She swallowed hard. For once she couldn't argue with him.

Skorpio hefted her effortlessly, to rest both of her ankles on his shoulders. This left her suspended and wide open, while the captain took advantage of the view—although it was her calves he was stroking. Tenderly. Teasingly. And when his fingertips found the underside of her knees, Lola laughed and bucked so hard he had to grab her to keep her from falling.

"Do you want me, Lola?"

God, that accent had her churning out the butter, didn't it? Even while he was humiliating her.

She nodded, feeling the give of Odette's breasts beneath her head.

Skandalis stepped closer, slipping his shoulders into the bend of her legs. He studied her slit; blew warm air over it to watch the wiry red hairs move.

Lola sucked air. Maybe it was better to let these two Greeks cavort and have their fun at her expense, because right now things were getting awfully quiet and . . . intense.

"What if I tickle you there with my tongue?"

She squirmed just thinking about it.

"Would you cry out for more?" he demanded in a voice she had to strain to hear. "Would you squirt your honey all over my face?"

Lola exhaled, her body tensing with need.

"Ask me for it, Lola," he continued in that sinuous whisper. "Tell me exactly what you want."

Lord, how embarrassing was *that*? Especially since she now realized it was Odette stroking her backside, breathing like she was close to climax. But she couldn't deny how much she wanted the man only inches from her . . . poof poof.

He could see the telltale pearls of dew. Smell them by now.

"Would you . . . would you flick the tip of your tongue around my . . . my clit?" she breathed, not believing she was saying this.

But what if he did it? What if he gave it to her just like she wanted it—even if Rio had done it without her having to ask? This man, of course, was being difficult—making her *pay*.

But if this excruciating sense of anticipation was a way to work off her debt, why not play along? Lola's pulse drowned out all rational thought. Might as well go for the full load.

"And then I'd like it if—would you stick your tongue up it?"

"Up what?"

Lola sighed with wanting and exasperation. "Stick your tongue up my—my slit!"

Scorpio raised his eyes. "What do you think, Odette? Myself, I like the word *cunt* better."

"Ah, *oui*," the woman behind her said. "Eet makes a poem zat way! Tongue up my—"

"Cunt," Lola wheezed, squirming all over. She'd never considered that word terribly poetic, yet that part of her was now getting *very* aroused. "Stick your tongue up my cunt. Fuck me with it!"

The captain moaned, licking his lips. He was quaking with need himself—

But no! He was laughing! Looking over top of her to share some private joke with Odette!

"Let's take her to bed, shall we?"

And damned if the two of them didn't walk up alongside that four-poster and *drop* her onto the rumpled bedclothes. Quicker than she knew what they were doing, Lola felt wide velvet cuffs: Skorpio was wrapping her ankles, while his accomplice bound her wrists in them. They seemed to enjoy that brisk, nerve-wracking noise the Velcro made as they adjusted all four of the cuffs.

Lola squirmed to get a better look, and then—

"Ready? Up!"

—her right arm and left leg were tugged upward, tipping her forward at an awkward—

"Ready? Up!"

—angle, until the opposite arm and leg rose to the same level!

"What the hell is—what're you—?"

Skandalis shrugged, wearing nothing but an infuriating grin. "I'm in the mood to tie one on, Miss Wright. I hope you are, too."

"But you told me to—I asked you for—and I asked you *nicely*!"

Lola struggled against her ties. She couldn't see their contraption, but she seemed to be hanging like a human hammock, from straps wrapped around those four wooden bedposts. She felt velvet crisscrossing beneath her bare butt to support her, too. Her hands were about a foot higher than her ankles; small comfort that they hadn't left her head dangling back.

"Did I agree to give you everything you wanted?" the Greek quipped. Then he reached for Odette, his black eyes snapping. "I'd much rather eat my little French pastry. Much rather rip off her uniform—"

Odette squealed with delight as he tore at her bodice, revealing those firm, pert breasts—and nipples that were painted bright red!

"—and scratch her snatch—"

"Oh, a poem you made! For *moi*!" the maid cooed. She planted one foot on the mattress then, to give Skorpio full access as he pulled her against his bare body.

Lola had little choice but to watch the Greek and his masseuse-cum-cleaning lady pawing at each other. Oh, he liked those cherry nipples, too, by the way he was cupping her while running his tongue around one of them! And that copycat Odette was thrusting them at him! Wiggling her hips against the hand at her crotch.

The captain kissed her then, at just the right angle so Lola could see their tongues dueling. Their faces flushed with passion, and she felt the heat radiating from their bodies.

Odette raised the hem of her short black dress, moaning her request. "Fuck me! Oh, yes, fuck me!"

As though those long, firm thighs in their patterned stockings and black garters didn't cry out loudly enough.

Lola clenched inside when Skorpio lowered his partner onto the bed. Her skirt billowed up over her torso to expose her, and he wasted no time tugging her ass to the edge and grabbing her calves. Her pointy-toed black heels wiggled beside his ears, and then *his* pointy thing went inside her.

Odette bucked upward as he pumped, his handsome face growing tight and shiny with need. Their guttural mutterings filled the room, as did the scent of their sweat and sex.

Lola could only hang there, suspended in her own sense of helplessness and . . . what was there about watching these Greeks go at each other? The porn flicks she'd rented with Fletch had *never* featured stars that could shine like these two. Such beautiful, fit bodies—such a passion for this pleasure they shared.

She'd never seen passion like that with Dennis, either.

Odette climaxed with a cry, and then Skorpio rocked to his own finish. They were oblivious to her, to everything but each other as he let her legs down so they could catch their breath.

Then the captain opened his eyes, still panting. He *winked* at her, the prick!

Then he added insult to injury by giving her butt a shove, like she was a kid riding sideways on a swing. The bed creaked with a rhythm that reminded them all of the same thing.

Would he leave her hanging? Surely this didn't fit his definition of swinging.

Lola was almost afraid to ask. She wasn't much for this suspension thing, but what would they do to her when they let her down? Wasn't it time for the phone to ring? Surely Captain Scandalous had ship business to tend to as they prepared the ship to leave this port.

"Why so jittery, my dear?" he crooned, as though he'd eavesdropped on her thoughts. Then he leaned forward enough to take her nearest nipple into his mouth. *Nipped* it, he did!

Lola surged forward, amazed—no, appalled—at how badly she needed release.

"Ah, such a desperate expression," Skorpio crooned. "Odette, it seems we've done a terrible thing, leaving Lola trussed up while we took all the pleasure for ourselves. How shall we make it up to her?"

"I know ze way!" she replied in that overdone accent. "Zat old song, how's it go? You take ze high road, and—"

"You'll take the low?" Skorpio's crowsfeet creased with mirth. "If that doesn't work, we can always trade. Or try something else."

The high road? The low? What in the hell were they talking about? It was some kind of lovers code that made it sound like they'd done this dozens of times.

Lola watched with apprehension as they went to the foot of the bed to approach between her spread legs. And yet, being strung up—totally at the mercy of these two nude lovers—added an edginess to the game. She had to play along anyway, so she decided to let go and let them have their way . . . so maybe she could get hers, too.

Lola did *not* figure on the maid's fingers slipping into her slit.

Nor did she guess Captain Scandalous would concentrate on her clit . . . the higher road.

And she was getting high, indeed, as he tongued the sensitive skin while ruffling the reddish hair above it. The sensations were so intense Lola could only moan and try to wiggle away: they were going at her, each with a separate agenda yet both trying to make her scream for it. Making her *take* it as they chose to dish it out, so they could witness her total surrender.

Surrender of body. Surrender of mind.

Surrender of control.

With both Skorpio and Odette between her knees, her thighs were wide apart and the handsome couple was only too happy to watch her struggle against their wiles. Oh, they knew what they were doing! They knew how to alternate between pressure and speed, between making tight, hard circles and then pulling away to just look into her eyes . . . and blow their warm breath on her wet, aching slit. Just when Odette would let up, her lover kicked it up a notch, his head bobbing playfully between her open thighs.

Lola clenched her eyes shut, gritting her teeth against the inevitable. The spasms were spiraling higher now, driving her wild with wanting—

And the sight of Skorpio, standing up as though he intended to take her the old-fashioned way, made her sink to another level of degradation.

"Yes, please," she pleaded, her body swinging with his rhythmic attentions. "Ram it up there and make me scream! Make me—"

When her head lolled back in anticipation, he did as she asked. Well, at least he took the matter in hand: Captain Scandalous plugged her with his thumbs, high and hard, while his fingers kneaded her mound.

Lola jerked and cried out. Again and again she spasmed and arched, until she wondered if she might black out from the sheer intensity of his attentions. It was pleasure and pain and spontaneous combustion and—

"Never forget that you are mine, Lola," Skorpio reminded her in that low, alluring tone. "Mine alone."

One final press of his thumbs sent her into a purple haze of oblivion.

When she awoke, Lola still hung suspended in those wide velvet cuffs. But she was alone. Had she been out for an hour, or moments? Her forearms and calves felt bloodless and numb, while her thighs ached from being spread so far for so long. Her butt was sensitive from rubbing the velvet sling that supported her. She had to pee, and she had to pee *now.*

Where the hell was everybody?

"Hey! Hey, you can't just leave me hanging here!" she hollered. "Get me down, dammit! I have to go—"

Aric entered the bedroom, taking his sweet time about it. Taking in her predicament like he enjoyed seeing her in this helpless, desperate position.

"So this is how the captain has put you in your place?" He ambled around the bed, studying those cuffs with his secretive green eyes. "Velvet suits you, Priestess. That black around your forearms and calves really stands out against your pale pink skin. You look like you're offering yourself up to the gods, as a sacrifice to—"

"Knock it off and get me outta here!" she snapped. "I'm just the one to teach you about sacrifice, little man!"

Cabana Boy—just to irritate her—stroked the velvet encasing one ankle, and then tickled the bottom of that foot.

"You smart-ass! Let me *down* from—I swear to God—"

Aric's loose curls shook with his laughter as he reached up the nearest post she hung from. "Patience, Priestess! Patience is a virtue!"

"Virtue, my ass! Get me outta this thing so I can piss!"

He was tall enough, with strong enough arms, to release both leg straps from their pegs and lower them at the same time. When her arms were freed, Lola had to gave her prickly limbs time to get the blood pumping again.

She looked around for her cocktail dress.

Damn that fake maid! Odette had not only made the bed beneath her, but she'd picked up the room, too. It looked like a picture in a travel magazine.

"They stole my clothes!" Lola gasped. "That new black dress and my best stilettos! Can you believe the *nerve* of that man, to abandon me this way?"

She used the bathroom and came out wrapped in a fresh towel. She was *tired* of being naked; vulnerable to everyone else's whims.

Aric was waiting, still looking way too amused about this whole thing. If he knew anything about where Skandalis and Odette had gone, he wasn't telling. He just strolled down the deserted hallway between the two suites with the key card in his hand.

"Tellya what," Lola muttered. "I've *had* it with surprises for one day! If I come within sniffing distance of a cigarette—"

Cabana Boy reached deep into the pocket of his long, loose shorts. "Camels okay?"

She stopped, staring at that oh-so-lovely pack he was holding out to her. Was it her imagination, or did that camel and the desert sand glow with a heavenly light? The pack was still wrapped, but she smelled that fresh tobacco with its hint of mint. If only in her dreams.

Lola inhaled deeply. After all these months of being such a good girl, she really shouldn't blow it now. "You—you got those for *me*?"

"No friend like an old friend, when things get crazy," he remarked as he opened the Aphrodisia Suite's door.

Now how was she supposed to interpret that? This same smart-ass kid who'd delivered her into the captain's clutches awhile ago was now being so damn considerate of her needs.

How did he know she smoked Turkish Jades?

She wasn't ready to ask him. Wayyyy too dangerous, to think Cabana Boy knew her so well.

Lola wasn't ready for what awaited her in the suite, either. There on the coffee table—like she might have laid them there last time she came in—were her purse and her cell phone.

12

As though that damn phone knew she was staring at it, it began to play a razzy-jazzy version of "Hey, Big Spender."

Was there a camera hidden in this room? How else could anyone calling her know the *moment* she'd come through the door?

And if they didn't have a cell signal before this—and if Dennis had stolen her purse and cell phone when he ran off with that floozy in Aruba, then how on earth—

"Maybe you better answer it," Aric suggested above the raucous music. He, too, was gawking at her cell like it might explode.

Half afraid to touch the damn thing, Lola finally reached down to—

The song stopped.

Lola gripped her towel, stepping back. The Camels fell to the floor.

"OK, so where'd you find my stuff?" she accused, glowering at her warden. "You put it here while the captain had me trussed up from his bedposts, didn't you? If you're trying to mess up my head, playing these little—"

"I had nothing to do with this! I swear!" Pale green eyes peered through his loose curls, imploring her to believe him. Cabana Boy looked as spooked as she felt.

They both jumped when the phone rang again.

This time Lola grabbed it. She flipped it open, but neither the caller's name or number appeared on her screen as that music taunted her. By God, those lines of odd symbols would *not* keep her from the answers she needed.

"Hello?" she demanded. "Look, if this little prank is your idea of a good time, you can—*Dennis?*"

Her pulse throbbed against the slender phone as she pressed it to her ear, straining to hear what he—or whoever—was saying between bursts of static.

"Talk louder! I can't—Fletch, if that's you—"

The voice sounded far away, and the signal was fading so badly she couldn't be sure it was anyone she knew. A few phrases sounded like a foreign language—like maybe a call from Caracas had been misdirected to her cell. But the way things were going, it felt right that her ex-fiancé would pick this particular moment to scare the bejesus out of her.

"Would you please repeat—if you need help—"

Click-click-click.

Then nothing.

Lola threw the phone at the couch and stood there shivering. She could've been standing in the ship's meat freezer, she felt so cold.

Aric frowned. "What was *that* about? Do you really think it was—"

"I have no idea. It went dead and I freaked."

For once, she was glad Aric was around. Had she been alone, she'd have run screaming into the hall—and as it was, she was now sweating with a nicotine fit that had pounced on her like a savage cat.

Lola yanked her purse open, driven by an overwhelming need to see if her security blanket pack of Camels had survived their misadventures. Fumbling, cursing because this purse she traveled with was so damn deep, she exhaled with sharp relief when her fingers found the suede cigarette case and the bulge of the Bic snapped to its side.

How many hundred times had she held this piece of paraphernalia, needing the ritual as much as the cigarette? She didn't care if Cabana Boy thought she was some crazed old junkie! She unsnapped the deep teal carrier and gripped the pack of Turkish Jades with a trembling hand, forcing herself to take long, slow breaths as she gazed at the layer of strapping tape encasing the pack.

It was grimy from being gripped, but by God she'd carried these little babies for months without being desperate enough to hack through all that tape—

Until now, maybe.

Except Cabana Boy was watching.

Lola swallowed hard. She willed her pulse into a lower gear, reminding herself that it was only a crank call; only her *assumption* that Fletch had made it. Her bad-ass traitor fiancé really wasn't worth the indignity of ripping this pack open to light up, was he? Especially in front of this impressionable young man, who was looking at her like he might call 911 any minute.

Letting out a shuddery breath, Lola tucked the Camels back in their case. The metal fasteners shut with a satisfying *snap*, and she gave Aric a tremulous smile.

"Thanks for not asking."

"Not a problem, Priestess."

He picked the phone up from the couch cushion to study its little screen; pushed the call-back button, and held the phone to his ear. Cabana Boy shook his head, and then pressed a few buttons to see what he could find out about the incoming call.

"Don't know what to tell you," he finally confessed. "I'm not getting a signal now."

This got Lola to thinking more rationally. "If Fletch was calling me from Aruba . . . would he be able to ring me because we're in port? But that makes no sense! If he took my purse and the phone with him—"

She studied her warden's smooth young face. Aric was keeping lots of little secrets, wasn't he? But hadn't she worked her way around hundreds of savvy, secretive men in her business? Cabana Boy still wore a highly mystified expression, so she would have to take the reins. Somewhere, they were making wrong assumptions—going nowhere fast, unless she consulted other sources.

Lola lifted the receiver from the phone on the end table. Of all the buttons and services to choose from, not one of them dealt with emergencies or security issues—as though passengers would never have those on this erotic fantasy cruise.

So she punched the 0.

"Good afternoon, Miss Wright! And how may I direct your call?" came a too cordial female voice.

Lola nearly came unglued again, until she realized the ship's operators would identify callers by the suite number. "I'd like to speak to Rio DeSilva, head of security, please."

There was a pause, so long Lola nearly hung up to try again.

"I'm sorry, but Mr. DeSilva cannot be reached at this time. If there's an emergency—"

"All right then, let me speak to the captain! Put on Skorpio Skandalis himself!" she blurted. "*He's* probably responsible for—"

"I'm sorry, but the captain cannot be reached at this—"

"Why the hell *not*?" Was this a recording or something?

The operator's sudden intake of breath told her she'd been unnecessarily rude.

"I—sorry, but there's been a creepy little—"

"Captain Skandalis is in the bridge and cannot be interrupted, Miss Wright," came a chilly reply. "He's preparing the ship to pull away from the pier right now, to sail us to Grenada. May I give him your message?"

Lola blinked sadly. Another day, another port of call she'd missed. It really didn't matter where they'd been or where they were going—except it was farther *away* from Aruba and, presumably, Dennis Fletcher.

"All right then," she sighed. "Please connect me to the concierge. Clive—"

"I'll ring Mr. Kingsley immediately. Thank you, Miss Wright."

Closing her eyes, Lola inhaled. Where was the take-charge woman who single-handedly ran Well Suited? Why was she getting so damn freaked about her phone ringing, when disconnections and wrong numbers happened every day?

Because once again the details aren't matching up. And I'm getting damn sick of it!

"Yes, Miss Wright!" came the Brit's familiar accent. "And how may I assist you on this fine evening, my dear?"

Was it? If she used Kingsley's chipper, unruffled greeting as her guide, why, she could believe there *was* nothing amiss. Her vacation could now proceed like it was supposed to—before Fletch messed it up a few days ago.

Lola sighed and got real. Took the direct approach. "Would you care to tell me how my purse and cell phone appeared in my suite?" she asked archly. "I was—*out* for awhile, and when I came back, I found them on my coffee table."

The concierge cleared his throat. "This is the same purse and phone Dennis Fletcher took from your room?"

"Yes! And there's no way—"

"You're quite certain those items weren't simply put away in a drawer, when your belongings got transferred to the Aphrodisia Suite?"

She hadn't thought about that. Hadn't even *found* all her stuff yet, what with the captain and Cabana Boy and DeSilva demanding her every waking moment.

So many men, so little time.

But it wasn't all that funny, was it?

"If Fletcher took my stuff," she mused aloud, rewinding her thoughts through the past couple of days, "and if he didn't return to the ship—because the man at the security computer verified that he didn't . . . then how have my purse and phone come back to me? And who put them here?"

There was a very lengthy pause. "I think you'd best come down to my office at once, my dear."

13

"Everyone's certainly gotten into the adults-only mode," Lola remarked as she and Aric got off the glass elevator. "Don't tell me I'm missing Nude Beach Night because of this damn *business* we're attending to."

The atrium, an open area for live entertainment and exhibitions, thrummed with men and women of all ages, peeled down to bare skin, dancing to the laid-back beat of the Kalypso Kingz. Others lounged in overstuffed love seats with tall, colorful drinks, flirting and flashing their attributes. A few more adventurous guests flaunted themselves on the open spiral staircase, wearing only their smiles and some interesting tattoos.

Cabana Boy surveyed the noisy crowd as though he experienced this incredible spectacle every week. Which he did.

"The evening's young, Priestess," he murmured, swaying playfully to the island music. "You could join the fun after we see Kingsley. If you invite me along, of course."

"Right. Like I'd parade myself naked in public."

She paused to gawk at the amazing variety of shapes and sizes on display, among fake palm trees and paper lanterns strung for this occasion. The noise level was pretty amazing, too, so she had to lean close to Beach Boy and talk loudly. "You'd have to pour more than a couple martinis down me to get *me* out there naked."

"I'll see what I can do."

She rolled her eyes as he took her hand and started toward the purser's desk. As they snaked between the dancers and drinkers, Lola had to laugh when several ladies called out to Aric to get naked and join them.

"Ladies and gentlemen!" a melodic voice came over the speaker system. "Ladies and gentlemen, if I may have your attention, *please*! This is Mike Mannering, your cruise director, and have we got the *fun* lined up for *you tonight*!"

The Kingz grinned, flashing white smiles on ebony faces. Their dreadlocks kept swaying, even though the music had stopped.

The noise level lowered to a dull roar.

"Next up, we've got speed dating! Yes, that would be speed dating *naked*," Mike clarified in his disk jockey jive. "Numbers and tables are now up for grabs in the Voyeurs lounge on Deck Six!"

Lola felt Cabana Boy's snicker against her back.

"No, we are *not* going there!" she warned him with a jab of her elbow.

"And poolside, our Kalypso Kingz will be set up and ready to play for—are you ready for this?" Mannering led them on in his carnival barker's voice.

"Ready!" some of the party animals replied.

"LIMBO-O-O-O! It wouldn't be Nude Beach Night without a *limbo* contest!" he crowed. "And volleyball! And of course, our drink of the day—Sex on the Beach—in our special flashing souvenir glass! See you poolside—or in the Voyeurs lounge—in fifteen!"

"Limbo? *Naked*?" Lola gasped.

"I could get that way for you in a heartbeat, babe. Say the word."

She turned to fire a pithy come-back at him, yet those glimmery green eyes and pouty lips made her bite it back: Aric was sounding half-serious. And it wasn't as though he hadn't seen *her* that way.

"Save it," she said. "I've got this business with Kingsley first, remember?"

Lola stepped out of the main aisle with him, to avoid the crush of moving nude bodies. A *lot* of guests were heading to Deck Six—and the Voyeurs lounge, no doubt—while several others were acting jazzed, daring their friends to enter the limbo contest. Calling out lewd reminders about where to slather their sunscreen.

It was a relief when a little Asian Guest Rep invited them behind the purser's desk, into some semblance of civility again. With all the skin on display around her, Lola felt overdressed in the jeans and camp shirt she'd hurried into after her phone chat with Clive Kingsley.

When the debonair concierge waved Aric off and escorted her into his back sanctum, however, she felt downright dowdy: there on his credenza sat a sewing machine. A dressmaker's mannequin beside it sported a gorgeous candy pink evening gown that shimmered with sequins and beads.

The Brit's blue eyes sparkled as he removed the cloth tape measure from around his neck.

"Just a little hobby," he murmured. "Something to occupy my inner child between guests' inquiries. A way to stay sane, after years of living at sea."

There it was again: that mystery about how a concierge could run a boutique—and indulge his inner child's *hobby*—while seeing to his official duties with the passengers.

But it was hardly her place to quiz him. Captain Scandalous was surely aware of Kingsley's personal pursuits—and, once she took a closer look at the gown on the mannequin, Lola had to admire his work. She knew a few tailoring tricks and basic sewing techniques, but *this* level of expertise made her feel like she was still struggling through her middle school sewing class.

"You made this dress," she whispered. She circled the flashy yet elegant gown, gaping at the minute detail of a beaded lace bodice designed for a *much* bustier woman than she would ever be.

"Why, yes, dear," he replied with a pleased grin. "And I also—"

"Made the gowns I chose in the boutique," she finished in awe. "Which explains the Kingsley Court labels I never connected to *you*, until just this minute. I really must be losing it."

She dropped into the chair in front of his desk. How many years had she chosen men's clothing, living by the labels? Yet this very obvious detail had escaped her.

Lola sighed sadly and set her purse on his desk. If she hadn't noticed something so obvious as this man's name in her new formal wear, she'd probably overlooked a few other details about him—among other things.

Maybe she'd gotten it all wrong, believing Fletch took her purse.

And maybe she was way off base, assuming Dennis had called on her phone awhile ago.

She gazed again at the dress, a confection that sparkled like wet watermelon candies. While *she* would never wear such a gaudy garment, it made her smile to imagine it on someone more flamboyant—like Dolly Parton, perhaps. And yet . . . the Brit's remark about choosing clothes she wouldn't have considered for herself came back to her. For all she knew, Clive Kingsley had steered her toward gowns Skorpio Skandalis would love to see on her—and then remove.

And for all she knew, this debonair Englishman was in just as deep as Captain Scandalous and Cabana Boy and—

Rio DeSilva?

Were *all* these men misleading her? Playing games to keep her off-balance and beholden to the captain?

Nah. That was her paranoia talking. She'd watched Fletch access her accounts and then con that busty blonde in the casino—and then kiss on her in that cocktail lounge. These men couldn't have faked those security tapes, or made up that itemized list of his hits against her credit card accounts.

Could they?

"May I check out your cell phone, dear heart? It'll require some delving into your call history, and I don't wish to intrude."

She blinked. Kingsley had seated himself across from her and was smiling pointedly. One more thing she'd missed.

"Sure, do whatever you need to."

With a nod, he surveyed the panel and pushed a button—immediately filling his sanctum with the striptease beat of "Hey, Big Spender!"

Lola grimaced. "Considering this Fletcher situation, maybe I should change my ring tone, eh?"

"Not a bad idea. No sense in recalling his dastardly deeds every time you receive a call."

Trying not to seem obvious, Lola studied the man on the other side of the lustrous mahogany desk. His deep blue uniform accented a fit physique as he meticulously punched his way through the systems on her cell phone. His chestnut hair was clipped into a tidy cap of curls, and his expression bespoke utmost integrity. Those blue eyes could pierce like swords when he concentrated—and as he handed back her phone, he was clearly as flummoxed as she by this latest turn of events.

"Far as I can tell, Miss Wright, your phone never left the ship. Or if it did," Clive added in a thoughtful tone, "Mr. Fletcher made no calls. I see no evidence of Caribbean area codes or connections."

Now she was really confused. "Which means?"

He shrugged, puzzling aloud. "Perhaps the perpetrator—perhaps not Fletcher, since he already knew your account numbers—merely took your purse long enough to rifle through it for your cards or cash, and then tossed it aside. Was anything missing?"

All you cared about was those Camels, remember?

Lola's cheeks prickled. "I—things happened so fast, I haven't even looked yet. Just a second."

Why did rummaging through a purse while a man was watching feel so awkward? Bad enough that Mr. British Efficiency had pointed up several loopholes in her logic; he now believed she was too stupid to keep track of her personal possessions, as well.

"Here's my wallet . . . maybe a little shorter on cash—but then, I bought a few odds and ends in Aruba, too," she sighed. "My driver's license and plastic's all here, though. And here's my passport—"

"Which should go immediately into your room safe, with the rest of your cruise documents."

"Yes, sir," she murmured sheepishly. Lola dug deeper, and down where Kingsley couldn't see, she caressed the suede cigarette case. She bit back that queasy *need* for nicotine again, when her fingers found the slickness of the fresh pack Aric just gave her.

Then she shifted her shades, a small address book, and her travel-size bottles of aspirin and hand sanitizer. "Everything seems in order. But I still don't understand how this stuff just *showed up* while I was . . . with the captain. They would've needed a key to get into my room."

Clive smiled cryptically. "If someone turned it in—say, at the gangway security station, or in one of the shops—a staff member could've identified you and returned it to your suite."

"Without calling me to the information desk—or here, to you?—to confirm that it's really mine?"

Kingsley looked directly at her with those cornflower blue

eyes. Was she naive to believe his expressive face would register too much emotion to deceive her?

"I assure you, my dear, that had someone returned it to *me*, I'd have notified you immediately," he said in that low, sonorous voice. "I'm so sorry this has happened to you, Lola. While I'm glad you're rid of that bad apple Dennis Fletcher, I'd hoped you could enjoy the rest of your cruise without such nasty repercussions."

Nahsty repp-ercussions. What was it about a Brit? More than just that rich, flowing accent, it was Clive Kingsley's *gentility* that made Lola feel so—so at *home* with him. So secure.

Not to mention very aware of the way he was looking at her right now, pondering something he wasn't sure he should ask about.

Fascinated by the play of his facial expressions, Lola leaned forward. "Yes? What are you thinking?"

Kingsley's eyes darted over to the dress on the mannequin. "I'm wondering if perhaps—because you *do* appreciate my design work, and you *so* deserve to have some fun—would you like to attend our gala staff ball? As my guest?"

Lola blinked. Now that he'd made the invitation, he was leaning forward with his hands clasped on his desktop, looking decidedly . . . predatory? Interested?

"I assure you that I'll in no way compromise your . . . *status* with the captain," he went on, as though he knew Rio DeSilva might be doing just that. "But I suspect once you enter that ballroom, and see *so* many colors and elegantly dressed dancers enjoying themselves, you'll have a grand time! It's our chance to get out of uniform and really dress to the nines—"

"Will Skandalis be there?"

Kingsley let out a short laugh. "Skorpio rarely appears at these functions, I assure you. Mostly because he and Odette—"

"So tell me about *her*. She's staff, right? So she would attend?"

Like a lightning strike, the concierge's attitude changed. "Attendance is never mandatory, of course. We can't mandate *fun*, now can we?"

Lola sat back, crossing her arms to wait him out. There was a better answer lurking behind his carefully composed expression; something about Odette that pushed Mr. Congeniality's buttons the wrong way.

But Clive rose. Their conversation was over.

"Please understand, Miss Wright, that while I'm doing *everything* in my power to solve this mystery involving Mr. Fletcher and his whereabouts," he assured her, "there are things I'm simply not at liberty to say. Please trust that you'll be the *first* to know when I learn more about him, or when I get word that your credit record has been cleared. Until then—"

He brought her up out of her chair with an extended hand and a suggestive smile.

"—may I count upon the pleasure of your company on Friday evening? Wear that aubergine-and-cabernet striped creation with the flounced cap sleeve. You'll be the belle of the ball, Lola darling."

Aubergine-and-cabernet striped. Right! Most guys would call it purple and maroon!

But then, Clive Kingsley wasn't like most guys, was he?

She watched, speechless, as this dapper man raised her knuckles to his lips. His eyes never left hers, awaiting her answer as his kiss tickled her skin.

What is it with me, swallowing every hook these guys dangle? Do I really want more trouble with Skandalis when—

Screw Skandalis!

Which is what I wanted before I knew about any of this other stuff, right? But all I've gotten is trouble for allowing my inclinations to—

"I'd be delighted," she breathed. Lola hoped he didn't misconstrue her hesitation—or see the wet spot in her jeans. Clive

Kingsley might have unusual talents, but that didn't change the way those blue-fire eyes and that resonant accent affected her, did it?

"Wonderful!" He looked like a kid who'd just finessed his first date—with his best friend's girl. Sly around the edges, but oh, so proper about it! "Take a nap and pamper yourself on Friday, so you'll be nicely rested. I'll ring for you around nine-ish."

What had just happened here? She'd come into this office scared and confused about the reappearance of her purse, and was leaving with another man on the string. A man whose "hobby" held all sorts of implications yet inspired her respect. He hadn't become a designer by dabbling at it in his spare time. Kingsley was *good*.

And then there was Aric, awaiting her in one of the hibiscus-print chairs facing the floor-to-ceiling picture windows that flanked the atrium. The few nude people left in this lobby looked too looped to move, and the canned music told her the Happy Hour activities were history. The ship had pulled away from yet another port city she hadn't seen—except for the lights of Caracas, now twinkling in the distance. Like a promise made between lovers in the dusk.

Like the assessing look on Cabana Boy's smooth, golden face as he came toward her.

"So you got the problem solved? You look a damn sight happier than when you went in there."

Shit. He could read her like the menu of the martini bar they were passing. Her warden was also walking a tad closer than before—and *not* just so he could grab her if she bolted.

"It's so quiet in here now," Lola remarked. She wasn't sure how much to reveal to him, or what might come next. Lord knows she'd had her share of excitement for one afternoon.

"The Kalypso Kingz are playing for the final round of the limbo contest—"

"*Still?*"

"Hey, there's more than one pole out there to play with, ya know?" he quipped. "But me, I'm savin' mine for *you*, my prim and proper Priestess."

Lola raised an eyebrow at him, yet the grin on those parted, pouty lips got her giggling. Although he was chuckling at *her*, Aric seemed sincerely interested in making her feel better. And he was pretty good at that.

"How about dinner? We can dress up and do it fancy at Chez Phillipe," he suggested, "or we could snag a really awesome pizza in the sports bar and watch the—"

"Room service," Lola breathed. A *ding* announced an elevator, and she was grateful that it was empty.

Suddenly, all this nonstop coming and going at somebody else's whim—plus the stress of this Dennis thing—was telling on her. She'd hardly had a moment to herself since Fletch ditched her.

"Room servisssssssss."

The word reverberated in the circular elevator, sounding like a lover's sigh as the door closed. As they rose, Lola caught three reflections of Aric's feline smile in the lighted glass walls.

"I'm likin' the sound of that room service thing," Cabana Boy murmured. Those low-lidded eyes focused on the vee of her blouse, as though he saw the two red spots beneath it. "It's one of those phrases that has . . . shades of meaning. Not all of them about food."

The elevator lurched to a halt, but Aric punched the STOP button before the doors opened. Then the lithe young man with those come-on curls slipped behind her, standing so close Lola could feel his erection through those low-rise shorts.

Damned if he didn't nibble the nape of her neck!

What am I, a magnet for it now? she wondered. *Must be wearing a neon OPEN sign that everyone but me can see.*

Lola held her breath as his lips fluttered lower, sending goose bumps all over her body.

Aric *was* a temptation. Young enough to keep her up—keep

himself up—all night, probably. A damn fine specimen, with those sultry smiles and that standoffish act he'd been playing—until now.

So why was he coming on to her more insistently?

He's Skorpio's snitch, remember? And gee, we haven't heard from our illustrious captain for at least four hours now.

Putting on her foxiest grin, Lola reached behind her.

"Maybe you ought to teach this thing some manners," she quipped, giving his cock a little squeeze through his pants.

Then she punched the OPEN DOOR button.

"C'mon, you know you want some. And *I* know you didn't get any from Skandalis," he razzed her. "I'm just trying to make it the vacation of your lifetime, ya know?"

Lola stifled a laugh. How many older women had he used *that* line on? What little game was he initiating here?

"Frankly, my dear, I'd rather have one of those awesome pizzas—*not* sausage," she teased. "And I really need some time alone to enjoy it."

"Not gonna happen."

"Look, I'd just like to—don't you have a girlfriend?" she demanded as he opened her door. "Can't you trust me when I say I'm going *nowhere* tonight?"

His chuckle followed her into the suite, where the room steward had again lit the mood lamps and turned down that king-size bed. God, it would feel so good to flop down on those cool, crisp sheets and forget about everything else!

"No, I don't. And no, I don't," he replied.

Aric flipped on his walkie-talkie and ordered them two loaded pizzas and a cold six pack of tall boys, like he thought it might be a long, boring night.

When he hung up, he gave her one of those sullen looks he was born for.

"I'm crushed at your rejection, Priestess," he breathed. "I was all ready to worship at the altar of your—"

"Save it."

Lola gave him a determined smile—and a motherly pat on the head. "I'm going to consult my Tarot cards after I eat, and that's not an audience participation thing," she stated, starting toward the bedroom. "So figure out a way to watch me without watching me, all right? Knock when our food arrives."

With that Lola left him behind, locking the bedroom door even though he surely had a key to it. She leaned against it to keep him at bay—and to keep tabs on what he was doing out there. She figured she'd let about a minute go by before—

Shit! It's only 7:00.

The red numerals on the bedside clock mocked her. The way she felt—with so many things that had happened to her again today—it *had* to be nine-thirty or ten! This entire damn day— her whole frickin' trip so far—made a mockery of her perceptions, didn't it?

It also did a fine job of pointing out how, after making such lovely, elaborate plans for her future with Dennis Fletcher, she really had very little control over anything at all.

Control? You thought you had control, little Lola? What a joke!

And what an unfortunate epiphany, too. Just when she thought she was getting into the game again.

Sighing, Lola dropped her purse tiredly . . . resisted the call of those Camels in it by lunging toward the turned-down bed and grabbing the two truffles as she landed on its pillow-top softness. Tomorrow's edition of the *Aphrodite Ahoy!* fluttered across the comforter, but reading it was the furthest thing from her mind.

The first candy split between her back teeth as she smoothed its green wrapper to read it.

Truth or Dare? What would your lover love?

She let out a sorry little laugh, and then opened the other truffle as she swallowed the thick, minty middle of the first one. The way things were going, the wisdom inside these candy wrappers might give more divine guidance than anything her Tarot deck offered up right now. And it sure tasted better.

This one was rum buttercream, so rich the filling clung to her tongue.

She closed her eyes, trying to get a handle on the feelings of disappointment and confusion that had her on the verge of a crying jag—or a cigarette binge. Here she was, holed up in her room on a warm, gorgeous Caribbean night, poking down chocolates and pouting. How stupid was that?

Defy authority—or logic—or even gravity! Break away with that Special Someone.

"Oh, Jesus," she muttered, ready to wad the foil in her fist.

But those words called to her again.

Defy Authority. Break away.

Didn't that sound like a helluva lot more fun than shuffling her cards while her warden pulled guard duty in the other room? They might as well be an old married couple—or she was acting like a very cheap date, settling for pizza and beer when there was a whole damn cruise ship to be had!

Lola sat upright, a new sense of purpose surging through her.

How much did Aric want her? How far would he go, really?

No, the real question is, how long and hard would he look for you, if you escaped?

She blinked, feeling all tingly. Now *there* was an idea!

Lola looked toward the door, ideas racing through her mind. In her line of work, she dodged propositions all the time—from men who were much savvier than Cabana Boy, with the money to buy whatever they wanted.

She was the queen of making clients feel wonderful about themselves, because she could make herself . . . invisible. They paid her the big bucks for the masculine, moneyed images of success they saw in the mirror after she dressed them—*not* for the fact that she was a green-eyed redhead whose panties they wanted to get into.

But that part still made the world go 'round, didn't it?

Lola slithered off the bed, a lynx in heat. She wiped the give-away grin off her face and quietly opened the bedroom door.

Stud Muffin was on the phone. His low voice and the way his arms wrapped around his slender waist told her he was *not* talking to his mama.

So he does have a girlfriend! Someone to distract him—from me!

"Aric, I—I've changed my mind," she announced in her most come-hither voice.

Cabana Boy pivoted to face her, burying the receiver in his tee-shirt. "Oh, yeah? How's that?"

"I've decided to shower and put on a strappy little sun dress, and take you up on your offer for a nice dinner," she continued, watching his facial expressions fluctuate. "I want you to show me all your favorite places aboard this ship! I want to shop! I want to be your Priestess and let you worship whatever you damn please, all right? But there's one condition."

His eyes grew warier behind those loose curls. "And that would be—?"

"Turn off your walkie-talkie and ignore the captain's commands," Lola challenged. "I want it to be just you and me, babe—for as long and as hard and as high as we can fly! I want to soar under the radar and into next week, got it?"

Thank God he didn't laugh in her face.

Instead, his lush lips parted in a tomcat grin. With a purposeful flourish, he hung up the phone and then flipped the switch on his two-way.

"That's more like it, Party Girl. I'll be ready and waiting," he crooned. "Accent on the *ready*."

14

"**G**oodness, Aric. You look stunning!"

Cabana Boy's pleated, pale green slacks skimmed the contours of his slender body to flow down endless legs. He wore an island-print shirt in pinks, beiges, and greens that brought out the sparkle in his silvery eyes. A different medallion twinkled at his neck—a gold serpentine chain with a large diamond-shaped crystal that lodged in the hollow of his collar bone.

He let out his breath, making the chain slither. Those eyes were lingering on all of her . . . attributes.

"Holy mother of God but you're hot, Lola."

Her jaw dropped. No one had *ever* said that to her! Not even Fletch in his more impassioned moments, or when he wanted a really huge favor from her.

"Th-thank you," she whispered. "It's just a sun dress I got on sale at—"

"Not the dress, Priestess. I'm talking about *you*," he murmured, circling her so he could appreciate her from all sides. "It's the way your auburn hair falls over your shoulders in those natural, loose waves. The way your eyes look all smoky and ready to play."

Aric peered at her from beneath his own sun-streaked mop. "Good thing you wanna fly under the radar. If Skorpio sees you tonight, he won't be turning you loose any time soon."

"Well, that's quite a compliment!" Lola felt like a prom princess, but refrained from batting her eyes at him. "After I decided to wear this, I wondered if it wasn't dressy enough for that Chez Felini place—"

"Chez Phillipe. But believe me, Phillipe will be so damn glad to see you, he'll have a hard time keeping his hands to himself."

Cabana Boy placed his fingertips lightly on her bare shoulders to toy with her double spaghetti straps, as though they—or what bobbed beneath her bodice—fascinated him.

"I hope you'll remember who you're with, Priestess," he said softly. "I don't fly under the radar into next week with just anybody."

Lola smiled up at him, indulging her fingers in the softness of his hair. "I agreed to attend the staff ball with Kingsley on Friday, but I'm yours tonight, Aric. All yours."

My, my but that's sounding cozy, Aunt Lola! Especially since you can't figure out why this young stud's giving you a second glance.

She sighed languidly. OK, so maybe their conversation sounded like the script from a sappy old movie. Except Aric seemed to believe it as easily as she'd said it.

And once she entered the dimly lit French cafe, where their adoring host Phillipe couldn't do enough exclaiming over their arrival, Lola understood Aric's remark about being a one-man woman. The raven-haired Frenchman, so debonair in his white dinner jacket, was indeed a hands-on kind of man: a hand on her upper arm as he escorted them between the tables, a hand on her ass when he gestured toward the chair Aric was to take. And a hand that lingered on her cheek as he took a really good look at her from kissing distance.

Lola held her breath: the heat of Phillipe's gaze penetrated her cotton dress, as though he were zeroing in on her Very Cherries with x-ray specs. And he was anything but apologetic about it.

He beckoned to another waiter. In low, rapid-fire French, gesticulating all the while, he instructed the younger fellow to take over his other tables. Phillipe was devoting all his attention to her and Aric, it seemed—and Cabana Boy didn't appear the least bit surprised.

"I believe we'll leave our selections entirely up to you, my man," he said as he handed back the menu. "You have excellent taste, and you know what women like. Please my Lola tonight, and you've done me a big favor, as well."

Was this the same kid who said "no problem" instead of "you're welcome?" Lola rested against the slatted back of her chair to look him over more closely. Maybe there was more to this pouty-lipped smart aleck than had previously met her eye. Maybe he could rise to whatever the occasion demanded—

Or rise to MY demands. Right here under the table, for starters.

Lola giggled.

"What?" his whispered. "I can see the cogs turning in that sexy head."

"Nothing. Just nothing," she teased. She was about to ask him one of those open-ended questions designed to make guys talk about themselves, when he pulled something large and sparkly from his shirt pocket.

"All right then, before we get any farther along, I need to give this back, Priestess. And I apologize for sounding so crude the other day, when I insinuated that the stone might not be . . . genuine."

Damned if Cabana Boy didn't slip Fletch's ring back on her finger, like a man who would be her fiancé himself. Or a man who'd made that move enough times to be downright smooth at it.

"You probably weren't far from the truth. Were you?" she ventured.

Lola watched the shimmer in those secretive eyes as Stud Muffin weighed his response. While it wasn't the most pleasant of subjects, she could rise above the humiliation it represented—for tonight, at least.

"Be honest, Aric. If you had a jeweler here on the ship look at it—"

"Joel's a pretty good friend. A guy I'd buy a diamond from, for the right lady," he replied with a rueful smile. "But yeah, it's a big chunk of CZ. I'm really sorry, Priestess. You deserve the real thing."

"Yes, I do. And thanks for saying so." Lola felt better—bolder—as she watched the colorful prisms play inside that rock when the light hit it right.

"In the back of my mind, I always wondered if Fletch had uh, taken some liberties when he bought this," she explained quietly. "Now that I know how badly he's ripped me off since we've been on board, I assume he not only bought this ring with money from one of my accounts—he allotted himself enough to pay for a huge diamond, and then pocketed the difference, as well. And then found a creative way to bury the expenditure among my other transactions."

Aric was still holding her hand, looking as eager and loyal as a puppy. "I hope they catch that bastard! I hope they tie him down so you can really get a piece of him."

She sipped the pink champagne Phillipe had poured, smiling wryly. "You know what, sweetie? Right now I don't give a damn about getting back at Fletch. Kingsley says my credit will be restored—"

"And Clive will see to that," Aric agreed with an emphatic nod.

"—so I just want to have some *fun*, already!" Lola continued. "I've lost way more than Dennis is worth, in stress and time and finances. No more throwing good money after bad!"

"Amen!" Aric clinked his champagne glass against hers, and as the *tiiiing* of the crystal vibrated between them, Lola took it as a turning point.

It sounded like a call to worship played upon some mystical temple instrument. And she was indeed the High Priestess.

Or maybe she was imagining things. God knows she was good at that.

But Lola couldn't miss the way Aric's eyes followed her champagne flute to her lips, and the way he watched her swallow . . . and the way he slipped his fingers loosely between hers, like he didn't intend to let her go.

"This is really nice," he murmured. "This is the way I wish it could always be for us, Lola."

"Why?" she blurted. "Sweetheart, I'm old enough to—"

"To forget that rubbish about age! Shall I show you how?"

Before she got his drift, Cabana Boy leaned closer and kissed her tenderly on the mouth. He tasted like champagne, tart and lightly sweet, with a hint of tingle even after he lifted his lips.

Lola sat absolutely still, eyes closed and lips apart. Waiting. As breathless as she'd been at sixteen.

So he kissed her again. He kept it very light and playful, with just their fingers and lips actively involved—

Unless we figure in this wet spot I'm making, she teased herself.

My God, she'd always thought he was cute in a beach boy sort of way, but now that he was kissing her—and it was *his* idea—Lola told herself once and for all to leave that age thing alone.

Who needed it? Age was just another number—like the ones Dennis rearranged all the time. When she looked back on this trip in a few months, Cabana Boy would remain a pretty fling she'd enjoyed on this cruise. A sweet reward for the way she'd been treated by that guy who gave her the fake ring.

Not to mention an attempt to trump Captain Scandalous.

When Phillipe cleared his throat, they moved apart so their personal waiter could set the first course in front of them.

"Our signature Parisian *soupe à l'oignon* for the lady," he said as he gave her a flirty wink. "And for you, *mon ami*, the *bouillabaisse* you can't get enough of. *Bon appetit!*"

Lola stifled a grin. While she wasn't surprised Aric was a regular here, where his friend was in charge, she wouldn't have predicted the fish soup. It didn't bear the slightest resemblance to pizza.

He watched her take her first bite of bread and stringy cheese and golden broth, and then close her eyes. "This is absolutely divine," she breathed.

She glanced at him, then gazed at the crisp linen tablecloth and the array of heavy silver flatware around her plate, which gleamed in the light from their table's candle. Lola let out a happy sigh.

"Thank you for this, Aric."

"It's my pleasure, Priestess. Even if I really wanted that pizza and beer."

They chattered through the greenest *salade aux épinards* she'd ever eaten, and on through a main course of *coq au vin* that was to die for. Way better than the chicken she brought home in a box.

And she'd been missing this cruise cuisine! Not to mention all the music and fun the others had been having all along! All because Dennis had ditched her and Captain Scandalous was making her pay for it.

"And for dessert, a classic cherries jubilee," Phillipe proclaimed. He got an obvious thrill from torching the brandy at their table.

"It is against the fire code to do this nowadays," he explained in a confidential tone. "But for *you*, tradition and taste must prevail over cruise company rules!"

"And the best part is, we're charging this to the captain's account," Aric replied with a wide smile. "So give yourself a generous tip, Phillipe."

The dark haired Frenchman went away chortling under his breath.

Lola, too, thought this was a fine note for the end of such a wonderful meal. "Where else are you taking me?" she ventured as they spooned down their ice cream.

While Aric had mentioned some great places—and she fully intended to enjoy them—she hadn't given up on that escape idea. It toyed with her the way a kitty swatted a catnip mouse, and Lola hoped her companion couldn't read any wavering devotion in her eyes.

Aric gave his spoon a long, suggestive lick. "We have an out-of-the-way watering hole called Improvisations, up on Deck Eleven. Jazz and trendy drinks. A panoramic view. I think you'll like it."

Lola nodded dreamily, leaning her chin on her hand to look at him. "And then?"

"You said you wanted to do the shops—and we've got everything from high-end jewelry to ship trinkets to duty-free booze," he enumerated. "Although I myself plan to remain, uh—*upright* enough to take you up on *your* offer."

"Which offer was that?" She put on an innocent smile, so she could watch him kick it up a notch when he returned it.

"To let me worship you, my Priestess," he breathed, lowering his eyelids. "I'll start with your face and your hungry lips, and burn my kisses down your neck until I'm taking those breasts into my mouth to—"

"It's the nail polish, isn't it? It's that siren red—"

"It's *you*, Lola."

Cabana Boy gazed directly at her, an expression every bit as potent as the way he'd finally called her by name. "From the moment I saw you in the suite, I wanted to *do* you—and do you up *right*."

Lola fought the urge to make another self-denigrating comment. It still didn't feel right, falling for what this kid was saying, yet she was drinking him in like the second split of pink champagne they were dawdling over. They sat like lovers who had nothing better to do than gaze into each other's eyes.

And how long had it been since she'd done that?

"Why me?" she breathed. She shifted in her chair, hoping he didn't get too honest and ruin this fine mood.

He shrugged, almost shyly. "Maybe it's time I raised my sights, Priestess. Maybe I should aim higher, rather than always going for the easy lay."

"Ah. You want a challenge."

"And you want a cigarette. May I light it for you?" he asked as he reached into his pocket. "I always thought that was such a seductive move in the old films. Continental, you know?"

That alone seemed reason enough to let him woo her with a flick of the Bic he was holding. Her gut clenched at the sight of the slim cigarette, and *need* overrode the nice pink high she was riding. It would feel so damn good to inhale. To feel that hot menthol warming her all the way down.

If he can talk you into a smoke, he can talk you into anything. You're breaking away, remember?

"Thanks, babe, but I'll abstain," she wheezed.

"Not from sex, I hope! That's what I'm after, you know."

He leered at her like a cheesy gigolo, making her laugh so loudly that everyone in the cafe turned to look at her.

Lola clapped her hand over her mouth, blushing.

But Aric was chuckling along with her. And damned if he didn't light up.

"I love it when you laugh," he assured her, the Camel dangling from his lips. "They say a woman who can cut loose with a really loud laugh will cut loose in bed, too. I love when that happens."

Lola followed his every move: the way his lids lowered and he caressed the cigarette while he drew in that first hit of nicotine. The golden tinge the flame cast on his fingers and face. The slither of that serpentine when he sucked a couple times.

She thought she was going to come when he blew the smoke slowly out his nose, watching her through the pale haze it made around his face.

Images of Aric in her bed . . . propped on an elbow to kiss her, with that boyish mop of hair brushing her forehead while he teased her bare skin with his fingertips . . . down there. God, she could feel the warmth of those hands, even though he kept them to himself right now.

Lola wondered if anyone would notice the wet spot on her dress when she stood up.

"Well, then," she murmured, determined to enjoy this game while it lasted, "I guess we'd better get on to that Improvisations place, and our shopping, so we can get to the good part. Right?"

"You got it, Priestess. Let's make ourselves scarce before Phillipe has to come out from behind that front desk with such a *peak* in his pants."

"Oh, I'm sure! It's not like he's been handling himself—"

"You need to get out more, lady. You have no idea what guys do when you walk past."

He glanced toward the desk by the door, as though to drive his point home. "But then, Phillipe's not the first guy who's ever played a whole damn pocket pool tournament while he fantasized about yanking down your panties."

Lola rose from the table, unable to keep a straight face.

Aric coaxed her body back against his, slipping his arm beneath her breasts. "You're not wearing any, are you?" he breathed beside her ear. "You're not wearing one freakin' piece of underwear under this dress."

"Please don't tell my mother."

"You little tease, letting on like—" He turned her and kissed her hard then, crushing her loose breasts against his body as he thrust his tongue between her teeth.

God love her, she sucked it. Just for the taste of his cigarette.

He let go with a gasp, grabbing her hand. "We're outta here right now, before I take you on that table."

The last thing Lola saw as he trotted her past the reception desk was Phillipe, wiggling his fingers.

And yes, he was *peaking* at her, too.

15

Improvisations was what Lola expected from a classy cruise ship bar: candles flickering on tables swallowed up in the near darkness. Vintage wallpaper, with framed pen-and-ink caricatures of greats like B. B. King and Springsteen. An inviting haze hung around the footlights at the bandstand, where a guitarist, a drummer, and a keyboard player jammed something soft and smooth.

The bar was hopping, as were the girls running the blender and mixing drinks. They wore tight white tank tops and pink satin boxers, and if their curly wigs hadn't been different wild colors, they could've passed for triplets.

Well, no—the blue-haired one's got bigger implants.

Lola snickered. The champagne was starting to hit, and she had to concentrate on walking so she wouldn't trip into her escort. He was gripping her hand, leading her between the crowded tables close to the stage.

"Petrocelli! Getcher ass up here, man!" the drummer called out. "Come and play with us!"

Whoever Petrocelli was, his name certainly brought everyone to attention. The bar babes chimed in with their cheers, while the guitar player and keyboard guy began that rhythmic *clap clap clap* that demanded a response from—

Aric? Her warden?

He was grinning big, stubbing out his cigarette, like it was him they were hollering for. And then he pulled her close again for one more kiss.

"Gimme some luck, Lola," he whispered as good-natured catcalls echoed around them. "Now that I've had a taste of you, I'm not sure my mouth wants to go anywhere else."

And just like that, he was striding onto the stage. The applause got deafening.

Lola dropped down into a chair, damn glad it was padded. What the hell was happening here? One minute they'd been slipping in for a drink, and the next thing she knew, the place had come alive like some big rock star was arriving.

Was she farther gone on the bubbly than she thought? Or had she been picked up out of reality and plunked down in a scene from an MTV clip?

Cabana Boy was reaching into an instrument case behind one of the big speakers, while the other musicians revved up a song introduction like he was going to *sing* or something. When he pulled out a—

Clarinet?

Lola choked. Her neighbor girl back home, Sissy Roark, got shanghaied into playing the clarinet for marching band because her brother had given up on it a few years earlier. She still recalled the awful squeaks and squawks coming from Sissy's open window, when she had to practice.

When Aric Petrocelli stepped up to the mike beside the guitarist, however, the crowd hushed. He was moving to the music, wetting his reed against his tongue—

And wouldn't you love to be the one he was tonguing?

Lola grinned, and realized Cabana Boy was grinning back at

her. He winked, the hot dog. Then he pointed his instrument above the crowd to play a showy run of triplets, his fingers flickering nimbly up a scale and back. As he swung his clarinet into a downbeat to start the song, the place came alive.

Lola perched on the edge of her chair, absently shaking her head when a blue-wigged barmaid asked what she was drinking. This kid was *good*! She didn't know all that much about music—took a few piano lessons because her mom made her—but there was no getting around the way Cabana Boy made that licorice stick sing.

Her feet couldn't hold still, and she couldn't help grinning insanely as her entire body took up the catchy beat. The kid put on quite a show for her, raising his shiny black instrument and *pushing—pushing—pushing* the tempo of a Dixieland jazz dance that brought everyone to their feet.

The clapping got louder, and it egged him on. Aric would've been flashing her a grin from beneath his tousled curls, had he not had his mouth full—

And Lola suddenly wanted to be his instrument. The way he was tonguing that thing, gripping it lightly as his fingers danced up and down the silver keys and his hips thrust forward like he was making love, *God* she wanted to be fifteen years younger!

No you don't. Now's your chance.

She blinked. Ever since he kissed her in Chez Phillipe, she'd felt a little sidetracked from her escape plan. But here where the lights were so low and everyone around her was up and dancing—and Aric was caught up in his own little world of passion—why, she wouldn't even be missed.

Lola looked around for the restroom. A natural thing to do, after a big meal where they'd downed two bottles of bubbly, and nearly three hours had passed since she left her room. He wouldn't think anything of it, until she'd been gone awhile.

She stood up, her limbs aquiver as she gripped her purse.

But she'd waited too long. The jazz dance ended on a trill

like the mating call of an exotic jungle bird, and when the wild applause died down, she got nailed.

"This next one's for Lola, my lady of the evening," Aric crooned into the mike. "I have to thank her for setting aside her objections to young turks, and tell her how glad I am that she came into my life."

Eyes searched the smoky darkness and found her gripping the table's edge, caught between going and . . . coming. Her smile wavered and she sat back down in a hurry. She couldn't very well leave when he'd dedicated this next song to her! So she leaned back, anticipating another virtuoso performance on his clarinet.

But no, Cabana Boy *sang* to her! That old Stevie Wonder classic, "You are the Sunshine of My Life," but with his own little dips and twists.

Damned if she didn't have to dab the corner of her eye. He was looking at right at her, crooning about how she was the apple of his eye, and that forever she'd stay in his heart. It was like having her very own James Taylor—with Rod Stewart putting the edge on his top notes.

"I had no idea," she rasped when he came back after the song, between fans who clapped him on the shoulders. "You never told me—"

"So now you know my deepest, darkest secret," he quipped, slipping into the chair next to hers.

A green-wigged barmaid brought him a cocktail—not to mention an up-close-and-personal view of the boobs bouncing beneath her white tank top. The serpentine around Aric's neck shimmied as he drank greedily.

Was it her imagination, or did the crystal at his Adam's apple wink like a little signal light?

The crowd was still clapping, coaxing him back up for another number, but Cabana Boy lifted her hand to his lips for a damp kiss that made her tingle all over.

"Go on up and play some more," she urged. Partly because she really did need to pee . . .

"I've been enough of a show-off here for one night."

"But they *love* you!" she insisted. "Play some more, if you—"

"I've got places to be and trinkets to see—with *you*, Lola. And besides," he added with raised eyebrows, "the more we keep moving, the more likely we'll stay under the radar. I play with these guys several times a week, so I'm pretty visible here."

Lola stiffened, glancing around to see if Skorpio or any of the security staff were here keeping track of them. He rose to go, so she took his hand and followed him out. It wasn't every day she got to bask in the adoration of her escort's fans—even if it waylaid her getaway for awhile.

Just outside the door, where there was a secluded little alcove, Cabana Boy pressed her to the wall and kissed her tenderly. He tasted like liquor instead of cigarettes now, but Lola kissed him back anyway. When else was she going to be the object of such attention?

"Thanks for being a good sport about that little musical interlude."

"And why wouldn't I be? It was so cool to watch you play!" she gushed, gazing up into his smooth young face. "And it's not like I get sung to every day, you know! And I—

"Thank you for that," she finished softly. "It made me feel really special."

His wistful smile made her ashamed for even *thinking* of ducking out on him. He smiled and clasped her hand again as they strolled toward midship where the shops were. If she pretended hard enough, she could believe Aric Petrocelli was at her side because he wanted to be.

But thoughts like that held her captive just like Captain Scandalous was doing, right?

"So how do you land a job like this, Aric?" she went on in a more purposeful voice. "I mean, *my* work looks downright boring and predictable compared to yours—and I certainly don't have clients clapping and cheering when they pay my fee. It must be like being in the movies."

He snorted, glancing at the passengers thronging the hallway up ahead. "Like with most things, it's who you know—or who you are—that gets your foot in the door."

"And which one worked for you?"

"Both." He waggled a playful eyebrow at her. "But then, it doesn't hurt to be a natural born gigolo, either. It's not like I can get many steady jobs playing the clarinet these days, right?"

Lola knew a dodge when she heard one. Just like she saw the logo for the ladies room up ahead as her chance to carry out her plan.

"See you in a minute," she announced, dropping his hand to beeline to the door.

Surely he wouldn't follow her inside! And even though she knew damn well Cabana Boy would be waiting when she came out, she could at least take a few minutes to think about how to give him the slip. A girl made better plans when her bladder wasn't full.

Like the restrooms of a fine hotel, this one was pretty swanky—a poshly decorated powder room with overstuffed chairs, and then the toilet area with its shiny gold faucets and fixtures. The louvered stall doors went all the way to the floor and had doorknobs instead of metal slides. All the doors stood ajar, so she was alone—except for the uniformed lady who was wiping the counter beneath the powder room mirrors.

The attendant glanced up and Lola froze.

That face in the mirror, smiling so politely, belonged to Odette.

16

Lola smiled and wavered only for a moment. She would *not* be waylaid by a bathroom attendant! Even if it *was* Odette, who was now smiling pointedly at her, maintaining nerve-wracking eye contact.

"Good evening," Lola rasped, skittering to the nearest louvered cubicle.

"Good evening, miss," followed her in.

And as she locked the door, Lola wondered what the hell she was going to do now. She'd be trapped in here all night, if Odette waited her out!

Lola sat down on the gleaming white seat. The bowl was so fresh, little soap bubbles still rode the surface of the water.

Now why on earth would Odette—the Captain's own personal masseuse—be cleaning toilets at ten o'clock at night?

Why would *any* of the housekeeping staff be cleaning during the ship's busiest hours?

So it *had* to be Odette, who somehow knew Lola was coming in here. She'd heard that Skorpio's captive had evaded his command performances for the past several hours, so she'd come looking!

But how did she know I'd be in this one?

No, the real question was, how would she get out? And why had she ever thought she could slip out of Improvisations to get away from Aric? Skorpio's employees were no doubt being paid very well to keep track of her, ever since she agreed to be his love slave.

Lola reached for that pack of Camels in her purse. Reminded herself she'd be in *big* trouble if she lit up in here, and just held the suede case in her hand to settle her nerves.

She sighed and sat there long after she'd relieved herself. Here in this louvered, locked stall, she could get some real thinking done without anyone peering at her from under the door.

If she was going to really get away from Aric, she'd have to make a more concrete, airtight plan. She'd have to have her ducks in a row and the means to get around—especially if she slipped off the ship tomorrow, when they docked in Grenada.

And wouldn't *that* be cool? To get away from the ship—

You'll need cash money. Your SeaKey won't buy one frickin' thing on shore.

But it'll still get you into your original room on the Promenade Deck, won't it?

Now there was a thought! Since she'd been moved to the Aphrodisia Suite after they'd set sail, it was quite possible no one else had been shifted into that room . . . which might make a good hideout, for awhile.

But she'd seen how many cameras and monitors the security crew had in operation. She'd be *so* easy to spot in every public area on the ship—

Unless you're wearing a disguise. Or a costume.

Lola thought back to those girls in the tank tops and colored wigs, and to Odette in her French maid's uniform—who, now that she'd settled down, and thought about it—may or may *not* be Odette.

She'd spoken politely. She'd shown no particular sign of recognition, or any indication of being on the prowl. With all the different nationalities on the ship's staff—so many young women with olive complexions and their dark hair pulled neatly back—there might be dozens who resembled Odette at a passing glance.

Lola thought hard, which was getting more difficult as the hours went by. Her champagne buzz was going flat now, replaced by the need for some real sleep.

And how likely was that? Cabana Boy might not consider snuggling in bed a legitimate way to fly under the radar, if he had a more exciting type of flight in mind.

If she could just figure out how to get ahold of—

Rap-rap-rap. "Miss, are you all right? Your young man, he is asking about you. About why it is you are taking so long."

Lola narrowed her eyes, wishing she could see through the door. "I'm fine thanks," she insisted. "Tell him I'll just be another minute."

"I'm here to help you if you need me."

Now *that* sounded like an Odette trick! What bona fide bathroom attendant would offer to help her that way?

Maybe someone who saw the startled look on my face when I came in her. Someone who has no clue I'm hiding out.

Lola held her breath to listen. Was the maid still outside her stall?

Was it Odette, or just an attractive look-alike?

Does it really matter? You can't spend the rest of the night in here!

Lola stood to smooth her sun dress. She turned to push the flush button, and then waited for the forceful *whoosh* to die away before turning the doorknob.

If Odette was waiting for her, she'd just have to take whatever that vengeful woman dished out.

When she stepped out of the stall, however, she was alone. All that lingered as evidence of her frightening encounter was the cloying scent of the attendant's disinfectant, masked by floral air freshener.

Lola glanced quickly around the other stalls and in the mirror above the sinks, but saw no one. She washed her hands and scurried out the doorless archway, back into the corridor where the night owls were getting really geared up. Most folks had put on clothes now, but a few die-hards were still partying naked.

"Trouble?" Cabana Boy quizzed her. He was leaning nonchalantly against the wall, his hands in his pockets.

Lola gazed up at him, wondering if he already knew who she'd met up with. After all, the cleaning lady had to come out this way, right past him. And since he, too, was connected to Captain Scandalous, it could well be he was still in touch—was making covert contact while she did things like . . . shower and use the ladies' room, without him.

And what if that wasn't Odette? What if her mind was playing tricks on her?

Then you're in a world of hurt, baby. You'll need to pull your act together in a hurry if you think you'll get away from this wily crew.

"Just a little case of mistaken identity," she murmured, testing the waters. "I thought for *sure* that was Odette cleaning the can, but that makes no sense at all. Odette wouldn't be caught dead swishing a toilet unless Skorpio was going to bend her over it to take her from behind."

Aric laughed. "Appearances can be deceiving," he quipped, slipping his hand into her bent elbow.

See there? You really do need a disguise.

So after Aric bought her a box of those truffles with the messages, she latched onto two airy, elegant scarves, a pair of dark sunglasses, and a lime green canvas hat with a flowery band tied above its broad, dipping brim. What a deal, in a shop where almost everything was ten dollars!

"That's all you want?" her escort quizzed. "We're charging this to the captain's account, you know."

Lola smiled—but then wondered if these high-tech computers would track her transactions, so the captain could keep track of her according to the purchases she made. A paranoid thought, but a possibility.

"Let's keep shopping," she suggested when she saw the sign for the ship's high-end jewelry shop. "Gee, if Skorpio's buying, maybe I need a new diamond. A real one this time."

Aric let out a little laugh, but they entered the shop anyway—a place where the display case spotlights made the fine gold and precious gemstones sparkle enticingly. She instinctively knew that the young man behind the counter was Aric's friend, Joel—a nice-looking guy of maybe thirty who was picking a variety of rings out of his main display cabinet for a man who seemed intent on something really showy.

"Let me see that one—the diamond with the tanzanite clusters," he was saying. He was balding from the forehead back and probably thirty pounds overweight, with the air of a computer geek or a scholarly type who didn't see the sun much.

"See, I met this really foxy lady at the speed dating this afternoon—"

Naked, Lola mused, trying not to imagine how this marshmallow of a man must've looked to the fox he was talking about.

"—and we hit it off immediately! I—I could see she had a lot of guys hanging at her table, probably fixating on her uh, fine attributes. But she's with *me* now!" he rhapsodized. "It's like we've known each other for years! So if I impress her with a ring—"

"This one should make a definite impression," Joel agreed,

fighting a smile. "Total carat weight of three point five for that diamond, plus the six tanzanites of a quarter carat apiece."

"Holy cow, this is gonna cost me—but dammit, life's too short not to take risks!" the guy replied. He was all aquiver, drumming the edge of the glass case with the pudgy fingers of both hands.

"If I may see your SeaKey, the ring's yours," Joel said smoothly. "And if for any reason your lady doesn't like this one, or needs it resized—"

"My SeaKey! Gretchen has my SeaKey because she—well, she's up in my room, getting ready to surprise me—"

Lola groaned inwardly. Caught the same dubious expression flickering across Cabana Boy's brow.

"—so I'll have to give you cash," the guy said, reaching for his back pocket. "That's better anyway, because Gretchen won't know what I paid for it."

"Sorry, sir. The ship's shops only accept your SeaKey. We're not set up to handle cash."

Marshmallow Man got that deer-in-the-headlights look. "Then I'll have to figure out a way to finesse it back—without her guessing that I'm buying her a surprise!"

"I'll keep the ring right here for you, sir." Joel called after him as he hurried out the door.

And Lola was hot on his heels.

"Sir! Sir, I might have an answer to your predicament!" she called after him. "If it's cash you've got—and a really flashy rock you want—let's talk!"

He turned, eyeing her and Aric warily. Pushing a bad comb-over back into place with jittery fingers. "How'd you know—"

"We were standing right behind you," she said, looking into his watery gray eyes, "and I couldn't help overhearing your conversation about wanting a really nice ring for Gretchen."

Lola flashed her left hand—and her finest smile.

"Now, I'm going to be straight with you, because Joel back there knows this is a high-dollar chunk of CZ that passes for a diamond to the average, untrained eye," she said in a confidential tone. "But I'm thinking maybe it's a better solution to your gift idea, because if Gretchen turns out to be as wonderful as you're hoping, you can always replace this with a genuine stone when you get married. And if it doesn't work out, well—you didn't blow so much of a wad on somebody who might just, uh—*present* herself well during speed dating."

Naked.

He blinked, and glanced toward Cabana Boy. "Let me take a look at this," he said cautiously. "You might have a point about—"

"Frankly, sir, it's been my experience that giving someone else access to your account isn't such a hot idea," she went on ruefully. "That's *exactly* why this ring's for sale. If Gretchen's not really up in your room—or if she made a few detours through the shops first—you might be amazed at how quickly your tab can tote up."

"Naw, she's not the type to—"

"Then you could go upstairs right now and slip this baby on her finger. Take up where your speed date left off."

"How much do you want?" he asked in a breathy voice. His forehead beaded with sweat, but he was fishing out his wallet.

"Well, the gold is eighteen carat, so I'd have to have at least—"

"I've got eleven c-notes in my stash—"

"—nine hundred bucks."

"Sold!"

Lola whipped the ring off her finger so fast Fletch's memory got whiplash. "I think you're doing the right thing. Hate to see a nice guy get taken to the cleaners when he's trying to follow his heart."

"This is great, lady. Hey, thanks a million!"

Lola watched him waddle toward the elevators, a hippo in hot pursuit, gripping the ring in his fist.

"Can you believe that guy?" she asked, shaking her head. "Buying a diamond for someone he met speed dating today!"

"'A fool and his money are soon parted,' as Kingsley would say," Aric replied with a little laugh. "But I can't believe you really *did* that, Priestess!"

"Why not? I was meeting a desperate man's need," she reasoned, "and I don't want to be reminded of my colossal misjudgment of character every time I see that CZ.

"So we both win!" she added, tucking the hundreds into her wallet. "I might as well go home from this trip with *something* to show for the time and energy I invested in the absolutely wrong man."

He shook his head, making that crystal wink again.

"I've gotta hand it to you," he said as they headed down the corridor. "You knew how to milk that guy. You can think on your feet . . . so maybe that mean's you can think *off* your feet, too. All stretched out on those cool, clean sheets up in your—"

"Oops, we're outta here, Priestess." Cabana Boy's voice dropped as his hands landed on her shoulders. "Don't squeal, baby. Just move with me."

Lola sucked air when he jerked her out of the main corridor. With all the grace of the dancing he'd done in the ballroom, Cabana Boy whipped her through a small door around the corner. She recognized the lobby area at the entryway to the ship's huge theater, before being steered into a small, tiled room that echoed with the slamming of the door.

"But—this is a men's room!" she gasped.

"Skorpio's coming."

"Oh. *Shit!*"

Aric put a warning finger to her lips. "Stay quiet. Hide in the stall if he comes in—but stand on the seat so your feet don't show!"

Her eyes widened. Lola hoped she wasn't breathing too loudly.

Her escort leaned toward the door, listening. Then he grinned, fingering its lever-style handle.

The lock button made a very quiet *click* when he pushed it.

17

Lola scowled, her pulse pounding. She hadn't noticed any of the *ladies'* restrooms having locks.

And how many of them have you visited on this ship?

True enough. And this *was* an adult cruise, so maybe those whispered stories about what goes on in public johns weren't just fantasies. Maybe guys really did get quickies and then walk away like they'd been . . . taking care of business.

This was a one-seater. Big enough for a wheelchair to roll where it needed to, but not much more. Which explained the lock.

She cleared her throat, hoping Captain Scandalous wasn't lurking outside the door.

Waiting.

Listening.

Laughing. Because all he had to do was whip out a master key and call the shots. Then he could whip out whatever he wanted—right here in the bathroom. Probably after he sent Aric away, like he loved to do. Or maybe he'd make the kid watch this time. They really were at Skorpio's mercy now, weren't they?

She let her breath escape very quietly.

Then Lola noticed that Cabana Boy didn't seem nearly as edgy as she felt. Matter of fact, he had an air of purpose about him, as though he'd really brought her in here so he could answer nature's call without her running away.

Aric wasn't really going to take a whiz with her standing here—*was* he?

Sounds like the perfect time to dash. He can't run after you with his pants down.

Cabana Boy turned toward the urinal on the wall—which put him in profile. Never taking his eyes off her, he whipped down his zipper. Unbuttoned, and then let his slacks slide down legs that had to be a thirty-six inseam. But who was counting?

With one smooth movement he scooped himself out of his stretchy black bikinis and took aim.

This had all taken a matter of seconds, yet it felt like slow-mo to Lola as she watched, fascinated while a bit embarrassed. Fletch had never considered pissing a spectator sport, thank God. She should turn away instead of watching him: what kind of woman would he think she was, if she got turned on in a men's toilet?

This is where you duck out, right?

Yeah, right into Skorpio's open arms.

"You wanna play with it, Lola?"

Aric's low voice rumbled like thunder as his words reverberated in the small, tiled room.

He was rock hard. Long and slender and sleek. Just waiting to be taken.

"I saw the way you watched me play my clarinet in the club."

He'd quit pissing, but he still stood there, holding himself out on display. "You really got into that song, and I thought,

'Cool! She understands my passion now!' Or at least one of them."

Cabana Boy's pouty lips parted in a sensual grin. "I bet you're a pretty fair player yourself. I'd sure like to find out."

Lola swallowed hard. He was asking for exactly what she'd told herself she'd never lower herself to do in a men's room. Especially if they had a lurker.

"But what if Skorpio unlocks—"

"Hey, he'll stand there and listen. Then he'll wait for his turn—*if* that was him," Aric said with a shrug. "When he isn't wearing his captain's hat, he looks like a lot of the other Greek guys from his engineering crew."

"But you said it was—"

"Better safe than sorry, right?" he cut in softly. "Better to step out of the line of fire—and as hot as you look tonight, Priestess, it was only gonna be a matter of time for us. You knew that when you said you'd be all mine tonight."

He wasn't bullying her. He didn't sound arrogant or high-toned like Captain Scandalous. He was just standing there with his cock in his hand and his pants around his ankles, watching her from beneath those sultry curls.

"I—"

"You don't have to swallow," he coaxed. "And Priestess, I promise if you just suck me—just play a little organ recital to take the edge off—I'll spend the rest of the night doing whatever you want."

"Anything?"

"Would Richard here lie to you?"

Lola giggled in spite of her jangling nerves. "Richard? You call it—"

"Just a fancy way to say *dick*, right?" he teased. "Not terribly original, but he's quite the party animal in the right lady's hands. Or mouth."

His throat sounded dry, and he gazed at her lips. "God, but

I've wanted you to take me in that sweet mouth so many times today."

His voice had dropped into that low, coaxing zone that would've brought Lola to her knees even if he hadn't been asking for a blow job. He wanted a dirty girl; a woman who'd do it anywhere, because she couldn't help herself. Because things got a lot edgier in a public place, where someone might catch them going at it.

Skandalis might have his ear to the door. And he'd just have to wait his turn!

Cabana Boy stepped away from the urinal and palmed off his tip, silently begging her with those low-lidded eyes. He shoved his island-print shirt up out of her way, revealing his slender, tanned body and the wreath of downy hair around his privates.

He didn't have a pale place where his Speedo would go.

Lola let her purse drop. Used the shopping bag as padding for her knees when she knelt.

She closed her eyes and opened her mouth.

When he slipped it in, Aric drew a breath that made her go all goose-bumpy. "Ohhhhhhh, Lola. Lolaaaaaa. . . ."

She closed her lips more firmly, savoring the taste of his warm, solid shaft and the way it filled her mouth. He moved ever so slightly, letting her take the lead . . . sucking air in anticipation when she took in his whole length. The tip of him touched her throat.

Lola relaxed. Took a breath, so her gag reflex didn't dampen the fine heat rising between them.

With one palm she fondled his balls, delighting in his softness there. Such a contrast to the rod she held in her other hand, at the base of it.

In and out he slid, smooth and slow and slick. She glanced up to see his eyes shut in impending ecstasy. The crystal in his necklace shimmered in the light from above the sink.

"Play me, Lola," he moaned. "Play me harder and faster now. Lick my tip. Run your tongue around it like—oh God yes, *yessssss*, Priestess!"

Hot now herself, Lola upped the pace. His fingers found her hair, so intensely she nearly stopped sucking him to luxuriate in his wild massage.

Is this how Rio would feel? How he would respond?

Her eyes flew open. Where had *he* come from, in this evening of flying under the radar?

Cabana Boy's cock got harder. He was shortening his thrusts, letting his head loll back.

"Please, baby, please," he moaned. "I'm gonna lose it soon—gonna lose my load—gonna—"

With a grimace, he climaxed. His body stiffened, and with each tremor he released more buttery cum.

Lola kept him in her mouth, looking up the length of his taut body. He was the most beautiful man she'd ever seen. And he'd entrusted himself; made himself utterly vulnerable to her.

Still quivering in the legs, he swiveled her head. "Spit, baby. I don't expect you to—"

Lola swallowed. Stayed on her knees as she let her fingers follow the curve of his butt.

Aric shook his head to clear it. "Wow," he breathed. "Wow, like—you *do* know how to play that thing, Priestess."

Cabana Boy wore an expression Lola had always been a sucker for: a look of utter amazement and gratitude. Which was way better than a victorious grin after a virtuoso performance.

Fletch had always been very proud of himself and had enjoyed splattering her chest so he could watch his cum dribble down her breasts. It was that guy thing, about getting a visible measurement. Then he'd ask if she'd felt how really hard he'd shot.

I won't miss that about him, either, she mused.

Aric was extending his hand, helping her stand up. Then he

slipped his arms around her and kissed her like he really loved doing it . . . loved hearing her moan and sigh for it.

His hand slipped into her sun dress to cup her. When he deepened the kiss, Lola's need for him surged.

"Hey," she whispered, "don't you dare start something you can't—

Bam-bam-bam! "Hurry it up in there, buddy! The show's gonna start!"

They froze, staring at each other.

"I'm not finished! Go someplace else!" Aric replied pointedly.

Lola's pulse raced, but that for damn sure wasn't Skorpio out there. Had Cabana Boy known that all along? Just used that ploy to get her on her knees in here?

Bam-bam-bam! "C'mon—I gotta go *now*!" the guy outside wailed.

Suddenly tired of head games, whether they were tricks played upon her or products of her own weary mind, Lola let out a disgusted sigh. She grabbed the canvas hat from her bag and crammed it on her head, before slipping the new sunglasses on, tag still dangling. It was one thing to be seen coming out of a men's room with an escort. It was another thing to be recognized for it later.

"Do what you want, but I'm out of here," she muttered.

She pumped the door handle down to pop the lock, and then, armed with her purse and shopping bag, Lola marched past the guy outside.

18

"Isn't my nephew a genius? Coaxing Lola into that bathroom—saying I was following them!" Skorpio whispered excitedly. "And having Odette's sister report to that ladies room. He deserves a raise, don't you think?"

DeSilva muffled a sigh as he watched the small monitor on their cocktail table. He should've taken this evening off. He should be doing anything but tracking Lola from the corner of the Voyeurs lounge.

But when the captain issues a command, a man who has a very large paycheck coming in another week does what he's told.

It gave him no joy to have Skandalis seated beside him now, catching up on Lola's newest adventure. Watching the images beamed in from the kid's crystal medallion to his portable screen.

"It was the best toy I ever bought, that wireless spy cam," the captain raved on. "Odette designed the medallion. She likes to wear it so we can watch ourselves making love on tape. But using it for *this* was a stroke of genius!"

He was squinting at the monitor, since the picture wasn't all that clear. But that was unmistakably the top of Lola's pretty head entering a door marked MEN, while Petrocelli steered her inside.

"She's not stupid," Rio remarked. "She'll figure out it's not you—or Odette—and then she'll catch you at your game."

"So much the better! She'll assume that she really has eluded me, and she'll get careless. And then I'll just have to punish her, won't I?"

The captain watched the monitor more intently, his eyes gleaming. "And besides, what can she do? I'm the captain! And she agreed to our little deal."

To keep from hauling off and punching him, or saying something he'd regret, DeSilva stroked his mustache. *Hard.* He'd had enough of this "little deal" because he saw no way for Lola to win it: the captain held all the cards.

"I got word that she's bought a hat and sunglasses," Skorpio went on. "And now that she's got that money from her ring, I'm betting she tries to leave the ship tomorrow when we reach Grenada—"

"Maybe she's just planning to tan on her balcony."

In the altogether. With me instead of Aric, he mused. Although he was pleased she got rid of that rock.

"—and I plan to be there with a little surprise. Women love surprises!"

Rio fought the urge to ask if he didn't have other things that needed tending to: even though he had the volume turned down, he suspected things would soon get hot and heavy, and he didn't want Lola to be *that* compromised. She deserved to have a little dignity left when the Skandalis family got finished playing with her.

"*You wanna play with it, Lola?*" Aric's raspy voice came through the mike in his cigarette pack.

"Now we're talking! I've got to watch this." Skorpio scooted his chair back, elbows on his knees, so his face was on the same level as the monitor.

Rio sighed. The picture only showed the tiled wall of the men's room, but he didn't need much imagination to fill in what was happening.

"*Hot as you look tonight, Priestess, it was only gonna be a matter of time for us. You knew that when you said you'd be all mine tonight.*"

"She overestimates herself!" Skorpio said, gleefully slapping the top of his thigh. "She thinks she can fly under my radar, but she's about to hit the wall!"

"*Ohhhhh, Lola. Lolaaaaaa . . .*"

Dammit, the kid was taking this way too far. The camera around his neck was pointed at where the wall met the damn ceiling now, and the way the picture was jiggling. . . .

Rio shifted in his chair to ease the ache in his cock. But it was like scratching poison ivy: the contact, the idea—just the thought that it needed scratching—made him itch for it. Made him want Lola even more.

It didn't help that she was just a couple doors down the hall.

While he hadn't figured her for the type to go down on a man in a public bathroom, deep inside, he loved her sense of adventure. Here was a woman being held captive by a very cocky captain, and she was defying him at every turn!

He admired her all the more for that, even as he saw the captain's hands moving in his pants pockets.

"*Oh God. yes, yessssss, Priestess.*"

Did Aric really have to call her that? It was a sacrilege to toy with Lola this way while referring to her in such exalted terms from the Tarot.

Of course, she *was* like the High Priestess: Lola lived by her intuition and creative forces, and ruled with all the power of the moon. And she certainly had men howling.

"DeSilva, how can you just *sit* there while we listen to Aric getting a blow job—"

"I don't enjoy eavesdropping on a very private, intimate act, sir."

Wrong thing to say.

Skorpio Skandalis made fists in his white pants pockets, looking at him far too closely.

"You want her for yourself."

There it was, the statement that summed up his desires perfectly. Dammit.

"You've had the idea she could be yours from the start. Even before she played that name-your-fantasy game with us," the captain asserted. Then he slapped Rio on the back. "Well, at least you're looking at women again. I was beginning to wonder if your preferences had changed—"

Rio stood up so forcefully his chair fell backwards, clattering against the wall. The bartender looked over, but DeSilva waved him off.

"So I'm right." Skorpio's eyes, black as panthers, looked ready to pounce. "You've been planning to defy my orders, even before Lola thought of it."

"I never said—"

"You don't have to, DeSilva. It's written all over your handsome Spanish face—and you're as hard for her as I am!"

Skorpio took his hands from his pockets, his laugh lines deepening as he considered his next move. "Better be careful, my friend. You have commitments. You have important life changes to make, and a woman like Lola—a woman who'd hock her engagement ring on a cruise ship, and then go into a men's room with a young stud like Aric—is the *last* person you need in your life right now. Leave her alone."

Rio knew a command when he heard one. He resented the way their fantasy with Lola was going way beyond the original game. Sure, Skorpio liked to have his fun with the ladies—and they flocked around him, every week a new batch of passengers with a few returning girlfriends vying for his attention.

Partly because he was the captain, but also because his good looks and magnetic presence gave the impression that he might be a very powerful Greek tycoon who wore dress whites for the fun of it.

Which was precisely right.

Which perturbed Rio every damn day, and rubbed him raw now that Lola had reawakened needs he'd ignored since Katya died.

"Bam bam bam! Hurry up in there!"

"Sounds like they've got company," Skandalis mused aloud. "I've got to move along anyway—Odette's not good at waiting, you know. But keep your eyes and ears open, DeSilva."

The captain stood up, adjusting himself so the pleats of his whites camouflaged his bulge better. "I'll expect a full report by the time we drop anchor in Grenada tomorrow morning, so I can plan my strategy. Lola needs some discipline that'll teach her to behave like a lady—at least while she's *my* love slave!"

His laughter followed him into the hall, echoing the inflated ego DeSilva wouldn't miss when he left the ship.

Pissed—as much at himself as at the captain—Rio flipped the little monitor off. He needed a long walk to clear his head.

A walk in the moonlight by yourself—out where you're sure to run across other lovers going at it. And what will that solve?

He paused at one of the automatic exit doors, torn between disappearing into the crowd around the pool—or going back down the hall, to come clean.

You can't let her catch you with this monitor. Not after what she did with Aric in that men's room.

He should help her, though. Lola responded to him—the kid was only her ticket out of that suite right now. A real man—the king of his castle—would rescue her before she played right into the captain's grasping hands.

* * *

I'm tired and I'm going to bed," she snarled as Aric slipped his key into the lock.

"But Priestess, you were just getting into the mood for—"

"Having a drunk stranger bang on the bathroom door kinda jarred me out of it, you know?"

Lola stalked into the suite ahead of Cabana Boy, tossing her purse, the hat, and her shopping bag on the couch. "And when I figured out it wasn't Captain Scandalous—and that you'd used that as your little ploy to get sucked in the boys' room, well, your stock went wayyyyy down with me, little man."

She watched him from the corner of her eye, gauging his reaction. Of course, why would he be upset *now*? He'd gotten what he wanted! And then left her hanging!

But she was so exhausted and disgusted she really didn't care.

"And how was I supposed to handle that guy?" Cabana Boy demanded. "I told him to get lost! It was *you* who had to open the door and—"

"You told me you'd do whatever I wanted for the rest of the night, right?" Lola snapped. "Well just zip it then—your lip *and* your fly! You get to sleep out here on the couch—"

"Oh no you don't—"

"—and I'm going in to collapse on that nice big bed. By myself! To get some sleep, for once!"

Aric crossed his arms, peering archly at her from beneath his loose curls. "Sleep was the last thing on your mind when you asked me to fly under the radar with you."

"That was hours ago! Dammit, leave me alone!"

She grabbed her bags and stalked into the bedroom. Gave the door a loud, satisfying slam. It was probably a waste of time, but she locked it, too.

What she needed was chocolate and a lot of sleep—

And what you really, really want is a smoke. You just don't want Cabana Boy to know you bailed.

Still leaning against the door, Lola reached into the plastic shopping bag for that wrapped package of truffles. With trembling hands, she ripped off the ribbon and peeled the foil off one. Popped it into her mouth before she could reach for those Camels—*two* packs of them, thanks to Mr. Nice Guy out there.

"So is it mint? Or butter rum?" his voice came through the door.

"None of your fuckin' business!" she said, although her mouthful of Black Forest nougat muddled the words.

"Ooh, we're getting touchy."

"No, *you* got all the touchy and I got cut off. Not to mention extremely embarrassed when I had to walk past that guy."

"And what's the little fortune say?" he crooned.

She cleared her throat ceremoniously. "If you kill him and dump him over your balcony railing, no one will ever find the body."

"All right, I know when I'm not wanted," he said in a mock sulk. "I'll just wait you out . . . eat cold pizza and sleep on this old hard couch while my Priestess gets her beauty rest. Would you like a beer?"

"I'd like you to shut up. I'm reading."

Things are not what they seem. Pay attention, the foil warned.

"No shit, Sherlock," she muttered, reaching into the bag again. This time it was dark chocolate with a honey-roasted peanut butter filling. Lola thought she'd died and gone to heaven.

"You're gonna get fat, Priestess."

"Fuck you. Go eat your pizza."

The second wrapper said, *Someone loves you more than you know. Find him.*

"Yeah, right. They're all after one thing," she muttered, rip-

ping into another one. She'd be better off switching to a cigarette. She could stand out on her balcony, and no one would
ever know.

"What's that, Lola? What are we all after?"

"Oh, just—"

She moved away from the door, popping the truffle into her
mouth. Mint, at last! Smooth and sweet and creamy, clinging to
her tongue and tingling all the way down her throat. As good as
the menthol in a Turkish Jade, but not the same kind of fix.

"You realize, don't you," he continued, "that eating more
than a couple of those truffles at once is a sure-fire way to get
diarrhea."

Her gut clenched. She swallowed the last of the candy faster
than she intended, and then choked on its richness.

"Hang on, babe—I'll be right there!"

Moments later, while she was still coughing and trying to
swallow, her door opened. A bottle of beer, so cold the sweat
ran down the side, appeared in the opening, with Aric's hand
wrapped around it.

"Drink this. I'll see you in the morning, when you're in a
better mood."

Damn that Cabana Boy!

But after he closed the door Lola drank it down, because the
carbonation cleared the gunk from her throat . . . and then the
alcohol kicked in with the sugar she'd just snarfed, and she was
ready to crash. Didn't much care what Aric did.

She stepped out of her sun dress. Saw the Tarot deck she'd
left on her table and picked it up, just to feel the slick newness
of the cards and to let the rich, luminous colors soothe her.
Sometimes, when she was very tired or a little tipsy, her brain
disengaged and her intuition kicked in. Then the cards fell together in patterns and pictures that meant more than when she
consciously laid out a spread.

Absently she mixed the cards in a loose pile on her table, then restacked them and cut them into three piles—her ritual for letting her inner energy pass into the cards. She fanned each pile across the table and without any thought or hesitation chose eight of them. Her lucky number.

When she'd restacked the rest of the deck, Lola laid out the cards she'd chosen. Court cards—a lot of them—caught her eye, and in this gorgeous deck the Kings and Queens, Knights and Pages were so beautifully detailed their facial expressions often suggested things, depending upon the situation she was dealing with.

Lola caught her breath. Why, that King of Swords had the same sly expression as Captain Scandalous! And didn't that Page of Swords—a young man she'd always found a bit too pretty in this deck—remind her Cabana Boy tonight? And surely that self-satisfied woman holding the falcon in the Nine of Pentacles had to be Odette.

And the Tower card! Always a sign of a surprise that struck like a bolt out of the blue. Surely it belonged just above that dubious trio in blues and purples, although she wasn't sure why yet. The Tower, with its bullet-shaped top, was *so* damn phallic it might have inspired the design for ancient dildos—and the way it was breaking at the top, a portent of doom, just seemed to *fit* somehow.

Lola looked at this grouping, too tired and upset to read anything definite into these images. The other cards she'd drawn felt much more compelling: The Hanging Man, dangling by an ankle wrapped in chains, and Strength—a long-haired woman with a chain around her lion's neck—seemed natural partners as well.

This left the King of Pentacles, a handsome fellow with a mustache, gazing off into the night sky—

Rio!

—and the Queen of Swords . . . a redhead who seemed to be recharging the sword in her hand as she gazed back at Lola with that sly, knowing look about her.

She'd always wanted to be more savvy, like this street-smart queen, but instead Lola usually felt intimidated by this Tarot character's sharp tongue and critical assessment of failure.

Her last card, The Moon, belonged above this second grouping as surely as the Tower looked right above the court cards representing Skorpio, Aric, and Odette.

Lola sighed tiredly. What did this reading *mean*? What were the cards trying to tell her?

She was too tired and looped—and too quickly sinking into a sugar low—to care. She turned out the light, fell into bed naked, and crashed.

When Lola awoke, the sun was streaming in from her balcony. The subtle movement she felt while they were sailing had stopped, which meant they'd already docked at their next port of call.

Rubbing her eyes, she wandered to the sliding glass door and stepped outside, into the brilliance. Not something she would do at home naked, but hey—adult cruises had their advantages, and she was feeling better rested than she had for days.

She realized then that Captain Scandalous was delivering his morning message: his voice came over the outdoor speakers on the deck below her, loud and clear and confidently Greek.

"Let me welcome you to Grenada, where the weather will be sunny and pleasant for those going to watch for whales—or for the snorkeling adventure on the party boat," he said with a chuckle. "As always, it is your responsibility to return to the gangway before five-thirty, so the *S.S. Aphrodite*—our proud jewel of the Caribbean—can set sail for Dominica at six o'clock sharp this evening.

"As a special enticement to go ashore and enjoy the unique

charm of Grenada," he added, "I myself will be handing out a passbook of certificates for discounts at the local shops, to one lucky passenger. It could be you! So come ashore and find me, and if your SeaKey number matches the one I've drawn, you're the winner! But then—you can't lose, if you're aboard the *S. S. Aphrodite*!

"We've now been cleared by the port authority," he added in that buttery-rich voice, "and I wish you a wonderful day in Grenada."

Lola gazed out over the harbor, lined with local market vendors, and then quickly went back inside. Those passengers walking down the gangway could *see* her if they looked this way!

But wouldn't it be fun to go with them? If Captain Scandalous was going ashore, making himself scarce enough that one lucky passenger would win his prize, this would be the place to make her break!

She would return, of course. This late in the game, she'd be stupid to pay again for air fare home, just to escape Skorpio and Odette or to get a rise out of Aric. And if she reneged on the deal, Skorpio might send her the bill for the purchases charged to his account—and he might be underhanded enough not to have her credit rating restored.

And then Dennis would win. And she couldn't have that!

Lola walked back to the table to look at the cards she'd laid out in her mental haze last night. One thing jumped out at her immediately—that the King of Pentacles with his happy smile was Rio, and that *she* was the Queen of Swords, with that red hair and such a secretive smile.

And gee . . . didn't the Hanging Man's chains belong around Aric's ankle? And didn't Strength's loose chain around that lion suggest that Cabana Boy needed to be tamed—

Or left hanging, she mused. *Like I was last night*.

Lola smiled hugely. She'd laid out these cards without conscious thought of their patterns or interpretation, but that

Moon suggested looking at things in a different, more imaginative light; seeing things other people didn't.

And Lola suddenly had a plan.

It was worth a try, anyway—if Cabana Boy cooperated. Was he still in her main room? Or had he taken a break, assuming she'd sleep the morning away?

Lola listened at the door and heard deep, even breathing, coming from the couch near her door. It seemed Aric was catching up on *his* beauty sleep, too, but she suspected he'd stayed up a lot later than she had.

Very quietly, she opened her door.

Good Lord, he was not only stretched out on her couch, snoring lightly, but he was buck naked!

In the dimness of this room, where the curtains were pulled against the morning sun, Aric looked like a painting done on the royal blue velvet of the couch: alluringly bronzed all over, with skin that just begged to be stroked and that mop of hair practically covering his eyes. He looked almost sweet and innocent, with his eyes closed and that cock dangling relaxed and limp between his slender thighs.

But she wasn't fooled for a minute! If he woke up, she wouldn't have a moment's peace—much less make her break for the shore. And yet her eyes lingered on his dick . . . recalling its length and strength last night, and the urgent way he'd responded to her sucking.

There was a certain *power* in having a man in her mouth—of controlling him and making him beg for it . . .

Lola re-entered her room without making a sound. Quickly she slicked on some makeup, and chose shorts and a top with the same colors as the flowered band of her new lime sun hat. She put the hat and the dark, oversized shades on, and then reached to the bottom of the shopping bags for the two scarves.

This was going to be *so* much fun! And if Cabana Boy woke

up too soon, she'd segué into a sex game and he'd never know her original intent!

Slowly, silently, she emerged from her bedroom with her purse. Laid it on the floor, ready to grab when she left. With her shades on, the curtained room looked even more secretive, and her warden seemed even more surreal as he lay before her, spread out like a banquet of soft, supple flesh. A temptation not to be missed!

Very slowly and carefully, Lola slipped the turquoise silk scarf under his ankles, which hung over the edge of the couch cushion because he was so tall. She tied a loose knot around them, and then paused to be sure he was still asleep.

Aric shifted, making that showy crystal medallion wink. He smacked his lips and resettled into his deep, even breathing.

So Lola tightened the knot, which would make him trip and fall first thing, if he tried to chase after her. And then, just for fun, she tied the other end of the long scarf around the table leg. Might as well give him something to fuss about when he awoke! Might as well give him a *challenge*, if he caught her sneaking out of the suite.

But of course he couldn't untie his feet with his hands also bound to the table, could he? Since he was lying on his side with both arms draped over the edge of the couch—and since he'd moved that end of the coffee table close enough to set his beer bottles on last night—it was too lovely a temptation to resist. Sweeter than that first deep drag on a Camel.

Lola nearly choked on her laughter as she lightly, lightly drew the hot pink scarf around his arms, knotted it next to his wrists, and then paused.

This is too easy! This kid sleeps like the dead!

She couldn't get careless, however. No sense in losing a whole day of freedom for a few moments of inattention.

So she stood contemplating him for a moment, listening to

him breathe. Convincing herself Aric Petrocelli was totally zonked out.

That's when she noticed his cock was getting hard. Little smart ass was only pretending to sleep! He was *liking* this game!

So she quickly wrapped the ends of the second scarf around the table leg and tied them in a tight knot. Then, to show him who was really in charge here, Lola slid across the center of the table on her stomach until she was within kissing distance of that willowy dick.

She indulged in a bit of playful contemplation, watching that thing spring to life as though its eye was looking down her shirt. Lola made a tight O of her lips, and slid down the length of him with one fast swoop.

"Jesus H. Christ!" he wheezed, arching toward her.

Knowing she had only a few moments when surprise remained in her favor, Lola swirled her tongue around him, concentrating on the sensitive ridge and the head that now throbbed hotly for attention.

"Yeah, suck it fast and hard," he breathed. "Oh, Lo—what the fuck—?!"

She pulled away with a playful slurping sound and stood up. Grabbed her purse and headed for the door, wiping her mouth.

"Untie me, you—! You can't just leave me here to—"

"Why not? You left *me* hanging last night!" she shot back with a giggle. "What goes around comes around, Lover Boy!"

Down the hall she hurried—then descended the center steps, in case the captain was using an elevator—and then she eased into the crowd of people heading toward the gangway.

Scents of sunscreen and fresh cologne filled the air, with so many guests crammed in this closely. Like everyone else, she fished out her SeaKey for the security monitor. Lola instinctively studied the guys in white at the exit, looking for a sandy-haired man with a mustache or a handsome Greek in a captain's hat. But she saw no one familiar.

When her card dinged in the computer, she realized the security staff would know Lola Wright was disembarking—but it would be awhile before Rio or Skorpio would realize she was missing. And how could they catch her? She was free to roam the island, with nine hundred dollars in her purse and all damn day to defy Captain Scandalous by being gone!

How cool was *this*? She gazed eagerly at the people filing down the gangway, toward the first real freedom she'd had— the first real sunshine and fresh air—since she'd left Aruba!

Happy island music rode the breeze and the sun warmed the back of her neck. A good night's sleep had put her in a fine, feisty mood. By God, she was going to shop, and walk, and eat in quaint local cafes. Maybe pay one of the cabbies at the pier to drive her around the island for awhile!

Lola had no doubt that Captain Scandalous would demand his due, when he learned she'd slipped his leash. But escaping felt so damn good, she didn't really care what the testy Greek would cook up as punishment for—

The crowd on the narrow gangway stopped, with people packed ahead of her and behind. The brim of her hat bumped the freckled female shoulders in front of her, while the guy behind her took advantage of the moment to rub himself against her butt.

What the hell was the hold up? Lola was short enough that she had to lean over the side railing to see if there was another security check at the pier, or if some sort of emergency had—

Her jaw dropped.

There was indeed a crisp white uniform at the end of the gangway, glad-handing each and every passenger—welcoming everyone to Grenada and checking SeaKeys for the day's winning number. As though he sensed her presence, the captain's gaze followed the length of the white metal walkway crammed with passengers.

Skorpio looked right at her. Flashed her a bright, victorious smile.

19

Rio switched off his radio receiver, shaking his head at the pathetic calls for help coming from the Aphrodisia Suite. Since the captain's quarters and this lavish hideaway were the only rooms on this corridor, he'd told Claudine to clean for her other guests first today, so he could take care of . . . business.

She assumed his business was with Lola, and he let her believe that. Because, if he played things right, it would be.

And Claudine—unlike her sister Odette—understood that his tip guaranteed her silent cooperation for the rest of this cruise. She'd smiled and stuffed the fifty down her front with a suggestive wiggle.

"Is more than I get from Mister Aric last night. *Thanks!*"

"You're welcome," he said, "because you'll be working for me, right? Mister Aric's acting like a low-life, and it's up to us to correct his wicked ways."

"Yes sir! He is—how you say? A major pain in my ass!"

When Claudine had strutted away, her walk ripe with invitation, it left this end of the hallway totally unoccupied. Except for him.

And Petrocelli, who seemed to be having mobility problems.

DeSilva paused outside the suite door to gather his thoughts—because after what he'd seen and heard last night, he'd had more than his share of *thoughts*. He passed his key in and out of the slot and opened the door.

It was even more absurd than he'd anticipated.

The kid was stretched out naked on the couch with his ankles and wrists tied in very colorful, very feminine, silk scarves, which Lola had fastened to the legs of the coffee table. The six empty beer bottles told the rest of the story, but he wanted to hear every last detail of it from Aric.

So he walked in, stopping in front of the table. His gaze followed the length of the kid's slim, bronzed body, lingering on his limp cock, before he let out a derisive snort.

"Looks like Lola really tied one on. Getting a little desperate, are we?"

"Hey—can I help it if I have to piss? Untie my—"

"Can you help it that a woman—the woman you were *watching*," DeSilva mocked, "took you hostage and escaped? How do you explain that?"

The coffee table jumped with his frustrated fumblings: his first show of any motivation, because the beer bottles clinked and clanked before rolling in six directions on the floor.

"I *knew* she was doing it!" Aric protested, as though any fool could figure it out. "I *let* Lola wrap those—it was part of the captain's plan to—"

"Don't blame Skorpio for this! It's your own damn fault you can't get up to relieve yourself."

Rio looked around the dim main room, stepping toward the open bedroom as though he had nothing more pressing to do. The rumpled bed and the sunshine pouring in Lola's balcony doors made him want to stay there the rest of the day waiting for her. Inhaling her scent from the sheets.

"Maybe it should be the captain who unties you," he mused aloud.

"Hey—don't do me any favors!" Aric jeered. "Somebody else would've found me! Claudine'll be coming in to—"

Rio let him blather on, pondering how much to reveal. After the way he'd treated Lola last night, Aric deserved the punishment—the humiliation—Skorpio intended for her.

Her essence beckoned him, into the room where the bright natural light reminded him of Lola's smile. Rio gazed at the big bed, and then saw the cards laid out on her table.

He paused to ponder them.

Not surprising that this woman would consult a Tarot deck—just as his mother did—or that she'd use cards with such rich, brilliant colors and beautifully drawn people. Not surprising, either, that whatever situation Lola had been considering, the cards were arranged in a pattern he recognized: the Skandalis family on one side, beneath the shock and surprise of The Tower, balanced by a King and Queen that made his breath catch.

They were well matched, beneath that Moon: a king who sported a mustache like his—and a suggestive grin, because he was gazing at the redheaded queen who *so* reminded him of Lola!

Had she chosen these cards consciously and arranged them this way? Or had the ancient wisdom of the Tarot determined them?

DeSilva chuckled at the Strength card, where the woman was leading the lion with a chain around his neck. Not much different from the medallion Petrocelli wore, was it? Clearly, the same chain could be used to leave the kid dangling like that Hanging Man, at the mercy of those who tormented him.

He ambled out into the main room again, restraining his grin. Devious ideas popped into his head, punctuated by Aric's grunts as he tried to pull free from Lola's knots.

"So how did you know someone would find you?" Rio

asked. He circled slowly to gaze at Petrocelli's nakedness—to taunt him as he struggled against the bright silk scarves.

All that frustrated jerking made Aric's limp cock bob in front of those goose-bumpy balls. Damned if he wasn't getting hard, as though he *liked* being Lola's victim!

Not the kid's best moment. Especially since he hadn't thought to knock the table over, so he could slip those scarves off the legs.

"The camera caught Lola tying me up!" he replied defiantly. "It was only a matter of time before Skorpio would've seen—"

"Skorpio has gone ashore," Rio remarked. "It might interest you to know that *I* have the monitor—and I watched your every gutter-level, mud-sucking move with Lola last night."

"Hey! She did the sucking, because she *wanted* to, DeSilva! Don't give me any bullshit about—"

"You told her Skorpio was coming! You had every advantage over her, yet you *lied* to get her into that bathroom," he replied in a rising voice. "You could just as easily have ducked into the theater, where it was dark and the crowd would've concealed you from the captain."

DeSilva glared down at the kid long enough for his disgust to register—not that he expected any signs of remorse. "But that doesn't matter now, since I'm not getting your signal anymore. Checked the battery lately?"

The slightest hint of concern flickered across his brow. "No way, man! I'm thinking it must be the—"

"No, you're *not* thinking. Or you'd've known better than to pull this wireless camera stunt on Lola!" Rio replied hotly. "When she finds out about it, she'll fry your hide, little man!"

"Why? I have my orders, same as you!"

"Yes, but the difference between us," DeSilva said tersely, "is that *I* have a conscience. And what I saw last night—the way you conned her into that john for a blow job—was about the lowest form of coercion I've ever witnessed."

He backed away, warming to this rare opportunity to get some licks in.

"She trusted you! All she asked was to have a good time and get out from under Skorpio's thumb," he went on, pointing an accusing finger. "But you had to be the hot-shot bodyguard. Had to use the hidden mini cam and mike, so the captain could take unfair advantage of her, too.

"But that's all over. The batteries are dead. I wasn't receiving a thing when I woke up this morning."

Rio looked the kid straight in the eye. No need for Aric to know that he'd turned the damn monitor on, but only to watch out for Lola's welfare. "It's just your luck I happened by—"

"Enough of the sermon, already!" Aric snapped. "Turn me loose, so I—"

"Nope. It might take me all day to find Lola and apologize for my lapse in judgment, when I went along with your uncle's scheming last night."

"You think he's going to be *impressed*, Mr. Nice Guy?"

"I don't really give a damn!" Rio fired back. "Another week and I'm off the ship. *You* have to be related to him for the rest of your life."

"Oh, for God's sake! Just untie my hands, so I can—"

Rio laughed, because it *was* awfully funny to see a twenty-three-year-old beach bum tied up naked on a couch! With soft, shimmery, *girly* scarves, no less. Petrocelli couldn't see his way out of his predicament because he was too busy whining. Pouting because Lola had won this one.

"Later, guy." He walked toward the door to further antagonize him.

"You can't just leave me!" the kid cried hoarsely. "If I have to wait until Claudine gets here, I'll bust a gut—"

"So relieve yourself," DeSilva said with a shrug. "You're a big boy, Aric. Figure out your priorities. Meanwhile, you can be sure the captain will get my full report on how you let Lola escape."

Rio went to the island-print shirt hanging neatly from the back of a chair, and fished out the pack of Camels where Aric's mike was hidden. When he opened the draperies—again to torment Petrocelli—he saw the line backed up on the gangway.

Then he spotted the white uniform; the raven-haired Greek who was keeping passengers from going ashore in a normal fashion.

"Shit," he murmured, pivoting.

"Problem?" Aric taunted. "Besides the fact that this couch is gonna get soaked if you don't—"

Rio leaned down and nimbly unfastened the crystal medallion. Stuck it in his shirt pocked and patted it flat.

"Duty calls for me, nature calls for you," he remarked lightly. "Have a great day, all right?"

Rio raced along the corridor and then bounded down the center stairway, skipping three and four steps at a time. If Skandalis was standing at the pier, then Lola hadn't gotten past him yet. She had to be stuck on that gangway, packed in there like a sardine . . . a captive the captain was just waiting to take.

He jogged to the security point at the ship's exit and flipped on his two-way. "Captain Skandalis? DeSilva here. We've got an emergency."

Rio cleared his way by ordering everyone in the crowd to one side. "Sorry folks, we've got a potential crisis brewing. Please let me through!"

From the open doorway of the ship, Rio looked down along the crowd and spotted Lola's bright green hat, right smack at the halfway point. She couldn't move forward, and she couldn't come back.

And when she leaned sideways over the railing to see what the holdup was at the pier, he couldn't miss the captain's crocodile smile.

Skorpio raised his walkie-talkie to his ear. "Yes, DeSilva? From what I can see, everything is perfectly under control. *My* control."

"You've spotted Lola," Rio agreed, "but you have no idea what she left in her wake. You need to get up here before we have a damn flood in the Aphrodisia suite. Your nephew—the *genius* who deserves a raise—is uh, all tied up. The wireless cam and mike have disappeared, and he has no idea where they are."

Skandalis stopped shaking hands to glower at him.

DeSilva sensed he'd better get down the gangway to rescue Lola before the captain got to her first.

But what was this? The packed passengers in the back half of the gangway were squeezing to one side—as though a miracle, like the parting of the Red Sea, had come to pass!

Rio stepped forward, squinting in the sunlight. When he saw that the miracle's name was George LeFevre, his nighttime security counterpart, he shut off his two-way. Skandalis didn't need to hear another word!

20

"**P**lease! I've got to *vomit*!" Lola cried, fluttering her hand in front of her mouth. "Please move! Please—I'm going to be sick—"

Which wasn't a lie. If Captain Scandalous grabbed her, it was all over. She wasn't sure how he'd managed to trap her this way, but it was a no-brainer that he'd make her pay for her sins.

"Please—let me by so—"

"Hey! Outta the lady's way!" a burly black guy took up her cry.

When he turned in the aisle, with his voice blasting at them like a bullhorn and his sheer bulk clearing a path for her, Lola believed in the intervention of angels. Even very large, very dark angels with southern accents.

"Y'all gotta move it now!" he sang out. "This poor little gal's about to hurl, and you don't want it gettin' *on* ya!"

Thank God for hats with floppy brims and big shades. Lola followed close behind this guy, keeping a hand to her mouth and the other one to her stomach, fighting the urge to look over her shoulder.

Skandalis would be pissed, but she didn't care. He had his games, and two could play them—by whichever set of rules worked at any given moment.

But then she caught sight of another white uniform, and a slender, golden face with a mustache.

Rio was looking right at her. Grinning. Either laughing at her predicament, or following orders from Skandalis to head her off.

She didn't have a rat's chance in a D-Con factory of getting away. Couldn't go backward; wasn't sure she should go forward.

Maybe the best answer *was* to hurl.

But then DeSilva grabbed her hand, thanking the man profusely for clearing her way.

Like they know each other, Lola realized. The guy went on inside before she got a look at his face, though.

But there was no time to worry over DeSilva having a huge black guy on his side. She was being led back through the security check point, past all the passengers waiting to disembark, so quickly she had no idea what was going on or how to get away if she needed to.

"Rio, if you tell me you're going to—"

He whipped her around a corner, away from other ears. "I'm saying I'm sorry for what you're about to find out," he whispered urgently. "And I'm saying Skorpio will be right behind us. Trust me, *querida*, and play along, all right?"

Didn't ask for much, did he? But even through her dark shades, she could see the concern on DeSilva's handsome face. Could feel the pulse beating in the hand that squeezed hers, and smell cologne made sharper by the heat.

"Where can we go?" she whispered.

"We're on our way."

Up the first set of stairs they dashed, to get out of the captain's immediate sight, and then Rio led her across to the ship's other side, into the Trade Winds Buffet. They wound through the crowd quickly, dodging guests with loaded breakfast trays and sloshing coffee cups.

Lola's stomach lurched. She'd had nothing to eat since the cherries jubilee Phillipe had flambéd at their table. The colorful displays of food—aromas of fried bacon, coffee, and fresh cinnamon rolls—made her whimper.

"You all right, Lola *mia*?" he asked over his shoulder.

"Just starving."

"Not really sick, though?"

"Not until I saw Skandalis down there running some cockeyed contest—and I realized *I'd* be the winner," she replied. "How'd he know it was *me* in this hat and shades?"

Rio's eyes closed with the answer to that. As he hurried her along, he snagged a banana from a centerpiece, and then led her around another corner at the end of the seating area.

They dashed up carpeted stairs into a lounge Lola hadn't seen.

The place was deserted. The lights were out, and nobody was behind the bar or at the piano. The scent of lemon furniture polish almost camouflaged the heavy smell of smoke that permeated the place.

Rio steered her into a booth against the side wall and slid in next to her. "Welcome to Whispers, our cigar club. It won't open for a few hours yet."

Again her stomach lurched, but with a different need now. She gripped the handle of her purse, determined not to reach for that suede cigarette case while Rio was watching.

"Interesting decor," she remarked, gazing at the dark red wallpaper flocked in black.

Around the walls, at eye level, ran a rough-cut band of carved marble that could've come from some ancient Greek ruin. A closer look revealed that the people were nude. Probably at an orgy.

The trio beside their table—a smiling woman with two aroused young studs caressing her breasts and belly—bore facial expressions that invited her to frolic with them. In the dimness, they seemed so lifelike Lola swore the lady winked at her. A dog lying to one side was looking right at her, too, with a face that was eerily human.

Lola blinked. Then burst out laughing when Rio tapped her hand with the banana.

"Thanks," she murmured, looking around to be sure no one heard them. Now that they sat side by side, she knew of a hundred things they needed to discuss.

Or not. The lips framed by that mustache were good for so many things besides talking.

"The frieze here is supposedly patterned after one in a temple honoring Aphrodite," Rio explained. "Legend has it that worshipers could become disoriented—or very aroused—because the figures on the walls seemed to whisper . . . *suggestions* to them."

He paused, fascinated by the way her fingers flexed when she peeled the banana . . . by the delicious O her mouth made when she took her first bite.

To think that Aric had felt her lips on his cock this way last night.

DeSilva shifted on the padded seat when he caught the banana's fresh scent, mingled with that of her sunblock.

"So I don't want to come here with Skorpio. Or with Aric," she mused aloud, "when there's a chance Captain Scandalous—or even Odette—is on the other side of the wall, listening."

DeSilva sat straighter. How much did she know about the captain's spying habit? Her pretty face, slightly flushed from the sun, showed no sense of disgust or betrayal. Yet.

I want you. You know I do!

Lola sucked air, staring at him. Honest to God, his lips hadn't moved!

"Motion detectors trip the audio effects at each table," he explained with a little grin. "The voices seem to change to match the situation, and no matter which booth I've sat in, the messages are never the same. A marvel of modern technology, wouldn't you say?"

Take me right here. Under the table.

Lola giggled, covering her mouth to control her bite of banana.

Rio gazed at her girlish grin, wishing he had time to pursue this playful thread of conversation—to sample the sweet, tropical taste that would linger on Lola's lips. Right here—or under the table, indeed. His cock was testing the seam of his pants, demanding attention like that damn banana got.

He glanced toward the doorway, clearing his throat.

"I want to tell you, before anything else happens today, that I'm sincerely sorry for the way you were treated last night," he said softly. "And I'm even sorrier that I didn't call it to a halt. I hope you'll forgive me for following Skorpio's orders instead of . . . listening to my heart."

Lola blinked, leaning closer. That was an *apology*—something she had to think about to recognize. Fletch believed that love meant he never had to say he was sorry—not that he had any concept of how sorry really felt.

But Rio seemed genuinely distressed. A little crease appeared between his eyebrows as he tentatively reached for her hand, which made her wonder if something awful was about to befall her.

His touch sent a tiny lightning bolt up her arm and all through her system, and Lola was once again aware of how *romantic* this Spaniard was. Rio seemed to wear his heart on his sleeve in a way that would make most American men shudder.

So how did he know what happened to her last night?

Do you want to hear my deepest secrets?

"I—I'm not sure I understand what you're saying," she hedged, glancing at that dog on the wall.

When it returned her gaze, she refocused on Rio, watching his eyes for signs of another head game. Or just body language that said he was dodging some important issue.

Rio sighed, looked toward the door to be sure Skorpio wasn't lurking there. It was risky, staying here this long, but he had to tell her the whole truth or Lola would believe he was only playing the hero, to look good.

He wanted to *be* her hero. The king of her castle.

"That medallion Aric was wearing?" he began, brushing her leg with his. An accident, yet it wasn't. He got a gratifying thrill when she nudged him back.

She nodded, already guessing where this would lead.

"It's a wireless mini cam. It belongs to Skorpio, so Aric—"

Lola closed her eyes against a wave of revulsion.

"So the captain saw *everything*," she wheezed. "Which explains how he recognized me in the crowd so quickly today. My shades and hat were on film as I was buying them."

Her voice faded and she put her mind into Rewind. "Which means he also saw me sell my ring—"

Rio nodded, restraining a grin about that one.

"—and then he saw what I did in the men's—"

Close your eyes and kiss me . . . down there.

Her expression curdled. Those recordings were starting to annoy her.

"Not really," Rio insisted, scooting closer. "The camera was pointed at the top of the wall during most of the . . . activity."

Lola nipped her lip. Rio *knew*.

And while they were all consenting adults here, it still bothered her that this kind, compassionate man had heard the grunts and groans . . . Aric's impassioned words as she'd sucked him to climax.

Which meant Skorpio had either blabbed or—

"This is why I'm apologizing, Lola," he breathed, praying she didn't walk out on him. He felt like a kid copping a feel in a dark theater, but putting his hand on her bare knee at least established the contact he craved.

"While it's true I was operating the monitor at the captain's orders—and he was sitting right beside me as we watched you," DeSilva went on, "I could've walked away. Could've told him where to put that monitor. But I didn't."

I know what you did last night. Do it again.

She looked away, batting back tears. "I'm sorry for what you saw."

Sorry didn't nearly cover it. She'd never felt more mortified in her life.

"Don't apologize, *querida*!" he whispered. "I heard how Aric conned you into that men's room, so it wasn't totally your idea, was it?" he asked gently. "I'm not telling you this to hurt you, Lola *mia*. I want you to know the facts, in case Skandalis and Aric deny them."

The smooth skin of her knee . . . a freshly shaved leg. Mother of God, but he wanted to run his hand up her shorts—which would be the *worst* thing he could do right now.

Higher . . . faster . . . harder!

Lola chuckled in spite of the way those damn voices seemed to be directing DeSilva's hand, not to mention this conversation. But even in the dimness of this deserted club, she could see how much he wanted her—and her wet panties cried out for his warm fingers to find them . . . to rip them off. But he was showing amazing restraint, for a man who drank champagne from her snatch the first time they were alone.

"You're not finished breaking the good news yet, are you?"

Rio smiled ruefully. He admired her for taking this so well; for not caving in or accusing him of anything. Yet.

"I also admit that, yes, we listened in on your conversations," he continued. "Because that pack of cigarettes in Aric's pocket—?"

An icky bubble of apprehension swelled up, like swamp gas in her gut.

"That's where he had his microphone."

"That little *shit*!" Lola scowled, slapping the table."That dirty, low-down—letting me think we could actually have some fun—evading Skandalis—and he was *recording* the whole thing! I'm sure the captain loved every fucking second of *that*."

"He was damn proud of Aric for setting things up the way he did, yes. Thought he was due for a raise."

"Yeah, well, *I* raised him—and I won't be doing that again!" She got so pissed she had to stand up—which forced Rio out into the aisle ahead of her. "That lying, sneaking little—"

Let me stick my tongue in your—

"Oh, would you just shut up?!" she rasped, glaring at the figures who frolicked on the wall.

That damn dog didn't drop his gaze. Like maybe he could smell where she wanted to be licked.

Lola closed her eyes, exasperated. DeSilva was going to think she was nuts, cussing the canned voices. And playing the drama queen wouldn't score any points with him, either.

She had to hand it to him, though: he was spelling it all out. Standing beside her—standing *by* her—while Aric had taken every advantage.

Lola sighed. "But then, I knew he was the captain's snitch, didn't I? I was stupid to think he'd lay aside his loyalties, just because some woman old enough to be his—"

"Shhhhh."

Rio listened carefully for intruders, with his finger on Lola's lips . . . wishing she'd kiss it, to show that she still accepted him. Still trusted him, even though this thing with Aric had blown his credibility. "I'm thinking we should go back to the suite—"

"You told Skorpio we'd be there?"

"No!" Rio replied, more vehemently than he intended. "But I did contact him on his two-way, right before you so creatively cleared your path back to the ship. I told him the suite was a disaster area, and that you'd taken Aric hostage."

Tie me up and go down on me, sweet thing.

Lola snickered. She was still peeved, but the timing on these canned voices was, well—uncanny.

"You were there?" she asked. "And you saw how I left him?"

Now *here* was an image worth getting in trouble for! DeSilva seemed impressed with her survival skills.

Rio smiled. "He was still wearing the camera, remember? I watched you tie him up, *mi vida.* I was cheering you all the way, hoping he'd—"

Lola's face fell. "Then . . . you saw what else I did to him. Again."

He took her hands between his, feeling the thrum of her pulse. What a woman she was, to feel remorse for giving another man the pleasure he himself craved. Just as he had regretted witnessing it last night.

"This time, you were getting even," he said with a wicked glint in his eye. "Our boy was in a world of hurt when I walked out on him to come after you."

"You left him on the couch?" She giggled, itching to kiss him.

"Damn right I did. He could easily have freed himself, but he was too busy whining about having to pee.

"And meanwhile," DeSilva continued, patting his shirt pocket, "I took the microphone and that medallion with the mini-cam. I want to be damn sure Skorpio never gets that advantage over you again."

"I . . . thank you," she breathed. She had an odd feeling someone was spying on them now. Or was it because that dog beside the lady's feet was still looking at her?

It *did* have a man's facial features. And it looked ready to talk to her.

"I'd let you have those devices for your own devious use," the security agent was saying, "but then you'd be even more of a target for the captain's vengeance. He's saying you need to be punished for . . . flying under the radar. Defying his authority."

"Why am I not surprised?" she murmured. She could've sworn that dog winked at her.

Hey, good-lookin'. I can smell where you're cookin'.

Rio coughed to cover his laughter. Lola's expression was priceless as she tried to pinpoint which of those carved figures beside the table had said that.

"So what would you like to do now?" he asked. "I'm going upstairs, because I want to be sure Skorpio has seen Aric in the predicament you left him in—tied with such pretty scarves, no less. So the kid can catch the lecture he so richly deserves."

"And to see if he's peed all over my couch."

"It won't be pretty, either way." Rio glanced around the cavernous club room again, wondering if he should mention an additional option. With a hand on her back, he started toward the door: it was only a matter of time before Skandalis either found them here or summoned him for some trumped-up assignment.

"You could go wherever you wanted to, Lola *mia*," he said in a low voice. "I understand why you wanted to go ashore today, after the games they've played on you. Now's your chance! The captain and Aric are upstairs—and I'll be there to distract them from your absence."

Lola's heart thudded hard at that idea, yet it went out to DeSilva, as well. He *understood*. He was bold enough to play devil's advocate and pretend she'd gotten away again, just to give her some freedom. He was willing to catch more trouble in her behalf.

If her imagination was once again playing her for a fool, well—so be it. She might as well mislead herself as wait for Cabana Boy or Captain Scandalous to do it again. Might as well go into that suite with Rio, because Skorpio would demand his due for this little prank, and it wasn't a bad idea to have a witness. Better yet, a confederate.

"I shouldn't pass up this rare opportunity to see my betrayer in such a bad, wet way," she ventured. "I hope we're not too late."

She paused, noting how the pattern of the Greek frieze repeated itself as it wrapped around the room. That dog was here by the doorway, too. Still looking right at her. Still ready to speak to her.

"Freaky," she murmured. "Just too damn freaky, that dog is."

DeSilva chuckled and took her hand. Before they reached the sunlight that came up the stairway, however, he pulled her into the last dark corner. The kiss that had hovered between them for the past hour drove her to her tiptoes, and his lips were there to catch it.

Her hips found a table edge . . . still kissing him as he lowered her backwards, Lola parted her legs so he could step between them. Rio deepened the kiss, swatting away the drink menu and ashtray, and whatever else had been there, until he'd coaxed her flat on her back.

The ridge of his erection left no doubt about what he *really* wanted while they exchanged sighs and unspoken vows about things to come, kissing—kissing uncontrollably. He rubbed his cock against her crotch, knowing better than to drop his pants— just as Lola grabbed his ass, knowing this was as far as it would go right now.

She tasted soft and eager, and the wet silk of her inner lips made him crazy for the lips farther down, where his cock could only dream of being. Rio kissed her with a hard desperation that shocked him, before he finally forced himself to stop. To get off her.

It wasn't nearly enough for Lola, either. He could read that need in her short, ragged breathing as she clung to him.

"I wish—"

"I do, too," he murmured against her ear, "and as soon as we can, we'll make that wish come true. Promise."

She nodded eagerly, her eyes taking up half her face.

"Meanwhile," he added, tracing the upper edge of her lush lip with his finger, "you have to be ready for anything, Lola *mia*. And you must believe that whatever I do, it's so that I can be with you again. As soon as we can."

Lola considered this, studying his slender face in the dimness. He was right, of course: neither Cabana Boy nor Captain Scandalous was very happy with her right now, and they'd both demand payback. Perhaps at DeSilva's expense.

"That's what I want, too," she replied softly. "Shall we go face them—together?"

Rio allowed himself one last taste of her. Then he took her hand again, blinking against the sunlight that poured through the picture windows.

You'll be back, a whisper followed them down the lounge's stairs. *You still want to fuck me, baby.*

Lola blinked. Then she walked a lot faster.

21

Things weren't pretty when she and Rio entered the Aphrodisia suite. Skorpio was muttering, overturning the sofa pillows and looking beneath lamps and behind the furniture. Odette stood at the window fuming, her arms crossed beneath her small breasts. Then Aric emerged from the bathroom—in her bedroom!— buttoning his shirt.

"You caused quite an uproar here," he remarked with a scowl. "If you think for one minute you'll get away with taking me prisoner, think again, Priestess!"

Lola stifled a laugh and let go of Rio's hand. The captain and Odette had turned to look at them, and it wasn't in her best interest—or Rio's—to appear too chummy.

"And why are you whining about this *now*?" she asked coolly. "Why didn't you make a fuss when I was tying you up? It wasn't like you were really asleep! You knew I was playing a little game with—"

"Little game?" Odette cut in. "It's no *game* that my medallion is missing!"

"Rio took it, I tell you!"

"But he told *me*—" Skorpio's expression resembled a storm at sea. "What's the real story, DeSilva? And why weren't you here sooner to clear this matter up? *You* were the one who warned me of the catastrophic conditions in the suite."

DeSilva felt himself losing it, so he took a moment to assess what sort of trap he might've walked into. He'd done nothing against regulations. But he also recognized the power of the ones who challenged him: it had never paid to get crossways between Skorpio and Odette. Even fully clothed.

"All right, so I got your attention with that story," he admitted. "And I got you up here to see how Aric had failed at his assignment to keep track of Lola. And yes, I myself removed the wireless cam and the mike because I thought they'd done enough damage."

Odette bristled. "But you have no right—"

"I am the chief of security on this ship, and I make decisions about the safety and well-being of our guests," he reminded her. "I've put your belongings in a safe place—"

"You did *not* have my permission to—"

DeSilva let out a short laugh at that one. "It wasn't my idea to *use* your medallion and microphone, Odette. I merely confiscated them so—"

"You're overstepping your authority," the captain snapped. The lines around his obsidian eyes rippled with displeasure.

"And you're going way out of bounds on this one, Skorpio!" Rio crossed the floor, clenching his fists in his pockets as he faced his superior. "For chrissakes, this is a fantasy—a game you're playing with Lola," he said in a terse whisper. "And she *won* this round, even though you had all the technological advantages! Lighten up!"

Skorpio scowled past him, nodding toward her. Pissed because DeSilva had divulged their surveillance secrets.

"You're taking her side, then?" the captain demanded. "Invoking your authority against *me*—the man who hired you—and in favor of Miss Wright? That smacks of insubordination!"

Lola wasn't standing for any more of this. She, too, stalked over to where the captain was standing. "And what do you call it when Aric lied to me to—"

"He was doing his job," Skorpio informed her in a coiled voice. "He was reporting to me as he was required to do, no matter *what* you asked of him. The fact that he got some... satisfaction from it is just another little bonus, isn't it?"

Lola's face blazed as bright pink as the scarf that lay knotted on the coffee table. Another day and another island were passing her by, because of this man's arrogance. And while she'd learned a few tricks—gotten a few illicit kicks—from becoming his love slave, she was still being *denied* what she'd originally wanted from this handsome Greek.

This whole situation was wearing thin.

"All right, *fine*!" she blurted. "Since this all seems to be because of me—because I agreed to this love slave scenario—I'm buying out of it now. Mr. Kingsley assures me my credit will be restored, so total up the tabs Dennis ran up. I'll pay you off and be done with these head games."

"Oh, no, Miss Wright, it doesn't work that way! It's my ship. And my game."

Skorpio circled closer, eyeing her as though he might tweak those Very Cherries for effect. "You're feeling noble, standing up for the man who would defend you even to the point of losing his job! But I'm having no part of it.

"And besides," he continued, from behind her now, "if I totaled up what you owe me for those three original designer gowns, and the French dinner—not to mention Phillipe's outrageous tip—you'd be appalled at how much more indebted you are than when we started."

The weight of his stare on her backside made her whirl

around to face him. "That's not your concern! It's not like I don't have the money to—"

"It's never really been about the money, my dear."

Captain Scandalous laughed like a man who was terribly pleased with himself. "It's time we had a discussion about obeying orders, Miss Wright. You need instruction on how to be the love slave of my fantasies, so that your debts may truly be forgiven."

"She needs more than *your* instruction," Odette chimed in with feline glee. "Since she seems so taken with Mr. DeSilva—and is distracting him from his daily duties aboard this ship—we should put her where she'll have some . . . *special* work to do."

"So! There you have it!" the captain crowed. "As always, Odette, you've cut to the crux of the situation! I'm entrusting Lola's punishment to you."

"And what did I do that was so wrong?" Lola spouted. "I merely requested the pleasure of Aric's company, and *he agreed* to my plan to—to fly under the radar for awhile. He *let* me escape today, yet I'm the one catching hell for it!"

"Oh, you're going to catch a lot more than that, Lola." Odette's voice had a distinctive edge to it. "You going to make so many new friends, you'll forget all about Rio. So he can do the job he's been hired for."

"A workable solution. Dismissed!" Skorpio said as he gestured for the security agent to precede him out.

DeSilva gazed at her one last time, and then he walked out ahead of the captain.

It was a whole new show, now that Odette was directing it.

22

Whispers, the cigar club, felt totally different now that it was open for business. The tables were filling with guests—men, mostly—and Lola noticed details she hadn't seen when she'd been here in the dark with Rio.

Signs behind the bar posted prices for lap dances, private massages, and other personal services. A jazz trio was playing cool, musky music that throbbed with a string bass's *step-step-pity-step*, catching her up in its heartbeat. The trumpet moaned a *wah-wah-wahhhhh* while the drummer in his dark glasses sat back smiling, making his cymbals shimmer with a *tssss-ts-ts-tssss* she had to grin at.

A spotlit stage with a chrome pole and a runway dominated the center of the room, so the marble frieze was now just a part of the scenery. If those nude Greeks—and that dog—were still talking, only the guests along the walls were aware of them.

Cigar club, was it? Yes, there was a display case of fine imported cigars along one wall, but Lola sensed Whispers smoked in a whole 'nother way from the venerable gentlemen she associated with such male enclaves.

"We'll be going backstage to find Miss Wright a costume," Odette informed the manager. "Be sure to keep her busy all afternoon and into the evening, Derek."

He was blonde and stocky; a scar along his temple gave Derek the air of a bouncer from a tough neighborhood bar, even though he wore a tux. He looked Lola over for several seconds longer than she liked.

"Deck her out however you want," he said. "But I can't keep an eye on her all the time."

"That's why Aric's here. We're teaching Miss Wright a lesson, about obeying the rules and being a team player—"

"Oh, she'll be an addition to our *team*, all right," he replied with an oily smile. "Fresh meat like her'll sell a lot of drinks and keep things . . . coming."

As Odette beckoned them to follow her across the huge room, Lola felt the manager's gaze riding her backside. She took Aric's sleeve, almost ready to reconcile with him.

"So what're they talking about?" she whispered. "This isn't where civilized men come to smoke and read their newspapers and get away from their wives, is it?"

"Oh, they smoke, all right," he replied, "but you're the one who'll be lighting their fires. Not that you'll have any trouble with that, horny little slut that you are."

Lola released him, incensed. "I beg your pardon, Mr. Petrocelli? Who was it that *lied* me into that men's room for his own—"

"Enough of your bickering," Odette snapped, turning to glare at them. "Let's get on with it."

The backstage area housed several curtained cubicles, which smelled of incense, sex, and secrets as she walked past. At the end of the hall stood a large closet. Odette swung open its doors to reveal costumes of all colors and varieties: she-devils and schoolgirls and fairy princesses could emerge from this armoire!

Matter of fact, a leather-bound mistress with whips and a Wild West saloon girl were eyeing her from the corner, where they shared a vanity and mirror. Had she not been here at Odette's command, Lola would've found all these outfits rather inspiring.

"It's *you*, Priestess!" Cabana Boy said with a chuckle. "The ensemble you were born to sport, so that all may worship you!"

He was holding up a gauzy body stocking with flared harem pants. The only thing that wasn't totally see-through were the silver sequined stars sprinkled here and there to catch the light. It would cover absolutely nothing!

"And here's your mask—like for Mardi Gras, except more alluring," he went on. "To keep our regulars guessing. To give you Priestess mystique and—"

"Enough rhapsodizing, young man," Odette interrupted. "The show's about to start."

Indeed, Lola heard the stage band playing a more provocative tune, as well as the clink of cocktail glasses above male voices raised in anticipation. Another girl came out of a bathroom, wearing a blue dress with a lacy white pinafore and socks, and a curly blonde wig.

"Better hurry it up, honey," she said in a gravelly voice that sounded nothing like her innocent get-up. "If you're dancin' with *us* this set, you've gotta kick some ass! No room for losers here!"

The other two laughed loudly, as though they already saw a big L painted on her forehead.

"But I don't know a *thing* about dancing in—"

"It's highly intuitive," Odette said with a smirk. "You'll start in a cage, where you can wiggle and writhe and do whatever it takes for men to bid on your service."

"Service," Lola echoed. "As in—"

"Whatever they want. Most of them love a good lap dance to start out, while some prefer a private dancer. Or, you could be performing with the pole onstage. Whatever they wish to pay for—which often depends on how *enthused* you seem."

Lola thought for a moment. There had to be a way out of this situation, which appeared more humiliating by the minute, considering her minimal experience. "What if nobody bids on me?"

"Then you'll be at the mercy of whoever Derek has waiting in one of those cubicles. Flat on your back."

Odette smirked as though she liked this idea. "And if I find out you've ended up this way, I'll tell Rio to come and see how the lady of his dreams is working off her debts! He'll love *that*, won't he?"

The raven-haired lady leaned closer, her feline eyes narrowing. "They pay to play, Lola. Our girls give them their money's worth—except in your case, all your credit goes toward your purchases on the captain's account.

"Too bad you've been so extravagant," she added, her tongue tipped with sarcasm. "You might have to stay all afternoon and evening, and come back again tomorrow!"

Laughter echoed in the open room again, and Lola cringed inwardly. This sounded like a bad B movie script, where the pimp was giving his speech to a new hooker about how she damn well better not cheat him. And how she better not try to escape his clutches, either, or some other bad-ass pimp would *really* show her what it's like to live in the gutter.

But then, this was just a game. *Wasn't* it? She was still a guest—she'd paid her fare long before she left home. So if worse came to worse, she could call it all to a halt. She could walk away and say no thanks.

And yet, as Lola quickly changed into the nothing little harem pants—with a crotch seam that wasn't sewn—and the top that fit like a second skin, she felt herself rising to her role. The music out front was revving up now, and the old bump-and-grind of that chicka-boom beat made her grin.

If Odette thought she was making Lola behave herself—well, she'd show them all! She'd become the Striptease *Queen*! The Come-On Honey they didn't think she had the guts to be! If they thought she'd give up or chicken out, well, they didn't know Lola Wright, or what she'd learned when it was Dennis Fletcher's games she was playing.

After all, who else sported Very Cherry nipples? Showing right through her sheer top, shimmying with every step she took! Odette's might be painted red, but she wasn't sticking them *out* there, was she?

Lola put on the mask, a stretchy turquoise cap that covered her tucked-up hair, with a glittery silver half-face that extended into Art Deco-style wings over her ears. The role was gelling in her mind: she was indeed the High Priestess, adorned in her costume spun of stardust and moonbeams—yes, with those red nipples peaking through to hold the attention of those who worshipped her.

She would *show* them! She would beat them at their own game and have fun doing it! After all, what happened on this cruise ship stayed on this cruise ship. She would never see these people again.

Except Rio. I'm doing this so I CAN see him ...

Or would the captain keep his Chief Security Officer so busy for the next few days there'd be no chance for the stolen moments she'd come to love? Maybe DeSilva would give up on her—

"All right—you're on, Lola! Get your ass in that cage!"

A wiry fellow with a cue-ball hairdo and a goatee—another bouncer type she didn't feel like challenging—steered her to an exit where a red metal cage awaited her. He opened its door.

She stepped inside, onto the small platform bottom, wondering how the hell she'd keep her balance when it started moving.

"Remember our rule, lady—you make the ride around the

room once without getting any bids, you damn well better shake that thing on your second ride, or you're outta here."

"Got it," she replied. Lola looked ahead and behind her, at the cages where the three other girls were getting in, hoping she was up to the competition.

"Let's *do* it!" the guy hollered. He pushed a button in a control panel and the four cages rolled along a track in the ceiling, out into the main room.

"Here they are, gentlemen! Our first ladies of the day!" a familiar voice came over the speaker system.

A cheer went up from the crowd and Lola blinked: the place was packed! And that was Mike Mannering, the cruise director, at the microphone.

The band cranked up, and when she saw how the other three girls were writhing and thrusting to the music, she did the same. Strobes were flashing to the raucous beat, and the cheering could've roused a dead man.

"Thirty for that one!"

"I'll go fifty!" a couple guys shouted, pointing to the raven-haired dominatrix in the first cage.

They were still rolling slowly, about ten feet apart, all four of them dancing to get the crowd stirred up. Which didn't take much.

Lola decided to up the ante: she placed her feet in the cage's spaces, spreading her legs and throwing her weight to make the cage swing.

"Oh, Blondie, baby!" another guy cried.

"I want the harem girl!"

"No, she's for me! A hundred bucks says so!"

"Make it two, and she's mine!"

Was she hearing this right? The other girls—Mistress Whips and Miss Kitty and Goldilocks—were much younger and more agile than she. But when the cages stopped and their doors slid open, five or six men were hurrying between the tables to help her step out.

She flashed them all her best come-on smile. "Good afternoon, gentlemen," she crooned in an exotic accent. "I am the goddess, Vahshi. Your every wish is my command. Your every prayer will be heard."

"Make that a five, and get outta my way, fellas!" the man with the bushy beard proclaimed.

Now that her imagination was kicking in, this was going to be a hoot—with five hundred dollars riding on it!

"Vahshi, sweetheart, I want you settin' on my lap and dancin' with Big Jim," her customer drawled. "He's got a hankerin' for some red-headed pussy, and you are *it*, darlin'!"

What did she do now? Lola gave Tex her most mystical smile, and took her cue from Miss Kitty, just a few tables over: the saloon girl's gyrations had her guy grinning like a kid at Christmas.

Licking her lips, she straddled her man's lap—not surprised that he then spread his legs and grinned like the good ole boy he was. She'd selected suits for his type a hundred times, so she felt right at home.

His hands went to her waist, so Lola raised her arms with an exotic flourish and pressed her palms together above her head, like a Hindu deity. The High Priestess at her best.

"Thatta way, sugah! Shake them cherries for me," he encouraged. "By God, you're givin' Big Jim the real what-for, and he's lovin' it!"

She didn't glance at his lap. Kept her eyes focused on his fleshy face . . . thinking about the slender Spanish features she'd rather be gazing at.

A shudder made her nipples jut out. The little stars in the fabric rubbed them with a suggestive friction.

"Yeah, baby, you got it," Tex rasped. "Wiggle them titties! Rub my face with 'em now!"

Since she was endowed with peaches rather than watermelons, Lola had to scoot closer—which put her right up against Big

Jim. He was still safely tucked behind that zipper, but even so, she knew he was huge—and that he'd seen the split in her harem pants.

Tex's fingers found it, too. As she wiggled to the music, brushing her breasts against his face, she felt him exploring her slit, teasing out her honey. For five hundred dollars, he probably figured he could—

"And that's the end of the first dance!" Mike Mannering called out. "Let's hear it for the girls! We'll take your bids for a pole dance now."

Lola slid off Tex's lap, flexing her thighs. It would be a longer, harder day's work than she'd anticipated, if she had to do much of this lap dancing.

She realized then that a slender man in a Zorro mask, clad in black leather, was Aric. He'd been behind her all along, and was now keying in Tex's SeaKey charge for her services.

It occurred to her then that Whispers took in a *lot* of money, since these gentlemen were flashing plastic instead of cash. The liquor was flowing freely enough that they didn't seem to care!

"That one!" somebody called, pointing her way. "Two hundred to see the harem goddess get herself off on the pole!"

"I'm sayin three! I want her to fuck the pole, too—but not till she wets my cigar!"

Lola blinked. The guy was looking right at her, unwrapping a stogy with a glimmer in his beady little eyes. Not a guy she'd care to go to the back room with.

So when Aric gave her a nudge, she approached the stage. Took the cigar and climbed the stairs amid hooting and cheering that rose to a deafening din.

Sometimes a cigar is only a cigar, she reminded herself, while her body swayed to the music. The band had gotten into her act by playing a reedy, Far Eastern snake-charmer tune, so Lola followed their lead. Her head jutted side-to-side while her arms rose and fell with the rhythm. Presentation was everything . . .

And then she realized what she was supposed to *do* with that stogy. *Where* she was supposed to dampen it, like some guys moistened cigars between their lips to make them burn longer.

She couldn't really believe she was doing this, but . . . with a seductive sway in her step, she approached the shiny pole in the center of the stage. Let her harem pants swing loosely around her body, loving the way the sheer fabric kissed her skin like butterfly wings and then fluttered away.

She stuck the cigar in her mouth, a phallic silhouette as she wrapped an arm around the cold pole . . . bent one leg around it and lowered herself slowly, so her pussy rode the chrome, exposed by that gap in her pants.

"Go, baby!"

"You do it, Vahshi!"

"Don't forget my cigar!"

With another suggestive grin, Lola hugged the pole while extending her other leg . . . opening herself to a crowd who'd spotted the split seam and clearly loved it. Ever so slowly she lowered the cigar . . . placed it against her nether lips—

"Stick it in!"

"Tickle your clit with it!"

A ripple of arousal sent feisty heat through her. Up here, away from groping hands and covered by a mask, Lola played her role to the hilt—and quickly dipped the cigar that far, too.

The room roared with male approval, and the fellow came up to claim his cigar. Five more guys were unwrapping theirs, watching her with avid eyes as she swayed and shimmied to the band's beat—swinging herself around the pole to tease them.

"Me next!"

"Here—mine's bigger!"

She threw back her head and laughed. Now this was *power*! Playing the temptress—the High Priestess and Temple Goddess— to those who truly appreciated her talents! The way things were going, she could tie one of *these* guys up, and they'd not only pay her the big bucks—they wouldn't bitch and moan like Aric had. Her man in black would *shit* at how much these guys would pay for that privilege!

The band played on and so did Lola. While she was vaguely aware that Miss Kitty and Mistress Whips and Goldilocks were plying their trade in other corners of the club, she had an avid gathering here at the edge of the stage. Watching her stroke herself with their cigars. Gazing at the gap in her pants and the bush pushing through it. Admiring the body she wouldn't dare display so boldly without the mask.

You should play this way with Rio. Now there's a guy who'll play along!

There he was, in her thoughts again. The band upped the tempo for a big finish, so Lola straddled the pole to rub herself against it, head thrown back and mouth open to fake a grimace of climax.

It was Rio DeSilva her flesh responded to. Rio who made her suddenly gush and catch fire—and then cling to the pole and the fantasy until the spasms became too real—too intense—to ignore.

The crowd simply disappeared. Maybe she got swallowed up in the noise, but all she heard was the *beat*—of the band, of her heart, of her body moving in a rhythm *so* in sync with the man who'd laid her out on a table here this morning.

She was panting, rubbing herself furiously, going over the edge as the Spaniard in her head thrust himself deep inside her, and—

"Hey, Priestess, let's keep it real, OK?" Cabana Boy said beside her ear. "Your turn's over. The next girls are ready to come out."

Lola blinked, stunned by the applause and the SeaKeys that clattered onto the stage. If she'd been quicker—more astute— she could've grabbed some and noted the names imprinted on them, for future reference.

But of course Aric was gathering them up to slide them through his scanner, to tabulate the totals she'd accumulated so far.

Blowing kisses at her fans, who cried, "Come back for the six-o'clock set!" Lola went backstage. Mistress Whips and Miss Kitty and Goldilocks strutted around her on their way to their lockers. Just another day at the orifice for them.

But as Lola stood out of their way, catching her breath while Zorro ran his calculator, she realized she'd never felt so *alive*. Was it the music? The applause and approval? The rush of playing her role to the hilt, in disguise?

Or was it Rio in your head?

While she'd never been a performer, much less an exhibitionist, she'd found a whole new energy she hadn't anticipated here. And she desperately wanted to share it with him.

Aric was gazing at her from behind that lean, mean mask like he'd never seen her before. "Way to go, Priestess. You were dynamite out there."

Glancing his way, she caught her reflection in the vanity's mirror and had to stare for a moment: was that really Lola Wright? The tailored female executive who dressed men for a living?

A spangled turquoise cap covered her head and hair, while the top half of her face hid behind a silver mask with wings that flared back over her ears. *So hot!* The outfit and mask gave her a sleekness from head to toe she'd never seen on herself, even though the flared pants and bodice spun from air would never be her choice in the real world.

Lola's pulse was pumping through her body and her breathing dove deep; her eyes looked wide and exotic behind the shimmering mask. It startled her when she realized how ethereal, how . . . *stunning* she looked.

She glanced back at Aric. His expression told her she'd mentally checked out for a minute, but she felt too brazen to care.

"What's a girl have to do to get fucked around here?" she breathed. "My God, I had a roomful of men hollering for me, *wanting* me! I've been with the captain and you and—and everyone's getting a piece of it but me! What's wrong with this picture?"

The little dressing room went silent. Mistress Whips, who had reapplied her eyeliner, and Goldilocks, refolding her white lace anklets, snickered at each other.

But another female voice overrode their humor.

"Well, well, well," Odette purred as she slinked from her dim corner. "Since the captain has informed me the name of the game is 'whatever Lola wants,' I'll pass your sentiment along to him. We'll see if we can't make your evening more . . . fulfilling, Miss Wright."

She seemed to float from the airless room, without visibly moving her legs beneath the silk caftan that draped her body so elegantly. Odette was a lynx on a mission now. Lola wondered if she'd set a whole new trap by blurting out what was on her mind.

It was Rio she wanted. But he was on duty, wasn't he?

From the conversation they'd had in the suite this morning, Lola could guess *he* wouldn't be the lover Odette went to fetch. She sat down on the bench beside Aric, taking the flavored water he offered her.

What sort of black magic would Captain Scandalous and the ominous Odette conjure up now?

23

The evening set began at six. As Lola rode her cage into the main room of Whispers, she noted that while some of the men from this afternoon were still here, several new ones had joined them, so the cigar club's main lounge was downright crowded. She doubted anyone could hear those suggestive whispers coming from the frieze around the wall, for all these other, more strident voices.

Like a beloved actress going onstage, she sucked herself in, waved regally, and bowed to acknowledge the applause and whistles of the men she'd serviced during her first set. A piano player and a couple more horns had joined the band, and Miss Kitty was stepping out of her cage in the far corner, twirling her boa to the honky-tonk ragtime number they were playing. Goldilocks was leaning out of her cage, swinging her long blonde hair—which gave the customers a good look at her exposed breasts. Mistress Whips had stepped smartly out of her cage; her stilettos tapped along the runway while she smacked men's eager, reaching hands with her riding crop.

"And now—by special request—" the cruise director bellowed over the microphone, "we have arranged for the return of the goddess Vahshi, in a command performance on our center stage."

The applause was deafening as her cage rolled along the track. She caught Aric's eye, raising her eyebrow in a question.

He merely shrugged. If Cabana Boy knew anything, he hid it behind his narrow mask.

With the spotlights crisscrossing the stage and the heavy haze of cigar smoke hanging like a blanket between the guests and the ceiling, Lola had no idea what she was in for—what sort of command performance was being required of her. It wasn't like she'd had any training as a dancer or—

But the music went from ragtime to a seductive Latin beat. The lights lowered, and so did the men's voices. Lola knew she'd damn well better do *something* besides standing here, looking clueless.

So she raised her arms gracefully, letting the rhythm sway her hips and dictate her moves . . . intuitively moving her body to best advantage. As she was gliding toward the pole, for an encore performance like the one that brought the house down earlier, she caught sight of him. His golden eyes were sending up flares she sensed before she actually saw them.

Rio.

He was standing in the entryway, still in his whites, leaning nonchalantly. But there was nothing relaxed about his focus: his gaze penetrated her soul as surely as she wanted him to penetrate her body. And yes, she could read *that* desire, as well.

Lola let out her breath, beckoning with an outstretched arm. Still following the beat of the sinuous music the band was playing.

He stepped forward, to wend his way between the closely packed cocktail tables—

But then another figure entered the stage from behind her on the right, and another someone approached her from the left. They, too, were masked, lean and gleaming in silver Spandex jumpsuits that rippled with their every step into the spotlight. Their movements were sure and graceful, their bodies attuned to the syncopated beat.

It was a man and a woman. Or was it?

Lola strained to see them from her restrictive eye holes, as she kept up her interpretive dance: they were svelte, like ballerinas, yet their silver suits bulged with provocative ridges between their legs.

Lola blinked. Instinct told her this was Skorpio and Odette, yet—

She pivoted to get a closer look at them.

With the spotlights behind her, she could focus more closely—not that it helped much. Damned if they weren't wearing spangled turquoise caps that covered their hair, just like hers. Same silver masks over the upper halves of their faces, with the same stylized wings. It was magic, the way they mimicked her movements: the three of them appeared to be performing as one for the crowd. Perfectly choreographed and costume-coordinated, like dancers who did this every day.

But it was sheer lust that radiated from their bodies when they moved in to touch her—to invite her hands into theirs—

And she was trapped.

The captain and Odette *had* her now, in more ways than she cared to think about. Lola felt the triumph in their grips; the sexual energy each sent through her body to the other. That untimely remark about getting fucked had come back to haunt her. And on this adults-only cruise, where "anything goes" passed for acceptable behavior, these two would stop at *nothing* to entertain this whiskey-swilling, stogy-smoking crowd.

Aric was moving among the audience near the stage, sliding SeaKeys through his scanner. A slender shadow in black. No help to her at all.

So Lola could only stay onstage and dance as though nobody was watching . . . wishing Rio wasn't, because she suspected Odette had summoned him here on some falsified excuse. So he could see her get turned every which way but loose, by the captain who'd declared her off limits to him.

Would DeSilva still want her, after whatever they did to her? Dammit, why'd she shoot off her mouth that way, just because she felt jazzed about her first performance?

Too late to worry about that now. Skorpio's grin flashed white in the spotlights as he pulled her into his embrace, matching his steps to hers with an innate grace that cast a sorcerer's spell.

Or was this Odette? The flashing strobes and crossing spotlights made it difficult for her to distinguish the details of gender. The identical jumpsuits had high turtleneck collars, and their smooth fit across the chest suggested sleek plastic padding.

Lola refused to bail or cave in. Fighting fire with fire was her only recourse—so she decided these chiseled lips and the hint of five-o'clock shadow belonged on Captain Scandalous.

"Skorpio," she whispered, narrowing her eyes at him. "Are we to be lovers at last? Here for everyone to see?"

"Whatever Lola wants," a sultry voice replied—but those lips didn't move, and the words came over the sound system from all directions.

They were miked! But was this him, or *her*?

Lola swiveled to catch the dancer behind her mouthing the words, but she got spun between then in a tight spiral. Had to concentrate on foot placement to keep from falling on her ass.

The crowd quieted as their dance became tighter and more sexual. The customers, too, were wondering if she danced with two men or a mixed double. Lola caught phrases and speculations, but they did nothing to help her.

"I dunno . . . that one's got a tight little ass."

"Yeah, but the other one's smaller-boned."

"But there's two cocks—and they're *cocked*!"

"Could be strapped on. Hell, maybe it's two women—can't see enough facial detail, with those masks and these strobes!"

Lola knew exactly where they were coming from. All she knew was that under their silver gloves, the hands of the dancer on her right felt larger and stronger than those on her left—but now they spun around her in pirouettes, releasing her hands only long enough to change positions!

Then things got gritty. While the captain held her—or at least Lola *thought* it was Skorpio—leading her in a series of erotic moves, Odette approached from behind. Lola felt the flexing of Skorpio's legs; his heat against her thighs, and the ridge of his dick rubbing her front. Odette was gyrating against her ass with an identical ridge, and Lola's shoulders were pinned between their two padded chests.

As one, the three of them moved, undulating to the music in a mesmerizing display of hunger that had the audience holding its collective breath. Speculating. Fantasizing.

Lola wished she could be out there *watching* this spectacle, and yet her senses were all on edge as she kept step between them, the goddess Vahshi and her two shimmering silver partners.

Without warning, Skorpio stepped back, grabbing her hands—thrusting her backwards into Odette's embrace. Lola knew better than to yelp when he swooped to grasp her ankles and bring them up beneath his arms.

As he inched forward between her legs, the men near the stage urged him on with lewd remarks.

"You go, guy!"

"Oh, man, don't you wanna be a dildo about now?"

"Dildo, hell! I want to be the guy who's about to take a piece of that redheaded action!"

Lola's pulse shot into a higher gear. The three of them circled slowly, with her body suspended between the wily lovers who'd surprised her with their games before. She was spread so far that her bush and pussy protruded from the open seam of her pants. The captain then hoisted her effortlessly, so her legs were bent over his shoulders at the knee.

"Oh, yeah—tongue-fuck her, man! Eat her out."

"Show me the honey!"

Still focusing on her role, Lola arched her body and kept moving in the dance—hoping this looked like a sensual, seductive ballet rather than some stupid skit they were improvising at the last minute. Skorpio was now so close his breath stirred the hair around her hole, which was responding with a wetness she couldn't believe.

"Come on, guy! We can't see through your head!" somebody protested.

"Yeah! Tell us what's going on—blow by blow! Every fluttering cunt hair!"

The captain laughed low in his throat. "Oh, it's a lovely sight, all flushed and pink and engorged with need," his melodious Greek whisper floated through the speakers. "Shall I tell you how she tastes?"

"Yeah!"

"Go after it!"

Again, Lola strove to maintain her Priestess persona. They hadn't called her Vahshi, the goddess, for nothing!

Letting her head fall back against Odette's chest, as though the three of them were a longtime love triangle, she moaned in anticipation.

"Please," she begged. "Lick my slit. God, I want you so bad!"

Skorpio moved in, flickering the tip of his tongue around her outer lips and then teasing her open hole with it. Odette was kissing her temple, murmuring impassioned phrases into her ear—like she meant them!—so Lola figured her best move was to let it happen. Fighting them, to maintain her dignity for Rio, was out of the question now that they were determined to make her scream for it.

"Oh, she's sweet—so hot and sweet," the captain announced with a sigh. "So wet and willing and musky, I can't get enough of her."

"Better plow her furrow, by the looks of that cock!"

"Hell, plow both of 'em!" somebody else chimed in. "The one at her back door ain't half bad either, you lucky stud!"

Lola nipped her lip to keep from laughing—and then yelped with the intensity of Skorpio's next kiss. He'd planted his lips on her cunt and was sucking and thrusting and nuzzling until the spasms warned her it wouldn't be long. She began to writhe uncontrollably, and the captain responded by upping his tempo and pressure against her heated cleft.

"Let go," Odette urged against her ear. "Let go and cry out—so I can have my turn!"

That thought alone, of Odette laving her this way, sent tremors through her insides like a small earthquake. Lola groaned, her head twisting of its own accord, and then her hips began to wiggle. Skorpio went for her clit then, circling it with his rigid tongue, until she bucked and cried out, her voice ricocheting around the high-ceilinged room.

"Yeah! Make her scream!"

"Let's see some more of that!"

Lola barely had time to catch her breath before Odette walked toward Skorpio, folding her throbbing body between theirs. Instinctively her arms went around the captain's neck, and when Skorpio shrugged, her legs slipped down over his shoulders—

And Odette caught them. Lowered her feet toward the floor . . . kept her legs spread. And then knelt between them.

The crowd was panting with her. The music had become very hushed and tense, like the soundtrack of sexy espionage. Lola couldn't see down there, with her chest pressed against the captain's, but she could envision Odette's lithe figure in profile to the audience . . . making the most of her long, feline tongue as she approached.

The first touch of that pointed tip made Lola squirm. With Skorpio holding her fast, kissing her with lips that tasted like her own juices, she could only comply. Could only stand there, wide open, while Odette's tongue worked its illicit magic from behind, through the open slit of her harem pants.

Still sensitive from that first climax, Lola spasmed and gasped, her body afire with the need—and being urged, from both directions—to come again. She broke away from Skorpio's heated kiss to cry out, grimacing toward the crowd.

"Please!" she bleated. "Take me hard! Take me now!"

She heard furtive rustlings . . . hands slipping under the tables nearby. When she could open her eyes, she saw that Miss Kitty, Mistress Whips, and Goldilocks were working the crowd by straddling laps and dancing, letting those horny men kiss their breasts and rub their erections against them for relief.

"Come on—take her, man!" a guy in the front row cried. "You've come this far! Come for real!"

"Yeah! She's beggin' you for it!"

"If you can't finish her, give *me* a shot!"

Skorpio flashed the crowd a grin. A born performer, he knew better than to disappoint his audience.

Was Rio still here, watching her behave this way? If he'd remained, would he stay to witness it when Skorpio claimed her body in a way he was forbidden to do?

The spotlights were in her eyes and she couldn't see the back of the room. A good thing, probably.

With an unerring sense of his observers' desires, Skorpio turned her so she faced the other side of the club, to take Odette's outstretched hands.

Odette leaned down, pointing her ass back, and Lola could only act as her mirror image: Skorpio was holding her hips, his body still swaying to the low, hungry beat of the band.

It got soooo quiet; the music was merely a whisper now. She heard heavy breathing—or was that her own? Lola felt Captain

Scandalous spreading her—placing his hands inside her thighs to get her into position—while Odette was guiding her arms lower . . . lower . . . until she stood with her palms mere inches above the floor, her ass pointed at Skorpio, and her legs lewdly spread.

Never had she been taken so overtly: her pussy was gaping, while wetness dribbled down the inside of her thighs. She was wide open to Skorpio's approach, holding her breath, waiting for him to enter.

The captain stepped closer; the music reduced to a slow stripper beat of the snare drum and the string bass, very sexy and low. Behind her, Lola heard the slither of a zipper.

His tip touched her ass; she felt his heat, and the reservoir of his rubber. Lola braced herself, praying he didn't enter her untried territory. Bad enough she was at his mercy—although every nerve of her body was twitching to the beat of that string bass and throbbing with a need so overwhelming, she didn't care how many eyes were watching or how many mouths were hanging slack, waiting . . . breathing with her in the anticipation of—

Odette suddenly planted Lola's hands flat on the floor, shoulder's width apart. With the agility of a gymnast, the woman crouched and then shot her legs between Lola's hands, so she was lying full-length beneath her.

The slither of another zip—

The men all around them gasping with anticipation and need—sucking air at what they could plainly see down there and she couldn't—

"We're going to kneel together now," Skorpio whispered, and his knees bent her legs from behind. "Hold us steady, or this will be a major fiasco."

Too scared to defy him—too damn curious about what would happen next—Lola did as he told her. Bearing their weight on her hands, she slowly lowered to the stage, with her knees landing on either side of the masked, silver-clad woman beneath them. Skorpio's knees were in there, too—opening hers farther.

And before she could protest—much less guess where this three-way would go—she felt the prod of a very hard, firm shaft nosing its way into the slit of her pants. Behind her, Skorpio had removed his glove, and his greased finger was teasing her asshole. It puckered in protest—

But the pressure of the prick beneath her, after so much heart-pounding anticipation, made Lola lunge to take it inside her. It wasn't hot, but it was hard and solid. Odette bucked upward to fill her with a dildo far larger than any man she'd ever had.

Lola clenched; closed her eyes. She was so close to completion—

That finger toyed with her; entered tentatively—

She gasped with the unexpected sensation of extra fullness—

And slowly, carefully, Skorpio eased the tip of his cock into her ass.

"Don't move," he whispered, his words reverberating in the breathless room. "Let us do it. Let us drive you absolutely insane with pleasure like you've never known."

Lola wasn't sure how it happened, but with one shaft coming from beneath her and another from behind, she became a core of throbbing, urgent need—a sensitive system of nerve endings all jangling at once. Her head flew back and she grimaced with it, a climax that rocked her so hard she imploded. Lola could only vibrate mindlessly as the spasms went on and on.

She was vaguely aware of hoarse cries around her, and wild applause. The band geared up again, signaling the end of this show, but it wasn't over until Captain Scandalous convulsed against her backside and Odette's sly laughter made her open her eyes.

"Be careful what you ask for," the woman whispered, her eyes shining dark beneath that spangled mask. "We'll give it to you—but it will always, always be on our terms. You know that now, don't you?"

Lola nodded mutely. It was all she could manage.

Later, as Aric escorted her upstairs, Lola had little to say. No surprise that she hadn't seen Rio anywhere after the show. He was probably so repelled by her brazen stage behavior, he would avoid her for the rest of the cruise.

Cabana Boy knew better than to say anything other than, "I'm whipped, Priestess. How 'bout a pizza and some cold—"

"Get me a medium, veggie with extra cheese. Two bottles of Rolling Rock," she specified as he unlocked the suite door. "I'm going to my room for the rest of the evening, and I *don't* want to be disturbed. Got it?"

"Loud and clear," he murmured.

His expression invited her confidence; matter of fact, he looked almost apologetic for the way things came down in Whispers, but Lola wasn't going there. She only wanted the company of her Tarot cards as she figured out the way she felt now—the highs of her first virtuoso performance, compared to the way Skorpio and Odette had once again twisted the rules of this game to put her in her place.

She wasn't sure whether to be pissed about their deception, or pleased that she'd crossed a new sensual line. But one thing Lola knew for damn sure: she was exhausted. Wrung out. Half inclined to rip open that pack of Camels before her pizza arrived, so that comforting old chemical high could help her sort out so many new feelings.

Including a heaviness around her heart. A loneliness far worse than she'd felt when Dennis ditched her.

Lola locked the bedroom door and leaned on it, dog-tired. Sorta sore. Claudine had turned down that big, heavenly bed, and a silky summer breeze drifted in from her balcony. The billowing sheers beckoned her to step outside and breathe in the fresh night—

She heard a quiet *fffffffft*. Saw the flare of a match.

Rio DeSilva sat in one of her patio chairs, his tiger eyes aflame as he inhaled to light his little cigar.

24

What was it about European men who smoked those skinny, dark cigars?

Lola froze, fascinated by the sight of him out there in the dusk. She stared at his seductive face, which glowed with the intensity of his red ember.

Hadn't she said she was tired?

Hadn't she feared he'd avoid her, after her grand finale in Whispers?

Just the way he lounged in that chair, with one leg cocked over the other knee, slumping enough that his head rested against the chair back . . . God, but he'd lit *all* her cravings with that match! DeSilva sat, motionless except for the flexing of those lips beneath that mustache, drawing on his cigar.

Drawing on *her*.

Lola could've been *blind* and still known how Rio's eyes beckoned. Could've *felt* that lusty summons, even if she hadn't noticed him yet.

And his eyes said he knew that.

Shaking with need—and for a drag on that little cigar—Lola

put a finger to her lips. Motioned for him to stay out there, and then pointed over her shoulder at the door.

She did *not* feel like sharing this surprise with Cabana Boy!

DeSilva didn't move. Just watched her, as that seductive smoke, which caught the glow from her bedside lamp, encircled his face.

She waited for Aric to knock on the door with her pizza and beer. Would he see Rio out there and then notify the captain?

That's why you locked the door, silly. So Aric wouldn't barge in. So he wouldn't quiz you about the cards.

Ah, her cards.

A smile spread over Lola's face, and she sidled over to her table. The spread she'd arranged the other night, with Skandalis and Odette on one side and Rio and herself on the other, was just as she'd left it. She could smile now at how the Hanging Man and Strength had allowed her to take her warden hostage with her scarves, just as those chains suggested.

But enough about Aric. She had a real man on her balcony, watching her. Waiting for her next move.

It was time for some cat-and-mouse. Time to see who came to whom. And who came first.

Sitting down at her table, Lola closed her eyes. She prayed for patience and guidance from the cards, to invoke the spiritual presence she required for true meditation. Then she prayed for an extra measure of *focus*. After all, what rational woman would be shuffling her Tarot deck when such a hunk had positioned himself outside her bedroom?

The cards felt smooth and slick and new. They whispered against the table as she mixed them in circular directions, face down, to transfer her energy to them. And now that she was preparing herself for a reading, what did she want to know? What question did she want the cards to answer right now?

What's going on, REALLY, with Rio? she queried silently. *What do I dare reveal to him?*

She gathered them in handfuls, stacking them; held the deck loosely between her hands, until her heartbeat pulsed through it. Then—because it was part of her ritual, and because she felt Rio watching—she divided the deck into three stacks. Instinctively picked up the middle one.

What's going on with Rio? What should I reveal to him? she repeated in her mind.

One by one, she laid the cards face-down in the ten positions of the Celtic Cross. Her fingers itched to turn them over, to study their possible meanings but—

Lola sighed longingly. She could feel the suction—damn near tasted the warm hit from that cigar—every time DeSilva inhaled. He was letting the smoke drift out through his nose, little puffs of temptation she longed to share with him, even if he didn't know what he was doing to her on a chemical level.

Tap, tap. "Pizza's here."

Lola blinked. Slowly, as though she didn't know she was being watched—*hah!*—she went to the door. "Just leave it right there. With two of those Rolling Rocks, please."

"You've seen me in your cards, haven't you, Priestess?" Aric whispered. "I'm that guy on the Nine of Cups, about to make all your wishes come true."

Shit! Who knew Cabana Boy would be into Tarot?

"More like the Page of Wands," she mused aloud, "bringing me a message, loud and clear, with that *wand* that nearly split your zipper in the elevator."

"Hey! Pages represent *boys*, and I—"

"You are *so* right, my little love slave," she purred through the door. "Now go scarf your pizza and leave me to my divination. We Priestesses must perform our rituals and renew our powers, you know. *Alone.*"

She waited for the scrape of the cardboard box against the bottom of the door, and the clinking of two bottles. Then Lola waited several seconds more, for the sound of his breathing to leave. It made a damn funny image: Aric's ear on the other side of the wood, slightly higher than hers.

Quickly she whisked the food inside and relocked the door. Lola set the warm box on the end of the bed, looking right at Rio as she pulled up the first steaming wedge of pizza. Thinnish, air-bubbled crust with lots of mushrooms, olives, red peppers, and *cheese*. Lord she loved the hot, gooey cheese that dangled out of her mouth as she took that first heavenly bite!

She had to hand it to him: Cabana Boy knew what a woman wanted. At least in a pizza.

Lola tipped the cold, green bottle to her lips, saluting Rio. Seducing him by just standing there for a moment, focusing on her food.

Or so she told herself.

He gazed back, nursing that cheroot like he might sit out there all night.

So she'd let him.

Or so she told herself.

Lola returned to her table with a second slice on the small plate Aric had provided, to study her Tarot spread. She'd better interpret the cards before things got ratcheted up a notch, somehow.

Somehow? Silently, Rio entered her bedroom, his slender mustache rising with his sly smile. The shirt he wore looked clean and white against his skin, but old enough that its cotton would be very soft. It was already unbuttoned, and when he let it fall down his arms, Lola could feel its caress against her own skin.

She shivered. Studied her cards again.

Yeah, right, like I have any idea what they're saying, with a half-naked man helping himself to my pizza . . . slipping onto my bed, while I sit here wishing he had a piece of ME between those long, slender fingers.

The first card in a Celtic Cross spread represented her, and when Lola turned it over, she gasped. The High Priestess danced above the ocean in her dress woven of stardust.

How did the cards know my new nickname?

How did the cards know anything? The way they fell into place spooked her more often than not—which made her connection to them seem valid.

Feeling Rio's gaze, she quickly flipped the other nine cards and noted the mix of positives and negatives . . . some very impressive messages in some very compelling places. Since her question concerned that man on her bed, who was reaching for more pizza, Lola's heart pounded into double-time: the sixth and tenth positions, which involved her future, showed The Lovers and the King of Cups, a major player when it came to love and emotions.

And who, come to think of it, bore a striking resemblance to—

"Tell me what they mean, Lola *mia*," he whispered against her ear. "Your face tells me the cards have revealed some startling, but exciting, predictions."

She may have won their little game of cat-and-mouse, but with Rio DeSilva leaning over her shoulder, bare-chested, crooning in an accented voice that smelled of pizza and beer and tobacco, Lola was a goner.

She closed her eyes against a welling up of every need her body knew. Then she glanced toward the door.

"He won't hear us. He's watching TV," Rio breathed, tickling her neck. "It's between you and me now, *querida*, and I won't allow Aric to intrude."

How did he know that? What did he see in these card positions? Or was he bluffing, to get her interpretation of *between you and me*?

"I—I'll place a clarifying card on each of these," she stalled.

She dealt from her pile again, going backwards from position ten this time. How could she admit she'd asked the cards about *him*?

"Such vibrant colors and images," he murmured, leaning lightly against her shoulders. "My mother would love this deck. She's been a psychic advisor for most of her life—but I recall little of what she's told me about the Tarot. Basics about some of the positions, maybe. And if this card is *you*—"

Rio caressed the High Priestess with his digit, following the arc of her nearly bare body.

"—then this gallant Knight with his uplifted goblet must be me. Is that how you see it?"

Lola let out a weak laugh. "Well, your visual interpretation of the cards is often as accurate as their traditional meaning, so—"

"So that means this is also you and me, in The Lovers card—making love in the ocean, no less." His low chuckle sent shivers all through her body. "And here's that goblet again, on the Ace of Cups, but it resembles a communion chalice. Doesn't take a rocket scientist to know that's the eye of God sanctioning the commitment. Am I close?"

She sucked in her breath. Rio was standing *oh* so close, she felt the heat of his bare stomach through her blouse. DeSilva was far too perceptive to lie to—and she'd never had the poker face for deception, anyway.

"The Lovers is about relationships, yes, and about choices," she murmured, "while the Ace of Cups suggests the beginning of a new—"

"Romance," he finished, lightly kissing her temple. "You have a way with these cards, don't you? Is that why the King of Cups is smiling toward the card at the top, where he sees a home with a wife and a daughter?"

Lola closed her eyes at the intensity of his voice. "The Ten of Cups is often called the 'happily-ever-after' card, yes."

Rio's hands closed over her shoulders and he took a long, deep breath. Was he actually trembling? Did he see his resemblance to that smiling king with the slender mustache?

Or was there something about the happy family in the other card that touched him so deeply?

She felt him shift gears then, maybe not wanting to reveal his deepest secrets any more than she did. "And this position—the past, isn't it?"

"Or energy that's passing away." Lola paused, fingering the two cards as their meanings suddenly hit home. "When the Six of Cups is reversed—turned upside down that way—it can indicate an unhappy childhood—"

"Was it?"

Rio crouched beside her table to gaze up into her eyes. "What happened to you, sweetheart? Did your parents divorce, or—"

How did he *know*, dammit?

Lola blinked, not wanting to get maudlin. Lord, how many years ago did that happen? She'd moved beyond that long ago. Learned that lesson and grew up to become an independently successful woman, right?

Or so she told herself.

Lola sighed. Rio would keep looking at her until she answered.

"I heard my parents having this awful fight one day—worse than usual," Lola amended. "And that's how I found out they'd *had* to get married, because—because I was on the way."

Rio's brow furrowed. His hand shot up to cover hers. "So you've spent more than half your life feeling responsible for your parents' breakup? That's a helluva long guilt trip, Lola *mia*."

Her head fell forward so her hair hid the wetness in her eyes.

DeSilva rose to pull her against him, holding her close to his heart. "So let me guess. You became a wild child to compensate—"

"Hardly. Boys didn't like me nearly as much as I liked them."

His sardonic laugh said he didn't believe that. "So you fell for any sign of affection or approval. Maybe gave yourself to men, thinking that if they responded to you, it must be true love?"

Lola shook against him with a single sob. Did he think she'd agreed to Skorpio's game to seek the captain's affection? His acceptance? Rio might as well be reading from her files in the shrink's office—except he was much more compassionate than Dr. Frinkel had been back then. And a *lot* better looking.

With another tender kiss, he pointed to that beautiful High Priestess again. "You sell yourself too short, Lola *mia*. A woman—a *goddess*—who can dance above the waters this way should never have settled for a loser like Dennis Fletcher."

Damned if he wasn't tapping on that Five of Swords card; the card about overkill and victory at the expense of others. It hadn't escaped her that the fellow with all the swords in his arms, lording it over his fallen competitors, looked a lot like Fletch.

"Why are you calling him a loser?" she challenged. Anything to salvage a *little* dignity from this man who knew too much. "Dennis is a very successful financial advisor. Works with clients in the Fortune 500—"

Rio raised her chin between his hands so she had to look at him. His expression was a mixture of disgust and . . . concern. He was *worried* about her. Too kind—too much a gentleman— to ask for details.

"Lola," he rasped.

His eyes shone with a light so piercing she had to look away.

"Lola, when we were downstairs watching those security tapes of him, do you have any idea why I stopped them so abruptly?"

She swallowed hard. Shook her head.

"In the next few seconds, that blonde must've said something that provoked him, because he—Dennis Fletcher lost his cool and took a *swing* at her!" he said with a harsh sigh. "Did he hit you, Lola? Because if he did, so help me—"

"I—I told him if he *ever*—"

Oh, who was she fooling? That Eight of Swords—the "fear" card—illustrated the way she'd blindfolded herself and built her own prison, when it came to dealing with conflict.

"I knew better than to make him mad," she murmured.

Color rose in the Spaniard's cheeks. But instead of lecturing her, Rio exhaled. Looked at the spread again.

"Those negative influences are in your past, *mi vida*—passing out of your life into *this*."

His finger landed on The Lovers, so ecstatically caught up in their moonlit revelry. "And I say we make it come true. Right this minute."

"But—what about—what're you—?"

Rio's seductive smile gave her a rush better than nicotine or melted chocolate or cheesy pizza. "The advantage of being Chief of Security is knowing how and where to catch some private time, away from the passengers," he whispered, his voice ripe with promise. "My favorite way to relax is with a dip in the spa's pool, after it's closed. Care to join me?"

A midnight swim? The sensual challenge in Rio's tawny eyes sent her senses spinning. "That sounds wonderful. Let me get my suit, and—"

"No, no," he murmured, teasing her with his wicked grin. "No suit. *Naked* is the only way to swim."

25

The look on Aric's face was priceless when she and Rio came out of the bedroom together. And the security agent was ready for him.

"Once again you've failed to provide adequate protection for Miss Wright," he lectured. "Her balcony door was wide open! You didn't even *think* to check the suite for intruders when you entered—which is crucial, since we don't know who returned her cell phone and purse."

Cabana Boy kept his retort to himself, although he was eyeing Rio's unbuttoned, untucked shirt.

"Ah, no response. Which is exactly what you'll have if Skorpio or Odette comes sniffing around," De Silva said pointedly. "Unless, of course, you'd like me to tell the captain about this latest mistake. Don't wait up."

Rio took her arm, and down the hall they hurried, giggling like kids. When the elevator door closed, they kissed like teenagers at home with no parents, descending deeper into the realms of sensual pleasure.

Was falling for Rio—because he could read her cards and her

needs—really any safer than letting Captain Scandalous, Kingsley, and Cabana Boy toy with her?

But they were all just escapes from the reality that Fletch had left her with, weren't they? When the cruise ended, she'd return to Real Life alone, but with her credit and reputation intact. No harm done.

Then DeSilva pulled her hard against his bare chest. His hand spanned the back of her head as he kissed her with such passionate abandon, Lola couldn't remember if they were going up or down. And she didn't care, as long as those lips didn't leave hers.

His hand closed around hers again, *tight*, as they hurried down the dimly lit corridor, past those ornate double doors to the Goddess Spa. It paid to play with a man who had a master key!

Like thieves in the night, they stole into the glass-domed enclosure, where the only light came from the red EXIT signs and the two spotlights under the dark aqua water. One entire side of the pool was a waterfall, which filled the solarium with a hushed, continuous whisper, like the call of the sea.

Still clinging to his fingers, Lola gazed at the beautiful pool, surrounded by shining white tile and chaises with colorful floral-print pads. This was living! Had Fletch not run off—had she not given over her week to Captain Scandalous—she would've come here to indulge herself in these serene, herbal-scented waters. Would've treated herself to Miss Christy's massage without being humiliated by Odette's idea of—

"You're having doubts, Lola *mia*? I assure you the doors are locked. We're totally alone."

Lola gazed up into a face so ripe with desire, on a man so ready to wipe away her pain with his pleasure, she went blank for a moment. Couldn't think of one single reason she wasn't the luckiest woman in the world right now.

"I—I've never gone swimming in the altogether before," she confessed.

"Then who better to introduce you to such total freedom?" he whispered. "This is an honor, indeed."

His zipper sang a slow, sensual song as he lowered it.

"And since you were the one exposed when we enjoyed that champagne on your balcony," he continued, "I'll bare myself first this time. You might change your mind, and go back upstairs to Aric."

Lola held her breath. DeSilva sounded so playful, like he couldn't wait to be with her, even after—

"I . . . I thought you left Whispers this evening because that uh, dance routine might've turned you off to—"

"I left Whispers," he said, his tawny eyes afire, "because I was ready to shove Skandalis out of the way, Lola *mia*. You were the most amazing woman I'd ever seen up there."

Her jaw dropped. She moved her mouth to protest, but he laid a finger across her lips.

"Don't argue with a man who's determined to pleasure you, Lola. You deserve pleasure—and love," he added wistfully. "You deserve the best of that, too."

His khakis slid down his long, lean thighs and he stepped out of them. Folded them loosely over the nearest wicker chair. The Spaniard's body was a luscious golden brown all over, and while he wasn't overtly muscular, DeSilva had the lean, deceptive strength of a tiger when he strolled over to fetch them a couple of towels.

Smiling, enticing her to follow, Rio then walked to the edge of the pool. With his back to her, he slipped his hands down the sides of his black bikini briefs . . . gave her quite a nice shot of his ass as he lowered them.

He slipped something into the crotch, and playfully shot them at her like a rubber band.

Lola's laughter echoed in the glassed enclosure, high and girlish. She was so caught up in snatching those bikinis from the air that she missed DeSilva's dive into the pool. So clean and quiet it was, the surface barely rippled. Then he swam like a slender, golden sea lion beneath the water's aqua surface.

When he bobbed up in front of her, grinning and tossing water back from his face, she could only stare. The ship's security agent resembled one of those native cliff divers who searched exotic waters for pearls.

He rested his shapely arms on the edge, grinning up at her.

That slash of mustache looked even more wicked, now that it was wet. He was a very sexy *bandito*, about to steal her—

What? What was Rio DeSilva after, really?

She reached into his bikinis and pulled out a foil packet. And while Lola had always regarded condoms as a necessary inconvenience, this one told her *exactly* what he wanted. Its subtle message went beyond penetration: like his edgy smile, it bespoke *possession*.

"Your turn, Lola *mia*," he whispered, extending his hand. "The water's perfect. Like warm, liquid silk against my bare skin. But cool enough to feel refreshing."

With a final glance around, Lola lowered her jeans. "You just want to see if my Very Cherry nipples'll stick out when I hit the water."

"And what do *you* want to see, my little mermaid?"

She tossed her jeans on top of his khakis, and then her blouse. She almost left her panties on, to feel the exhilaration of him pulling them off.

Was she silly, acting this coy? After all, he'd seen her the other night . . . had lapped champagne from the most sensitive crevice of her body.

And that silver packet in her hand spelled everything out, didn't it?

Rio DeSilva looked ready to swallow her whole. Lean and predatory, even though he'd made no attempt to hustle her, the way Skandalis had.

Following his example, Lola turned and mooned him a good

one as she tugged her skivvies past her thighs and calves. When they ringed her ankles, she waved at him from between her parted legs.

His lips twitched. "Lola," he said in a low growl.

She went wet without getting near the water.

That primal way he said her name unlocked a gate to some erotic frontier. While she'd gotten secret thrills from the games Captain Scandalous played, *this* man spoke her body's language. This drop-dead gorgeous lover made no bones about how badly he wanted her, and how he intended to *have* her.

Now.

At last.

Lola walked to the steps at the shallow end. *Paraded* herself like some hot, tropical temptress who fully intended for the water to steam when she stepped in. She stood with one hand on her hip and the other on the silver railing, watching his reaction to her grand entry.

By the time she was knee-deep, DeSilva had slipped beneath the water, like a heat-seeking torpedo.

By the time her bush was submerged, Rio resurfaced. Shook his wet hair back and then stepped between her legs without giving her any say about it.

He moved into her—grabbing her backside—and then hoisted her high, so her hips landed against his shoulders. His moan echoed around them, and when his lips found the skin of her belly, Lola's head fell back. Thrusting out her chest with wanton abandon, she realized he'd pulled her into the same pose as The Lovers card in her Tarot deck.

This man didn't miss a trick.

This man was too damn good, and she needed to take him seriously.

Rio was backing deeper into the water, still nuzzling her. It felt so different, the way he kissed her there—like he couldn't get enough of that fleshy ridge she couldn't lose, even when she got skinny. When Fletch had touched her tummy, she sensed he was sending a message about excess flab—

Forget him, OK? her thoughts prodded.

As Rio DeSilva massaged her with his mouth, the scrape of his mustache and light stubble awakened new sensations. Something told her she was in for a lot of those—

Like being *dropped*! And then caught against him again, face to face.

God, he looked hungry. For *her*.

Lola wound her arms around his wet neck, reveling in the slick heat of his skin against hers as she kissed him deeply. He thrust his tongue between her teeth, initiating penetration . . . possession on the first level. He coaxed her legs around his body without breaking the kiss, and walked them through the warm water, waist high.

With every step, his erection rubbed her in just the right place. Rio stopped, long enough to undulate suggestively, while his hot mouth sought out a hotter response.

He deftly turned her in the water. Lola gasped with the loss of lip contact, grasping the edge of the pool to steady herself . . . to give her hips more leverage when his hands explored her inner thighs. His cock was prodding her backside, a constant reminder of what he intended to do—of how slowly and purposefully he would claim her until she lost all pretense of being Lola Wright, Independent Woman.

"Lola . . . Lola *mia*," he murmured against her ear.

Guiding her legs so they wrapped loosely around his, he began to sidle sideways. "Do you like this, *querida*? I want it to be like nothing you've ever known before, our loving."

Lola moaned. He was caressing her breasts now, leaving her so very *open* beneath the water, wondering when that cock would make its move. It felt firm and insistent, and in no huge hurry to end this playful exchange.

"Hold on."

His hands spanned the front of her ribcage and slowly descended, pressing into her flesh to prolong his caress. When his fingers dipped below her waist to ruffle her muff, she giggled and squirmed back against him.

DeSilva groaned and rubbed more insistently. "Put the foil crimp between my teeth," he suggested. "Let's open that little package and play with what's inside."

Reaching over her shoulder with it, Lola could only stare: the white, even edge of Rio's teeth, bared beneath his curled lip, looked so damned *animal* she nearly spasmed.

His eyes locked into hers and he tugged, silently suggesting she do the same. The condom was a hot hibiscus pink, and when it appeared in the opening, she plucked it from the foil.

"Now take it underwater. I'm going to thrust between your legs so we can put it on. Together."

Again his eyes wouldn't let her go. As though hypnotized by his novel suggestion, her hand followed his directions while her heart thudded wildly.

He slid lower behind her, his gaze shifting to the way her lips formed an O when his shaft parted her nether lips to rub firmly against her clit . . . out and back, as he matched the motions to his breathing.

And she was taking every breath with him, too mesmerized not to. When his hand found hers, he guided it to his tip. Closed his eyes and exhaled with slow ecstasy as their fingers worked the sheath over the warm, hard length of him. Instinct told her to hold on, to stroke it until the little ridge rested against his sac.

For a few moments he gloried in her touch, his long lashes quivering with the effort to control himself. His fingers found her needy spot then, and like a key sliding into a well-oiled lock, they entered her open hole to explore. Their writhing escalated to a dizzying height before he cupped her hard and held absolutely still.

"Do you like it when water shoots against you there?"

Lola blinked, woozy with want. "I—I have no idea."

"Then it's time we found out."

Rio inched sideways along the side of the pool, letting her bob in his arms as he approached the jet where the warm water shot in. The current pulsing against her thigh made anticipation ripen inside her, just thinking about how that rolling *force* would feel against her pussy.

"We'll start high," he murmured, "to let you get used to the feel of it. If it's too much, you can always ask for *me, querida*."

The sensation of that billowing warmer water shooting against her belly made Lola's eyes widen. She gasped, but then relaxed in Rio's loose hug as her body grew accustomed to the whirling, tight current. It pummeled her, yet it was also a massage. And when she moved to see how it felt on different parts of her exposed body, curiosity got the better of her.

She raised up. Held her breath as the jet of water shot against her mound. God, this was like nothing else she'd ever—

When it hit her clit, she cried out.

Lola dropped down again to remove herself from that intense pressure; sucked air to regain her sanity. Rio was rubbing against her backside, breathing faster as their bodies slid in rhythm.

"Do you want me inside you?" he pleaded. "Take your time, Lola *mia*, and—"

She found the warm, rounded tip of him with her fingers. Letting the water bear her weight, Lola slid herself down the entire length of him in one smooth move.

Their moans rose to the domed ceiling, like those of mating wolves in the night. Rio pumped her slowly, bracing his forearms against the rim on either side of her. Lola curled against him as though they'd done this dozens of times, letting his *up* meet her *down* . . . positioning herself so he hit all the right spots inside her.

"God, this is so, so—"

"We could finish this way," he rasped, "or if you want to really shoot the moon, go for that jet again. I'll feel it, too, while I'm inside you. We'll—"

Her body took his dare. No other lover had ever suggested such brazen stimulation—maybe fearing it would eclipse his own power over her.

But Rio DeSilva had never been into power games. He truly pursued her pleasure before his own.

Lola inched lower, gripping him inside her, feeling his chest harden against her back as he, too, awaited the intense stimulation. The jet shot at her belly now . . . at the indention between her pelvic bones, just above her mound . . . and then Rio brought his knees up against the back of hers, bending her legs to his.

Was it like the sudden adrenaline surge of a roller coaster? Or like shooting straight up into mindless bliss? All Lola knew was that they were moving together, forward and back against that flume of water, and that such intense pleasure might make her insane.

But then, sanity had always been highly overrated, hadn't it?

Their screams ricocheted around the glass dome above them, yet she was unaware of making any sound. Her eyes squeezed shut and her head fell back to bump against Rio's shoulder. His stubble brushed her cheek when he grimaced, panting with the effort to control himself. The low grunt that began in his belly worked its way up into a keening cry, which sent her even higher, into a soul-shattering climax.

They collapsed against the side of the pool, away from the rush of that water jet. Rio's head rested on her shoulder and his hands grabbed for hers on the cool tiles in front of them.

"Lola *mia!*" he wheezed. Only this time it was a declaration of triumph, rather than just an endearment.

"You got that right," she rasped back.

Because no matter what happened after this cruise ended, part of her would always be Rio's. Any man who came later would have a damn hard time topping *this* trick!

"If I hurt you, or if—if the jet was too intense—"

"Is there a limit to pleasure?" she queried breathlessly. "Is there such a thing as too much fun? Or too much love? Or coming too hard?"

His body shook with laughter. "Excellent questions, *mi vida*. And I hope you'll want to love me again and again to find the answers."

Lola reveled in the tenderness of his lips on her temple; the way he ran his tongue so lovingly around the shell of her ear as his breath tickled her damp skin. Had somebody told her she'd make love in a public pool this way, naked, she'd have laughed in their face.

But that was before DeSilva dared her to experience herself so fully as a woman—as that High Priestess who danced above the water, arching back in ecstasy because she gave herself over to it completely.

She turned within his loose embrace, to smile at him. He was so damn beautiful, with his wet brown hair clinging to his bronzed face, and that boyish grin flickering on his lips, and that pirate's mustache. How had she ever attracted him?

Not that it mattered. There'd be no letting go of him now.

"Thank you for this," she whispered. "I—I never knew—"

A *thunk*, *thunk*, *thunk* made them jerk and look toward the glass wall.

There, not fifteen feet in front of them, stood Odette. She was peering in, her face pressed to the glass in a wicked leer.

Wiggling her fingers in a gleeful wave, she loped away. Probably to tattle to the captain.

26

When Skandalis summoned her to his quarters the next morning, Lola braced herself. Aric and Odette both knew who she'd been with last night—in direct defiance of Skorpio's orders that she remain *his* lover. She fully expected to be cuffed and stuffed into the ship's jail.

Or set out on her ass, now that they'd docked.

If this was Friday, they must be in Dominica. The local authorities would have a field day with an American woman who'd been put ashore without her passport or purse—which is the way Captain Scandalous would play it.

Yet when Skorpio opened his door and waved Aric on his way, the Greek's expression remained amiable. He smiled at her; invited her in with an eloquent gesture that made his deep green robe ripple on his body. His black eyes snapped as he drank her in, and the flare of his nostrils suggested he was sniffing her up for sex more than for punishment.

He didn't say a word.

Lola didn't know how to interpret that, but she refused to fill in his silence with nervous chatter. Bad strategy, that was.

This captain, suave and inscrutable, could mesmerize his prey so skillfully the victim never knew what hit her. Maybe it *excited* him that she'd been doing it in the pool with DeSilva! Maybe it was part of his plan, to hold the threat of deportation over her head, hoping she'd defy him. A show of his personal power.

And Lord help her, Skorpio Skandalis reeked of a power far headier than his cologne. Lola reminded herself she'd better play it his way again today: being at the mercy of a masked man in a silver jump suit had felt dicey, true—but in Whispers, there'd been *witnesses*. Here, it was just her and Skorpio.

Dangerous. Very, very dangerous.

She breathed deeply and kept her gaze fixed on his. Ready to submit and accept her fate—but not without challenging him first!

A morally upright woman would've walked ashore before this little adventure began, in debt but with her honor intact. *So much easier!*

But then, this adults-only cruise and the devil-get-screwed deal she'd made with Skandalis were never about remaining upright, were they? She'd stated her fantasies outright, and he'd agreed to them. He was like the Emperor or the King of Swords in her Tarot deck: all-knowing, and all about control.

Maybe he didn't know about Rio. Odette played this game by her own rules, after all.

And maybe he did know, and would use this knowledge against her when it would cost her the most.

Skandalis let a single finger drift down her cheek.

"You look relaxed and happy today," he remarked in that musky accent. "So much lovelier than when we first met."

Now *there* was a trap if she'd ever stumbled into one!

"Thank you, sir," she murmured.

The corner of his mouth quirked. That finger continued its lazy journey along her jaw, inciting little riots with the edge of his manicured nail.

"Let your hair down," he said in a voice she strained to hear.

Lola reached up, not wanting to obey in too big a hurry. This man was all about seduction, so slow, sensual moves worked to her advantage.

Was that *swishing* in the other room a brush in a toilet bowl? Claudine was probably cleaning, since Odette didn't impress her as the potty-swishing type . . . which meant she might be in for a different surprise altogether. Lola hadn't yet met the house girl who left those truffles on her turned-down bed, but if Skorpio had hired her, she was bound to be attractive.

Probably playful, too!

Still holding Skorpio's obsidian gaze, Lola plucked the hairpins Aric had arranged her curls with, and let them *ping* to the foyer floor. Ever so elegantly, she loosened the covered elastic band to pull it free. Shook her head then, letting her auburn waves fall in artful disarray around her face.

Skorpio inhaled, still tilting her chin; keeping his finger firmly planted to remind her who was in charge.

"I considered having you clean for me today," he remarked softly, "because a woman should do *some* work for the man who's forgiving her debts."

"'Forgive us our debts, as we forgive our debtors,'" Lola quipped—and then wondered if that was wise.

But the captain's laughter sounded low and rich and smoky. Made her wish for a cigarette.

"Yes, my darling, you should say your prayers when you're alone with me. While I drive a hard bargain," he said, coaxing her closer with that single digit, "I drive my cock even harder when a woman excites me. And you *do* excite me, sweet Lola. You have from the moment we met."

"So why did you shove it up my ass yesterday?" she whispered. "Why didn't you *face* me, to fuck me like a *man*?"

His kiss snapped her head back. Skorpio Skandalis was

forty-something but fit; tall enough that Lola had to toe-dance to hold her own against that fabulous mouth. There was nothing pretty or romantic about this kiss: she was all give and he was all take.

And wasn't this what she'd wanted, since the first time she saw him on her TV? Captain Scandalous was living up to every fantasy, the way he held her so hard. The way he took control, to make her lose it.

He was shrugging out of his robe, so Lola yanked it down his bare back, over his firm, muscled ass. He was rubbing his cock against her, too, making it quite obvious that *this* time, he would grant her fantasy. *This* time Lola would get whatever she wanted from him!

A red flag in her mind warned her to proceed with cautious abandon, however: he was chauvinist enough—Old World enough—to believe she should "know her place." And Skorpio would put her there whenever it pleased him—because he *could*. Because he was the captain, and he made the deals on this ship, no matter what her fantasies dictated should happen between them.

And then, without knowing how it happened, she *was* between them—between Skorpio and that damned Odette! Where had *she* come from?

This time she wasn't masquerading in that French maid uniform with a faked accent, or concealing her gender in a padded jump suit. Nope, Odette was as naked as her partner in passion, and she was now behind Lola, peeling away the layers of clothing Skorpio had unbuttoned in his eagerness.

When Lola tried to protest, she got nowhere: his lips remained firmly fixed on hers, claiming her mouth in a most egotistical, arrogant way.

But God, could this man *kiss*! And when she tried to wiggle out of his embrace, to resist Odette's advances from behind, why—he merely wrapped his arms around her more tightly! Giving her what she wanted, he would say.

Except he wasn't talking.

He was making her his prisoner in the most sexy, sensual way. Holding her captive—so Odette could have another go at her!

She then became the filling in a very hot sandwich: Skorpio was making full frontal contact and getting harder and more insistent with his prodding, while behind her, Odette rubbed against her butt. It was a more alluring massage than Lola dared to think about—but then, she didn't spend much time thinking about making love to women! Her initiation with Miss Christy— and that dildo act in Whispers—was as close as she cared to come to that.

So of course Captain Scandalous sensed her hesitation and let Odette call the shots from behind.

Maybe this was his punishment for her little escapade in the spa pool. Or maybe he realized how she detested the idea of doing it with another female, so that was what he'd mete out for her penance. But probably, he was just doing it because it excited him, watching two women who wanted *him*, really.

Odette eased her agile hands between Lola's body and Skorpio's, to flatten them over her breasts. Slowly the naked woman behind her squeezed her sensitive flesh, taking her nipples between her fingers and flicking them with her nails.

Lola bucked, trying to pry herself from Skorpio's hold. But he was having none of it.

"Lola, my darling, you're so hot and ready for me," he whispered against her ear. "I love it that you want me so badly. Rub yourself against my cock. Feel how hard it is, from wanting you, too."

She obeyed him immediately—except then Odette pressed forward with her pelvis. Lola felt like the meat in a cheeseburger, getting squeezed by someone very hungry. Including the part where the juices dribbled out.

Then the exasperating woman insinuated her hands lower, to play in Lola's pubes, as though she found that feathery hair terribly erotic.

"Oh, Lola," Odette whispered in her other ear. "Lola, you've gotten Skorpio so hard! He obviously adores you as much as I do, so it's only fair that you get your turn with him this time. Open your thighs—"

Lola's legs obeyed as though an invisible cord had drawn them apart, like curtains at a window.

"Yes, yes! Now thrust forward—"

Odette's hands slipped lower, to strum Lola's delicate sex lips with the sure grace of a harpist who knew how to make beautiful music.

And indeed, Lola began to moan in a rising sing-song that amazed her. Was she really falling for this? Did she believe Skorpio would really make love to *her* this time?

It wasn't so bad, this sandwich act . . . very warm and sexy— until Skorpio kissed her again, and then placed his face on the other side of hers to kiss Odette! Right next to her ear they were, bumping against her cheek as they went at it as passionately as the captain had been kissing *her* moments ago.

How humiliating! This raven-haired pair was now fully engaged from the neck up, and Lola could only stand between their hot, pulsing bodies and *let* them carry on this way!

Not that she was uninvolved. Her juice was now running down the insides of her thighs.

When Odette found this puddle with her toe, she giggled.

"Skorpio," she whispered, "our Lola has sprung a leak. In the interest of your floor, I should stanch the flow of this cum, don't you agree?"

Without any warning, Odette let her go and Skorpio spun

her in his arms. Lola gasped with the sudden change of sensations: as the captain wrapped his muscled arms around her waist, thrusting against her backside, Odette knelt in front of her.

The slender woman spread her legs until Lola stood with her feet more than shoulder-width apart. Wide open she was, powerless in Skorpio's embrace as he kissed behind her ticklish ear—and that damned mistress of his stuck out her very pointy tongue and started to explore.

Around those wet lower lips she probed, pushing up Lola's mound with her hands to get better access. Her clit ached enormously: it had felt Odette's prying fingers before, so now it felt deserving of *everything* the feisty woman offered it.

Odette nipped and suckled, making Lola squirm even more. This woman knew precisely where to put that tongue and those lips! And for how long, and with how much pressure.

If she closed her eyes and pretended, it could be Rio giving her this tongue job.

But Rio was on duty during the day. And if she hollered for help, Cabana Boy knew better than to intrude on her behalf—and he'd be cheering his Greek boss on, anyway.

So it was just Lola, struggling to maintain a shred of dignity. It was Lola, squirming and grunting, proclaiming her disgust and frustration while her body sang another song altogether.

Why were spasms spinning like a tornado inside her, just as they had with Rio in the spa pool? Her body was so damn fickle, when it came to whose attentions it would respond to! She was behaving like such a slut—

But then, hadn't this been part of the deal all along?

Once Fletch had abandoned her, and she'd revealed her deepest fantasies to Clive, the captain, and Rio, she could do any damn thing she pleased on this cruise! She'd never dreamed that would include getting caught in this kinky three-way she couldn't escape.

But she couldn't say they'd taken her against her will, either: once she'd tasted those smooth, intoxicating Greek lips ... heard Skorpio's moan in that rich, smoky accent, Lola was hooked. Odette was like the meringue on the lemon pie—light and frothy, but a very fine topper for the main filling.

So by God, Lola intended to enjoy the whole piece!

The captain was now panting against her backside, so she gave him some relief: she rose up on her toes—and he slid between her legs!

"Oh, yes! I can have you both now!" Odette exclaimed.

And damned if that woman didn't alternate between sucking Skorpio's cock and licking Lola's slit, when he retracted to give her another pump. With her legs spread this way, the captain was rubbing some very sensitive tissues. Lola could only gape when his reddish-purple tip poked out beneath her bush, as Odette licked him like a lollipop.

How many firsts had she experienced this week?

But who was counting?

So Lola gave herself over to them, deciding it was no real shame to be enslaved by her body's responses to Skorpio and Odette. It would be odd if she did *not* respond to such a pretty, provocative pair.

Odette was now lapping at her thigh with that tongue. Slim and damp and pointed it was, as it snaked its way up to her midsection.

Here, Odette stopped. Rolled her face against Lola's belly.

"So soft, so lovely and warm," she murmured. "So much better today, skin to skin, than hidden beneath costumes."

With her eyes closed, and that mane of blue-black hair swaying with her every caress, the Greek female made a fascinating sight. It wasn't like Lola had planned to be suckled by an older woman, yet when Odette's lips closed firmly over one nipple, she let out a long, languid sigh.

"Why did you remove the polish?" she asked, her voice tinged with disappointment. "I adored that shade. She-devil red it was—like mine!"

Lola smelled another trap here: her Very Cherry peaks had vanished with all the rubbing Rio gave them in the pool. She wasn't about to go *there* in this conversation!

But her breasts betrayed her, aching for Odette to continue her liquid caress while Skorpio cupped her to make them stick out lewdly. What an illicit thrill, to be caught between these two, the object of their adoration!

"Lola," he murmured thickly. "We admire your sense of adventure. Your willingness to share your fantasies, to try things our way. So—"

Captain Scandalous gave her breasts another thorough fondling while his erection teased her from underneath.

"—we would all have more fun if you'd surrender to your wayward inclinations. Be the Lola you are with Rio DeSilva!"

A *huge* red flag shot up—but it was too late for caution, wasn't it? The captain had her where he wanted her, physically and psychologically. Odette was still working on her, too. Damn that tongue, making her nipples salute!

Lola had no choice. No escape.

"Wh—what would you have me do?" she asked, in a sycophant tone Lola Wright *never* used in real life!

"Ahhhhh . . . now you're talking!" he crooned. "Thrust yourself forward, my dear. Aim your body toward Odette after I sit us down."

The captain fell backwards, making her laugh nervously when they landed on the edge of the bed. Bad enough that he was now in control, and Odette was loving it. He would start giving orders, she sensed. Once a captain, always a captain.

"You have two hands, Miss Wright. Stroke yourself."

Lola 's eyes widened. It was one thing to pleasure herself

when she was alone. But to caress her most intimate parts while Odette—her nemesis and competition—watched?

"Yes, please," the lovely woman pleaded. She was kneeling in front of them now, her face alight with a provocative sexuality. As though to reassure her, Odette leaned back on the rug, let her long legs fall open from the knees, and began to caress her own inner lips.

They were dusky pink, in contrast to her olive skin. And that brazen black Mohawk shifted with each stroke; a mesmerizing effect, Lola had to admit. She found herself staring at those two busy fingers, at the slickness which made a wet, suggestive sound in the quiet room. Odette smelled . . . well, *ready*.

And then she felt herself giving in to a temptation like she'd never known, and to inclinations that came out of hiding from deep inside her.

Still watching Odette, Lola slipped her hand between her thighs. Skorpio eased her back against his chest as they sat on the edge of the bed, so she was wide open at Odette's eye level. Wide open and melting from the heat of that woman's gaze. She found her pubes, and began to manipulate the folds of damp skin.

"Yes, let me watch," Odette rasped, her fingers increasing their speed. Her hips were quivering and Lola could see the dew on her scarlet nails while that hot skin grew pinker . . . more inflamed from watching *her* as she caressed herself.

"Stick some fingers inside," Skorpio breathed. "Let me guide you—"

The man was shameless! He not only slid her fingers into position, but inserted his own along with them! Lola felt very full and hot and needy, and as her hips ground against the Greek's, he, too, got more involved in their play. Odette was so damned *into* this little game, her eyes went shut and she was moaning like she wanted to explode.

Then the woman sprang from the floor, so inflamed she had to put out that inner fire. She pushed them both backwards by giving Lola a shove on her chest.

Skorpio grunted, chuckling as he went down with Lola on top of him, while Odette positioned herself between their four legs. Rubbing and riding—writhing like a snake trying to shed its skin—Odette now lay directly on top of her.

And dammit, Lola felt herself beginning to spasm. Rising from both ends at once, frustrated yet fascinated, because Skorpio held her so tightly around her chest.

"Let me—"

"Take it!" he said hoarsely. "Take her, Odette! Fuck her—be relentless! Make her come!"

His partner was only too willing. The beauty with the black hair straddled their hips, and Lola got a massage from above and below. Her poor body didn't know who to respond to: Odette's weight rested against her pubic bone, and she could feel Skorpio's erection stroking where her fingers had been moments ago.

They were all panting, but Lola cried out first. What a desperate, despicable—downright delicious!—predicament, to be held prisoner between them, until she could take no more! And then to have her hips wiggle like they'd never stop—

Next thing she knew, Odette was tossing her aside, onto the bed. Lola protested, but before she could move, the other woman had slung her long leg over Skorpio and impaled herself on his manhood.

Triumphant, she hung on like a bronc buster, raring back so her breasts jiggled with each thrust and her hips angled forward with each rampant stroke. Thoroughly amused and aroused, Skorpio grabbed her hips to set the tempo up a notch or two, until he was buried deep inside her.

Their climax was like nothing Lola had ever seen in the best porn flicks. But dammit! Skorpio had promised himself to *her* today! They'd led her to believe that "whatever Lola wants" was the theme for this encounter!

Wasn't it? Or had she only imagined the captain wanted her? Was he using that velvety voice and those midnight eyes to lead her into thinking whatever he wanted her to believe?

With a wicked laugh, Odette fell forward onto the handsome captain. He kissed her with gusto, obviously as enthralled by their lovemaking, and their deception, as she was.

Then they both looked at Lola, so alone on the crumpled coverlet yet mere inches away from them. Odette's lip curled.

"Too bad you didn't learn your lesson onstage yesterday. This is only *part* of your penance for what I saw in the pool last night," she said in a menacing whisper. Her eyes glowed like a cat's and she looked ready to unsheathe her claws. "If you think you can sneak around with Rio, and no one will know you've reneged on Skorpio's generous bargain, you're a bigger idiot than I thought, Lola. Now get out of my sight."

Odette stood up, making Lola feel even lower.

"Aric's waiting for you. *He* wants you, too—but don't think you'll get away with *that*, either!" she continued her tirade. "This ship is a fish bowl, and all the little fishies report to the big ones."

She crossed her arms beneath her breasts, a bitch in heat moving to the finale. "And from where I see things right now, you rank right up at the top of the water, Miss Wright. With the floaters and the *scum*."

How was *that* for afterglow? While Lola was no quitter, it was time to make herself scarce. She slipped off the bed, yanked her rumpled clothes from the floor, and went to the front room to get dressed.

Of course Cabana Boy was there to witness her degradation. His upper teeth indented that thick lower lip as he controlled his—what? Laughter? Humiliating remarks? Lola suspected he'd watched them the whole time, bringing himself off, just because the people on this ship seemed to play that way. Monkey see, monkey do.

Monkey strum, monkey cum.

"Get me out of here," she muttered, disgusted because she'd fallen for Skorpio's tricks again. "And get me a—"

Grinning, Aric pulled a cigarette pack from his shirt pocket. "Light, Priestess?"

Was it a sincere offer, or that damn microphone again? She swatted the Camels from his hand and stalked down the hall.

27

An ivory envelope was tucked under the suite door, with her name printed in a perfect calligraphic script. Tonight was the formal ball Clive Kingsley had invited her to!

Lola grinned. Not surprising that the charming Brit would write as properly as he behaved. And who could forget the hint of promise in his debonair voice when he'd mentioned this event?

It had to be more fun than getting screwed over—rather than screwed—by Skorpio, didn't it?

"So, Aric dahling," Lola teased when he peeked over her shoulder, "what's a girl have to do to get her favorite stylist to give her a fabulous new 'do for this ball tonight?"

Cabana Boy shrugged, yet she saw a secret shimmer in those pale green eyes. "Just part of my job, ma'am," he replied in a petulant voice. "And God knows if I don't do my *job*—"

"Oh, stop whining." Lola ran a flirtatious finger down the alluring indentations of his bare chest. "If you didn't enjoy fixing my hair and face, you wouldn't have done it last time—or even hinted you knew how. You can't fool me!"

Damn that smirk! It was a silent reminder of how Captain Scandalous had just deceived her. Again.

"Whatever you say, Priestess."

He mocked her with a bow, and she playfully kicked his butt. Then Lola went to her closet, glancing outside in the vague hope she'd see a handsome Spaniard smoking a little cigar on her balcony. She whipped out the dress of eggplant—no, *aubergine* and *cabernet*—stripes Kingsley had recommended, turning to Aric again.

"This is it, slave boy. Make me look fabulous, and maybe I'll reward you with a little something," she tossed over her shoulder as she entered the bathroom.

She was *not* expecting Cabana Boy to drop his pants and follow her into the shower.

He adjusted the water temperature to something warmer than she preferred, and then squeezed a generous dollop of body wash into her scrubbie.

"If you want to have the best time tonight," he murmured, massaging her back with suds, "you should forget about making it with Kingsley. He's not your type."

"And who are *you* to presume what my type—"

When Lola pivoted in the shower's spray, her earlier suspicions were confirmed in Aric's grin. "So. Our concierge, the designer of knockout ball gowns, doesn't *ball* the clients he outfits."

"Dear old Clive has some singular tastes, yes."

Aric's gaze raked over her bare body as he continued his scrubbie massage over her breasts, watching the swirl of white, lacy bubbles coat her skin like a tight-fitting cami. "But nothing else on the ship matches this event for sheer *spectacle*. He's into glitz and glamor."

Lola had to grin at the word *spectacle*, because here in the steam, Aric Petrocelli resembled that remark. Young and smooth and tanned and gorgeous and oh-so-nonchalant about his body.

His gold chain shimmered wetly—no crystal camera on it this time—and while he sported an erection, he wasn't putting any moves on her.

"So are *you* coming tonight?" she asked.

He smirked at her double-entendre. "Wouldn't miss it."

What did she see in Cabana Boy's eyes? While he obviously wasn't just washing her as part of his *job*, the lowering of his languid eyelids suggested secrets about to unfold. And while she was wishing for one night without any *nahsty* surprises, Lola had to admit she was having more fun paying off Fletch's debt than she would've had with the man himself. For one thing, she wouldn't have had this sleek, sexy young man tending her personal needs . . .

Aric was now kneeling on the floor of the shower, his saturated curls clinging to his head as he brought the scrubbie up the inside of her thigh . . . and higher . . . until he held the bright green, soapy muff against her own.

With a brazen grin, he started rubbing her *there*, in suggestive circular motions. He locked his gaze into hers.

"You are so *hot*, Priestess," he whispered.

Lola's breath caught. Had he really said that—about *her*? Or was the hiss of the shower disguising his words? "I—you surely can't mean—"

"I mean, the shape of your body—the softness of your skin—the way your sex smells," he said in that husky young voice. "Well, I'm signing your dance card early, Lola. Don't take this wrong, but Clive had ulterior motives for inviting you there tonight. Not for sex—although they say he's an all-night kind of guy."

"You think sex is the only reason I like men?" she teased.

But then her moan echoed in the shower stall. Cabana Boy was coaxing her legs farther apart, until she had to lean back against the wall because he was so relentlessly *washing* her. Down There.

His chuckle sounded villainous. And indeed, the kid got her excited to the point she needed him to finish what he'd started—was ready to prop her foot on his shoulder and demand some tongue—when he stood up.

Grinned at her.

Pivoted her in the spray, gently ducking her head so he could lather and rinse her hair. As he shut off the water, he pressed into her for a quick kiss before opening the shower door.

"No time to foo-foo around," he said lightly, grabbing one of the plush ivory towels. "Have to get the Priestess ready to be seen. Have to make her nothing less than stunning, so Clive can show her off."

It sounded like window dressing, didn't it? Was something wrong with this picture?

Even though she'd told herself—and Cabana Boy—that he was way younger than she preferred, Lola wouldn't have kicked him out of the bathroom had he propositioned her right now.

But he didn't. Just dried her nicely, limiting his reactions to an admiring smile. But damned if he didn't extend his arm across the door when she was ready to leave the steamy, white room wearing only a towel wrapped around her hair.

"Just so's you'll know," he said in that low, throaty voice, "there's nothing in this world hotter than a woman who keeps herself charged up. Guys can tell she's willing—not easy, just *aware*. Ready to be a player. But ready to walk away if he treats her like a cage is waiting, once he gets her home."

"A cage?" Lola pondered this as they walked into the bedroom. "That sounds like something from Whispers. Pretty kinky."

"Not if he treats you like a dog, it's not."

That was cutting too close to home! Lola slipped into the thick terry robe hanging on the closet door, eyeing him pointedly. "Let's leave Fletcher out of this, shall we?"

"You got it. Sit your pretty ass down and let's turn the Priestess into Cinderella."

Lola wasn't sure she understood his mixed metaphors, but she couldn't argue with Aric's results. This kid had poked fun at Kingsley's nontraditional talents, yet he himself had gotten extensive training in cosmetology.

Again he wound her wavy auburn hair into a chic knot, this time pulling a single tendril loose to hang at her right temple. Again he worked a miracle with the eye shadows and foundations in her makeup case, using subtle strokes and quick flicks of his fingertips to create a look so polished—so professional— Lola could only stare at the transformation in her mirror.

By the time he escorted her downstairs, in that exquisite dress that whispered with each step, she felt like a billion-dollar baby. Felt herself radiating positive vibes and yes, the message that she not only loved looking this fabulous—she could make good on the assumptions every man in the room would have!

Kingsley was clearly bowled over.

"My *word*, Lola darling," he breathed, circling her in his inner office. "I imagined this gown as a showpiece on you, but you've outdone yourself! I can't wait to introduce you to others, who've been *so* eager to meet you."

"Actually, it was Aric who—"

But when she glanced around for Cabana Boy, he'd disappeared.

"No doubt he's gone to get himself ready," Kingsley said with a rich chuckle. His blue eyes danced as he smoothed the gown's angel-wing sleeve, and then tucked her arm beneath his. "It's going to be a night like you've never known, dear Lola."

What could she say? They hadn't even arrived at the dance, and here she was strolling down the corridor of a luxury liner, wearing a dress that sold for more than she earned in a week, with the man who designed it! A night like no other, indeed!

Kingsley was decked out in a Caribbean blue tuxedo with a

sequined jacket that was a cross between Elton John and Elvis, yet his sense of glitz made her giddy. Not a single one of her clients would try that jacket on—*nobody* else she knew would venture out in formal wear so outlandish! Yet this Brit looked *so* in his element, so confident in his elegance, it was a thrill to be with him. To be whisked into a ballroom she'd never seen in the ship's diagrams, in her travel catalog.

When Clive opened the door for her, Lola's jaw dropped.

It wasn't just the huge ballroom, which had been transformed into an island paradise with neon palm trees and fiber-optic parrots that flashed in a succession of bright colors. And it wasn't the scantily clad triplets who called themselves Three Way, singing their hearts out to a beat they throbbed to—although Lola had to admit they gave *sister act* a whole new twist.

No, it was the roomful of people like she'd never seen in real life: slim young room stewards and waiters dressed in sophisticated tuxes with blinding white shirts, all dancing like they'd done time onstage and were damn proud of it. Some of the men—even older staff members—sported dinner jackets of peacock, and chartreuse, and even an electric shade of rose, yet here in this fantasy ballroom they looked exquisite. Absolutely stunning.

But the women! Such elaborate hairdos and out-there makeup . . . lean or lush, these ladies filled out ball gowns that outdid Cinderella a thousand times over, with sparkling trims and colors that outshone an electric rainbow.

Lola couldn't help gawking. Except for Kingsley, she didn't see a soul she knew, yet she wanted to meet every one of these attendees and hear their stories. Not just because they came from so many countries, but because they were glorified servants living their night life to the hilt.

"It's as though you not only created each gown expressly for the woman wearing it," Lola observed with awe, "but the dress now determines who she *is*. The same way this ultra-sophisticated gown has transformed me. Taken me from Portland to Paris for the evening."

The concierge beamed at her. "Thank you for noticing that, darling," he crooned as the music grew more raucous. "It's quite the ego trip, to say I designed most of the gowns in this room—as well as some of the more colorful tuxes. It's a whole realm of psychology in itself, color is. Don't you agree?"

"Oh, yes. While I'd never have chosen this gown for myself, it works a magic I hadn't anticipated," she mused, watching the crowd dance.

How can the wait staff afford this designer formal wear? her rational side cut into the fantasy.

But Lola decided not to ask. Better to compliment Kingsley than to question the priorities of those he'd outfitted.

A sparkly gown of candy pink caught her eye then, and she waved excitedly. "Why—that's Miss Christy from the spa! In the dress you were finishing the other night."

"Makes her complexion just *glow*, doesn't it?" Kingsley agreed as the masseuse grinned back at them. "And no ordinary gown would handle her *assets*."

Miss Christy *was* sticking out in all the right places—including the slit that opened all the way up to her tailbone, exposing lush butt cheeks swathed in iridescent stockings!

"Good Lord, she wouldn't even have to undress to—" Lola mused aloud. She watched the busty blonde shake her booty as she sang along with the triplets. "Miss Christy only has to lean over, and—"

"One could discover a whole new galaxy, complete with two moons," Clive quipped. He glanced toward the stage, nodding to the music's catchy beat. "This band gets everyone up and moving, but I'm sure you've surmised that Randi, Candi and Dandi are not among my clients."

She laughed at that one. The three skinny blondes crying into those mikes, jiving as the girl-gang band behind them played heavy-metal, wore bikinis to show off their tattoos and piercings. When the drummer segued into a solo, the trio yanked off their tops to reveal their nipple rings and chains, which began swinging in sync, like miniature jump-ropes, when the triplets shimmied together.

"Oh. My. *God*!" Lola blinked, gawking outright. "How do they—?"

Clive rolled his eyes. "Far be it from me to improve upon *that* talent! But seriously, dear Lola, I'm so very flattered that a professional clothier like yourself finds my designs distinctive."

The concierge shifted then, to stand between her and the stage, so she wasn't distracted by those gyrating butts and boobs.

"I've checked you out online, Miss Wright," he continued in that low, melting-chocolate voice she'd first been drawn to. "I truly admire the way you've made yourself the empress of menswear. Hoping, of course, you might want to feature *my* designs in your Well Suited shops. Or on your web site, perhaps."

Her stomach did back flips when Clive's sparkling blue eyes held hers captive. What was it Aric had hinted, about him being gay?

And why are all the really interesting men not interested in women? she mused with a sigh.

Lola didn't have the heart to point out that these gorgeous Kingsley Court gowns didn't figure into her menswear collection—not the way Clive was challenging her with his aristocratic grin.

But then he bowed slightly, stepping back. "I know this has taken you by surprise, and that such a decision requires careful thought. I'll await your answer patiently, Miss Wright."

"Thank you! I—" Once again the Brit's gentility left her breathless. "I hope you'll understand that I'm not writing you off if I—"

"And I hope *you'll* understand, dear lady, that as the host of these events, I must oversee the details that keep our staff coming. So to speak," he said as he bussed her temple. "Please help yourself to the buffet, and to a glorious time tonight! If you're open to surprise and delight, that's what you'll find here."

What could *that* mean? Lola watched him step deftly between the dancers, blowing kisses and wiggling his fingers at nearly every person in this crowded room. She saw Joel the jeweler waving back, resplendent in a turquoise tux, while Phillipe the maitre d' did his own version of the Wave, making the sequins on his red jacket shimmer like rubies.

It struck her then that the women far outnumbered the men, which was interesting since most of the staff in the dining rooms and serving the staterooms were male. And it struck her as well that she'd never seen a room full of such *dazzling* women—all shapes and sizes, yet beautifully coiffed and elegantly dressed and dancing to display themselves. Not a one of them was behaving like a lowly galley gopher or toilet tender: these ladies lived large! They knew how to shake it and make it!

Like they practice in front of the mirror.

She smiled, realizing that she, too, was swinging her hips to the music, even though she ordinarily refused to dance by herself or in a group of girlfriends. Lola began studying the faces then, looking for Cabana Boy. Hey, if he was going to be her warden, even in the shower, he could damn well dance with her like he'd said he would!

"We've gotta take our break now," Candi, Dandi, and Randi called out as one, "but we'll be baaaaaaaaaack!"

Applause rippled through the crowd. Some of the guests went for the buffet table, while others stayed on the dance floor awaiting the next song . . . preening themselves like the sequined peacocks and exotic cockatiels they resembled. Maybe scoping out the crowd for partners to slip away with?

But when the Rolling Stones blasted through the speakers, belting "Lola" at full force, a loud whoop went up. The neon ballroom decor and those fiber-optic parrots flashed at full tilt and the rest of the lights went out, so the mirror balls could rule like sparkly, spangly moons.

Lola shook her head, grinning at that old song she'd been teased about all her life. Most of the guests were singing along now, about how girls would be boys and boys would be—

"How is it that everywhere you go, Lola *mia*, the music hails you as the queen of the evening?" a mellow voice asked beside her ear.

She turned, only to be caught up in Rio's fast, passionate kiss. His eyes, when he released her, blazed with the flash of a mirror ball—or was it because he couldn't stop staring at her in this dress?

"Well," she murmured, shaking her hips to his rhythm as they began to dance, "while I'm guessing you requested this song, I *am* the queen, you know!"

Rio grinned enigmatically. "One among several, *querida*. But perhaps I shouldn't stray into that territory right now. Even though these formal evenings for the staff are a regular event, it took me two or three visits to figure it out."

Lola considered this, but not for long. While she'd heard several insinuations, they were of little concern to her—especially since this handsome Spaniard had shown up to dance, just when she needed a partner.

How lucky could she get?! DeSilva was decked out all in white: tails, trousers, a shirt with a Mandarin collar and button studs like diamonds. He flashed her a sensual grin as he moved in for a slow dance.

She realized then that she could gaze into this man's hazel eyes forever, and still not see all the fascinating things he was.

Just as she sensed Rio wanted to remain that focused on *her*. And for that long.

But no, she was letting her imagination run away with her—with her heart, which galloped like a wild mare chased by a stallion.

Except Rio was pulling her closer now. Swaying to the sultry beat as he admired her with those tawny, tender eyes. Sad eyes, yet so damned magnetic.

"Lola *mia*," he whispered, "you're the most beautiful woman I've ever met."

It came out unembellished, except for the flutter of his long lashes.

And as Lola was swept along by his magic, dipping and gliding without conscious thought, she nearly forgot her manners.

"I—thank you," she breathed. "It's not like I hear that every—"

"But you should. Because it's true."

An exaggerated sigh came from the couple on their left. Her awareness of Rio was still shimmering down her spine as Lola glanced over to behold a boldly coiffed, elegantly sheathed young lady in green. As the mirror ball flashed, it seemed to her she recognized that dress—

And then Lola noticed the glimmer of those lush cinnamon lips . . . the eyes that shone like moonlight as they invited her in—

By God, if another woman on this ship comes on to me, I'll—

"Aric!"

Had *she* said that?

Lola glanced at Rio, who didn't miss a beat. He balanced and swayed so she could stay in position to study her assumption, that the attractive person to her left was really—

My God, she'd blurted out the truth before she knew!

Lola's jaw dropped when she saw that yes, the green sheath was the gown she'd gotten from Kingsley and yes, it was Cabana

Boy wearing it so well! His sinuous sway made the satin ripple; made the loose cap of curls he'd done up in glittering pins look extremely . . . feminine.

Her breath escaped with a slow *hiss*. Did this explain why her warden, so aloof yet suggestive, *stopped* before his come-on became sex? It really *wasn't* because she was old enough to be—

Hell, I'll never be old enough to understand this! I saw this kid's cock in the shower, so how'd he tuck it out of the way to wiggle into that dress?

Aric grinned, loving her discomfort yet behaving like a perfect, well—*lady*. Then he—she—danced away, disappearing between the other couples in the arms of a tuxedoed partner.

Lola stared at DeSilva, totally flummoxed. "If nearly all these women are wearing gowns Kingsley designed," she reasoned in a halting whisper, "and if Aric looks better than I ever will in that green one . . . are you telling me that *none* of these women are really female?"

"If you're upset or offended—"

"No, no, just—"

What *was* the word for how she felt right now? Shocked? Flabbergasted? Astounded?

Humbled. Definitely humbled.

Lola sighed. "It's just that all those cute waiters and room stewards I've seen surely can't be here masquerading as—I've never looked that glamorous in my *life*!"

"Begging your pardon, *mi vida*, but—"

"No, let's save the begging for Cabana Boy," she wheezed. Then she managed a shrill laugh. "Who knew so many men on board could elevate cross-dressing to such an art form? This brings a whole new context to Kingsley's definition of *menswear*, doesn't it?"

DeSilva kissed her cheek, listening attentively.

Lola shook her head, still shell-shocked. "He called me the Empress of Menswear moments ago," she murmured, "yet *he* wants to be the king of queenswear! Holy shit. This is too much."

She felt Rio watching her as they swayed to the song's hypnotic beat, but she couldn't stop gawking at the other couples . . . speculating about which women really *were*, and which ones camouflaged themselves in this mirror-balled darkness to live out a fantasy she'd never dreamed existed.

After all, the guys wearing these colorful tuxes were part of this gay masquerade, too. And now that she studied them more closely, some looked a lot like girls.

Talk about a turn-around. Or at least for Lola it was.

And there beside the buffet table, Clive Kingsley stood watching her. His expression, so genteel and British—so damned handsome—told her he knew she *knew* now. Those blue eyes followed the way she danced in Rio DeSilva's embrace, but Lola sensed he was more interested in the way his creation draped and flowed with her movements.

So much for *that* fantasy.

"Do you suppose Miss Christy and I are the only natural women in this room?" she ventured. She gazed up at Rio, aware of how *male* he was as he effortlessly steered her between the other couples.

He chuckled. "You're sure those aren't implants?"

Lola let out an exasperated laugh, thinking back to her escapade in the spa. "I had the distinct impression Miss Christy was *all* woman, after the way she handled me during my massage—"

She caught sight of the masseuse then, a chesty confection who glistened like a cotton candy princess. Miss Christy danced with partner wearing a slim-cut tux of traditional black, whose dark hair hung loosely at collar length. Much like Rio's.

"Is he? Or isn't she?" DeSilva whispered.

Lola shook her head as the song came to an end. The tattooed triplets resumed their places on the stage.

"I have no idea," she murmured. "But after the way Kingsley asked about selling his designs in my stores, he's got *balls*, inviting me to here to make his point!"

"I've got balls," Rio whispered. He ran his tongue along the shell of her ear, pulling her closer. "I've got a point, too—and I'd definitely like to *make* it, Lola *mia*. Somewhere the security cams won't catch us."

28

Lola's heart pounded hard as he whisked her out of the ballroom and into the elevator. Oblivious to the guy making a room service delivery, Rio thumped a numbered button and then pressed her against the wall. His kiss felt absolutely ravenous—as desperate for attention as she was.

Had dancing among all those gender-bending couples whetted his appetite for a real woman? For *her*?

Or did it matter? For Lola, it was enough to be alone with him again—at least she was after that blue-uniformed Filipino got off. It was enough to know DeSilva had the same sort of surges and urges she did, from the moment they'd laid eyes on each other.

"I guess that guy delivering the food didn't want to dance?" she asked.

The elevator doors slid open and they started down a plain, narrow hallway.

"Kingsley doesn't invite everyone to his galas. You have to be *special*."

Rio slipped his key into the door, and then held her gaze before allowing her into his room. "I like Clive a lot, but I'm glad I'm not on his guest list. I'd have to keep sending regrets, and he doesn't take rejection well."

"Are we talking hissy fits and crying jags?" Something she needed to know, if she were to consider stocking his Kingsley Court clothing.

"Not in public. But a few times when his *friends* have departed for bluer waters—or told him to go jump overboard," DeSilva added with a grin, "our Kingsley's given a whole new meaning to the phrase 'drama queen.' Not a pretty sight."

He slipped his hand beneath her chin then, lowering his face until his lips were a mere inch above hers—until she rose on tiptoe to kiss him. Then he backed away.

"Understand, Lola *mia*," he whispered, "that all talk of other men stays outside this door. The only queen I want to think about right now is you."

Again he kissed her, until she saw stars and felt fireworks sizzling up her bare back. With his mouth still holding her hostage, Rio eased her into the room and fell against the door to close it. His hands roamed all over her, caressing and coaxing, lighting little fires with his fingertips. When he'd cupped her bare breasts beneath her dress, he reached back to unzip her.

Lola held her breath. Oh so slowly he was easing that zipper down, tugging with one hand and placing the other on her exposed skin. He switched positions with the quick pivot of a man on the dance floor, nailing her to the door with his mouth.

Deftly he slipped the angel-wing sleeve over her arm. Her dress slithered down, leaving Lola bare except for her whisper of an excuse for panties.

She slid her hands beneath his white jacket. It landed on the floor.

Rio moaned against her mouth, kissing her more passionately as she unbuckled him. Behind her, the secretive ripping of foil spurred her on, and Lola shoved his trousers past the shaft that had been making his point ever since they'd left the ballroom.

She blinked. What kind of man didn't wear underwear with a tux?

A very randy Spaniard!

And just how did he propose to—

Very quickly—and up against the door! Omigod—

Lola gasped when Rio's mouth pulled away from hers. He was hiking her up in his arms, to let her shoulders fall back against the wood—to wrap her legs around his waist, while he gazed into her eyes like he was going to set her on fire.

"Lola," he rasped.

The sound of her name spoken in that accent—so lazy and laid-back, yet so damned hot and bothered—made her insides quiver. Somehow he'd already sheathed himself. He'd lowered her just enough to feel that warm, insistent tip at her opening. Even through his latex and her silk, he felt hot and damp.

Or was that her own wetness?

"Yessss," she replied, yanking the crotch of her panties aside. "Really hard this time. I want to scream with—"

Rio thrust inside her, cradling her ass in his hands. She cried out with the force of his need, with the way his fingers indented her flesh. She would feel branded forever, long after he let go— if he ever truly did. She would crave this kind of rough-and-tumble ride every time he took her now.

God, he wanted her! So badly he couldn't even take off her panties—used them to stimulate her clit, and to accentuate the clandestine feel of this tryst. Anyone walking down the hall could hear what they were doing.

"Tell me when," he commanded, his shirttail flapping around their grinding hips. "Tell me how badly you want it."

"Not yet! Not—" Lola raised her knees, so she could maneuver her legs over his shoulders.

He held her suspended, at his mercy as he relentlessly drove his cock into her. This angle intensified their heat, and Lola thought she might pass out from sheer ecstasy.

Yet when he saw her strappy sandals beside his face, he grinned. Nipped her ankle.

"You love it this way!" he remarked in a smoky voice. "You got all excited, thinking about those odd couples and their—"

"I creamed the moment I heard your voice," Lola corrected him. "You could've spread me on the buffet table and snarfed me down like—"

"Shrimp cocktail. A feast in itself," he teased.

His golden eyes were shining with need. He was still moving inside her, subtle circlings to make the band of her panties rasp against his shaft. "But I have this maddening fantasy to devour you like a hot fudge sundae instead, *querida*. Right after I take your edge off."

Was that a promise or a dare?

As DeSilva pumped faster, the slapping of their skin and their mingled musk sent her soaring into a world of want. When she closed her eyes, there was only the maleness of him, claiming her, and the way she flexed and squeezed . . . bore down against that mindless whirling, that irrevocable ache that begged to be sated.

Her head fell back and she surrendered. Rocked and curled in on herself, and then spun away into space until her body went slack.

Panting, both of them. Reeling from an eclipse of his sun and her moon until it was safe to see again.

When she peeked at him through one slitted eye, Rio laughed.

"I wasn't kidding about the ice cream and the chocolate sauce," he said, holding her close. He walked very carefully, kissing her and then disengaging her hips. "I'm going to fetch it now, while you arrange yourself on my coffee table. You're my dessert, sweet lady."

Dessert? As she gazed up at him, Lola wasn't believing this

guy. He'd just popped his cork and poured her out, as well, but he was going for more!

She rested on the cool glass top of his table, listening while he rummaged in his fridge. Yanked off her soaked panties to cool herself beneath the lazy ceiling fan. The hum of a microwave ended in a *beeeeep*.

Were they in Rio's quarters? Except for the light coming in from the other room, the place was dark. She couldn't tell much about her surroundings, except they were much smaller than her suite and not as nice.

Not surprising, yet she was curious about the way this man had personalized his rooms: colors and wall decor, and what he had sitting around on his shelves, would reveal a lot about the Spaniard who remained a mystery even after she'd made love to him. Twice now.

Well, going on thrice: Rio was looking down at her with a devilish grin, ice cream carton and chocolate sauce in hand. A can of Reddi-wip rested in the crook of his elbow. His hair brushed loosely against the tabs of his collar.

"Let's not smear chocolate all over that nice shirt," she hinted.

When he set down the ice cream to finish undressing, Lola reached toward the open carton. She hooked a finger into the softer stuff around the edge, and then—looking him right in those tiger eyes—sucked on it.

Mmm, butter brickle. Not that she'd figured him for a plain vanilla type.

"Do that again," he whispered. "I like watching my food play with herself."

She laughed, gesturing lewdly before she licked her middle finger clean.

"Eat me," she challenged. Those nerves were beginning to curl again.

"Oh, I intend to. Every sweet, fucking inch of you, Lola *mia*."

He'd said the F word—in that same cultivated tone that bespoke lazy Mediterranean afternoons in open courtyards. So far removed from the way most men used it, she squirmed at the images it brought to mind: his lips roaming all over her, while his tongue would drive her wild in all her favorite places, too.

It was so good to be with a real man, wasn't it? Cabana Boy in the shower had been a nice work-up, and an admiring Clive to dress her to the nines was fine, too. But when it came right down to it, who could pass up a guy just wild for making love to her, in every way he could think of? In ways no other man had imagined.

When the first dollop of ice cream plopped between her breasts, Lola sucked air.

"Don't you dare move," DeSilva instructed, letting another scoopful fall to her middle. "I'm creating a masterpiece much more delicious than Kingsley's."

"And more satisfying than Aric's," she wheezed. It was a real effort to lie still when that third melting ball of butter brickle landed on her navel.

"We can't expect a boy toy to fill a man's shoes—or my woman's pussy. Can we, *querida*?"

God, what was it with the way he said those words? Rio DeSilva no doubt spoke English as his second language, yet he caressed the words in all the right places . . . had called her his woman! In such a romantic way, she yearned to believe it.

But the warm drizzle of hot fudge on her belly distracted her. Like liquid velvet, it drifted along her skin and pooled in her belly button until she was giggling and wriggling—

"Ah! I'm not finished!" he said. "If my creation slides off onto the floor, I'll make you kneel and eat it—naked, without a spoon. Maybe with your hands tied behind your back.

"And then we'll have to start all over," he added solemnly, "so I can have *mine*."

Ooooh, something yipped inside her when he talked that way! She was *so* tempted to sit up and lay him one across those wicked lips, just to defy his orders. Just to make him *make* her do as he'd said!

But Lola behaved herself. Practiced the patience of a saint as he shook that can of whipped cream so slowly, he must've been waiting for the damned ice cream to melt, so she'd *still* have to lap it up while he watched her.

Just the furtive spurt of air escaping the can, and then the squirt of thickened cream from the nozzle had her laughing. God, he was circling her boobs with it! Zigzagging around those mounds of ice cream, along that river of fudge sauce— down to *her* mound.

He drew a new pair of panties for her. A thong, really, the way he trailed the cool, white cream between her lips.

"Would you *eat* already?" she teased. "My God, Rio, there's enough sundae here for—"

"For both of us to enjoy. One way or another."

He knelt beside the table, his chestnut hair swinging around his face and his golden body taut.

"One for you," he intoned, spooning some ice cream and fudge sauce up to her mouth. "And one for me."

Lola closed her lips around the spoon, thinking how goofy this was—how it had been years since she'd allowed herself so much sugar and—

"One for you," he repeated in that low, sexy voice. "And another for me."

His mustache flickered as he swirled his ice cream around in his mouth, watching her. Her lush body was smeared with pale golden cream and umber fudge, with crinkly streams of Reddi-Wip melting down her pert breasts and into that rust-colored fur between her lovely legs.

That she was actually holding still for this amazed him.

But then, he'd seen Lola Wright in action for five days now

and considered her a miracle in motion. A mixture of minx and Madonna who—

He was getting way ahead of himself.

"You're a treat, Lola *mia*. Thank you for indulging my fantasies," he murmured. "Thank you for playing along without fussing about fat and calories and—well, it's a joy to be with someone who can play like a child and love like a woman. Who doesn't give a damn about getting messy or—"

She shushed him with her finger. Held absolutely still, even when his next bite of ice cream slipped from his spoon back onto her stomach.

"Whoever she was," Lola whispered, "she's not here now."

His Adam's apple bobbed. He nodded solemnly.

"And besides," she teased him, "you're going to lick every drop of this stuff off my body! And then you're gonna kiss my cherry until I say you can stop. And then you'll ram that banana inside me again, so I can squeeze the cream out of it. When you promise me a sundae, DeSilva, you damn well better *deliver*. Got it?"

Her wink made him laugh out loud, chasing the ghost of that other woman from the room.

"Whatever Lola wants," he said, spooning up more of the melting ice cream. "Your wish is my command, sweet queen."

It went quickly then, the fudge sauce he smeared with his spoon and the dribbles he lapped from her skin as she quivered from giggling so hard. Whipped cream caught on his mustache when he licked her midsection, and she smeared him up good when he stuck his tongue in her belly button and made her double up.

Deep, chocolate kisses . . . the abrasion of brickle bits when he sucked them from her nipples . . . the rumble of laughter in his chest as he assaulted her with lips that kissed up the remaining sludge, on his way down to where her legs waved in the air with her laughter.

Her toes curled inside her high-heeled sandals. If she lived forever, she'd *never* forget these sensations, or the man who'd brought them on.

DeSilva paused at the apex of her thighs. Even when her slit was white with melted cream, he could smell her sex. Her *need* to be refilled.

His spoon clattered to the floor. He scooped her into his arms and tossed her on the couch, his movements desperate. When his fingers parted her and he lapped the length of her slit, Lola cried out. She grabbed his ass, wanting that cock that bobbed just beyond her reach, so Rio swung his leg over.

When she took him in her mouth, the Spaniard let out a few words in his native tongue and then went at her, until they were both writhing out of their minds. Somehow they slid off the edge, and somehow Rio broke their fall.

And then he rolled them over on the rug, so *she* was on top. Confined between the table and couch, yet feeling freer than she'd ever known sex to be.

Lola dug the toes of her shoes into the rug as he brought her off with those powerful tongue strokes. And then she let DeSilva have it, payback for the way he'd so mercilessly made her his dessert. With his shaft in her hand, she concentrated on the warm, smooth tip of him, sucking hard, until his breathing got ragged.

He erupted in her mouth.

"I'll get you for that!" he rasped. He rousted her up off the floor before she was ready, smacking her ass to steer her toward the bathroom.

"*What*?" she protested. "I gave you exactly what you wanted!"

"Twice! In one night!" he mocked, twisting the handle of the shower faucet. "I'm not twenty anymore, you know!"

"And your *point* would be?" She grabbed him again as warm water sprayed around them. He was limp, yes, but he was laughing like he was way happier than he'd been for a long time.

Rio kissed her, like some wild thing much younger than twenty getting his first taste of sex and wanting a big gulp of it. Then he held Lola against the wall of the shower, watching her breasts rise in rhythm with his as the rivulets of water ran in wet patterns on their skin. His fingers found *her* again, too, and he strummed her like a guitarist who truly loved his instrument.

"If I die from this tonight, will you miss me, Lola *mia*?"

It went straight for her heart, his question. But it wasn't the time to answer it—not when he was revving her up, to see if she'd come again. Even in the steamy dimness, she could read that challenge in his eyes.

"If you die from this tonight, Rio *mio*," she teased, "I'll know you went out a happy man."

"You've got that right. You've got it *all* right, *querida*."

Her low chuckle echoed in the shower stall. "That's why I'm . . . Miss Wright. Get it?"

Rio slipped his fingers inside her, making her arch backward against the wet wall. "Oh, I got it, Lola. So now I'm giving it back to *you*. If you ever think I'm finished, I'll make you think again."

Thinking was the furthest thing from her mind—if indeed she had anything left in her head. Her pussy was still sensitive from their previous escapades, so in a matter of moments she was yelping and thrusting against his palm again.

Absolutely amazing, how bad Rio DeSilva made her want it. Had she found a lover who could keep her coming back for more—or just coming—more times than she could count?

Lola only had enough strength to let this handsome man massage her body with lemon-scented soap, and then caress her all over to rinse it off. Her knees felt so rubbery, she didn't fuss when he wrapped her in a towel and carried her to his bed.

Never had a man made her feel so special. So desirable. So crazy for sex.

As she lay limply, watching Rio turn on the light in his closet, Lola realized that every flat surface of this small bedroom displayed framed photos of a little girl. A dozen pictures, at least.

She rolled closer to the night stand, squinting in the dimness. Wow, this kid was a cutie—and she flashed an endearing smile that looked awfully familiar, minus the mustache.

Lola's heart dropped into her stomach. "Your daughter?" she wheezed.

God, had she fallen for a married one? A devoted daddy, no less?

Rio ran his finger fondly over the photograph nearest her head.

"My Chloe," he murmured, his voice thick with emotion. "And after next week's cruise, I'll be leaving my post on the *Aphrodite* to become her full-time father. At last!"

A lump the size of Texas rose into Lola's throat. "I see."

29

Stupid, stupid, stupid! her inner voice chided. *Why WOULDN'T a man like Rio be married? God, he could have any woman on the face of the earth!*

"Her mother was an international model," he went on softly. "A woman who stunned the fashion world with her beauty."

See there? We're not talking about some small-potatoes American businesswoman here.

Lola sat up, feeling drained and queasy and—well, *used*.

But Rio wasn't finished rubbing her nose in it. He grabbed her shoulders, leaning down so she had no choice but to gaze into those golden eyes and see the love light there. Burning for someone else.

"I loved her madly," he breathed. "But Katya didn't want to be tied down. Didn't tell me about our child, until I saw the two of them together in a magazine ad. I—I couldn't miss the resemblance."

Her eyes widened. The man who sat down on the edge of the bed was more than naked now. He'd exposed himself from the inside out. Lola's hand went to his knee before she knew what it was doing there.

"Helluva way to find out." She felt Rio shaking, as though the wound still oozed. "How old was Chloe then?"

"Almost three. Katya's career was skyrocketing, and she'd refused my offers of marriage so many times—"

Rio paused to catch his breath, like a mountain climber unprepared for the higher elevation. "Motherhood had seemed the farthest thing from her mind before we broke it off. She'd always been so—so *careful* not to conceive."

"But she had your baby. Wow."

Lola closed her eyes to let out a long breath. What a roller coaster ride, coming out of a triple loop-de-loop of mind-blowing sex, into a discussion about international relations. And his *child*.

"I—I can see you're crazy for Chloe," she murmured. "And I can't fault Katya's taste in partners—can certainly understand how you got under her skin, so to speak."

DeSilva's eyes flashed sadly.

"I wasn't the only habit Katya had that way. She was very young when she came into so much money and fame. The endless cycle of photo shoots and stress and cocaine . . ."

He paused to gaze at his little girl again. "More stress as she became more in demand, so more drugs bombarding a body she kept fashionably anorexic.

"Not even Wonder Woman could've survived such abuse," he continued in a thin voice. "She was only twenty-eight."

"I'm so sorry," Lola squeaked.

She grabbed his hand, feeling bad about the tragedy this man still suffered—and yes, feeling bad for herself, too. She'd fallen for that 'Whatever Lola Wants' fantasy, forgetting that all these men vowing to make it come true had real lives off the ship. Same as she did.

Lola found a smile for the pretty child who'd inherited her father's long lashes and tawny eyes, and whose chestnut pigtails were the replicas of Rio's hair, too.

"But lucky Chloe, to have a daddy like you," she made herself say. "Where will you live? What will you do, now that you won't be a security agent?"

His handsome face eased into a smile.

"My family's estate in the hills above Palma, Mallorca, will be a wonderful place for Chloe to grow up," he said in a hopeful voice. "For the first time, she'll have the stability of a home, and she can make friends! She'll have a father who adores her. I—I confess that I'm overjoyed, while feeling overwhelmed, as well."

Rio looked up from the photograph, his eyes ablaze with more than the lamp light. "I want to do right by her, Lola *mia*. Raising a six-year-old . . . alone . . . is a lot different from spoiling her senseless on the weekends we've spent together."

Alone. That word quivered between them as Rio DeSilva's gaze deepened.

Was it wishful thinking, or was this man pondering her possibilities? Wondering if she'd take that wild, uncharted journey into parenting with him?

She bit her lower lip. Looked at Chloe again to lessen the intensity of his golden, high-beam eyes. Felt so damn jittery, sitting against him, that she got off the bed to study the other photographs he'd collected over the years.

God, I need a smoke.

No ashtray on the night stand. Shit. One of those sexy little cigars sounded pretty good about now, but she'd have to keep acting interested in these pictures. This was his daughter; a part of him that would never go away, no matter how the script of her fantasy went.

Here was Chloe and a very thin, chic European woman— Katya, obviously—in an ad for high-dollar moisturizer.

Now, Chloe blowing out the five candles on her cake, and then with her little arms and legs wrapped around Rio as he held her, sleeping sweetly, against his shoulder—

You're doing it again! You'd say "how high?" in a heartbeat, if DeSilva asked you to jump!

Where had *that* thought come from?

Lola tugged her towel tighter around her breasts, caught in an emotional whirlwind. She hadn't even known Rio a week! Hadn't she sacrificed enough of herself, for a relationship with another man who'd betrayed her trust?

Swallowing hard, feeling Rio's gaze following her around his room, she kept after herself. Steeling herself against a sad little smile that resembled her own at Chloe's age.

How could five minutes of looking at this kid, listening to this wounded daddy's tragic tale, make her forget all about the business she'd built from scratch? Why did menswear suddenly seem so shallow, compared to mothering?

And why was she even *thinking* about the questions this Spaniard was asking with his eyes? He'd brought her here for mind-boggling sex, to catch her in a weak moment so he could trot out his personal life. Reel in a mommy for Chloe, before she knew what hit her. How conniving was *that*?

And you're falling for it, too, honey. Hook, line, and sinker.

"I—I wish you and Chloe all the best," she replied resolutely. She set the last photo down with a decisive *thump*. "I wasn't much older than that when I found out my mom only married my father because I was on the way."

Now why had she let *that* puppy out of the crate again? Were her mouth and mind going to betray her, just like her body had?

But she couldn't unsay it, could she? The man sitting naked on the bed, already baring his soul to her, would pester her until she spilled the rest of her story, too. It was only fair.

DeSilva was already up and wrapping his arms around her.

"I've been thinking about this a lot. Wondering how any parent could let a sweet, sensitive girl hear such a thing," he clucked against her damp hair.

Lola had to laugh at that one. "Well, if this sweet, sensitive girl hadn't been listening at their door, she might not've found that out. But then, it was pretty hard not to hear them fighting.

"I hated it when they went at each other," she murmured, revisiting those hostile scenes in her mind. "At that age, when you think the whole world revolves around you, it's easy to believe you *caused* the problem. Especially when snatches of their conversation, with your name in it, wake you up at night."

Dammit, he was holding her close now, swaying with her to console the frightened child she'd been. And she was clinging to him.

"I'm so sorry, Lola *mia*," he whispered. "You were so very young to be learning about issues that even grown-ups can't handle well."

She shrugged, craving his warmth despite all the warning sirens wailing in her mind. "It was no surprise that Dad walked out on us. Or rather, he just didn't come home for nights at a time, until it stretched into forever. I figured that must be my fault, since—"

"How could that be? You couldn't help it they were careless with their passions," he asserted. "And with your feelings, as well, it seems."

He lifted her chin. Gazed down at her with eyes that pooled with compassion. "My mission with Chloe has always been to love her completely. To prove to her again and again that she was *not* an accident, and that neither of us could've prevented Katya's death."

"A tall order." Lola closed her eyes, trying not to get lost in the clean, fresh scent of him, and the way his warmth made her feel so . . . wanted. She'd had damn little real loving, and this was getting dangerous.

"I used to dream about going after Daddy," she went on wistfully. Too late to turn back now, wasn't it? "I believed that if I could be smarter in school—if I could bake him his favorite cookies whenever he wanted, or sing well enough to travel in his band—I'd be good enough to win him back. Good enough to make him stay."

"Oh, Lola—"

"I know, I know," she added when his scowl bent that sexy mustache downward. "With years of practice and therapy, I've figured out that I was plenty good enough all along. It was *Dad's* problems, and Mom's, that made them split. He just never gave me credit for the things I did well. Same as Fletcher."

Well, she'd jumped in head-first now, hadn't she? Just begging to get hurt again, the way she was playing for Rio's affection.

"No, Lola," he said, holding her very still now. "You haven't given *yourself* the credit you deserve. Few women could've created your menswear empire, or gotten this far in life on their own. And yet, where it counts, *querida*, you've never rewarded yourself for your success."

DeSilva gazed into her green eyes, so large and lovely he wanted them to be his looking glass from here on out. Did he dare state his case more specifically? Would he scare her more than he already had?

"High time you found a man who appreciates how loving and competent you are," he said, stroking the damp strands of hair from her face. "A man who treats you like his queen by day and loves you like a mistress by night."

What she wouldn't give to *believe* his lines, spoken in that Mediterranean eloquence that caressed her all the way down to where she needed him most. Rio DeSilva instinctively knew how to excite her mind as well as her body. And he was making himself so available, so open to her, with gentle kisses that accentuated what he was saying.

But this was sounding a lot like that fantasy he and the captain cooked up in Kingsley's office, after Fletch left her.

"I need some time—and some sleep! Good grief, it's nearly three," she murmured, looking at his bedside clock.

It sounded lame, probably, but now that she was worn out from their lovemaking and relaxed from that shower, going to bed sounded heavenly. *Alone*.

Right after she took a Camel ride.

She looked into Rio's face, haunting in the lamp light. "Thank you for what you've given me tonight—and for something to think about," she said. "Especially for believing I could be what you're wanting in a woman . . . in a mother for your Chloe."

Okay, maybe that sounded presumptuous. But if DeSilva took offense or shut her down, well—she knew better than go any farther with this cozy little scene, didn't she?

He pulled her against his bare body for one last, fabulous kiss.

"I promise you things will get better, Lola *mia*. We don't have to live lonely any more."

God, how she wanted to believe that.

30

I want a man who can keep me coming all night long.

Had she really said that?

God, did we really DO that?

Lola lit her next cigarette from the red ember of the one still in her mouth. The ash tray on her table was overflowing, and she hadn't eaten or dressed yet. Every time Cabana Boy came to her bedroom door, she curled her lip at him.

"Hey! I can get you more smokes. I can order up lunch," he said in a wounded voice. "What the hell happened last night?"

"I saw you in my dress, for one thing." She glared at him, disillusioned with herself, mostly. "You keep your secrets and I'll keep mine, okay?"

He rolled those pale green eyes—the drama queen unmasked—and went for the phone in the living room. "I'm calling room service. Last chance to say what you want."

"Stay outta my face. And outta my closet!" she called after him. "Go out and play with the guy who delivers your food, why don't you?"

"Soooooo, the Priestess must've struck out last—yeah, hi, Julio. Aric here, up in the Aphrodisia Suite."

His voice had gone softer and he turned his back, which suited Lola just fine. She shut the door and locked it. Didn't really care what or who he wanted to eat. Just wanted some time to *think*, for chrissakes.

Ten straight hours of sleep hadn't fixed what was wrong, and as Lola riffled her Tarot deck, the cards weren't sliding together right, either. Telling her she was too impatient—trying to force things when a lighter touch, a better head, would set things right again.

Like that was going to happen.

She'd fallen for Rio DeSilva that first moment she met him at the gangplank, and he'd been nibbling away at her ever since. She'd told herself he was just for sex—the flavor of the day—because at the end of the cruise he'd be history.

But he had to take her to his room. Had to let her see all those pictures of the little girl who was *so* him. And so cute. And so alone.

Stop it! Look what you're doing to yourself!

Lola stared at the cigarette wedged between her quivering fingers, and at the turquoise pack with only two Turkish Jades left in it. It was the pack she'd carried in her purse, wrapped in tape, for nearly a year. The Camels Aric gave her were long gone.

Disgusted, she stubbed it out, which made the ash tray overflow. Pissed with herself, she swept the whole crumpled mess off the table with one swift flick of her wrist. Watching the flecks of ash catch the sunlight as they drifted toward the floor gave her a feeling of great satisfaction.

But not for long. After all these months of going without, she was on one helluva nicotine trip and couldn't hold a thought or a feeling for more than a moment at a time. Too damn jittery.

She closed her eyes and tried to mix her cards again. They

felt cool and detached, and their edges butted into each other instead of dancing gracefully between her hands.

Like you and DeSilva, doing the tango in perfect sync—
Forget him! He'll never happen for you.

Lola let out her breath. Went limp in the chair. Let her mind wander into that state where associations and images appeared on their own, rather than consciously bringing them up.

"What's going on here? Why am I such a mess?" she muttered. It was her question for the cards, and when she laid them out in a Celtic Cross, the pictures made the answer perfectly clear.

They were all men.

Several of them were upside down—guys hated that!—and these reversals explained why she felt so conflicted.

"Pretty well tells the tale, doesn't it?" she muttered, considering the positions and what the cards meant there. "I'm that Knight of Swords, searching for the truth—crossed by that sneaky Seven of Swords guy, who is really Dennis. And I'm asking this question because that man in the reversed Four of Pentacles *so* reflects my loss of control. Like I ever had any."

Lola sighed, shaking her head over how the cards portrayed her predicament so accurately. There was that Five of Swords in the Past Energy position again—Fletch, who'd started this whole mess. And there was the Knight of Wands in the Present . . . the bold fellow in red, whom Rio had identified as himself in her last spread. Uh huh.

The Future and Final Outcomes positions showed *her* losing it—losing her hold on all she tried to juggle in that Two of Pentacles reversed, and caught up in the conflicts of that Five of Wands. Come to think of it, the five guys batting at each other could well be Captain Scandalous, Aric, Kingsley, Fletch and Rio. And as if that weren't enough negative news, the overturned treasure chest in position seven said she saw herself getting dumped, losing everything. That King of Cups—the guy

Rio had identified with, as the *winner*—was now pouty and moody in the ninth position. Stuff she had to work through.

At least she could laugh at the Ace of Wands in the eighth place: even reversed, that rod with the fiery tip looked too damn phallic between those masculine hands: others saw her as their tool, and they were using her to get their jollies.

And what can we learn from this?

Lola drummed the table with her fingers. She hated it when her head played teacher.

It's a game to them! Next week, with a new slate of guests, they'll be pulling the same sexy stunts to relieve the monotony of life on the Love Boat.

Yeah, but how often did a passenger disappear to Aruba and leave his fiancée to pay off his debts?

Her fingers turned into a spider creeping toward those last two Camels, and she had to sit on her hands.

The real question is, how many women has Rio DeSilva made love to all night long in his room, and spilled his guts to afterward? How many potential mommies has he romanced?

And why did she want to be the one he kept?

Lola stood up. Went to her balcony and gazed out over the port of St. Thomas, with its brilliant blue water, and honking horns, and streets crowded with cars and shops and shoppers. The sunlight was so brilliant she had to squint to look at the other cruise ships docked along the harbor's edge—

Yet all she could see was Rio's face, in the glow of that little cigar he was lighting. She felt the shimmy of goose flesh where he'd kissed her and lapped champagne, that first night she'd been out here with him. Lola had hoped to take home some unique accessories for her clients, yet the only souvenirs she'd accumulated were sensations. Pretty pictures in her head. A knot in her heart for a six-year-old.

Intangibles, yet they tore at her.

Was there no place she could go where she wouldn't see

Rio? He'd been in her dreams, wild and relentlessly male, and now he was intruding on her thoughts every time she didn't focus on something worthwhile.

Like that could happen.

She imagined a sprawling Spanish villa among the trees, in a wash of soft watercolors, where DeSilva would lavish his affection on her, and always talk in those romantic, accented undertones. She saw Chloe laughing and playing—grabbing her daddy's hand, but then taking *hers*, too! The sensation had felt so strong at times, Lola swore little fingers gripped hers in her sleep.

Which explained why she'd grabbed her Camels in the wee hours: something to do with her hands.

But why should she believe these dreams would come true? Her romantic visions of Dennis Fletcher certainly hadn't panned out. And for all she knew, Rio's pretty hints were part of the script to indulge the fantasies she'd spelled out to the concierge and the captain. All a part of his charm.

And who was to say Captain Scandalous hadn't had his spies out, so he could punish her for spending last night with DeSilva? Aric might've ratted on her as soon as she'd left the ballroom—even though this gave Cabana Boy the night off to enjoy his own fun and games. In *her* dress.

It occurred to her then that Skorpio hadn't summoned her in nearly twenty-four hours.

Lola smiled. Lifted her face to the sun and soaked up its warmth while the breeze played in her hair. High time she got to enjoy this luxurious suite, since she'd *paid* for this trip, after all!

Or does this mean Skorpio's up to something? Probably scheming up another scenario where he used his body for bait and then let Odette have her.

Shaking her head at her worst-case imagination, Lola leaned on the railing. She'd made that stupid love-slave deal, so now the only diamonds she got to look at, in this port renowned for its jewelry bargains, were the sparkles on the water.

Damn shame she'd locked herself into her room, when there was a whole ship to explore . . . other people to meet, who weren't determined to humiliate her. This was the last day of her trip, so she might not have many more chances to act like an everyday cruise tourist.

Which meant living a little!

Which means taking control of your time—your life—again! Not being available for men who make you to dance to their beat.

Half an hour later, with her auburn hair hanging in its naturally wavy state and an attitude as fresh as her makeup, Lola opened her door.

Cabana Boy looked up from his crossword puzzle. "*Oooh*, Priestess! Can I borrow that cami?"

"Get your own—in a different color," she teased him. "Now—I'm due for a nice lunch and one of those big, chichi drinks of the day. So if you'll tell me the best place to have a little fun—without running into your boss—I'll be on my way."

He quirked an eyebrow. Ran his finger along the Across clues, like she hadn't asked him anything.

"Six-letter word beginning with H. Means a highly attractive young—"

"Hottie."

Lola planted her fists on the sparkly sash of her low-rider capris, aware of how it called attention to her hourglass curve. Aware she had to fight fire with fire while dealing with *this* hottie. She tapped the toe of her kitten-heel sandal.

"Look, Big Boy—I'm sick of hanging around, wondering what Skandalis has in mind for making my day miserable," she informed him. "Since you seem *so* enamored of me, the least I can do is spring for a drink. Are you coming?"

One silvery-green eye rolled her direction. "No funny stuff? No disappearing acts?"

"Hey—if DeSilva's bribes aren't high enough for you—if the captain doesn't pay you enough—bitch to *them*. It's not like I *asked* for a baby-sitter."

Aric's gaze wandered back to his crossword. "Ten-letter phrase—starting with that H from 'hottie'—meaning 'tinkling musical instruments from the underworld—'"

"Hell's bells!" she cried. "I'm outta here! If you can't keep track of me—"

"Damn, you're good! How'd you *know*, without even seeing—"

Lola was out the door and picking up speed when Cabana Boy, barefoot and wearing only his low-slung boxers, caught up to her. He pushed back his curly mop, grinning.

"Now isn't this better?" he razzed her. "Inviting me for a drink instead of acting like you don't wanna be seen with me?"

The elevator opened and Lola took the back wall. Even knowing what she did about this kid, it was hardly a sacrifice to have him squiring her around. That dog tag on his suntanned chest rose and fell with his breathing as he gazed at her from between his rumpled, curling bangs.

"So if I asked you to come home with me, how much would it cost?"

Cabana Boy's low laughter made her insides tingle. "More than you can afford, Lola. Nice try, though."

"Fine! Since you probably have a higher net worth than I do, *you* can buy the first round."

She crossed her arms, looking up at the digital floor numbers to keep from snickering. It felt damn good to be throwing her weight around again, taking charge. "And it better be someplace classy. Not the cigar club, and not the sports bar."

"You don't like jocks?"

"I'm with *you*, aren't I?"

31

Aric ushered her off the elevator, his thumb slipping through her back belt loop. The loose span of his hand on her ass established his control over her, while giving everyone else in the atrium the impression they were an item.

Lola played along, though. How often did she get escorted by a hottie who couldn't keep his hands off her?

And as they entered a dim, intimate alcove where the sign outside flashed FEDORAS in neon red and purple, she had to admit he had taste in watering holes. The barmaid and the two waitresses wore nothing but black lace boy shorts, sky-high stilettos, and black felt fedoras with red bands, which angled jauntily over their flowing blonde hair.

"Guess I don't have the qualifications to work here," she murmured.

Aric nodded as the nearest lovely waved them toward a table. "Why not? Your boobs are every bit as cute as theirs."

"But I have red hair. Clashes with the hat bands."

Cabana Boy's arm slipped over her shoulders as he scooted

against her in the booth. He was laughing with her, maintaining that fantasy that they were a couple of good-timers whiling away an afternoon after a wild night in the sack together.

It felt pretty damn fine to bob her head to the happy island music playing in the background, while they awaited a menu. Lola gazed at the sleek ebony tables, and wing-back chairs upholstered in rich cranberry leather. A hideaway like this could help her forget about a hard-ass like Captain Scandalous, and her emotional tug-of-war with Rio DeSilva. Here—with enough drinks—maybe she could find a solution to the bruised feelings Fletch had left her with, and get on with her perfectly fine life in the business lane.

"Bring us a pitcher of your rum punch. Orange slices and cherries in our glasses," Aric instructed the waitress, "and a plate with extra fruit. It's a health thing, ya know?"

The blonde smiled like she knew better. "Nah, it's a fruit thing. A real fresh fruit thing."

Lola wasn't sure whether to laugh or cough. She settled for relaxing against the high leather back of the booth . . . just a nice mental float, anticipating rum punch like you could only get in the Caribbean—

Until she saw the blonde bringing their pitcher to the table.

She wasn't the one who took their order, because this fox in the fedora had much bigger, bouncier boobs and walked with a wiggle that said she knew it, too. But it wasn't this blonde's attributes that made the little hairs tingle on the back of Lola's neck.

She gripped the edge of the table, staring to be sure.

But yeah, that was the bimbo she'd seen on Rio's security tapes! The busty blonde who'd lured Fletch off the ship with her big bucks and her big—

The bitch he'd called his soul mate! With the villa in Aruba!

"You have your *nerve*," Lola rasped, "sashaying to my table as though—"

"Lola, what the hell—?" Aric was staring at her like she was a snarling, two-headed dog.

"What'd you do with him?" she demanded.

The waitress set their pitcher on the table, frowning prettily. "Sorry, ma'am, but I don't understand—"

"What part of *barracuda* don't you understand?"

Her rising voice had the other customers turning to peer at them, but she didn't give a damn.

"Where'd you leave him?" she demanded. "We were all set to—and he drained my accounts because of—you scheming, filthy—luring him to your seaside villa to—"

The waitress stood tall, her slender hand poised at the edge of her boy shorts while the nipples on her D-cups pointed at Lola like exclamation points.

"Begging your pardon again, but—"

"Don't *give* me that! I *saw* you!"

Lola shoved Aric out of the booth ahead of her before he could hold her down.

"You used your credit card as bait! In the casino, and at the ATM!" she exclaimed, pointing her finger like a pistol. "You laid it right out there so Fletch could slip it into his pocket—and then you could catch him with it, and use it to lure him off the ship and—"

Cabana Boy was standing beside her, trying to settle her down. He actually looked embarrassed about all the people watching them. "That's pretty tall talk, Lola, since you weren't actually there to—"

"I *saw* her!" Lola shrieked. "She was playing fast and loose at the Caribbean Stud table, and then she—"

Instinct—*something*—took hold of her arm and Lola let the bimbo have it! Slapped her soundly across one cheek, and then—

when Blondie was off-guard—brought her other fist up to finish telling her what a no-good conniving whore she was.

But the waitress grabbed her hand before it connected. With one quick twist, she pinned Lola's arm behind her—and then sent her to the floor with a strategic sweep of her high-heeled foot.

"Call Security," the blonde barked toward the bar.

"You don't have a stiletto to stand on, honey," Lola wheezed, "because it was Security who showed me that tape of you and Dennis—"

Blondie planted a foot on Lola's chest and put some weight on it. Right under her rib cage, where that damn six-inch heel might puncture her lung if she stepped any harder.

"Get off me!" Lola cried. "You know I'm right! You know who I'm talking about! *Don't* you?"

"I don't know who you think I am, honey, but letting women *hit* on me isn't in my job description," this she-cat in the hat declared. "We'll let somebody else handle this, since you apparently left your manners at home."

By now Lola realized that the other passengers were watching their squabble with great interest. Like maybe bets would start changing hands any minute now.

"You better let me up," Lola said, grabbing Blondie's ankle. From this angle, those two full-bodied peaks bobbed above those black boy shorts, which seemed a loooong way up the bent, shapely leg that held her to the floor.

Lola gripped harder, determined to get that pointy heel out of her chest. Thinking it was a shame that such a high-toned floozy had better taste in shoes than she did in men.

"Dammit, I told you to—"

"And what seems to be our problem, Fedora?" a familiar voice came from the doorway. "This is the last place I expected a . . . confrontation between two lovely women."

Ever so subtly, Blondie ground her heel deeper into Lola's chest. "It's not every day I'm accused of luring a passenger's man away—or smacked in the face, either."

Rio DeSilva was standing beside the woman he'd called Fedora, his hands clasped behind him as he stared sternly down at her. From here, his face seemed a looooong way from Lola's, and his white uniform made him look very, very official. And very pissed off, to find her in this position.

Or was that a flicker of something else in Rio's eyes?

Had that blonde bitch *winked* at him?

With so many eyes glued to her as the bimbo in the hat told the security agent her version of the story—punctuating the important parts with little stabs of her stiletto—Lola felt the teensiest bit mortified.

What if she was wrong?

After all, the three chicks working here looked enough alike to be classier versions of the Candi, Randi and Dandi who sang at the staff ball. Was it possible she'd made a mistake, calling this Fedora person—

Oh, Lord, was she the owner of this club?

—the loose, no-good floozy who'd stolen Dennis away?

"I'll take care of it."

"Thank you so much, Mr. DeSilva."

And with those so polite, businesslike phrases, the entertainment was over. Fedora removed her foot, and Rio leaned down with his hand extended.

"I can get up myself, thank you," Lola informed him. "If I didn't know better, I'd think Aric brought me here because he knew—"

And what if he *had*? What if Cabana Boy had known all along that—

Since the beginning, she'd suspected all the men making her work off Fletch's debt were keeping secrets. This certainly seemed to prove it.

It was all Lola could do to keep her mouth shut until they were outside the lounge.

"All right, dammit, where is Dennis *really*?" she demanded in a whisper. "And who brought my purse back the other day?"

DeSilva's brow puckered. "You saw his note, Lola *mia*. He said—in his own handwriting, was it not?—he was going ashore in Aruba. Not coming back."

"But I saw her with my own eyes!" Lola retorted, pointing toward the lounge's doorway. "That—that Fedora bitch was the one who lured Fletch away with her big—and left me to pay his frickin' bills! He left *me* for those two bouncing—"

She sighed, exasperated. She was getting damn tired of riding this staff elevator: no room to move away from men who tried to confine her, and seduce her, and *intimidate* her in here! No frickin' air to breathe, the way they all stood right up against her like they wanted to yank down her pants and—

"I'm sorry you're upset, *mi vida*."

Rio's endearments irritated her even more. His golden gaze bored into hers, and she made herself break the eye contact, to keep some semblance of self-control. He was way too powerful—way too potent—when he stood this close to her.

"If you'd like to see the security tape again, we can go to—"

"I want answers, dammit! And I want them from you!"

Lola wrapped her arms around herself, wishing she hadn't worn such a snug cami with only pink lace covering the tops of her cleavage. "*You*, with all that pretty talk about your woman being the queen of your castle, and taking care of motherless little Chloe, and—you've been bullshitting me all along, and you know it!"

That's what hurt the worst: finding out just how far Rio had gone to cover for his colleagues, while letting her suffer the consequences of Fletch's desertion. As though her compromised credit wasn't punishment enough! As though her feelings counted for nothing!

And because every hallway in this fricking ship looked the same, she didn't know where DeSilva was taking her—

Until he opened the door on all those photos. That sad-eyed little girl who smiled so much like her daddy was more than Lola could handle.

"I thought you *liked* me," she whimpered, turning her back on the face that beckoned her from so many picture frames.

"Oh, it's gone way beyond *like*, Lola *mia*," he murmured as he glanced both directions down the corridor. "Do you think I make wild passionate love to every woman I meet? As though you were just my flavor of the day?"

She glared at him. How dare Rio express her own earlier thoughts during this high-stakes situation!

"Maybe I don't know you as well as I thought I did when I let you—"

"Before you say another word, please come inside," he insisted in a low voice. "It's one of the few places on the ship where security cameras can't incriminate us."

She flashed back to that awful hour she'd watched Fletch in the casino, with that *soul mate* he'd found. Lola still swore it was that Fedora bimbo from the cocktail lounge. But even without *her* in the picture, those security monitors had shown Lola just how public all the areas aboard the *Aphrodite* really were.

"I suppose now you'll tell me I've got cameras hidden in my suite, too," she asserted hotly. "Spy cams behind the vanity mirror, and—and probably in the damn shower head! Is that how you get your grins, Rio? Watching women use the bathroom?"

He closed the door, sighing. "Your anger is speaking so loudly—"

"Damn right I'm mad! And when that bitch put her foot between my boobs—"

"—that you can't hear yourself think," he continued in a

low, flowing voice. "You have no idea how badly your accusations are hurting me, *querida*. As though you don't trust me anymore, after all the beautiful moments we've shared."

Lola raised an eyebrow. "Smearing me with butter brickle and hot fudge ranks as a beautiful moment?"

"Absolutely."

He *almost* said that with a straight face. It was the flicker in his sexy mustache that told Lola he still wasn't coming clean.

"It was your complete trust in me—the way you remained on my table, open to whatever I teased you with, that made the occasion so special."

Rio focused those soft brown eyes on her, looking like a puppy who'd been put out on the road by his owner.

"I've never met a woman who made me *think* of such a thing—much less allow me to try it," he continued quietly. "And you laughed along with me. And then shared your deepest personal concerns after listening so lovingly to mine. This is something I've never had with a woman, Lola. It made me feel special. *Loved*."

Lola swallowed hard. He sounded sincere. Seriously involved with her.

But did she dare believe him? No sense in adding insult to injury—building herself up with that hopeful expression on Rio DeSilva's gorgeous face—to walk ashore tomorrow feeling like the world's biggest idiot.

He stepped closer, his hands on her shoulders and a kiss on his lips that begged for her to return it. Lola *wanted* to believe again—wanted her faith in men and herself restored. Those golden-brown eyes invited her to a place where that could happen.

Rio lowered his long lashes, parting his lips to exhale lightly. He smelled of those sexy little cigars, and a flush colored his golden cheeks.

Didn't he look like a man ready to risk everything—to *ask*

the questions that played with his expressive eyebrows? Wasn't that visible pulse in his neck a sign of how vulnerable he felt?

Lola closed her eyes. Let out the breath she'd been holding, along with the inhibitions and doubts that would keep her from feeling the truth in his kiss. She opened her mouth, to better taste him—to respond more fully to whatever invitations DeSilva sent without saying a word.

If she kept quiet, she would hear his heart speak.

Rio's mouth lighted on hers, lifted, and then settled in for a fine frenzy of a kiss. With a soft moan, he pulled her against his body and placed a hand behind her head.

And Lola surrendered. She would go anywhere with this man—as long as he promised to love her this way, no matter what. Over the years, she'd learned that a man's kiss foretold everything she needed to know about him as a lover and a partner. That other guy . . . what's-his-face, who'd left her . . . couldn't kiss her this way if his life depended on it. Never took the time to taste her inner lips, and tease her tongue with his, and—

The door opened so suddenly it slammed back against the wall.

"Well, *this* certainly tells the tale, does it not?"

Skorpio Skandalis let out an edgy laugh when she and Rio jumped away from their kiss yet remained in each other's arms. The captain's obsidian eyes flashed wickedly as he looked from her to his security agent.

"I'm sure you realize, Miss Wright, that this is the final day of your cruise. Your last chance to repay my generosity—for allowing you to remain aboard my ship, and to work off the bills you've run up in the spa and the boutiques."

The captain crossed his arms, looking very impressive in his crisp white uniform. And extremely pissed.

"But what have we here?" he asked sarcastically. "My love

slave—in the arms of another man! In direct defiance of our agreement! Not only have you disobeyed me by becoming involved with Mr. DeSilva, but now you've attacked my sister, as well!"

Lola's jaw dropped. That blonde in the fedora and the boy shorts—wearing those ice-pick stilettos—was Skorpio's *sister*?

Well, that made things pretty plain, didn't it?

"This was all a set-up!" she cried, pointing at him. "Don't you *dare* presume to charge me for spa time *you* ordered, and—"

"That's enough out of you, young lady!" Captain Scandalous said, pointing an ominous finger back at her. "I have been *very* patient all week! Hearing reports, yet giving you the benefit of the doubt when you—"

"You could at least listen to Lola's side of this," DeSilva undercut him. "From the first, you had all the advantages of knowing—"

"And *you*!" the Greek proclaimed, filling the room with his anger. "*You* have ignored me at every turn, DeSilva! How am I to maintain security aboard my ship when *you* are holed up with one of the passengers? Which is *expressly* forbidden by the Code of Employee Conduct, as you know!"

"And I take full responsibility for that part of—"

"And you'll take a full hit in your final pay next week, as well!" Skandalis cried. "All these years of trust and friendship—a career of great integrity—tossed overboard! Because of this—this *woman*! The one you stole from *my* service—"

Rio stiffened to his full height, which put him a head taller than his superior. "Lola owes you nothing, and you know it! Just as you know how much she lost before *you* ever caught her up in your web of—"

"Enough! Out!"

Captain Scandalous was looking at Lola now, pointing toward the door. And while he resembled a fiery, commanding

Greek god handing down the law from Mount Olympus, Lola knew this was no ancient myth. No play on her emotions. This guy was serious!

"And just where—"

"Straight to jail! Where I can keep track of you until we dock tomorrow!"

The jail? How was she supposed to—surely he didn't expect her to—

"Begging your pardon, captain," Lola jeered, "but this cruise was *paid in full* before I ever set eyes on you! You have absolutely no right to—"

"I'm the captain, Miss Wright. I rule."

His midnight eyes didn't flicker. No sign of teasing or winking or "your wish is my command" from this arrogant bastard standing in the doorway, staring her down. In fact, he reached for his walkie-talkie.

"George! I need an escort for a disorderly passenger," he barked. "It seems DeSilva isn't doing his job, so I'm putting you in charge of security until we're in port tomorrow."

Just like that, Skandalis relegated her to jail, and into the custody of another man. Rio looked no happier about it than she did, but a glance at all those photos reminded her DeSilva had more at stake than she'd previously considered: if he was going home to play daddy, his final paycheck might be pretty important. He talked about the family estate like a man who came from old money, but her career dealing with influential men—and those who just wanted to look that way—had taught her that appearances could be deceiving.

Before they could appeal to Skandalis again, a burly black fellow with a shaved head, a gold front tooth, and a diamond stud in his lip came to the door. He took one look at Lola and sneered.

"So this is the little lady goin' to the lock up? Not a problem, sir."

Lola took one look at Mr. Muscle and all inclination to lip back at him disappeared. His blue uniform shirt bulged at the buttons—but not because he had any loose flab on him. This guy could crush her with one hand. Looked like one of the superhuman villains from a James Bond movie—only George was very real!

She glanced at Rio for reassurance, but he dropped her hand. Apparently refusing to challenge the captain any further.

So, hey! Sit in the jail cell tonight, clear out tomorrow, and never look back! How hard can that be?

Lola didn't want to think about how hard it was to walk out of this room, without the slightest sign from Rio DeSilva that he intended to finish their previous conversation. Or that he intended to make good on all the promises he'd dangled in front of her.

Captain Scandalous just kept staring at her. Willing her to leave.

Why had she found him so drop-dead gorgeous while she watched that orientation loop on her stateroom TV? Skandalis was the most self-absorbed, pigheaded despot she'd ever met. Way more in love with himself than any woman could ever be!

George motioned for her to go first down the hall. Once again Lola was ushered into that damn staff elevator. This time, her escort nearly filled the thing with his shoulders. Just stood there as the stainless steel cubicle descended through the lower levels, looking at her with a bovine expression that made her glad she'd be leaving tomorrow. No sense in letting any more *Aphrodite* guys try for a piece of her!

The doors opened on a narrow, grim corridor that had to be in the very belly of the ship: the lighting was minimal and the decor was nonexistent. Pale gray walls, and carpet of the same shade but darker.

Get used to it, she told herself. *The jail won't be much like the Aphrodisia Suite, either.*

But again, what did it matter? Tomorrow she was out of here.

Lola walked slightly ahead of Big George, because there wasn't room for them to walk side by side on this level. A beefy paw rested on her shoulder—as though she might *run*! She didn't dare shrug out from under it.

Up ahead, she caught sight of the security office where Rio had shown her those monitors. Beyond it were a couple of closed doors marked ISOLATION. They were painted a dull putty like the walls; no way to see in or out of them.

So ships really do have a jail. Or solitary confinement, anyway.

Lola sighed. At least this way, she didn't have to pack all her stuff. No doubt Aric was already loading her suitcase . . . probably keeping a few souvenirs, so he could wear them later. Tomorrow they'd dump her off on the pier in San Juan, along with her luggage, and this would all be behind her.

But what the hell was this in front of her?

George was pushing his metal key into the the first door's knob lock. But when he swung it open, she saw a figure seated on a bunk in the shadows.

Lola stared into the dimness. "I beg your pardon, George, but there's already someone in this—*Fletch*?!"

The man gazing back at her sported a pale grizzle around his jaw, uncombed hair like a haystack, and rumpled clothes that were smelling mighty ripe. But she recognized those eyes! And right now they were saying she was in for more surprises— probably things she didn't want to know—than she'd anticipated.

"Dennis Fletcher," she rasped, "what the hell are *you* doing here?"

32

"**G**uard, you can*not* put this woman in here with me!"

George's diamond stud flashed when he snickered. He blocked Fletch's escape with his linebacker body.

"Captain's orders," he said with a shake of his neckless head. "Cain't nobody go against what The Man says."

"Well, I'm not going in there!" Lola spouted. "This whole week has been one trick after another, and now—and *you* started the whole damn thing with that Dear Lola note! *Didn't* you, Fletch?"

The slender man in the cell—the man she'd almost married—looked at her like she was six shades of stupid for asking that.

But it was all falling into place, wasn't it? The man who'd ripped off her accounts had been nowhere near a villa in Aruba. No self-respecting woman—certainly not a fox like Fedora—would be seen with him, in this condition.

And where does that leave YOU, honey?

She didn't want to think about that. She didn't want to re-hash all the moments of agony and humiliation this man had caused her with his casino habit this week. Not to mention those other irritating habits she'd been way too willing to overlook over the past few years, thinking she loved this guy. This *loser*. Thinking married was better than single; selling herself short by settling on Fletch. Just because he was a flashy dresser who lived on the edge.

"*So?*" she demanded. "What do you have to say for yourself, Mr. Rip Off? Where's that soul mate now, when you need her most?"

Dennis glared at her, and then at the gorilla in the doorway. "I see no reason to explain anything to you, Lola. Not with the captain's goon listening in on—"

"Who you callin' a *goon*, smart ass?" George demanded. But instead of stepping toward Fletch to collar him, he reached back with an arm the size of a small tree and grabbed Lola!

"Just for that, why, you're gonna be bunkin' with this chickie here! I'll let *her* give you the what-for, while I see to the rest of this ship!" he crowed. "I gotta job to do, and I don't need your *sass*, man!"

With an agility that amazed her, Big George whipped her into the small room, stepped out, and slammed the door. Then he stood outside for a few moments, chuckling like he found this hugely funny.

"Ta-*ta*, ya'll! Don't bother cryin' to *me* to get outta here, coz we be dockin' way early in the mornin,'" he teased them. "Got no time for little children who fight and cry like spoiled-ass brats!"

His footsteps faded as he made himself scarce in a matter of seconds—as though he knew what kind of a job they were going to do on each other and wanted no part of it.

Lola stood with her ear to the door until she could no longer follow his progress. How could a man that big disappear so fast? And where had she heard his voice before?

And how 'bout that captain? Sending her down here to this hellhole, knowing damn well Dennis Fletcher was—

And he's known it all along. It's his ship and he rules, remember?

Lola licked her lips, trying to slow her wild thoughts, still spinning on a nicotine high.

And if Fedora was that boobsy blonde Fletch supposedly left the ship with—and Fedora runs the cocktail lounge—and Fedora's the captain's sister—

Well, the pieces were falling into place now, weren't they? And the picture they painted was *not* pretty.

Lola's breath escaped in a rush. She turned then, not wanting to have her back to Fletch. Gazing through the darkness at him gave her a chill, even though the air in here was growing warm and fetid.

As her eyes adjusted, she could see the room was only big enough for that bunk against the wall—which Dennis sat on—with about two feet on the end and on this side to stand up in. Wayyy too close for comfort.

Lola fumbled beside the door, greatly relieved to find a light switch.

"Dammit! Why'd you—turn that off!" Fletch protested, shielding his eyes with his arms.

She wanted to, when she saw him. While some men looked fashionably seductive—or downright hot—with a few days' growth of bristle on their faces, Dennis wasn't one of them. His eyes were bloodshot. He smelled like B.O. and unwashed laundry. Curled in on himself like a cornered animal, Fletch bore *no* resemblance to the Fortune 500 mover-and-shaker she'd known back home.

She looked away, determined not to talk just to fill in the silence.

Some villa, huh? Doesn't even have a pot to piss in.

So of course, she had to go now.

And God, how she wanted a smoke—except she'd left her purse in Fedora's when DeSilva escorted her out. Not that she'd lower herself to sucking on Camels while Fletcher jeered at her for falling off the wagon again. *He* looked like he'd fallen into a puddle of something, so it was no wonder the classy blonde with the big knockers abandoned him.

Lola wanted out, too. So she started talking to keep from thinking how creepy it was in here. To get this over with.

"Like I said before," she began in a coiled voice, "you started this whole fiasco when you scribbled that note and had it delivered—from here in this cell, right? So I wouldn't come looking for you! But our relationship was a lie wayyyyy before that, wasn't it?"

Fletch rolled his eyes, shoving his hair back from his eyes. It was a gesture she knew well—and come to think of it, it usually preceded some bullshit story he was concocting so she wouldn't ask any more questions.

"So how many other women have you ripped off, Fletcher?"

Lola crossed her arms—*again* wishing she'd worn more than this lace-trimmed cami that showed more cleavage than Dennis needed to see.

But she couldn't let him know how his presence bothered her—sickened her—now. Not until she finished grilling him and he was one overdone hot dog. Then she'd cook the captain, and his chesty sister with the cutesy name, and Cabana Boy, who'd led her merrily down this primrose path—not to mention Rio DeSilva. Head of Security.

Keep him out of this! Keep your head on straight while there's a chance to get answers.

Fletch was playing the strong silent type. Didn't look inclined to say a word unless she pried it out of him, as he sat farther back against the wall.

"All right, I'll ask you again," Lola said. "How many women have you ripped off, Fletcher? And don't give me any bullshit, because I *saw* the security cam tapes from the casino!"

Fletch flashed her an exasperated look, his shrug exaggerated.

"So if you've seen everything, why ask *me*? If you can't handle the truth—why ask at all?" he jeered. "Never could take a hint, could you? Never had a *clue* what was going on!"

"And why do you sound so proud of that?"

Lola stood before him with her fists against her hips, out of his reach but close enough to glare directly at him.

"What I saw appalled me, Fletch! The way you played that blonde like a violin and then slipped her ATM card into your pocket, like you'd done it a dozen times before!" she said, her voice rising with her temperature. "The way you *kissed* her in the bar, like—like you had another pretty fishy on your line! Until you took a swing at her!"

Another piece clicked into place: Lola felt like she was finally seeing the big picture, no thanks to any of those men who'd supposedly been helping her!

"But that was Fedora, the captain's sister," she reasoned aloud, "and she takes shit from *no*body. So you landed here."

She paused to collect herself. Fletch was right about the way she asked questions and then fell apart when the truth wounded her. And she did *not* want him to see how badly he'd hurt her. Did *not* want him to concoct another cock-and-bull story she'd swallow just because it was easier. Cleaner.

"So why the big fairy tale about finding your—your *soul mate*, and then running off to her villa in Aruba?" Lola asked.

But her voice wavered, dammit. And her hands were so jittery she had to keep them fisted so Dennis wouldn't know how strung-out she felt, now that the morning's nicotine binge was wearing off.

He snickered. Shook his head as though he'd always figured her for such an easy mark, it wasn't even sport to take pot-shots at her.

"I wanted you to get disgusted enough to realize it would never *work* for us!" he cried. "I walked away a dozen times, but no—you wouldn't hear of that! You're Lola Louise Wright, and by God you have to be *right*!"

His voice echoed angrily in the little room and he stood up, ready to get his licks in.

"You see a challenge and you have to rise above it!" he scoffed, raising his arms dramatically. "You perceive a problem, and you have to *fix* it!"

"And your point would be?"

Dennis Fletcher, red-eyed, whiskered, and panting, suddenly resembled a deranged drug addict. Had she created this monster, by believing she could fix *him*, too, once they were married? What he said was making sense—finally—but couldn't he have found a better way? A better time?

Like, *weeks* ago, when she was booking this cruise?

"My *point* is, I did you a favor! I let you make your cruise plans, on this adults-only ship, knowing that if I ducked out, you might find a guy you'd be *good* with!" he explained.

His grimace of derision—his belittling tone of voice—were real eye openers. Lola could hardly believe this raving maniac managed huge investment portfolios for corporations far wealthier than she. Mr. Charisma had disappeared, and his stand-in was scaring the bejesus out of her.

"Any man with eyes would make a play for you, Lola! And from what I hear, my plan has worked!" he continued, laughing sarcastically. "I knew you wouldn't go even a *day* without latching on to some other poor fool—because you can't! Lord love you, Lola, you're a woman who has to have a man, even if you create him out of sheer fantasy. You'll see what you want to see, to avoid being alone!"

She went slack against the wall, like a balloon who'd lost all her air. What Fletcher said confirmed some of her deepest, darkest self-doubts and she wanted to just crawl into a hole—with a carton of Camels—and not come out until they docked in San Juan tomorrow.

Wait a minute! That's bullshit and you're stepping in it!

Lola sucked in a deep breath, gathering her scattered thoughts. Fletch was up to his old tricks, making it look like this was all *her* fault, so he never had to admit his own wrongdoing! Creative management, he'd be calling it, when it was out-and-out lying! Not to mention theft!

She'd been blinded so long by his golden-boy charisma—by her own mental movies of the happily-ever-after she wanted—that she hadn't realized how far gone she really was.

Or how despicable Dennis Fletcher could be.

"You were doing me a favor," she echoed, shaking her head at such stupidity. "So that's why you wrote me that lovely note—*after* you maxed out all my personal and business accounts. *After* you wiped out my credit, and my credibility as a businesswoman. *After* you sneaked up to the room while I was in the shower, to swipe my purse and cell phone, so I couldn't contact you!"

Lola was starting to shake, so she braced herself against the wall to keep herself together. By God, Dennis would answer to her!

"Well, then," she went on, her voice deceptively calm, "if you haven't been impressing the thong off that bimbo soul mate—at her villa—what'd you do with all my money?"

His mouth snapped shut. He shoved his hands in his pockets.

"The concierge showed me an itemized list of your charges, Fletch," she continued. "You didn't lose it all at the Caribbean Stud tables, because you bought things at the boutiques. Surely not gifts for *me*, because you were doing me such a *favor!*"

"It's none of your business, what I—"

"*Excuse* me?"

He backed away from her advance, his eyes widening when he hit the wall. "I had no idea that blonde was—who *knew* she was an undercover—?"

"Oh, this is rich, Fletch." Lola gripped his stubbled chin, bumping his head back against the wall. "Are you telling me you used your *old* honey's money to buy your *new* honey some trinkets? Little gifts to tell her how *special* she was—before you stole *her* plastic?"

It was sad, how gratified she felt, watching his eyes widen as she put pressure on his chin and jaw. Sad, too, that Dennis could've shoved her away with one hand if he wasn't so wrapped up in all his stories—if he didn't actually *believe* he'd done the noblest thing by walking out on her.

"Okay, so I fucked up!" he rasped. "I—I just wanted to look in your purse for the plane tickets, so I could be out of your life for good! So you could keep enjoying yourself—your trip—and never have to mess with me again. Honest to God, it all started when I was looking for my tickets—"

"Where *you're* going, Mr. Fletcher, you won't be needing plane tickets."

The voice from behind them was cool and smooth and female. When the door opened, Fedora stepped into the cell, smiling tightly.

"I'll take it from here, Lola," she said in a low, competent voice. "I don't know what sort of story this guy fed you in that note, after I arrested him, but I bet your cruise was a lot more fun without *this* loser leading you on."

Lola's jaw dropped when she caught the reflection from a gold seal on a badge this gorgeous blonde was flashing.

"Fedora Skandalis, International Investigations," she said with a big smile. "I've come to deliver you from Dennis, and to explain a few things."

33

"You dirty double-crossing bitch!"

Fletch suddenly recovered, shoving Lola out of his way so he could get in Fedora's face.

Ms. Skandalis, decked out in her white uniform—crisp slacks that hugged her butt, with her shirt unbuttoned down to the crack between those double D's—gave him a smile that would've smoked any other guy's shorts.

"And it's a pleasure to see you again, too, Mr. Fletcher," she crooned. "I'm sure you won't mind if I remove your room-mate, to allow you the total privacy you so richly deserve."

Fletch really lost it then. His face looked like a raw beefsteak he could've grilled with his temper. "You have no fucking right to hold me here! I'm an American citizen and I demand legal counsel!"

Fedora looked ever so elegant with her streaky blonde hair in an updo and gold star earrings dangling from her ears. Way too classy to be dealing with the likes of Fletch.

"Indeed, Mr. Fletcher, when we dock on American soil to-morrow, you'll meet men just *itching* to read you your rights and bring you to due process—for identity theft, and fraud, and those other games you play with people's money."

The agent smiled, but Lola noticed how she stood tensed and ready for anything Fletch might do next.

"You're not just a stateside crook now!" Fedora went on boldly. "You've elevated your status to international extortionist! Which should look very impressive on your resume, don't you think?"

Fletch made a gross sound in his throat. And spat on her!

That big black guy, George, rushed in from the hall then. He shoved the two women toward the bunk, so he could take his turn at Dennis.

"You and I's gonna have us a talk about how to treat a lady, Mr. Fletcher!" the burly man muttered. "Right after botha these ladies you've done dirty have left the room. Now back off! Don't try nothin' funny, 'less you wanna be singin' soprano in the penitentiary choir. You get my meanin'?"

Fletch stumbled backwards into the wall with the force of George's shove, and Lola lost no time stepping out of the cell. While she'd known Dennis had a nasty temper, because he'd scorched her with it plenty of times during their rocky romance, she was appalled at what she'd just seen.

"I am so sorry," she murmured as Fedora wiped the gob of spit from her face. "I knew he could be a jackass, but that was inexcusable, what he did to you."

They started down the hallway, and the woman in white smiled like it was all in a day's work.

"At least you found that out before you married him, right?" she asked. "I'm sorry if this escapade has upset you, Lola. We wanted to get that jerk locked up—and out of your way, so you could enjoy your vacation."

Once again they got into a staff elevator, but this time Lola was aware of a spicy, enticing perfume—and the presence of a beautiful woman who was still a mystery to her.

"You'll have to excuse me if I sound clueless, after the way Rio showed me those security tapes, and—and jeez, I'm really sorry I tried to punch you out, too!" Lola sputtered. "It puts me down there on Fletch's level, and that's not where I want to be."

When Fedora smiled, Lola sensed she was being studied by an undercover officer who fooled a lot of people with that flowing blonde hair and those big bazooms. She pushed a button and the elevator doors closed.

"Apology accepted. I can understand your frustration, hon," Fedora said. "You've had bits and pieces, while the rest of us have seen the big picture. We knew from Day One how this would pan out. Mostly."

Fedora grinned ruefully at her. "It was Fletcher's ATM activities and his behavior in the casino that caught our eye. DeSilva was watching him on the monitor. Told me I'd better get this guy out of the casino, before he pulled a really big fast one. Sorry I was too late to save you some humiliation, and the hassle with the credit card companies."

Lola cogitated on this. "So you were undercover, letting Dennis—"

"Using my bogus credit card as bait, playing easy to take," she replied. "And when I mentioned my villa on Aruba—a story as fake as my fingernails—Fletcher bit. Followed me off the ship, where George LeFevre was waiting to arrest him. Since we brought him back on board and put him in the brig—"

"His key card didn't register on your security computers. So it appeared he really did run off with a new soul mate, to her villa on the island."

"That's what he said in that note?" Fedora snickered at that one.

"And of course he did it so I could spend the rest of my cruise finding a guy I might really make it with," Lola added, almost smiling herself.

"Mr. Nobility, eh? You've gotta love a guy who thinks only of *you*."

"Yeah, I can see that now." She glanced at the lighted number above them when the elevator dinged. "Thanks a lot for—"

"No need to thank *me*, hon. My brother Skorpio set this all up."

"Now *there's* a man who plays fast and loose with a woman's fantasies! But I've wanted to ring his neck a few times this week." Lola thought about adding more as they stepped out into the atrium's bright sunlight, but that was a score she had to settle with Captain Scandalous himself.

Fedora was chuckling, lighting up that model-perfect makeup with her natural glow. "He's an original, one-of-a-kind, to be sure. And I hope my son Aric did his best to make you feel—"

Lola gaped. Cabana Boy was this woman's *son*?

"But you're not old enough to be—"

Fedora squeezed her arm. It was the gesture of a woman who wanted to befriend her, without making her feel embarrassed or beholden. A nice thing to consider, now that she wasn't pressing the heel of a stiletto into Lola's chest.

"I had Aric when I was too young to understand the consequences of sex, or the responsibilities of motherhood," she said quietly. "My brother saw that I finished my education. Then he hired me for his security force."

"And the night club is yours, too?"

"Nice cover, no?" She grinned, showing even white teeth that looked so perfect against her honey-colored skin. "Much more fun than having to play cop all the time, since we have so few problems with passengers. Dennis gave us some practice with our procedures and security skills."

Lola shook her head in amazement. You just couldn't look at this fox when she was wearing boy shorts and a fedora—not to mention stilettos that made her legs look a mile long—and think you were being monitored.

"So who returned my purse?" she asked.

Fedora rolled her big brown eyes, which sparkled with mischief. "The captain did. Because it was yours, of course—but partly to see how you'd react. As you've probably realized, he enjoys a good game of cat-and-mouse.

"Well! Here we are at Mr. Kingsley's office. If you have further questions, just give me a call." Fedora flashed her a dazzling smile. "I've returned those gifts and supplies Dennis bought in our boutiques, by the way. You'll be seeing a credit on your final account statement."

Lola took the card she offered, nodding. "So what'll happen to Fletch?"

"The Feds have plans for him. They've been following his activities for awhile, waiting for him to pull some stupid stunt they could haul him in for. I'm sorry it had to happen this way, Lola."

"Yeah, but what if he'd gone through the ceremony and I found out—too late—what a real bad-ass he was?"

There was a scary thought! But it was getting easier to smile about, now that Fletcher was locked up.

Lola shook the hand Fedora offered, and watched her walk away. Pretty amazing, that story about the gorgeous Greek woman who could've gone the way of other pregnant teenagers, had it not been for a big brother who loved her. This cast a whole different light on Captain Scandalous—not that Lola was ready to forgive him! He still had some explaining to do.

"Ah, Miss Lola! So good to see you looking relaxed—and free!"

She turned toward Clive Kingsley, who came from behind the purser's desk with a dapper British grin and several pieces of paper.

Did she really look relaxed? Free? She was itching for a cigarette, now that she had so much new information to process.

But that would wait for later. Kingsley was handing her a

print-out on letterhead that bore the *S. S. Aphrodite* insignia, with a little bow.

"Your final statement, my dear," he intoned, "along with the faxes from the credit card companies, which confirm the reconciliation of your accounts and excellent credit status. And here's a check to cover items returned from Mr. Fletcher's spending spree."

She glanced at the itemized statement—so very Kingsley, the way it had PAID IN FULL across the bottom, in his calligraphic script. And the check—good Lord, he'd just handed her more than seven thousand dollars!

Lola gaped, feeling extreme relief yet jealousy, too: Fletch had never spent this much on trinkets for *her*! What on earth had he bought that first day—from *her* accounts—?

But what would she gain from asking this dapper concierge? No sense in getting upset to the point she'd need those last couple of Camels upstairs.

"I—this is all very—"

Lola gazed at this bastion of British sanity, and then threw her arms around him. "Thank you so much for your help, Clive. I don't know what I'd have—"

"Clever puss that you are, you'd have landed on your feet eventually, Miss Wright," he crooned. He tightened his hug before releasing her. "I hope you'll accept those gowns as a token of my admiration and esteem."

"Oh, but I'll pay you for them when I get—"

He placed a gentle finger on her lips. "Believe me, the captain's paying me well for my part in this Caribbean caper. He's rather enjoyed it, you know.

"But of course," he went on with a twinkle in those blue, blue eyes, "if you'd carry my Kingsley Court formal wear in your stores, I would be forever grateful."

Lola sighed. "You design the most gorgeous—but you realize I only carry clothes for—"

Men. And why was that?

She nipped her lip, thinking quickly. His line *would* give Well Suited a whole new definition of *menswear*, wouldn't it? And Lord knows the clients—of whichever persuasion—who bought Clive's tuxes and ball gowns would gladly pay her the big bucks for accommodating their exquisite, impeccable taste.

Or they'd bring their women along to buy them. Kingsley had class and panache—as a man, and as a designer—and Lola had no doubt his clothes would sell from the get-go. This could be the biggest opportunity for expansion, with the least amount of effort, she'd ever been offered.

She plucked the card from between his fingers, noting the logo that matched the labels in her three gowns.

"I'll contact you as soon as I get home," she said, shaking his hand firmly. "It's been a real pleasure meeting you, Clive. You've just handed me a whole new way of doing business."

He smiled again, still keeping a few secrets. But she was used to that.

"Please enjoy your suite and all the privileges of being our guest on your last evening with us, dear Lola," he went on in that voice that still reminded her of hot fudge . . . but not quite as exciting as what Rio had smeared all over her. "You'll understand, I hope, that as we approach San Juan and prepare for disembarkation, Captain Skandalis and Mr. DeSilva will be occupied with ensuring everyone's security. Damn shame so many rules and regulations came about after the September Eleventh disaster—"

"It touched every one of us, didn't it?" Lola smiled, letting go of his hand. "Thanks again for all your help. I need to pack, so I can set my luggage out in the hallway before I go to bed."

It felt funny, using the regular elevator to go up to the Aphrodisia Suite. And damned if she didn't make a wrong turn when she stepped off it, and ended up in the corridor on the ship's other side.

She laughed at herself. What she needed was a Cabana Boy to escort her from place to place, in the manner to which she'd become accustomed!

Matter of fact, she was hoping Aric would accept her invitation for a nice late-night dinner—or at least a good pizza and a beer—when she got her clothes packed. She felt like celebrating, now that her life was falling into place again!

But when she entered the suite, its stillness echoed. The rooms felt empty, even though the lamps were lit and a little bag of those chocolates awaited her on the turned-down bed.

No sign of Aric.

And when she opened the closet, she discovered only the third dress Clive had provided her—the one so filmy, it showed every freckle and hair.

"Holy shit," she muttered, yanking open the drawers—which made a hollow rattle because they were all empty!

Then she saw the note on her table:

Priestess, I knew you'd be busy squaring things away, so I packed your things. Have delivered your luggage downstairs, so it will receive preferential treatment when you disembark tomorrow.

It's been my pleasure—so, okay, I gave you some crap, but I really did enjoy tricking you out and spending time with you! Have a good trip home and a wonderful life.

That little shit! He'd packed her things, all right, except for that one peekaboo dress—which no decent woman would wear in broad daylight, much less to fly home in! And then, before she could say goodbye and thank him, he'd given her the kiss-off!

Lola dropped onto the bed with a sigh. Even though she knew better, she looked out the balcony door. He'd left the sheers open so she could enjoy the view of the night as they sailed toward San Juan.

But nobody was out there smoking one of those sexy, dark cigars.

Lola opened the bag of candy. She popped a truffle into her mouth, carefully flattening the foil wrapper.

You're about to get lucky. Really, really lucky.

"Yeah, right," she sighed. A Lucky would taste pretty good right now, considering how Cabana Boy had also taken the last of her Camels.

34

Early the next morning, Lola sat downstairs in the huge lobby among hundreds of other passengers, waiting for the blue group to be called. Feeling right at home in that color, because what had she really gotten out of this cruise? She was going home without a ring or a husband—

Oh, quit bitching! Fletch would've ruined your life!

—and she'd eaten only one meal in the ship's dining room—

—But look at the parties you went to! Who else got to witness so many guys playing dress-up?

Now she sat among all these tired looking strangers, who were waiting to be herded to the pier to reclaim their luggage, and then herded through Customs and into buses for the airport. She'd planned to wear her cami and capris from yesterday, but apparently Aric had returned to take them for himself while she was dead asleep, the little shit.

She felt out of place and overdressed—if you called being exposed in all this see-through fabric *dressed*. The only thing that saved her tits and ass from being extremely visible was the pink silk scarf she'd bought before she'd tried going ashore. At least Cabana Boy had left her *that*.

Hey—you don't have panty lines!

Yes, how considerate of Cabana Boy, not to leave her even yesterday's panties. She didn't want to think about what *he* was doing with them. Now she'd have to scrounge through her suitcases before going through Customs—in a huge room surrounded by all these people—to pull out real clothes to put on in the restroom. Was she a class act, or what? And what if she missed her bus to the airport then?

"Mr. Roger Delahanty!" a nasal female voice came over the loud speaker. "Mr. Roger Delahanty, please report to the purser's office immediately to settle your bill."

Holy shit, that could've been me! They really DON'T let you go till they've got your dough.

A man lumbered down the crowded aisle then—and it was Marshmallow Man! The guy she'd sold her ring to! Was *he* the one they'd just called, to settle up for things that naked speed-dater had charged to his account?

Lola slumped back in her upholstered chair, grinning a little. Thanks to Clive Kingsley's persuasive efforts, all her accounts were restored. She even had money in her pocket! And yeah, she was heading home with three designer gowns she never would've bought for herself—not to mention plans to include his designer lines in her stores very soon.

And you did have a few little adventures, like in the spa, and the captain's quarters, and the pool, and on that coffee table.

But she shut out those compelling images of Rio DeSilva. She'd finally fallen asleep in the wee hours, realizing he wouldn't be coming to her room. And now that they were docked, he was checking in with the local port authorities. The staff was also preparing to take on another load of passengers within a matter of hours, for another cruise like this one.

Chances of seeing Rio ever again ran between slim and none.

"All those passengers in the blue group may now exit through the main doors," that nasal voice came over the speaker.

Lola stood, with dozens of others, ignoring their stares. Kingsley's sheer, elegant gown sparkled in the sunlight that poured through the floor-to-ceiling windows. Her bare legs were blatantly displayed below the scarf, and yet . . . under different circumstances, she'd be feeling as ethereal as a fairy queen.

Could she help it these gawkers were dressed in slacks and natty shirts? Could she help it this exquisite gown was absolutely *all* she had to wear?

Lola slipped on her shades and quickly joined the queue heading toward the gangway to get out of here.

That's what she wanted right now—out of here. Her fantasies had gone as flat as day-old champagne. Never again would there be bubbly like the stuff Rio DeSilva had licked from between her legs—

Oh, just start chain-smoking and stop your whining!

But of course, smoking wasn't allowed in the baggage claim area, or during the Customs inspection, or on the bus. She'd have to wait it out—head for one of those glass rooms in the airport, where the other slaves huddled, puffing as though their lives depended on those white coffin nails. Stoking up on nicotine, praying they'd survive their flight without a meltdown.

Things really were simpler when she didn't smoke. She really would quit again. Soon as she got back home. Back to reality.

Customs went amazingly fast because, bless his heart, Cabana Boy *had* given her luggage preferential placement.

The bus ride to the San Juan airport was uneventful, even with a prissy old lady in the seat beside her, who couldn't stop staring at her see-through evening gown. Lola felt like a Cinderella who'd been yanked from her fairy tale world to be plunked down in the steam-heat reality of San Juan as only tired, returning travelers knew it.

She got off the bus. Waited at the curb among the thirty some others for her bags—which of course had been shoved to the very back of the cargo hold, because they were loaded first.

Lola panicked, watching dozens of people streaming to the ticket windows. Her return flight had been scheduled so tightly she barely had time to pee, let alone change clothes, before boarding her plane. If she missed this one, it meant an entire day's delay.

Finally the bus driver hauled out her deep green suitcase. She yanked up its plastic handle and then rolled the large bag behind her, cussing the way her gown wound itself around her legs. Kingsley had designed this elegant dress for strutting down fashion runways, rather than racing frantically toward the airport to—

Squealing tires scattered everyone around her, and Lola looked up. A white stretch limo skidded to a stop at the curb, and pedestrians scurried to stay out of its way—gawking as a huge, dark chauffeur in a pinstriped suit hopped out of the driver's side.

He was wearing oversized shades, as shiny as his clean-shaven head, yet something looked familiar about him. He grinned like he *knew* her, which made his lip sparkle when he opened the limo's doors. His riders must either be running wayyyy behind, or he was fetching some very impressive guests.

But wait! That was—

"Miss Wright! Lola! I'm so glad we got here in time!"

She froze in front of the automatic doors, forcing irritated travelers to wheel their luggage around her. What the hell were Captain Scandalous and that damned Odette doing here?

"And don't you look stunning?" the French pussy purred, looking her up and down.

Before Lola could smart back at her, Skorpio grabbed the handle of her suitcase and wheeled it out of the doorway!

Lola's heart thudded. "Look, I—I'm running late for my flight—"

"Ah, but we haven't all been properly introduced, my dear," the captain crooned, in the same voice that had first led her astray. He was smiling at her, deepening those laugh lines in his tanned, handsome face. Even in navy slacks and a striped sport shirt, Skandalis was turning ladies' heads. Any one of them would've gladly missed her plane to hear him out.

Lola gave the attractive pair an exasperated look. "I—I *know* who you are, and—"

"Ah, but this lovely woman, Odette," he said, slipping his arm around her slender waist, "isn't really my chamber maid, you see. She is the Chief Financial Officer of Skandalis Shipping. And my wife of thirty years!"

Lola's eyes widened to the size of half-dollars as she returned Odette's enthusiastic handshake.

"And after being married to Skorpio for so long," his raven-haired goddess said with a laugh, "I'm sure you can understand why we play our little games to keep each other amused."

Amused? Hell, she'd never seen a couple so hot for each other!

"I put up a good front," Skorpio continued in a confidential tone, "but my Odette is always in control. She lets me look, and pretend to play into other women's fantasies, but she keeps me on a very short leash."

Captain Scandalous leaned closer then, his onyx eyes shining as though he could see through her hot pink scarf. "I truly *wanted* to fulfill your every request, Lola, but—"

"We've come to wish you a safe journey home!" Odette chimed in, stepping possessively closer to her man. "And we've got to run, dear! We're shopping for some new toys before the *Aphrodite* sails again this afternoon!"

The *S. S. Aphrodite*.

Lola gaped when it came to her: the S. S. stood for Skandalis Ship.

So Captain Scandalous wasn't just another pretty Greek face, he was a damn shipping magnate! He played by his own rules on board, because he *could*! What a life, to live on a luxury liner belonging to a fleet he *owned*!

Lola could only shake her head in amazement, watching the two of them scamper toward a taxi. She was still seeing Odette in that skimpy French maid get-up with the black garter belt, clutching a toilet brush—

"On behalf of Fantasy Cruise Lines, I'm inviting you back on board, Miss Wright. To compensate for the . . . unfortunate complications during your Caribbean getaway."

The air rushed from her lungs. That satiny Spanish accent came from the limo behind her—and she now felt the tall, warm body that went with it. He was standing so close, she could've reached back to grab his—

"Rio!"

Lola whirled around to gaze at him. God, but he was gorgeous in his whites, with his sandy hair blowing in the breeze. Those golden-brown eyes latched onto hers like they never wanted to let her go, and she caught the scent of his little cigars. It was like one of those moments in a romantic movie, where the guy and the girl, fated never to see each other again, suddenly came face to face.

"But on behalf of Don Rio Benito DeSilva," he continued in a silky whisper, "I'm inviting you to share my last week aboard the *Aphrodite,* so we can get better acquainted. To see if we are indeed . . . well suited."

Lola let that reference to work pass right by her.

"Your place or mine?" she rasped before she thought how tacky that sounded.

Rio's laughter made his mustache flash like a stiletto blade. "I believe, if I pull a few strings," he teased, "the Aphrodisia Suite could be our hideaway, yes, *querida.*

"Although," he continued in a low voice, reaching for the knot in her scarf, "the way you look in this dress, Lola *mia*, I might have to have you right here and now."

"On—on the sidewalk?"

The Spaniard let the lightweight silk drift down her arm as he beheld what was revealed beneath the gossamer gown.

"I believe our friend Kingsley has spun this dress from little more than air and fairy dust," he whispered as he gazed at her. "The fabric is so fragile, I don't see how it holds in those peaks you're pointing at me. But then, fairies do possess unique powers, do they not?"

Lola laughed so loudly, at an image of Clive flitting around like Tinker Bell, that passersby looked at her. And then they flat-out *stared* at what was showing beneath her dress.

She hadn't had time to grab any panties.

Rio ran a fingernail down the fabric, making it sing a suggestive song all the way down to where her nipple met his caress.

"But enough about our clever concierge," he whispered. "I'm thinking stretch limos were just made for lovers like you and me, Lola. And if George—I believe you two have met, yes?"

Lola forced her gaze away from DeSilva to look at the driver, and then covered her startled laughter with her hand.

"Y'all aren't gonna *hurl* now, are ya?" the big man teased, flashing his gold tooth and his diamond lip stud when he grinned.

Lola shook her head giddily. She recognized him as the other security agent, of course—but she hadn't realized that this same broad body, in an island-print shirt, had cleared her path up the gangway that day she'd tried to escape from the ship.

"Yes! Well—if Mr. LeFevre will take the long way, driving us back to the *Aphrodite*," DeSilva added with a pointed look at the driver, "I believe we should begin getting much better acquainted. Right this minute."

"And once we're settled in—once we're sailing," Lola said, while the mood was warming up so nicely, "will we be together all night long?"

Rio's warm hand rode the curve of her ass as she stepped into the limo ahead of him. It was a gorgeously appointed car, with a bar and a small TV and a nice sound system—

But who needed all that? The man sliding into the rich leather seat beside her was looking at her as though his gaze alone might make her dress go up in smoke. Never in her life had she been with a lover who wore his emotions so plainly in view. And who so openly adored her.

It made her dizzy, just thinking about a whole week with Rio DeSilva. Oh sure, he'd have to work some, but without Skorpio and Odette ordering her around, telling her what she couldn't do, why, she could cruise the Caribbean this week and not feel she'd missed a thing if she didn't see any of the islands. Or even the elevator.

Rio reached inside her gown to cup one aching breast, unbuttoning his shirt with his other hand. "My mantra for this next week—forever, if you wish, will be 'whatever Lola wants . . . whatever Lola wants, Lola gets.' That's how much I intend to love you, my queen. Will that be enough, do you think?"

Lola sighed her way into his kiss, reveling in the feel of his fingers as they relieved her of her dress. The limo door closed behind them, dimming the interior into a private rendezvous. The long car purred into motion.

But then Lola lost track of everything except the splendidly naked man who was easing himself between her legs as he deepened his kiss. She tasted tobacco on his inner lips, and sucked his tongue like it was a cigarette. Here was a man who truly understood her tastes!

Whatever Lola wants—forever? Now *there* was a fantasy worth trying for!

She laughed low in her throat, opening to Rio as she realized how prophetic Fletch had been in his kiss-off note.

Have a nice life, babe, he'd scribbled.

Lola moaned as Rio DeSilva thrust inside her. Just this once, she was going to do exactly as Fletcher said.

And here's a look
at Jami Alden's DELICIOUS,
available now from Aphrodisia . . .

Suddenly a large, proprietary hand slid around Kit's hip to flatten across her stomach. She didn't even have to turn around to know it was Jake. Even in the crowded dance club, she could pick up his scent, soapy clean with a hint of his own special musk. Without a word he pulled her back against him. The rigid length of his erection grinding rhythmically against her ass let her know her dance floor antics had been effective.

What she hadn't counted on was her own swift response. Sure, he'd gotten the best of her in the wine cellar, but she'd written it off as a result of not having had sex since her last "friend with benefits" had done the unthinkable and actually wanted an exclusive relationship. She'd had to cut all ties and hadn't found a suitable replacement in the last six months.

Tonight, she'd only meant to tease and torment Jake, give him a taste of what he wanted but couldn't have. Now she wasn't so sure he'd be able to stick with that game plan. The memory of her gut wrenching orgasm pulsed through her, her nerve endings dancing along her skin with no more than his hand caressing her stomach and his cock grinding against her rear. His broad palm slid up until his long fingers brushed the undersides of her breasts, barely covered by the thin silk of her top.

She was vaguely aware of Sabrina raising a knowing eyebrow as she moved over to dance with one of the other groomsmen.

Without thinking she raised one arm, hooking it around his neck as she pressed back against the hard wall of his chest. Hot breath caressed her neck before his teeth latched gently on her earlobe. The throbbing beat of the music echoed between her legs, and she knew she wouldn't be able to hold him off, not when he was so good at noticing and exploiting her weakness.

"Let's go," he whispered gruffly, taking her hand and tugging her towards the edge of the floor.

She wasn't *that* easy. "What makes you thing I want to go anywhere with you?" she replied, breaking his hold and shimmying away.

A mocking smile curved his full, sensuous mouth. "Wasn't that what your little show was all about? Driving me crazy until I take you home and prove to you exactly how good it could be between us?" To emphasize his point, he shoved his thigh between hers until the firm muscles pressed deliciously against her already wet sex. "What happened earlier was just a taste, Kit. Don't lie and tell me you don't want the whole feast."

She moaned as his mouth pressed hot and wet against her throat, wishing she had it in her to be a vindictive tease and leave him unsatisfied, aching for her body.

But her body wouldn't let her play games, and she was too smart to pass up an opportunity for what she instinctively knew would be the best sex of her life. Jake was right. She wanted him. Wanted to feel his hands and mouth all over her bare skin. Wanted to see if his cock was as long and thick and hard as she remembered. Wanted to see if he'd finally learned how to use it.

And why not? She was a practical, modern woman who believed in casual sex as long as her pleasure was assured and no strings were attached. What could be more string free than a hot vacation fling with a guy who lived on the opposite side of the country? And this time she'd have the satisfaction of leaving *him* without so much as a goodbye.

Decision made, she grabbed his hand and led him towards the door. "Let's hope you haven't oversold yourself, cowboy."

"Baby, I'm gonna give you the ride of your life."

Outside, downtown Cabo San Lucas rang with the sounds of traffic and boisterous tourists. Jake hustled her into a taxi van's back row and in rapid Spanish he gave the driver the villa's address and negotiated a rate.

Hidden by several rows of seats, Kit had no modesty when he pulled her into his arms, capturing her mouth in a rough, lusty kiss. Opening wide, she sucked him hard, sliding her tongue against his, exploring the hot moist recesses of his mouth. Her breath tightened in quick pants as he tugged her blouse aside and settled a hand over her bare breast, kneading, plumping the soft flesh before grazing his thumb over the rock hard tip.

Muffled sounds of pleasure stuck in her throat. She couldn't ever remember being so aroused, dying to feel his naked skin against her own, wanting to absorb every hard inch of him inside her. She unbuttoned his shirt with shaky hands, exploring the rippling muscles of his chest and abs. He was leaner now than he'd been at twenty-two, not as bulked up as he'd been when he played football for the UCLA. The sprinkling of dark hair had grown thicker as well, teasing and tickling her fingers, reminding her that the muscles that shifted and bulged under her hands belonged to a man, not a boy.

Speaking of which . . .

She nipped at his bottom lip and slid her hand lower, over his fly until her palm pressed flat against a rock hard column of flesh. The taxi took a sharp curve, sending them sliding across the bench seat until Kit lay halfway across Jake's chest. He took the opportunity to reach under her skirt and cup the bare cheeks of her ass, while she seized the chance to unzip his fly and reach greedily inside the waistband of his boxers.

Hot pulsing flesh filled her hand to overflowing. Her fingers closed around him, measuring him from root to tip and they exchanged soft groans in each others mouths. He was huge, long and so thick her fingers barely closed around him. It had hurt like a beast when he'd taken her virginity. But now she couldn't wait to feel his enormous cock sliding inside her stretching her walls, driving harder and deeper than any man ever had.

She traced her thumb over the ripe head, spreading the slippery beads of moisture forming at the tip. Her own sex wept in response. Unable to control herself, she reached down and pulled up her skirt, climbing fully onto his lap. She couldn't wait, her pussy aching for his invasion. God this was going to be good.

If anyone had told her twelve years ago that someday she'd be having sex with Jake Donovan in a Mexican taxicab, she would have called that person insane.

Pulling her thong aside, she slid herself over him, teasing his cock with the hot kiss of her body, letting the bulbous head slip and slide along her drenched slit. She eased over him until she held the very tip of him inside . . .

The taxi jerked abruptly to a stop, and Kit dazedly realized they'd reached the villa. With quick, efficient motions Jake straightened her skirt and shifted her off him, then gingerly tucked his mammoth erection back into his pants. With one last, hard kiss he helped her down from the van and paid the driver as though he hadn't been millimeters away from ramming nine thick inches into her pussy in the back of the man's cab.

Kit waited impatiently by the door, pretending not to see the driver's leer. Like they were the first couple to engage in hot and heavy foreplay. Jake strode over, pinning her against the door as he reached for the knob and turned.

And turned again. He swore softly.

"What is it?" Kit was busy licking and nibbling her way down the strip of flesh exposed by Jake's still unbuttoned shirt. He tasted insanely good, salty and warm.

"I don't suppose you have a key?"

She groaned and leaned her head back against the door. "I didn't take one." There were only four keys to the villa, and when they went out they all made sure they had designated male and female keyholders. Unfortunately tonight, Kit wasn't one of them, and apparently, neither was Jake. "What time does the housekeeper leave?"

Jake looked at his watch. "Two hours ago."

He bent over and picked up the welcome mat, then inspected all the potted plants placed around the entry for a hidden key. Watching the way his ass muscles flexed against the soft khaki fabric of his slacks, Kit knew she was mere seconds away from pushing him down and having him right here on the slate tiled patio.

He straightened, running a frustrated hand through his thick dark hair. Eyes glittering with frustrated lust, he muttered, "There has to be a way in here."

"Through the back," Kit said. All they had to do was scale the wall that surrounded the villa. The house had several sets of sliding glass doors leading out to the huge patio and pool area. One of them was bound to be unlocked.

With a little grunting and shoving, Jake managed to boost Kit over the six foot wall before hoisting himself over. Holding hands and giggling like idiots, they ran across the patio. But Jake stopped her before she reached the first set of doors.

"Doesn't that look inviting?"

She turned to find him looking at the pool. Wisps of steam

rose in curly tendrils off the surface. The patio lights were off, the only illumination generated from the nearly full moon bouncing its silver light off the dark water. A smile curved her mouth and renewed heat pulsed low in her belly. "I could get into a little water play."

He pulled her to the side of the pool and quickly stripped off her top. Kit arched her back and moaned up to the sky as he paused to suck each nipple as it peaked in the cool night air. Her legs trembled at the hot, wet pull of his lips, her vagina fluttering and contracting as it arched for more direct attention.

His hands settled at the snap of her skirt. "I like this thing," he said as he slid the zipper inch by agonizing inch. "Kinda reminds me of those sexy little shorts you wore that first time—"

Her whole body tensed. She didn't want to think of that night right now, didn't want to think about the last time she let uncontrollable desire get the best of her. Her fingers pressed against his lips. "I'd rather not revisit unpleasant memories."

She caught the quick hint of a frown across his features but he hid it quickly as he slid her skirt and thong off, leaving them to pool around her feet.

"In that case," he said as his shirt slid off his massive shoulders, "I better get down on creating some new ones."

Damn, the woman knew how to hold a grudge. But the sting Jake felt at Kit's reminder just how unpleasant she found the memories of their first time quickly faded at the sight of her in the moonlight, fully nude except for her stiletto heeled sandals.

With her long legs and soft curves, sex radiated from her pores like a perfume, sending pulses of electricity straight to his groin. His cock was so hard he actually hurt.

In the clear moonlight he could make out the sculpted lines of her cheekbones, the dark sweep of lashes over her blue eyes, the full curve of her lips. Her dark hair swung forward over her shoulders, playing peekaboo with the tight, dark nipples.

His hands followed his gaze, tracing the taut, smooth plane of her abdomen, coming to rest just above what he'd felt before but hadn't seen. Her pubic hair was a dark, neatly trimmed patch over plump, smooth lips. Her breath caught as he combed his fingertips through the silky tuft of hair, inching his way down but not touching the hot silky flesh that lay below.

He was afraid if he touched her he wouldn't be able to stop himself from pushing her onto a nearby lounge chair and shoving his cock as hard and high in her as he could possibly go. His hands trembled at the remembered feel of her soft pussy lips closing over him, stretching over the broad head of his penis as she straddled him in the cab. If the driver hadn't stopped, he knew he would have lost control, would have fucked her hard and fast until he exploded inside her, ruining his chances of proving he'd learned anything about self control in the past ten years.

So instead of dipping his fingers into the juicy folds of her sex, he knelt in front of her and removed her lethal looking sandals before shedding his slacks and underwear. Taking her hand, he led her into the pool.

He pulled her against him until her breasts nuzzled his chest like warm little peaches, reveling in the sensation of cool water and warm skin. He kissed her, tongue plunging rough and deep, just the way he wanted to drive inside her. He couldn't believe after all these years he was here with her again, touching her, tasting her. She tasted so good, like vodka and sin, her wet mouth open and eager under his. One taste and he regressed back to that horny twenty-two year old, shaking with lust and overwhelmed by the reality of touching the woman who had fueled his most carnal fantasies.

Greedily his hands roamed her skin, fingers sinking into giving flesh as he kneaded and caressed. He wished he had a lifetime to spend exploring every sweet inch of her. Kit gave as good as she got, her hands sliding cool and wet down his back, legs floating up to wrap around his waist. He threw his head back, clenching his jaw hard enough to crack a molar. Hot, slick flesh teased the length of his cock, plump lips spreading to cradle him as she rocked her hips and groaned. He backed her up against the smooth tiles that lined the sides of the pool. One thrust, and he could be inside her.

"No," he panted, "Not yet."

Water closed over his head as he sank to his knees, drowning out everything but the taste and feel of her. Eyes closed, he spread her pussy lips with his thumbs, nuzzling between her legs until he felt the tense bud of her clit against his face. Cool water and hot flesh filled his mouth as he pulled her clit between his lips, sucking and flicking until her hips twitched and he heard the muffled sounds of her moans distorted by the water. A loud buzz hummed in his ears, and occurred to him that he might pass out soon from lack of air.

Surfacing, he sucked in a deep breath and lifted her hips onto the tiled ledge. She drew her knees up, rested her heels on the edge to give him unimpeded access to her perfect pink cunt. He parted the smooth lips with his thumbs, lapped roughly at the hard knot of flesh, circling it with his tongue, sucking it hard between his lips as her pelvis rocked and bucked against his face. Every sigh, every moan, every guttural purr she uttered made his dick throb until he was so hard he feared he might burst out of his skin.

"Oh, God, oh, Jake," she moaned. Another rush of liquid heat bathed his tongue and he knew she was close. The first faint flutters of her orgasm gripped his fingers as he slid inside, clamping down harder as the full force of climax hit her.

Kit stared up at the bright night sky as the last pulses shuddered through her. Taking several deep, fortifying breaths she risked a look at Jake. His dark head was still between her thighs as he rained soft, soothing kisses on the smooth inner curves. Tender kisses. Loving kisses, even.

Oh, Christ, she might be in really big trouble.

She could never remember responding to a lover like she did to Jake. Then again, she'd never had a lover treat her like Jake did, either.

Her last partner was exactly the type she liked. She told him what she wanted and he listened, bringing her efficiently to satisfaction before finding his own.

But he hadn't looked at her like she was the most beautiful woman he'd ever seen. He hadn't run his hands over her skin like he wanted to memorize every inch of her. He hadn't buried his head between her legs and licked and savored her pussy like it was the most succulent, exquisite fruit he'd ever tasted.

And he sure as hell had never made her come so hard that her vision blurred and her body felt like it was wracked by thousands of tiny electrical currents.

She heard the sound of water splashing, and her stomach muscles jerked as Jake held his dripping body over hers. Bracing himself with his hands, he came down over her and kissed her with the tenderness that almost made her want to cry.

Crap. What was wrong with her? This was Jake, the man who'd so rudely introduced her to the world of slam bam thank you ma'am. To give him credit he'd proven—twice now—that he could make her come. Really, really hard. But still. It was just an orgasm.

The smartest move would be to get up and leave before she fell victim to this weird hormonal anomaly. But her brain had ceded all control to the area between her legs that still throbbed and ached to feel all of Jake buried deep inside her.

And to think men got a bad rap for being controlled by their dicks.

She draped a lazy hand around his neck and slid her fingers into the wet silk of his hair. Then he was gone, water splashing as he levered himself out of the pool. She could barely summon the energy to turn her head to watch him dig around the pockets of his pants.

Moonlight cast silvery shadows on the muscles of his back and shoulders, illuminating the drops of water cascading down his long strong legs. A renewed jolt of energy rushed through her as he turned, his cock jutting out in stark relief. Though she couldn't see his eyes, she could feel him watching her as he rolled on a condom with slow deliberation. Stroking himself, reminding her that in a few moments the whole of that outrageously hard length would be buried deep inside her.

She rolled to her knees as he waked toward her, reaching for him as he got close. He brushed her hands away, slipping back into the water and pulling her in with him. The cool tile was hard on her back as he pulled her close for a rough kiss. He lifted her leg over his hip, burrowing the tip of his erection against her. "I can't be gentle," he murmured. "I've waited too many years to have you again."

Waited years? What did he mean by—

The thought was abruptly cut off by the sudden, swift presence of him shoving inside her. Even though she was wetter, readier, than she'd ever been, the sheer size of him caught her off guard. Stretching tight slick flesh, pressing deep, and just when she thought she couldn't take any more he drove in another inch.

Her mouth opened wide on a silent scream of pleasured pain, her startled gasps swallowed by his mouth as he pumped inside her with his cock and his tongue. Towering over her by several inches, he surrounded her, dominated her. She'd never felt so invaded, so claimed. She wasn't sure she liked it. But her body did.

She felt herself easing, softening around him, relaxing to take him deep with every surge of his hips. "Oh Kit," he groaned, the helpless note in his voice prefectly matching the way she felt. Suddenly he pulled out, ignoring her embarrassing wail of protest as he spun her around to face the edge of the pool.

Gripping her hips so hard it should have hurt, he thrust in from behind, whispering all the while how beautiful she was, how hot and tight her pussy felt around him. Whispers that faded into groans as his hands reached around to cup her breasts, pinching her nipples hard enough to make her yell as she pulsed and clenched around him. His hips pumped faster now, short shallow strokes interspersed with long deep plunges as he gasped and heaved behind her.

Bracing her hands on the tile wall, Kit pushed against him, working herself on his swollen shaft, pushing him so deep she felt him at the base of her spine. Her climax hovered around the edges of every stroke, knotting and tightening low in her belly. Suddenly he stiffened behind, a low roar bellowing from his chest as he jerked heavily inside her.